THE SUBSTITUTE

JOHN CATAN

DartFrog Plus

Published 2020

Printed in the United States of America
Print ISBN: 978-1-951490-63-8
eBook ISBN: 978-1-951490-64-5

Library of Congress Control Number: 2020915402

Publisher Information:
DartFrog Books
4697 Main Street
Manchester, VT 05255

www.DartFrogBooks.com

Join the discussion of this book on Bookclubz. Bookclubz is an online management tool for book clubs, available now for Android and iOS and via Bookclubz.com.

*For my mother, Ronnie Catan, PhD,
who taught me by example that I can do anything.*

CHAPTER 1

Magne ducked behind a thick marble column to shield himself from an onslaught of steel-tipped projectiles. The sound of steel striking stone pierced his eardrums as the darts ricocheted all around him.

"You know, my brother wouldn't mind being chased and shot at so much. Hell, he might even get a kick out of it. It's the socializing that would kill him," he said with a laugh to his partner.

Leo was back at headquarters, listening through an earpiece while she tried to gather intelligence on two things. One, who was trying to kill Magne, and two, how to get him to safety. So far, neither was going well.

"Later, Magne. You need to get out of there."

A sharp sting—something grazed his forehead. He felt his face, checking for blood. He pulled back, wincing as the hissing shots grew louder. A rapid succession of darts bounced off the column. They were closing in.

His vision blurred, as if he had too much to drink. But it wasn't because of the agency's annual gala event he'd just left. Was the dart poisoned? Or a tranquilizer? As an agent, Magne was used to being in harm's way, but now that he was back in the states and among friendlies, being ambushed was the last thing he expected.

He eyeballed the entrance to a long hallway about a hundred feet across the empty lobby. He knew from prior briefings that there was a secure room at the end. There was a turn immediately after the entrance, which would provide additional cover if he could get to it.

At least a half-dozen men, dressed in black suits and armed with air guns, continued their steady advance toward Magne's position, stopping to take cover every few steps. Magne didn't have his gun, but they didn't need to know that. Their footsteps on the marble floor drew closer as he glanced at the hallway again. If he bolted, he might make it. More shots hit the column. He couldn't stay there any longer. He'd have to make a break for it, but needed a distraction if he was going to have any chance of pulling it off.

There was a heavy, decorative candle on the end table next to him. A stun-grenade would have been preferable, but this would have to do. If he was lucky, it would take them a few seconds to realize what it was—or in this case, what it wasn't.

He took a deep breath, grabbed the candle, tossed it toward the enemy agents, and ran, arms pumping, heart pounding, straight for the hallway. He crossed the threshold and slammed against the wall just before he could take the turn. The impact dazed him, but he had to keep moving. Bolting for the end of the corridor, he stopped at a sliding door and punched in a code. The door opened to a small, windowless room. He sealed himself inside; the whisper of steel gliding on steel gave him a fleeting notion of safety.

He slid to the floor. "Leo, how long 'til backup arrives?"

"Should be less than ten minutes."

"Good, I'll sit tight."

"Did you know that you bring up this idea of your brother assuming your identity every time you come close to being captured?"

He smiled. "It would almost work."

Leo sighed and her voice softened. "You miss him."

"We used to do everything together." Magne ran his hand over his cropped black hair.

An explosion echoed through the room, shaking the walls. Plaster dust billowed around the entrance.

Magne glanced at his watch. "Don't know if you heard that, but they've got explosives."

"You've got to get out of there."

"I can't. Not from here, anyway." He backed away from the door.

"What can I do?"

"Find my brother. He's got to take over for me."

"Are you kidding? It'll never work."

"The agency is splintered. If our team finds out I've been taken or killed, it will swing the balance of power in Aluerd's favor."

"But Davyn thinks you're dead." Leo hesitated. "And he's not trained. He wouldn't last two minutes."

"I just got back from deep undercover." Magne coughed. "I'd be on a mandatory decompression. He'll be glad-handing and socializing at black tie affairs."

"I... I guess."

The room rocked as chunks of plaster fell from the walls around the door, and the air filled with dust. He covered his mouth with his shirtsleeve.

"They'll be in here any minute."

"Magne, hang—almost there—"

"I'm losing your signal. DARPA has an office near the university where Davyn teaches. Contact Dan McQue. He'll help you. Magne out."

CHAPTER 2

It was midmorning, and the university library's main hall was busy. Students gathered around the tables and worked on their papers, homework and research. A few talked softly. Mrs. Dawit, the head librarian, wore her gray hair in a bun. In her late sixties, she carried her reserved and weathered beauty with a stylish dignity. She scanned the room, occasionally pausing when she thought something might be amiss. When all appeared to be in order, she'd pinch her lips, slowly nod, and continue her survey. The hall was humming, quiet and productive. At least for the time being.

On the second floor, in a remote conference room, thirty-two-year-old Professor Davyn Daeger leaned over a large leather-bound book, minding his place with one hand and transcribing in his notebook with the other. He pushed back his dark, unruly hair and turned a page over, then back again.

He looked out of place, or more accurately, time. He wore light brown corduroy pants and a white cotton dress shirt, complete with a vest that would have suited H. G. Wells. He had no laptop, no cellphone, no technology newer than the turn of the last century. Even his pocket watch and chain were antiques. He was a walking anachronism.

He liked this quiet space. He liked the books, and the way they smelled, and most of all, he liked how it sheltered him from interruptions. Especially those that came from his students.

Davyn heard a click and the brush of wood on carpet as the door swung open.

He glanced up to see his teacher's assistant's trim figure lingering in the doorframe before she entered. She was an undergrad minoring in his chosen field of anthropology. Her long blonde ponytail bounced behind her as she sauntered over to the table where the professor was working. He shook his head and returned his attention to his book.

With no provocation whatsoever, she asked, "Why are you so nice to Mrs. Dawit?"

Davyn didn't bother to look up.

"Hello, professor," she said in a singsong voice.

"You didn't you come clear across campus to ask me that, right?"

Lily leaned over and rested her arms on the table and smiled at him with the cocky air of a kid sister put in charge while her parents were out for the evening. "Yes.".

"I could just as easily ask you why you always dress in shades of blue and wear purple sneakers."

"Sure, go ahead."

Davyn weighed his next move carefully. Any miscalculation could prolong her visit. "If I answer, will you leave me alone?"

She put her chin in her hand and appeared to give the question some thought. "Maybe. But I may have a follow-up question for you. It depends on how you answer."

He felt himself sinking deeper into what he had come to call the "Lilia tar pits." The term was based on the famed La Brea Tar Pits, a tar trap that consumed animals as they wandered by, minding their own business. Before they knew it, they'd find themselves trapped in a futile struggle against the oozing, sticky mess. He'd been down this road before and knew it was usually best to stay calm and provide a quick and short response, then hope for the best.

He set his pen down. "Well, let's see. She's smart and she actually enjoys helping people." Davyn paused and thought for a moment. "She's a better person than I am, and she's a sharp wit." Davyn leaned back in his chair, crossed his arms, and thought for another moment. Lily looked a little surprised by his response, but smiled and leaned in closer to listen as he continued. "She's a widow. Her sweetheart of forty years died recently. I'm sympathetic to that, so I treat her with—extra care, I suppose, would be the right term."

Lily leaned back. "Aw. That's so very sweet."

Davyn threw a suspicious glance her way. "No, it's very logical. Everything I've just said has been a statement of fact." He looked away. "Besides, the nicer I am, the more helpful she is." He paused.

"She brings me gift cards for coffee from Bakersfield's Cafe. Maybe... Maybe I just do it for free coffee."

She squinted and appeared to give that some thought. "No, I don't think so," she said, sounding quite sure. "Plus, you never use those gift cards. There must be a hundred of them in your desk drawer."

"You were going to ask a follow-up question." He shifted his gaze to her. "And then leave. Remember?"

She swallowed hard. "Oh, yes." Then her eyes brightened. "You answered correctly, so I need a favor."

He returned his attention to his notebook. "Quickly."

Lily stood up straight and put her hands on her hips. "Bukka, my boyfriend, needs tutoring for an exam on Friday. If he doesn't pass, he'll be thrown off the team!"

Davyn, nose still in his notebook, replied, "There are tutors on campus."

She folded her arms and stood, not saying a word.

After a few moments, Davyn gave in and looked up. He needed a way to get her to go. Maybe Bukka couldn't afford a tutor. He added, "I'll even pay for it."

She pulled out a chair and sat down, accidentally bumping the table and shifting his books. "I don't think you're allowed to do that. And it's too important a test. If he fails, he'll just—it'll be terrible. The test is on research methods, and no one knows that better than you. And I promised him, and he really likes you." She smiled and raised her eyebrows expectantly.

He pulled the small arrowhead he always carried with him from his pocket and began rubbing it with his thumb, as if trying to stroke away his tension. He glanced at her, then back at his book, and drew a deep breath. "Anything else?"

She nodded. "Yes."

Davyn rubbed his forehead. The tar pit had won this round.

"You need to promise to be nice."

He smirked. "You remind me of my kid sister."

She looked down at her outfit, straightened her blouse and smoothed her pants. "I know. You've told me that, and that's the only reason you put up with me."

He flashed a faux smile. At least, he thought he did. He never really knew what his face was doing. He'd smile for a picture—or, it *felt* like a smile—but then he'd look at the photo, only to find he'd given the camera a death stare.

Davyn knew he was awkward, but didn't mind. It helped keep people away. Like a porcupine's quills, fear of awkward moments encouraged people to reconsider before trying to speak with him. Sometimes he'd even deliberately make things uncomfortable. As an anthropologist, he found people's reactions in such moments fascinating.

"So, you'll do it? You'll do it!" Lily clasped her hands and beamed as if Davyn had actually said yes. "Thank you!" she shouted and jumped up from her chair before running out of the room.

He shook his head and sighed, then went back to his book. Out of the corner of his eye, he noticed a shadow blocking the light coming from the hallway. Passing shadows were fine, but this one had stopped. Who now?

Mrs. Dawit entered. "What was all that noise? I didn't tell her you were in here. She figured it out on her own. But you must find somewhere else to set up, I'm afraid. There's a conference starting here in fifteen minutes."

Davyn closed his notebook. "Okay, Mrs. Dawit. Thank you for reserving the space for me."

Mrs. Dawit handed Davyn a gift card for a free coffee. "I brought this to help quell your disappointment at losing your room. There are shortbread cookies in my desk drawer. I would have brought some with me, but I came straight from Mr. Bakersfield's coffee shop. Feel free to pick some up as you pass by."

He collected his books and started on his way out. He stopped and without turning around, replied, "Most people just call it Bakersfield's Cafe."

There was no response. He turned and looked back at Mrs. Dawit.

She fiddled with her broach, then looked up at Davyn and pushed her chin out. "That is what I said. Now shoo."

Davyn smiled and walked out the door.

Leo spent the five-hour drive trying to figure out how she, a stranger, would tell Davyn that his dead twin brother Magne isn't really dead. *And oh, by the way, he's a secret agent who's been kidnapped, and you need to assume his identity to help rescue him.*

Her stomach was twisted and tight as she reached the DARPA campus, an unremarkable collection of one- and two-story commercial buildings nestled in a wooded area in central Maryland. She parked her car and glanced at her watch. It was 10:00 a.m., almost ten hours since Magne had been ambushed.

She was there to see Dan McQue, who, Magne assured her, could put her in touch with Davyn. The plan seemed so crazy, but Magne had never let her down before. She trusted him, and that would have to suffice for now. But even after she found a way to speak with Davyn, she worried how he'd react.

She'd been awake for the last twenty-four hours. Maybe after she got some sleep it would make more sense, but she doubted that. She opened the car door and hurried to the security desk in the main office building.

"I'm here to see Dan McQue. He's expecting me."

The security officer smiled and asked for her ID. She rifled through her bag and pulled out her driver's license and showed it to him.

He nodded and picked up the phone. "There's a Kaleo Sandalwood here to see you." He hung up and pointed at the waiting area. "He'll be down to see you in a few minutes. Feel free to have a seat."

Leo ignored him and rocked back and forth on her heels while she waited for Dan to arrive.

A few minutes later, a man she assumed was Dan exited the elevator and approached her. She expected someone closer in age to Magne, but he had at least thirty years on him and was balding.

"Kaleo?"

She extended her hand. "Yes, but you can call me Leo. You must be Dan."

He shook her hand. "So, what's going on?"

Leo glanced around the lobby and then whispered, "As you might expect, I really can't say."

He motioned toward the elevator with a nod of his head. "My office is secure. We can talk there."

Minutes later, Dan opened the door to his roomy, windowless office. A large desk covered with stacks of papers, books, and disassembled electronic components, including what looked like the insides of a robotic human arm, sat in the corner.

He closed the door. "Okay, you can talk freely now."

Leo took a breath. "I need to get a message to someone on campus. I can't be seen there, and I can't call. The message has to be delivered covertly, and I need to speak to this person one-on-one."

"Can't you just have a letter delivered? I know someone who is on campus frequently. He's trustworthy, has government clearance, and he knows the security protocols. He could deliver it for you."

Leo shook her head. "The news I have for this person is too extraordinary for a written note. I have to speak to them. They won't believe a note. They'll think it's a prank or something. Magne said you'd be able to help."

He rubbed his chin. "What if we deliver an encrypted phone? The one I'm thinking of changes its frequency and encoding regularly. That would work."

Leo shook her head again. "It would look suspicious if they detected it on campus."

"I'm guessing you need this like yesterday? How much time do we have?"

"None. I need something today." Leo took a stuttering breath and closed her eyes, then looked Dan up and down. "Look, this is confidential, but Magne said I can trust you. He's gone missing."

Dan's face dropped. "Oh, I'm sorry. I didn't realize." He rubbed the back of his neck. "I might have something that will work. Traditional surveillance wouldn't detect it, and no one would expect it. It's unorthodox, but given the restraints we're working with, it might be our best option."

He opened a key-box on the wall and rifled through it before lifting a set of keys. They walked down the hallway to the elevator. After descending several floors, the elevator doors opened to a dark hallway. The lights buzzed on when they stepped out and made their way down the hallway, past dark, empty offices. Dan stopped at a steel door with a placard that read "B LAB."

"Blab?"

He chuckled. "Uh, that's B lab. We've changed the naming convention for the new labs. We're in the old area now. The good news is, I can work in Lab F now without feeling self conscious about my waistline." Dan smiled as he unlocked the door and pushed it open.

He followed her in and waved his arms around until the lights came on, illuminating limited areas of a midsize, square room with walls that were probably white at some point. Or maybe it was the lighting that made them look grey. Leo picked up a faint musty odor, like unfinished residential basements sometimes have. She crinkled her nose and rubbed it.

He led her to an area with some scattered computer equipment cabinets, which were mostly empty. Colored network cables dangled from the ceiling. All the equipment was off. Dan flipped some switches, and one of the servers lit up. He used some canned air to blow the dust away.

"Probably should have done that before I turned it on. These haven't been used in ages." Dan offered Leo a seat, then claimed an old office chair. "I have two ideas," he said as he switched on a terminal monitor, displaying only a flashing cursor. Leo watched without expression. "I want to show you something that I think we may be able to use. This technology has been around for a couple of decades, but it really never took off, and almost nobody knows about it. It works like a laser, only, instead of light, it transmits condensed sounds waves in a beam. When the sound beam hits a person's head, their skull vibrates, and it reconstitutes the sound. It may sound scary, but it's perfectly safe."

Leo looked around the lab. "Where's the transmitter?"

He pointed. "It's that small dish on the shelf over there. See it standing up with that wand sticking out of it? I know it doesn't look like much, but wait until you experience it. I promise you'll see it in a new light." He pointed to the floor at a red circle about the size of a serving dish, with a big red X in the middle. "Please step over to that red circle on the floor over there and step inside."

Leo stood up and stared at the spot. She opened her mouth to speak, but paused. "You're absolutely sure this is safe?"

"It's one hundred percent safe. It's just sound."

She walked over to the circle but stopped short of stepping inside. "The crosshair doesn't help."

Dan smiled as he typed on the keyboard. "I would never put you or anyone else in danger." He looked at her. "How tall are you, Leo?"

"Five feet, 8 inches."

"Okay, I'm just going to tweak the settings here a bit, and in a moment, I'll initiate the sonic pulse and then you'll hear my voice. The experience will be a bit odd, as you won't have a sense of where the voice is coming from."

She stepped into the circle and scrunched her shoulders. "Okay, ready."

He cleared away some manuals and pulled a joystick toward him. He glanced at Leo, then focused on a circle on the monitor. As he moved the joystick, the dish with a wand made a whirring sound and moved around until it pointed at Leo.

"In a moment, I'll press this button and say something. I've added in a ten-second delay. After that, you'll hear what I said, but it will come from the transmitter." He flipped a couple of switches. "Okay, stand by." Dan pressed the button on the microphone. "Hello, Leo. This is Dan."

A counter on the monitor clicked down. 10, 9, 8... Dan turned and looked at Leo. Leo held her head still but glanced around, anticipating the signal. Dan watched the monitor until the counter reached zero.

"Did you hear anything?"

"No, nothing." Her shoulders relaxed.

"The calibration's probably off. Let's try it again. I'll make the adjustments while it's transmitting. When you hear my voice, I want you to call out, and I'll lock on to that position." Dan punched some keys to set the playback to a continuous loop. "Okay, ready?"

Leo took a deep breath and nodded. "Ready."

A sign wave wiggled on the monitor as the voice transmitted from the hypersonic sound transmitter. Dan adjusted the joystick, trying to focus the sound beam on Leo's head. A steel shelf behind

Leo began to vibrate and clatter. "I hear something, but it's not you. The shelving unit behind me is making a noise."

He stood up and walked over to where Leo was standing and positioned himself between the vibrating shelf and the transmitter. He bent his knees and shifted side to side, then stopped abruptly and looked at Leo.

"Hang on a sec..."

He walked over to the joystick and bumped it up diagonally, once, twice.

A smile broke over her face. "I hear it!" Then her eyebrows scrunched. "Man, this is weird." She tilted her head to the side. "Davyn is going to freak out." Her gaze moved around the room, her eyes wide. "He won't know what the hell is happening. He's going to think he's losing his mind."

Dan tapped a few buttons, and the transmission stopped. "I know. That's why the first thing that you say needs to be something to reassure him."

"Oh, and what's that, exactly?"

"Hmm?"

"What should I say to reassure him?"

"That's an excellent question. I don't know, and as I'm thinking about this, it will be hard, maybe even impossible to know what he's heard." Dan scratched his head. "I can rig up a camera so you can see his reactions. Remember watching hockey on TV in the old days, before large screens and HD? You couldn't see the puck, so you'd have to watch the player's reactions. A player would skate toward the goal, maneuvering his hockey stick like he had the puck. He'd get close to the goal and take a shot, then zoom past the goal. You couldn't see the puck. The only way to know if he scored was by watching how the players reacted."

Leo crossed her arms and raised an eyebrow.

"Look, I'm skeptical too, Leo. But given the constraints, I don't see any other options."

She bit her lip and nodded slowly. "What about the camera transmission? Won't that raise a red flag like the phone you suggested earlier would?"

"It'll use standard channels. It won't trigger any alarm bells. You will need a script of sorts. I'm guessing you can't share the nature of the communication with me, but I have some ideas about the protocols I'd like to share with you."

"A script makes sense. How soon can we have this system in place?"

"We'll have to locate the target and determine what location might work. Sorry, what's the target's name?"

"It's Davyn Daeger. They're twins."

"Wow, okay." Dan scratched his chin. "The system and remote camera will run on a battery, so we won't need an external power source, just somewhere inconspicuous to place it. I'll get my guy to see if he knows Davyn and where he spends most of his time."

"Probably the library, based on what Magne's told me. That or his apartment. Not sure. It won't be a nightclub, I can tell you that much."

Dan flashed a brief smile and a nod. He looked at the red circle with the X, where Leo was still standing. "I'll start my guy on staking out a location, then I'll need to get this thing calibrated, so we have a chance of hitting Davyn in the head."

Leo's eyes shot up at Dan, and he shook his head.

"With the transmitter. Sorry, I meant with the transmitter."

Leo wanted to laugh, but she was too worried about Magne and whether this plan would work. She half smiled instead. "Ugh, Davyn is going to freak out."

CHAPTER 3

L ily sat at a small desk grading papers in the lecture hall. She knew the dean of the anthropology department would sit in on today's class, observing Professor Daeger as part of the assessment to help determine if he'd get the promotion from associate to full professor. The thought made her queasy. The professor was accomplished at giving speeches, but little things would sometimes distract him, and he'd lose his focus.

Professor Daeger stood at the front of the lecture hall, writing on the blackboard. There was a lectern at the front and a small stage where he stood during lectures, with about 150 seats arranged stadium style, stretching to a second entrance in the back of the hall.

A few dust particles lingered in the early afternoon sunlight coming in through the windows. It was 1:30, half an hour before class. Professor Anne, Lily's psychology professor, stepped in the lecture hall's doorway and knocked lightly on the doorframe. Professor Daeger didn't notice and continued his work at the blackboard, while Lily stood up from her desk and waved.

Professor Anne smiled and waved back. She told the students to call her that because she felt using her last name was too formal. She was tall. Not quite as tall as Professor Daeger, but close. Lily thought they would make a nice couple if he weren't so odd. She was not exceptionally beautiful. Pretty, to be sure, but she had a certain something about her.

Lily walked over to Professor Anne. "Hi, professor. What brings you here?"

She stood up on her toes, then lowered back down, gazing over at Professor Daeger. "I came to see the professor, actually."

Professor Daeger stopped writing on the chalkboard and looked at them over his shoulder, stone-faced.

Lily narrowed her eyes at him, then turned back to Professor Anne with a smile. "Well, come on in."

Professor Anne stepped in but remained by the door.

"Was there something you needed?"

Lily shot an eyebrow raise his way. "She wants to speak with you, professor."

She knew he liked her, but he was socially awkward, to put it mildly. Since Professor Anne was a psychology professor, maybe she could fix him. Or at least understand his weirdness.

He lowered his hand but remained facing the blackboard. "How can I help you?"

It was weird. He stared at the blackboard like a robot or something.

Professor Anne shot a warm smile his way. "I was hoping to speak with you privately."

Lily looked at her, then at Professor Daeger. "Um, I need a drink. Anyone want something from the cafeteria?"

"That's okay, Lily. I'll go speak to the professor by the blackboard. You don't have to leave."

Lily admired her confidence and take-charge style, and she suspected that Professor Daeger did, too.

Professor Anne walked over and put her hand briefly on his shoulder. He hesitated, looking at her hand without expression. Lily sat back down and pretended to grade papers, but kept peering over at the professors, trying to listen in. *Shoot. Why is he so odd?* The two spoke for a few minutes. It was mostly Professor Anne doing the talking. Professor Daeger would nod occasionally, and he might have said a few words. It was hard to tell. Lily was sure that Professor Anne liked Professor Daeger, and she was pretty sure he liked her, too, but his actions were always so stilted. He'd never make any progress if he didn't loosen up.

Professor Anne pushed her hair back over her ear and laughed, then touched his shoulder. *Holy crap, he cracked a smile.* Lily kept her head down, but couldn't look away. He said something that made Professor Anne laugh. Just when Lily thought he might be making some headway, she started to walk away.

She waved at Lily and smiled. "Bye, Lily. See you in class."

Lily watched her leave, then hurried over to Professor Daeger and punched him in the arm.

He stopped writing on the board. "Something I can do for you?"

"She likes you."

"Who?"

"You know who. She likes you and you like her, so why are you so—wait." Lily's mouth dropped open. Then she blurted out, "Are you gay?"

He went back to writing on the board. "Define gay."

"You know. I mean it's fine if you are of course, but do you like men?"

"I don't like anyone, really."

"Why can't you ever provide a straight answer?"

"A straight answer?"

She slapped his arm. "You know what I mean."

He turned to her. "No, really, I don't."

The professor was really quite charming, if somewhat obnoxious when he acted this way, but at least he was engaging in conversation. He usually just ignored people.

Lily folded her arms. "Yes, you do."

"Holstering your slappers?"

"Look, it's fine if you're gay. I was just curious."

"Thank you." He continued writing on the board.

Lily shifted her weight to one leg and put an arm down, still holding her shoulder with the other. "So, what did Professor Anne say?"

"She said—" He stopped writing and looked Lily dead in the eye. "You can't share this with anyone." He scanned the room to make sure it was clear before he whispered, "It's a secret."

Lily's eyes opened wide, and she nodded.

He went back to writing on the blackboard. "I don't spend enough time interacting with students."

Lily's shoulders dropped. "But everyone knows that."

"Uh-huh."

"So, all she said was you have to interact more with the students?"

"Yeah, I think that's what she was getting at."

"Well, that is important."

"Yep, and obvious."

"Maybe she just wanted to talk with you. Like I said, she likes you. Everyone knows it."

"Well, I like her, too. She's funny, smart and unconventional."

Lily leaned in and nodded her head rapidly, hanging on each word.

"But I can't get in a relationship right now."

Lily's eyes bulged. "What? Why?"

He continued writing. "Because class is starting soon, and I have to get this on the board before the dean arrives."

Lily huffed and went back to her desk.

Lily glanced at her watch, then at the students assembled in the lecture hall. She noticed a student with his hand up. Professor Daeger sat behind the lectern reading, apparently unaware of the time or his surroundings, so she cleared her throat to get his attention. He didn't notice.

"Professor Daeger," she said. He didn't appear to notice that either. She looked at the student, then back to the professor. "Psst, Professor Daeger." He looked around until he saw the student's hand in the air, but said nothing. He just stared at him expectantly.

The student lowered his hand. "Sir, it's 2:05. Class is supposed to start at 2:00."

Davyn shrugged and set his book down, then walked out to the stage and started speaking. "Just sixty thousand years ago, there were five different species of humans sharing the planet. Well, sharing might not be the right word. They were in deadly competition with one another. They lived in small groups and subsisted by hunting and gathering. They were also nomadic, so there was ample opportunity to run into each other."

He paced the stage as he spoke, and the students settled into their chairs.

"As part of my research, I make tools and weapons. Occasionally, I go hunting with these tools."

Five students' hands immediately shot up, then six, seven. The professor wandered around the front of the hall, continuing the lecture, oblivious to their questions. Lily also took an interest in what he'd just said and set the papers she was supposed to be grading aside.

She leaned forward in her chair and called out, "Professor Daeger?"

The professor continued, unaware of the interruption.

"Professor Daeger," she repeated. He didn't respond. Lily cleared her throat and raised her voice. "Professor Daeger."

He stopped abruptly, as if awakened from a dream. He peered out at the students and squinted. At least ten of them had their hands up. He turned to Lily, seeking some direction, and Lily bit her lip.

"Professor, some students have questions they'd like to ask you."

"Yes, I see." He looked around and then pointed at a young man. He wagged his finger, in small, slow circles that grew bigger and more exaggerated, until he was flicking his hand like he was trying to shake off a dab of mayonnaise.

The kid pointed at himself. "Me?"

The professor blinked a few times, then nodded.

"Um, professor, did you say you make your own hunting tools and go hunting with them?"

Davyn looked around the lecture hall but didn't reply.

The student leaned forward in his seat. "What type of tools? What do you hunt? Where do you go?"

The professor scratched behind his ear and thought for a moment. He looked at his watch. "I fashion projectile points from stones." He started pacing again. "Where was I?"

More hands went up, but he looked back down at the ground and continued the lecture. Lily, however, noticed how excited the students were.

"Professor. You have more questions from the students."

Davyn stopped walking and put his hands in his pockets as he took a deep breath. "There's a lot to cover. I don't think we have time."

Lily stood up, made her way over to him, and touched his elbow. "What if we just take a couple?" Lily nodded to the first kid who'd asked a question. "You had a follow-up question, sir?"

The student put his hand down. "I have a bunch. Professor, what kind of animals?"

Davyn looked at him, then at Lily. "Rabbits, sometimes deer, turkeys. It depends on what I'm researching."

Lily nodded. "And where do you go hunting?"

"In the woods." He looked at his watch again.

She nodded an exaggerated nod as if trying to extract the information from a child. "Uh-huh, so what do you eat?"

He shrugged. "I eat what I kill."

"What if you don't catch anything to eat?"

He stretched his neck and looked at the student who had asked the question. "I don't eat. If I don't catch anything there's nothing to eat."

"Why don't you just bring food with you?"

The professor's eyes rolled back as he turned and walked toward the back of the stage with his hand covering his mouth. He faced the class again. "I have to get into the headspace of these hunters, at least to the extent that I can. For that to happen, the stakes have to be there. The Clovis people didn't have protein bars waiting for them at camp if they failed. There have to be consequences. I don't know how you can understand a people if you don't live in their shoes."

Lily admired his earnestness and dedication and the skill required to do it with such primitive tools, even if she didn't like that he hunted animals. She pointed to another student.

The professor glared at Lily. "This will be the last one."

Her eyes grew big, and she nodded.

The student said, "Do you use spears? You said projectile points. How do you use them to hunt?"

"For big game, I attach them to sticks I've cut and shaped for maximum strength, flexibility and precision."

"So, spears, then?"

"You can think of them as spears—"

"You throw the spears at the animals?"

The professor sighed. "I use a tool called an atlatl." He walked to his desk and picked up a yardstick. "The spear sits on the atlatl," he said, holding the yardstick near his ear. "Then you use it to throw the spear."

"And that kills them?"

"No, I still have to chase them down."

"How do you chase down a wild animal?"

The professor sighed. "Humans aren't fast, but they have great endurance."

"You can chase down a deer?"

"Not a healthy one, but if it's injured or weak, yes."

One student sitting in the back yelled, "Someone ought to tell Professor Anne to fake an injury. Maybe Professor Daeger will catch her then."

The lecture hall erupted in laughter. Lily laughed, too, but the professor didn't seem to get the joke.

Just then, a man entered the lecture hall and stood quietly in the back. It was the department's dean, Rupert Puddington. He was in his late fifties, balding and heavyset. He didn't look happy, but the truth is, he never did. His mouth appeared to be forged in a persistent frown. The years had carved out deep lines, like the spaces between a ventriloquist dummy's mouth and face that allowed the mouth to open and close. Even his eyes were sour, always squinting like he'd just drank homemade lemonade but forgot to add the sugar.

Lily lowered her head, walked back to her desk, and sat down.

The professor's face turned red and looked out over the full lecture hall. Lily bit her bottom lip and went back to grading papers. An awkward silence descended over the room and the air suddenly felt very thin.

"I'm sorry," the dean said. "Am I interrupting something?"

The professor moved over to Lily and whispered, "You should have just let me give my lecture. Where did I leave off?"

She furrowed her brows and whispered back, "I was just trying to help. Everyone's looking. You were talking about hunting—with projectiles."

Dean Puddington glared from the back of the lecture hall as Professor Daeger cleared his throat. "Uh, right. Clovis Points," he stammered. "A remarkable stone, really." He pulled the arrowhead from his pocket and held it up. "One that can be fashioned—is fashioned. I mean, was fashioned, into tools and weapons, by the Clovis people. Who are in North America—were in North America—thirteen thousand, five hundred years ago." His voice changed at the end and he sounded like a game show host announcing a prize.

The professor must have realized how ridiculous that sounded, because his eyes got big and he fixed his gaze on the floor. Lily felt her ears burning, and looked down at her papers. Davyn continued, but he was jumping between topics. Lily rubbed the back of her neck and winced. She tried to look at the professor, but she just couldn't.

Finally, he shook his head. "Okay, that's enough for today. Class dismissed."

Lily thought about telling him that the class had only just started, but as bad as things were going, and as flustered as he was, she thought it might be better for him to just cut his losses and regroup.

The kids in the class gathered their books and slowly walked out. The dean shook his head and descended the steps toward the professor. Lily kept her head down and worked on grading those papers. At first, the professor looked like he might make a break for the door, but then stood there as if frozen.

The dean forced a smile. "You've done some amazing research, Davyn, and the university is lucky to have such a smart and talented member of our faculty."

The professor forced a half smile, but it quickly evaporated.

"I know you've given speeches on the circuit. I've seen some of them. In person, and on video. The speeches are brilliant." He folded his arms. "What happened today?"

The professor looked around as if searching for a reply. He put his hand out, like he was going to physically offer a response, but nothing came to him. A few seconds passed, but they felt like hours.

"Uh, well, the students had questions, and—" The professor grabbed his shoulder and cracked his neck. "Then you came in." He looked around. "Let me give it some thought and get back with you," he said, grabbing his bag as he hurried out the door.

Dean Puddington glanced over at Lily. She looked up and smiled as he approached her. "How long have you known Professor Daeger? What's he like to work for?"

Lily stood up. "Well. He can be very funny. And he's helpful. He tutors my boyfriend, Bukka."

"He does tutoring?" The dean crinkled his brow.

"Well, on special occasions. My point is that he likes to help the students." Her voice rose at the end, as if she was asking a question. The dean didn't respond, so she continued, "He's really a great guy—I mean, professor. He's just a little rough around the edges." She smiled. "He needs a polish."

The dean frowned. "He needs more than a polish, I'm afraid."

Lily watched him leave, then grabbed her books and stood up to go, too. Professor Daeger was going to tutor Bukka in the library in less than an hour, but she needed to speak with him first.

CHAPTER 4

Davyn sat in a recliner, reading a book in an otherwise small, empty, windowless reading room on the second floor at the university library. The lights were off, except for a floor lamp that created a gloomy island of light around him. An observer would have no way of knowing that it was noon on a bright sunny day. Lily opened the door and turned on the overhead lights. Davyn shut his eyes tight, shook his head, then blinked a few times. He looked up briefly, then put his hand to his forehead to shield himself from the light as he went back to reading.

"Sorry, Count Dracula," she said, strolling over to where he was sitting.

Davyn continued reading. She moved her head around, trying to get in his field of vision so he'd look up, but his only response was a sigh. She laughed.

"Thank you for agreeing to tutor Bukka."

Again, Davyn didn't respond.

"It means so much to him."

Davyn furrowed his brow and set his book on his lap. "Is that today?"

Lily squinted. "You know perfectly well it is."

"Well then, tell him to bring his A-game. I don't have patience for anything else. I just want to get this over with."

Lily pulled up a chair from a nearby table and sat down next to him. She stared at him until he looked up and acknowledged her. "I want you to promise to be nice."

Davyn leaned back as if shocked. "Am I ever anything but nice?"

She pursed her lips. "I've seen you cut people down like a combine mowing grass."

Davyn pondered her curt reply for a moment, then, without expression, went back to reading.

"It's important to me—and to Bukka."

It was clear he she wasn't going to go away until he agreed. Davyn turned the page in his book and glanced at her. "Okay, cross my eyes and hope to die."

Lily furrowed her brow and cocked her head. "Cross your eyes? That's not how it goes."

Davyn's jaw dropped and his eyes got big. "You mean I've been saying it wrong all this time?"

Lily leaned back in her chair. "You know perfectly well it's 'cross my heart and hope to die.'"

Davyn shook his head. "No, no, I'm quite sure it's 'cross my eyes.' After all, what does one do before dying? They cross their eyes." Davyn crossed his eyes and stuck his tongue out as he mimicked a dying man. He let his book drop to his chest. A couple of spasms later and he was out. Gone.

Lily laughed. "You can be so funny sometimes. Honestly, no one knows what to make of you."

Davyn lay motionless.

Lily got up and collected her bag. "Okay, I'll take that as a yes, you'll be nice to my Bukka. He'll be here in twenty minutes, so somebody better give you some CPR." She laughed and walked out the door.

Davyn smiled, then returned his recliner to a sitting position to continue reading.

Davyn moved to a large table in the library's crowded main hall to wait for Bukka. He didn't do it to make it easier for Bukka, just to help speed things along and get the tutoring session over with. The table could easily hold six people, but Davyn wanted to make sure he could maintain his personal space. If Davyn were to be asked how much space he preferred, he'd have replied the orbit of Neptune, unless Pluto happened to be farther away at the time in its highly eccentric orbit.

The clatter from a book turnstile spinning rapidly and ejecting books when it nearly toppled over drew Davyn's attention to the front of the library. Bukka's muscular six-foot-seven frame was hunched so one hand could hold the top of the turnstile as the textbooks under his other arm slipped out, one by one, and fell to the floor. *That's one way to distribute books to the community, I suppose.*

Davyn watched as Bukka awkwardly slowed the turnstile and then steadied it. A few students, who'd been standing nearby when the circus that is Bukka began, helped him gather the scattered books and return them to their places.

Once things settled, Bukka thanked his helpers and craned his neck to look around the library. Spotting Davyn, he waved so enthusiastically that he almost dropped his books all over again.

Bukka arrived at the table and plopped the books down, splaying them out like a deck of cards. He then proceeded to pick up one of the heavy wood chairs, swing it out and around with unusual ease—like someone waving off a bug—then place it down and sit.

He wore a perpetual smile. Even when his face was resting, there was a hint of it. The sides of his mouth curved up like a dolphin's.

Davyn's face, on the other hand, looked like he'd just eaten a bad potato salad. "Hello Bukka, it's nice to see you."

"Hello, Professor Daeger. Thank you so much for agreeing to tutor me. I've been studying, but it's hard. The work, all these books. And the practice, you know. Football. It's just all a lot."

"Yes, the studying and the football. That will take its toll. I guess."

"Did you play football in college? I mean, before now. Not as a professor, I mean. When you went to college."

Davyn paused and chewed his lips, squinting. "Bukka, I think you're a nervous talker. There's nothing to be nervous about. Why don't you open your book to the section where you want to begin, and we'll get started?"

"Sure, oh sure. Where was it?" Bukka thumbed through the textbook with his head almost inside it. The pages fanned past his face, nearly brushing his nose as they shot by.

Davyn stood up, took a deep breath, and stretched.

Bukka stopped flipping pages and looked up from his book. "Is everything alright, Professor Daeger?"

Davyn forced a smile, but only the left side of his face responded. Then he stretched some more. "Yes, I just need to move a little. My back hurts from sitting. Old sports injury."

"So you did play." Bukka leaned back in his chair. "What was it Professor Daeger? Football?"

"Rugby. You don't have to call me Professor Daeger."

Bukka went back to looking through the book. "What would you like me to call you?"

A disembodied voice called Davyn's name. It seemed to simultaneously come from everywhere and nowhere. Davyn jerked his head to the side and looked around at the students, then across the way at the wall of bookshelves.

"What?" Davyn said, still searching for the source. He winced and looked for the source of the voice.

Bukka repeated, "I said, what would you like me to call you?"

"Who is this?" Davyn continued scanning the room, trying to find the source of the voice.

Bukka looked around and noticed the other students peering at the professor.

"Um, are you talking to me, professor? You're acting a little weird."

"Bukka, do you hear that voice?" he whispered.

Bukka closed his book. "Look, you don't have to make fun of me. You could have just said no when Lily asked you. She told me about you playing dead earlier and how you stayed that way 'til she left. I may not be that bright, but I can see what you're doing." He collected his other books. "I'll just leave."

"My brother?" Davyn said as he continued searching the room.

Bukka stood up and his shoulders dropped as he turned and walked toward the entrance.

The commotion drew Mrs. Dawit's attention. She looked over at Davyn from her desk and her jaw dropped. She put her hand to her mouth and watched as he paced, his eyes darting around the room, then hurried over to him.

"Davyn?"

"Do you hear that, Mrs. Dawit? That woman?"

The students in the main hall stared disbelievingly at Davyn.

Some gawked and pointed, while others kept their heads down and pretended not to notice. Mrs. Dawit put her hand on his arm, but he pulled away. He paused for a moment, gazing around the room again with wide, glazed eyes and furrowed brows.

"Davyn, what's come over you?"

Davyn heard the disembodied voice say, "You are the only one who can hear me. I need you to stop talking and drawing attention to yourself. Act normal, and stop moving or you'll lose the signal and you won't be able to hear what I have to say.. Your brother is not dead, but he is in danger."

Davyn shook his head and started for the library door. The voice went silent.

He picked up his pace and exited the library. The cold air stung his face. He sat down on a nearby bench, bent over, and held his head in his hands as if to keep his thoughts from exploding outward. *What the hell was that?*

A group of students walking toward the library stopped abruptly.

"Is everything alright, professor?" one of them asked.

Davyn put his hands on his legs and rubbed them slowly. He looked at the students, then at the ground. "Yes, yes, I was just...a little befuddled."

The students laughed. "Okay, just checking," one of them said as they continued on their way. Another kid whispered to the other, "He can be so weird. This is the first time I've ever seen him outside."

The chill crept in around his face and chest. He pulled his collar up around his neck before standing up, taking a deep breath, and heading back into the library. As he walked past Mrs. Dawit's desk, she looked up at him.

"Davyn, what is it?"

Davyn didn't respond, but kept walking until he reached the table from earlier and sat down. He looked around the room and noticed several students peering up at him from behind their books. He grabbed one of his books and began thumbing through it. Glancing up, he saw Mrs. Dawit staring at him. When she realized she'd been caught, she looked away. He thought about what he must have looked like, the way he acted when he heard the voice. He picked up the rest of his books and headed for the rear exit.

Davyn walked down a narrow hallway toward Mrs. Dawit's office. He didn't like explaining himself to others, but he knew that Mrs. Dawit deserved an explanation, and he wanted to put what happened in the library behind them. Surely she was wondering if he'd done mad. The door was open, but he stopped before entering and considered having the conversation at a later date. No, he thought he'd better take care of it now.

Mrs. Dawit sat at a wood desk across from a large bay window, where the sun radiated in, illuminating tiny particles of floating dust. She didn't notice him as she thumbed through a rolodex. The room was quiet, except for the soft ticking of a clock on the opposite wall. A passing cloud obscured the sun, and the room grew dark.

This must be how a ghost feels. Okay, enough of your weird thoughts. Time to normal up.

Davyn took a deep breath and knocked on the door. "Hello, Mrs. Dawit. Do you have a minute to speak with me?"

She smiled and stood up. "Always, for you, Davyn. Come in." She extended her hand toward a chair opposite her desk.

Davyn put his hand out. "I'll stand, thank you." He stayed by the window and clasped his hands in front of him. "I have a trip coming up this weekend," he said. He was avoiding the topic he came to talk about: the voice he had heard in his head.

"Yes, you told me. A hunting trip, with sticks and arrows and things, right?"

"Yes, that's right. I'll use the tools I made to mimic the ones our ancestors used during the late Pleistocene era, about 12,000 years ago." Davyn turned to the window and gazed out at the trees in the park. His hands moved like he was tracing the contours of the tools he described. He took on a new energy when he spoke about the things that mattered to him. "I'll hunt game like they did." He stopped and folded his arms. "It's not the same game, of course. By game, I mean megafauna, the very large animals that used to inhabit North America."

Mrs. Dawit furrowed her eyebrows, then smiled. "You sound like you're teaching one of your classes."

Davyn scratched behind his ear, then rested his hand on his neck. He stared at the ground. "Sorry. I thought you might be interested."

"I am." She smiled at him. "But you've told me all about this before." She pushed her Rolodex away from her and sat up straight. "You seem a little, um, on edge today."

Davyn looked out the window as she spoke. It was a nice view of the park, but the weather was turning, and it was getting cloudy.

"Have a seat, Davyn."

This time, Davyn turned and walked over to her desk, pulled out a chair, and sat down.

"What was it you wanted to speak about?"

Davyn hesitated. He looked up at the ceiling, then back at Mrs. Dawit. "I caught wind of something—I heard it from a teacher here on campus." He leaned forward. "That I might be up for a promotion."

"That's wonderful, Davyn. You're so talented. The university is lucky to have you."

Davyn looked down at the desk. "I only have the job because of my brother."

"That's not true, Davyn. You should know that."

Davyn cleared his throat and scratched at his elbow. "Um, you've been here a very long time."

Mrs. Dawit cocked her grey head to the side and raised her brows.

"Sorry, I meant longer than I have. I thought maybe you might have some tips on how to—you know, get the promotion." The way his voice rose at the end made it sound more like a question.

Mrs. Dawit put her hands in her lap. "Well, start by asking yourself why you want it."

"Oh, I know that. It's so I can focus on my research and not have to teach the kids."

She shook her head. "You don't want to say that. Just focus on the research. Leave the part about teaching out of it."

Davyn pursed his lips. "What else?"

"Well, just the usual things, I suppose." She paused and looked out the window, her eyes moving side to side as if she were reading a book. "You publish regularly and you bring in funds from the National Endowment. That will benefit you." She picked up a pencil and tapped it on her desk, then put it back down and looked at Davyn. "You have all the qualifications. Except for one."

Davyn leaned in.

"You need to do a better job of interacting with people. Your colleagues, superiors and, yes, students."

Davyn's face dropped as he leaned back in his chair and slid into a slouch.

Mrs. Dawit sighed. "I know it's not your favorite thing."

She opened the drawer where she kept her cookies and looked down at them, then back up at Davyn. His brows were furrowed, his arms crossed. She shook her head and closed the drawer.

"Why can't I just write and publish? Why do I have to teach? I'm just not good with people."

Mrs. Dawit pursed her lips. "Now Davyn, you know the answer to that. Once you're a full professor, you can focus more time on your research." She shrugged. "But for now, you must teach. And you can be good with people. I've seen it."

Davyn shook his head dismissively.

"Your students seem very interested in your course. Try engaging with them. Take some questions. You might find that you enjoy the interaction."

Davyn let out a laugh. "I tried that." He shook his head. "Didn't go so well."

He stood up and went back over to the window.

"There's something else bothering you, Davyn. What was all that commotion in the main hall earlier?" She leaned and tilted her head so she'd be in his periphery. "You acted as if you'd seen a ghost."

Davyn sighed. "That's really what I came to talk to you about." He turned around to face her. "I recognize how this may come across—and I assure you I'm not crazy." He scratched behind his ear. "At least I don't think I am. Of course, if I was, I would probably say the same thing." Davyn stared at the floor.

"Go ahead, Davyn. I'm listening," she said, her voice softening.

He walked back to her desk and sat down. "Earlier, when I was tutoring Bukka, I heard a voice."

Mrs. Dawit leaned forward, put her elbows on her desk and nodded. "Well, the library was very busy. That's not surprising."

Davyn squinted but said nothing.

"What did the voice say?"

"It didn't come from any of the other tables. It didn't come from anywhere. It came from everywhere and nowhere." Davyn stopped himself. "Look, I'm just going to say this and then we can talk about what it means, because I already know it sounds crazy and, trust me, it gets worse."

Mrs. Dawit fixed her gaze on him and gave a gentle nod.

Davyn waited a moment before continuing. "The voice told me that my brother is alive." He let out a short, jittery laugh and shook his head dismissively.

Mrs. Dawit cocked her head and frowned. "I knew something was troubling you, Davyn. I can help you. Get some help for you, I mean."

Davyn let out a laugh. "I don't need help. Not the help you're referring to, anyway," he said, pointing at his head. "I know what I heard, and I figured out how they did it."

"Knowing how who did what?"

"I don't know the who, but I know the how."

Mrs. Dawit raised an eyebrow. "And how did they do it?"

"They used something called a hypersonic sound transmitter. It's real. I can show you articles. The real question is why they'd use one and why they'd want to communicate with me." Davyn paused. He wanted to choose his next words carefully. As it was, he knew he sounded like someone talking about space aliens. "I mean, why do they want to communicate with me?" He crinkled his nose. *Ugh, that definitely didn't help.*

"Davyn—" She drew a long breath. "I'm afraid that makes little sense. Why would, um, people—we are talking about *people*, right?"

Oh boy. "Yes, of course."

Mrs. Dawit stood up and walked over to Davyn and leaned against her desk. She placed her hand over his. "You have a promotion coming up and I heard about how your class went the other day."

Davyn slid his hand out from under hers and placed it on his lap.

"I think the stress is probably getting to you. It happens to everyone." She paused and looked at Davyn more closely. "Maybe you need to take a few days off. Relax and unwind."

Davyn sat in his chair and thought for a few moments. *Maybe she's right. But the voice was so clear. There was no way it was my imagination. Either way, Mrs. Dawit won't be any help, and talking about it just makes me sound crazy.*

"Davyn?" she said, waving a hand in front of him.

Davyn shook his head. "Maybe you're right, Mrs. Dawit. I'll head home early tonight after class and get some rest. I'm sure everything will be better tomorrow." He picked up his bag and headed for the door. "Thank you for listening. I'm sorry if I upset you. I'll be fine."

CHAPTER 5

Davyn paused and took a deep breath before approaching the table in the library's main hall, where he'd heard the voice in his head. He strummed his fingers on the table, scanning the opposite wall, looking for a sign of the transmitter. If it was somewhere on the wall of books, it was hidden well. Maybe he should go search the other bookracks. But there were too many, and there were four floors of them. Just looking up at them all was dizzying. If he tried to search them, he'd look like a nut. Maybe if he stayed where he was, he'd hear it again. Then it would simply be a matter of getting someone else to hear it, too. At least he'd know he wasn't crazy. He let out a slow, sputtering breath as he sat and waited for the voice to return.

A tap on his shoulder sent a chill down his spine. He swung his head around, eyes wide. *Lily.*

"I'm angry with you," she said, her voice tight.

Davyn shook his head. "Look, Lily, about what happened with Bukka. It wasn't deliberate."

She put her hands on her hips and leaned in toward Davyn. "He's humiliated. He thinks you did it on purpose."

Davyn's mouth opened, but nothing came out. The stressful events of the day were gathering around him like a developing storm.

Lily hissed, "I don't know what's going on with you, but please talk to Bukka and explain what happened."

Davyn jolted upright in his chair. He'd been agonizing over whether the news of his brother and the voice in his head were real, and the fact that the voice suddenly stopped and there was nothing to do but wait for it to come back again. And now, he was being admonished by his teaching assistant for being too distracted to tutor her boyfriend. It was too much. He felt his face get hot and his throat tighten.

"Look, I didn't want to tutor him to begin with, and I don't have time for this. I have real issues to deal with, and Bukka isn't one of them."

She gave him a sharp look, then frowned and swallowed hard. "You are a really terrible person sometimes, professor." Her eyes welled up, then she turned abruptly and stormed away.

Davyn sighed and shook his head. He gave one last look at the wall. No sign of the transmitter. He packed his things and lifted his backpack to his shoulder and shuffled off to his empty conference room on the second floor. It had been a very strange day.

He walked into the dark room without turning on the lights and plopped his bag on the table with a thump. He sat down and stared ahead at nothing. After a few minutes, there was a light knock on the door. He looked over and saw the silhouette of a man standing in the doorway.

"Professor Daeger?"

Davyn swallowed hard and squinted, trying to make out who it was. He responded cautiously. "Yes. What is it?"

"I have a letter for you."

Davyn still couldn't make out who it was. "Leave it on the table there, next to the door."

The dark figure placed the letter on the table and walked away. Davyn walked over to the doorway and stuck his head out. He saw a thin man dressed in a suit turn the corner. He thought for a moment about going after him, but decided instead to read the letter. With the very tips of his fingers, he picked it up by the corner and placed it on the table where he'd been sitting earlier. Turning on the light, he saw there was nothing on the back. He used a pencil to flip it over. On the front, someone had written his name. He pulled a multi-tool from his bag, picked up the letter, and shook it gently. He felt a little silly; it was probably just a letter. He put it back down and sat with his hands on his legs, unsure how to proceed until he let out a huff and just opened it.

To: Professor Davyn Daeger

I tried to contact you earlier today using an unusual method. My fear is that you did not receive my message in its entirety. I am securing a more reliable means to communicate with you and will be back in touch. I apologize for the cryptic nature of my messages, but the reason for all of this will become clear. For your safety and theirs, please do not discuss this matter with anyone. Please be patient. Your questions will be answered very soon.

Mrs. Dawit called out to Lily as she walked past her desk, so she stopped. "Yes, Mrs. Dawit?"

"I wonder if I might have a word with you."

Lily shrugged. "Um, sure."

"Let's go in my office." She extended her arm to point the way.

Lily walked down the hallway and stepped inside the office. She stood by the window and looked out. "You have a beautiful view from here."

Mrs. Dawit walked past Lily and sat at her desk. "Yes, it is lovely. Looks like it might rain, though." She opened up her top drawer. "Oatmeal cookie?"

"No, no, thank you."

Mrs. Dawit motioned toward a chair by her desk. "Please, have a seat. Everyone seems to want to stand and look out my window lately. Maybe I should just move my desk over there."

Lily sat down and looked around the office. "I like your clock."

Mrs. Dawit smiled and leaned forward. "How do you like working with Professor Daeger?"

"Um, it's okay, I guess. He's not an easy person to get to know."

"No, he isn't." She leaned further forward like she was about to tell a secret and whispered, "But it is worth it if you do. I don't want to be telling tales out of school, as the expression goes, but I think it's important for you to know that Davyn has had a very difficult time of it. He experienced a terrible loss—well, it was a very terrible loss and it's stayed with him, I think—and it makes it hard for him to—" Mrs. Dawit paused. "He lost his brother, that's all I'll say. Please don't share that with anyone."

"I see. I won't tell anyone, of course. How long ago did, did— when did his brother pass?"

"I don't know. It's been a while, several years, I believe. But it haunts him. I think he feels like he's somehow responsible. I've really said too much. I'm sorry. I just feel like he's a good person inside and, well, you know how life can be."

"Thank you for sharing that with me, Mrs. Dawit. I know how important you are to him."

"Well, you are to him, too. I see how he pushes you to learn. It may seem like he's teasing or being curt, but in his own way, he's helping you. He only does it because he sees your potential." She sat back in her chair. "He just ignores most people."

Lily looked down at the desk and nodded. "I understand." She was still angry, but it seemed smaller now in contrast with what she had just learned about the professor, and she felt a little ashamed. Rain started tapping on the window.

Mrs. Dawit looked outside. "Here comes the rain." She sighed, then looked back at Lily. "He likes you, and he likes me, but we're really all he has, so it's important that we put in the extra effort."

Lily nodded. The air felt dry and the room was quiet, with only the sound of the ticking clock and the rain on the window to break the silence. Lily leaned closer to Mrs. Dawit. "This doesn't feel like the right time to bring this up, but maybe you can give me some advice on how to deal with him. He can be really mean sometimes. Bukka is the biggest, sweetest man, and Professor Daeger humiliated him today. Poor Bukka feels just awful about the whole thing."

Mrs. Dawit tilted her head. "Don't be so sure that Professor Daeger did what Bukka said." She brushed some crumbs from her desk into her hand. "I'm not saying Bukka's wrong, only that he may have misinterpreted what happened. Davyn's—I mean Professor Daeger's—sense of humor is a little..." She searched for the right word as she dumped the crumbs into a wastebasket. "Out of the ordinary, maybe. And sometimes he's the only one who gets it. Earlier, though, when he was tutoring Bukka, his behavior *was* very strange. I think something is bothering him and I don't think he was teasing Bukka."

"You're probably right, Mrs. Dawit. Maybe I should give the professor the benefit of the doubt." She paused for a moment. "I still want him to apologize to Bukka."

Mrs. Dawit nodded. "Just keep what I told you in mind and move slowly. He's not an easy person to get to know, as you said."

"It is funny, though," Lily mused as she stood up.

"What is?"

"It's funny that he's an anthropology professor, but he doesn't like people."

Mrs. Dawit smiled. "He'd think that was funny. I must tell him that one. He'll appreciate the irony."

Lily nodded and looked down at Mrs. Dawit's desk and saw a gift card from Bakersfield Cafe. "The professor likes the gift cards that you give him. I see him carrying one with him everywhere he goes."

Mrs. Dawit squinted. "Hmm, have you seen him actually go to Mr. Bakersfield's?"

"Oh, um—" Lily stopped herself. She meant that the professor used the cards as bookmarks, but she'd better not say that to Mrs. Dawit. It would hurt her feelings. Not to mention he probably had a hundred in his desk drawer.

"Lily?"

"Sorry, I just thought of something."

Mrs. Dawit raised an eyebrow.

Lily noticed her reaction. "It's nothing." Lily waved her hand, but ended up using it to cover her mouth when she let out a snort. She hunched her shoulders and looked away, turning slightly red. "Excuse me."

Mrs. Dawit crinkled her brow and walked over to Lily. "I give the cards to Professor Daeger to encourage him to go out more. At least for a coffee. But I never see him there. Have you?"

"Um, no, I don't think so. Maybe."

"Don't tell this to anyone," Mrs. Dawit said, looking around the room as though someone might be hiding and listening behind the fern. She looked Lily in the eye and whispered, "I think Mr. Bakersfield has a crush on me."

Lily smiled and nodded. "That wouldn't surprise me at all."

Mrs. Dawit smiled back. "He gives me the cards to get me to come in more, I suppose. Then I give them to Professor Daeger to get him to go out more." She appeared to ponder that for a moment. "It's a strange circle."

"Doesn't Mr. Bakersfield wonder why you don't use the cards when you buy coffee?"

"Oh, I don't know what he thinks." She waved her hand, dismissing the notion. "I'm not a schoolgirl, you know. Dating is for young women and men like you and Bukka."

"Oh, that's not true, Mrs. Dawit. I'm sure you'd enjoy each other's company. You should go on a date with him."

"Oh, posh." She turned a light shade of pink as she fiddled with her broach. She tilted her head. "We do have pleasant conversations when I see him."

Lily beamed. "See, that's what a date is. You just do it somewhere other than Bakersfield's."

Mrs. Dawit fanned herself and straightened her dress. "Enough about that for now." She stood up straight and cleared her throat while Lily tried, with little success, to suppress her smile. "I think getting out would be very good for Professor Daeger's mood. Don't you?"

"Yes, I think he needs that very much. He's always alone and hardly ever talks to anyone."

"Good." Mrs. Dawit picked up a gift card from her desk and reached into her center drawer to pull out two more. "You and Bukka should take him there. Today is good." She handed the cards to Lily and pressed them into her hand.

"Oh, I don't know. I mean, he should definitely go out, but I don't know if I want to go with him."

"Why not? He likes you."

"He says trouble follows him when he goes out. He refers to himself as a sh—" She glanced at Mrs. Dawit. "Um, a poop magnet."

"Nonsense. That's just Professor Daeger being silly. Take the cards and go. It'll be fine."

A loud thunder crack shook the windows and Lily gasped.

Mrs. Dawit gazed out the window. "Maybe after the storm passes."

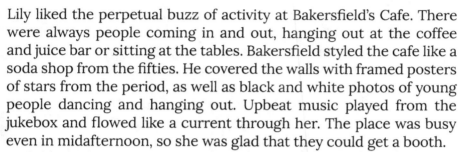

Lily liked the perpetual buzz of activity at Bakersfield's Cafe. There were always people coming in and out, hanging out at the coffee and juice bar or sitting at the tables. Bakersfield styled the cafe like a soda shop from the fifties. He covered the walls with framed posters of stars from the period, as well as black and white photos of young people dancing and hanging out. Upbeat music played from the jukebox and flowed like a current through her. The place was busy even in midafternoon, so she was glad that they could get a booth.

"Thanks for the coffee, professor," Lily said, as she toasted him with her coffee.

The professor winced. "You're welcome. Mrs. Dawit's given me dozens of these gift cards. I had to get rid of some."

"Oh, well... Thanks all the same." She smiled and toasted again.

He rubbed his temple and grimaced. "Do you have to do that?"

"What?"

"Toasting. It's annoying."

"Lots of people toast. It's a tradition with a long and storied history."

He pulled his arrowhead from his pocket and began stroking it with his thumb.

"I learned that in class the other day," she said, glancing at the stone in his hand.

"I'm glad they're covering all the important topics."

"Let me see that rock."

"What rock?"

"The one you're always stroking."

"It's an arrowhead."

"I know. Made of rock. Let me see it."

He placed it in her hand, and she examined it. She ran her finger up the side. "Look at this groove you've carved into it. Why are you always rubbing it?"

Davyn stared off. "It helps me relax."

Lily looked past the professor at Mrs. Dawit as she entered the cafe.

"Mrs. Dawit's just came in."

"Good, make sure she sees us. I don't want to have come here for nothing."

Lily scrunched her face. Pop music started playing over the speakers. "I love this song. Don't you love this song, professor?"

"Why does a fifties-themed shop have to play pop music?"

Lily swayed back and forth to the music. "They play fifties music, too," she reassured him.

He reached into his backpack and pulled out a book.

Lily's eyes bulged, and she stopped swaying. The pitch of her voice rose. "What are you doing?"

"If you can dance, I can read."

"No, you can't," she chastised him. "Put that away."

Davyn set the book down on top of his backpack. "How long do we have to stay here?"

"At least until Mrs. Dawit leaves." She looked at his backpack. "That's a nice bag. Is it leather?"

He nodded.

She squinted, glanced between him and the bag. "It looks different from others I've seen."

"It's goat leather."

Lily snorted and covered her mouth. "Really?"

He nodded.

"Why would you use goat leather?"

He blinked deliberately and shrugged. "I like goats."

She cocked her head. "You mean you hate goats. That's why you have them made into bags."

"Actually, this one's cruelty free. You should appreciate that."

Lily smirked. "How can it be cruelty free?"

He glanced at his pocket watch. "They wait until the goat dies of old age before they use the skin."

She shifted her gaze from the bag to him and raised her brows. "You're teasing me because I'm vegan."

"No, actually, I'm not." He put his book back in the bag. "I have to use the restroom," he said as he stood up and walked away.

Lily shuffled over to his side of the booth and opened the top flap of the bag. She read the label. Cruelty free/Fair trade.

She closed the flap and returned to her side of the booth.

When the professor returned, Lily cleared her throat and squared her shoulders. "Professor, I'd like you to apologize to Bukka. For what happened."

"That wasn't my fault."

"But he thinks you were making fun of him."

"I wasn't."

"It doesn't matter, his feelings were still hurt."

"But I'm not in the wrong."

"Sometimes it's more important to be kind than to be right."

"Okay, you can tell him I wasn't making fun of him."

"You should tell him."

The professor didn't respond. He just stared out the window. Lily thought she'd start up a new conversation and to try and get him talking.

"I think you need to get out more. You're always cooped up. You should get out into the world, instead of just reading about it. You don't have to go far. You can—oh, I don't know—volunteer. Feed the homeless or something. Volunteering always makes me feel good."

The professor didn't reply.

Lily looked around the cafe and sighed before continuing in her efforts. "Professor, did you hear me? You could feed the homeless, and you'll feel better."

Davyn looked at his watch and sat up in his chair. "Yes, I heard you. I can feed the homeless."

Lily peered at the professor, thinking that maybe if she talked about school he'd take more of an interest. "I was in philosophy class today. The professor quoted an old saying, 'If you want to go fast, go alone, but, if you want to go far, go with a team.'" She nodded.

Davyn sat for a moment then said, "What if you want to go far, fast?"

Lily scrunched her nose. "We didn't cover that."

"Maybe they'll cover it in tomorrow's class."

Lily frowned. "I really thought I had something there."

"Oh well."

"Oh my god." Lily's mouth dropped open.

"What?"

"Mr. Bakersfield is talking to Mrs. Dawit. They're so cute together. Look."

"I'm not looking."

"You're missing out," Lily shifted her gaze to the professor. Her eyes got big.

"What now?"

"She's looking over here."

"Okay." He turned and looked over the back of the booth at Mrs. Dawit and waved, then turned back around in his seat.

"What if she saw me looking at them?"

"She'll probably have you expelled."

"Ha, hilarious." She pulled her ponytail out from behind her and pulled it over her shoulder. "I hope he's not already in a relationship."

"He's not. He's a widower."

Lily and the professor had run out of things to say. Meanwhile, the sounds of people laughing and talking grow louder as the cafe filled in anticipation of the singer's arrival.

She jumped in her seat. "Oh, I know—I said something to Mrs. Dawit earlier, and she said you'd find it funny."

"Okay, what did you say?"

"I said I thought it was ironic that you study anthropology, but you hate people." She beamed, expecting a laugh from the professor.

He scrunched his face.

"I'm sorry. Mrs. Dawit thought you'd think that was funny."

"It is—kind of. Look, I'm tired. I think I'm going to get going." He reached for his backpack.

"Wait, we have to wait for Mrs. Dawit to leave."

He settled back into his chair and rubbed his temple again.

A heavyset man walked in and sat down at the table next to them. The professor watched him out of the corner of his eye but said nothing. Lily glanced at the man, then back at the professor.

Lily cleared her throat. "You know, your story about hunting really grabbed everyone's attention."

"Did it?"

"They had a lot of questions."

"Yeah, that's what screwed me up." He shook his head.

Lily put her hands in her lap and looked around the cafe.

Everyone else was having fun. She glanced briefly at the man that the professor had eyeballed. He looked angry and disheveled and appeared out of place in an otherwise joyful environment. A few minutes passed without conversation.

Lily looked at the professor. "Frankly, I don't know how you can kill and eat those little bunnies, though. That's partly why I went vegan."

"I don't hate—" the professor started to reply but was cut off by the man at the table next to them.

"Vegan?" His voice was deep and scratchy, and the expression on his face made him look like he'd just eaten something rotten. Lily smelled the stale odor of alcohol on his breath, and his eyes were droopy and glazed. "Why would you be vegan?"

Lily opened her mouth to speak when the professor said, "Health reasons."

"I was asking the lady." He swung his legs out from under the table one at a time, followed by his upper body. His movements were erratic. It reminded Lily of a zombie movie she'd seen once.

The professor looked at Lily, and she stared back with wide eyes. She shook her head subtly and whispered, "Don't say anything. It's not worth it."

The man walked over to their table, and the cafe grew quiet as everyone took notice of the scene. The man leaned down toward Lily.

"I asked why you're vegan." He coughed and wiped his mouth with his sleeve. "I'm just curious."

The professor said, "I'm vegan, too. Ask me."

The man turned to the professor. "Okay, why are you vegan?"

The professor shifted his eyes from Lily to the heavyset man. "You have a short memory." His voice was calm, almost sympathetic.

The man's head flinched back. "What?"

"Oh, you don't remember?"

"Remember what?"

"I had said that eating plants improves brain health and memory."

Lily bit her bottom lip and focused her gaze on the professor.

The man stood up straight and put his hands on his hips. "I don't remember you saying—" He stopped, nodded, then went back to his table and picked up the menu.

"Prime rib's on special today," the professor said, looking toward the guy, but not directly at him.

The man hesitated, then said, "Thanks." His focus stayed on the menu.

Lily's eyes were big. She shook her head again. "Don't provoke him," she whispered.

"I didn't. I told you I'm a shit magnet."

The guy stood up. "I think I'll eat somewhere else. Nothing here but coffee and muffins." He stood up and walked out. The professor smiled at him and nodded.

"What's a shit magnet, again?" Lily asked.

"If there's someone within a particular radius of me and they're looking to start trouble," he gestured at the heavyset man walking out the door, "they'll be drawn to me." The professor stared off into space for a moment. "That's what Magne used to say, anyway."

"Who's Magne?"

He focused back on Lily. "Never mind. I have to get going." He grabbed his bag and walked out the cafe's front door. Light rain fell, so Davyn turned up his collar. The man from the table was waiting for the bus. Davyn saw him and stood there for a moment. The guy looked Davyn up and down, then nodded at him. Davyn walked away, but his day wasn't over yet.

CHAPTER 6

Midday sun streamed through the library's windows on the fourth floor, covering most of the main hall. The rain had passed, and the warm sunlight cast an orange glow despite the dropping temperatures outside. Davyn felt a social hangover coming on as he headed past Lily and Bukka studying at a table in the main hall. He needed some time alone, and the reading room on the second floor would do just fine.

"Oh, professor," Lily called out.

Mrs. Dawit looked up from her station and shot a glare at her. Lily jumped up, covered her mouth and gave Mrs. Dawit an apologetic glance in return.

She tiptoed over to Davyn, periodically looking at Mrs. Dawit, and exaggerated her tiptoe movements when Mrs. Dawit locked eyes with her.

"Professor, Bukka is stuck and needs you to answer a question. The exam is tomorrow. It'll just take a minute."

Lily walked back toward Bukka, waving Davyn on to join her.

Davyn took a deep breath, then followed her and sat down at their table. "Make it quick. I only have a minute."

"Thanks, professor. This will be quick," Bukka said, sliding an open book in front of Davyn. "You mentioned when creating a control group, it's important to—"

Lily put up a hand to stop him. "Hang on, Bukka, I have to tell the professor something."

Bukka pinched his lips and leaned back in his chair.

"I was in the administration office earlier and I accidentally overheard something."

"What did you hear?"

"I think the decision on your promotion will be made on Monday, but I'm not sure."

"That doesn't really help me." He gazed off and bit his bottom lip. "But if it's true, I probably shouldn't take Friday off to go to the woods."

"I'm sorry I don't know more." Lily's eyes darted around. "But Professor Anne was part of the conversation. She would know. You should go see her."

Davyn stared at the table. "No, I don't like asking people for things." He turned to Lily. "But you could ask her for me."

Lily jerked back slightly. "What?" She scrunched her nose. "You're a big boy. You can go ask her."

Davyn shook his head, then regarded Bukka sitting back in his seat, waiting patiently and watching the exchange. "Okay, Bukka, let's get this over with."

Bukka leaned forward over his book. "My question is about control groups—"

"Hang on, Bukka." Davyn ducked his head down, but focused his eyes at the man talking to Mrs. Dawit at the other end of the main hall. It was his department's dean, Rupert Puddington. He was looking in Davyn's direction, wearing the expression that he always wore: a carved-in-the-face frown.

"What is it, professor?" Bukka said.

"The dean is looking over here," he whispered. "I need to make a favorable impression. Act like I'm being engaging."

Lily and Bukka turned to each other and simultaneously shrugged.

"How do we do that?" Lily asked.

"Follow my lead." Davyn sat back up, let out a laugh, and slapped Bukka's arm, then patted him on the back.

Lily burst out laughing and slapped Davyn on the back. Mrs. Dawit shot them all a critical gaze.

Davyn pinched his face into a grimace. Through grated teeth he whispered, "Too much. Take it down a notch—or ten." Davyn peeked up at Puddington. He was still watching them. "We're going for subtlety here. Got it?"

"Oh, sorry," Bukka said, placing his hand on Davyn's back and rubbing slowly. Lily followed suit.

"Get your hands off me."

Bukka and Lily quickly pulled their hands away and placed them under the table, like kids caught in the cookie jar.

"Look, never mind, just nod your head and act like you understand what I'm saying when I show you something in the book."

Lily and Bukka nodded.

"Wait for me to show you something. Oh my god, this is going terribly."

Davyn sat back up, but kept his eyes fixed on the table. He dared not look up now. He reached out with one hand and pulled a book in front of him, and opened it to a random page and pointed at it. Lily and Bukka simultaneously nodded.

Davyn slapped the book closed. "Okay, that's not working either." He slid the book away. "Just try to look happy to be here. Is he still there?"

Lily looked up.

"Don't look."

"You asked me to look."

"Yes, but don't look like you're looking. Look away."

Lily turned her head to Davyn.

"Don't look at me."

Lily leaned back and looked behind Davyn at Bukka, her eyes big and questioning. Bukka shrugged.

"Look, let's just go back to what we were doing when I sat down."

Bukka stole a quick glance at Puddington, then back down at his book. He slid the book in front of him and flipped to the page he had opened before. "He's leaving, professor."

"Thank god. I've gotta get out of here." Davyn looked back up at where Puddington had been and put a hand on his bag.

Lily grabbed his arm. "Wait, the question Bukka had—"

"Look it up in the book. I have to go talk to someone." Davyn stood up and headed for the exit.

Davyn walked down the long, empty hallway, glancing briefly at the numbers over the office doors as he passed. He was looking for room 3214, Anne's office in the psychology building. He needed to ask her if the decision about his promotion would be made on Monday. If so, he'd put off his trip. It was just after four in the afternoon, and he hoped she was still in the building. Davyn's heart rate increased as the room numbers got closer to the one he was looking for. He wasn't excited about seeing Anne so much; he didn't enjoy interacting one on one with people he didn't know well, which was almost everyone.

The next door was 3214. Davyn stopped and turned around. Maybe he could still persuade Lily to ask Anne for him. *No, I've got to start interacting more with faculty, and this is a good opportunity to do it. Besides, she likes me.* The corner of his mouth curved up, then dropped. *Oh Jesus, that makes it worse.*

Davyn tucked in behind a column just outside her office door and peered in through the glass window. He leaned further and saw her sitting at her desk, reading. He tilted his head. *I wonder what she's reading. She's a psychology professor. Could be anything, I suppose.*

He looked around at the rest of the office and noticed a poster with a quote on it. He tried to make out what it said. He was procrastinating, to be sure, but when things caught his attention he had a tendency to fixate on them until his curiosity was sated.

As Davyn was trying to read the quote, and figure out how it related to the accompanying image, Anne opened the door and it hit him in the head. Not hard, just sort of pressed into his face. He didn't jerk back. That would have been embarrassing. What happened instead was a sort of snowplow effect, with his face as the snow.

"Maybe you could close it a little," Davyn said through squished lips.

Anne pulled the door back, and Davyn's face peeled off the glass with a sucking sound. "Wow, that was weird."

"There's a quote on your wall I was trying to read." Davyn pulled the door the rest of the way open and stepped inside. He walked over to the poster and leaned in. "Ah, yes, I see. That makes sense."

Davyn continued examining the other posters.

"Is there something that I can help you with, Davyn?" she asked with a smile.

"Ah, um, yes. Yes, I had a question for you. Maybe you know the answer. You may not," he said as he perused the wall of posters. Davyn glanced sideways at her for a moment, then returned his eyes to a poster in front of him. He squinted.

Anne looked at Davyn, then at the poster. "Okay, did you want to ask me the question, then?"

"Yes, yes, I would." Davyn turned to Anne and looked her in the eyes, but it made his face warm, so he shifted his attention back to the poster and straightened his vest. "I have a trip coming up this weekend, this holiday weekend. And I was going to take Friday off to extend it to four days. Monday's a holiday." Davyn caught himself. When nervous, he'd either pad what he was saying or truncate it. Usually neither helped to clarify what he meant. He meandered toward the window. "I'll be out in the woods, like the woods out there." He pointed out the window. "The woods beyond the parking lot."

Anne looked out the window, then back at Davyn. Davyn took a deep breath and thought about what Lily had told him, that he'd have a better chance of getting the information he wanted if he was cool and charming. Charming to Davyn meant speaking formally, so he composed himself and said, "Maybe we can take a walk and talk. It feels very warm in here, and I can use some air. Perhaps you do too, um—would want to."

Anne smiled and nodded. "Sure, let me grab my purse and we'll head out."

It surprised Davyn she agreed, and he grew just a bit more confident, smiling and standing up straight. "That would be lovely, Miss Anne—" Davyn paused. "Miss Anne... I'm sorry. What is your last name?"

"Oh, it's Throp," she said as she put on her coat and looked around the room, as if making sure not to forget anything.

"Well, Miss Anne Throp, the..." He stopped again and pursed his lips. A wry grin spread across his face. "I see. Very clever."

Anne pulled her hair from under her coat and over her shoulders. "What?"

He turned to Anne, stood up straight, and cleared his throat. "I have to say, I'm a bit proud of Lily for this one. I guess I had it coming."

"Had what coming?"

"Misanthrope." He bit his lip and nodded. "I'm the misanthrope." His face turned crimson, and he looked down at the floor.

Anne pulled back slightly. "Is this about my name?"

"Good day, Anne, if that's your real name."

Anne's shoulders dropped and her mouth fell open as he turned away and walked out the door.

Dan sat in his office at DARPA, Leo strumming her fingers on his desk across from him. Her knee bounced up and down as she stared at her watch. It was early morning, and the sun wasn't up yet. After driving all through the previous night, exhaustion had finally dragged her into a deep, if brief slumber. Now, they waited for the delivery of the earpiece. Once Davyn had it, she'd finally be able to tell him that Magne is alive and enlist his help to rescue him.

Dan stood by the phone, "Should be any minute now." Leo rubbed her eyebrow and bit her top lip as her knee kept bouncing up and down. Dan took an unsteady breath. "Um, you said earlier that you're writing a book about dogs?"

Leo flashed him a quick smile but didn't answer. "Your guy is standing by to take this over to the university as soon as it's ready, right?"

"Yes, Sam is standing by. He's good. You don't have to worry about him. We just need that earpiece."

Leo hoped the new earpieces would be reliable. They were prototypes that used new technology, but hadn't been field-tested yet. She didn't want to use them, but after yesterday's failed communication attempt, she had no choice.

Leo stood up and stretched. "How much of what I transmitted to Davyn yesterday do you think he heard?"

Dan frowned and shook his head. "I don't know. Not much, I'm afraid. He was moving around a lot. I wish we had something better that we could have used."

"We will. Any time now. Did I mention I hate waiting?" It was true; Leo was a great tactician, but her lack of patience sometimes got her into trouble. She looked at the safety posters on Dan's wall. "Lasers aren't toys," she mumbled with a small laugh.

Dan smirked. "Safety posters don't have to be serious to be effective. Did you catch the reference to *Hitchhiker's Guide*?"

"Yeah. Funny."

"Hey, I don't mean to pry, but your accent's interesting. May I ask where you're from?"

"I get that a lot. I was raised in Oxford, England, then we moved to the mean streets of Brooklyn. My uncle used to tease me and say my accent had a curious effect on people. He'd say if I asked someone if they'd like a cup of tea, it would sound courteous and eloquent, but with this subtle undercurrent that made them feel like they'd better accept to avoid trouble."

The phone rang, and Dan snatched it from its perch. "Yes?" There was a brief pause. "I'll be right there." Dan hung up the phone.

"Is it the—"

"Yes. I'll be right back."

He returned a few minutes later and held a small package out to Leo, who was already holding scissors. She grabbed it, cut it open, and slid two smaller boxes out, handling them like baby chicks. She opened one and examined it.

"Is that the model you were expecting?"

"It better be, I haven't seen the new models. I'll know as soon as I get it open." She opened the box and peered inside. "It definitely looks different from the earpieces we've been using."

The earpiece was small, white, and about the size of a pea with a tiny loop on one end. When placed in someone's ear, it would be invisible without an ear scope.

She set it down and pulled out the spec sheet. "Top secret, yada yada... This is it." She put the sheet down. "Call your guy."

Dan picked up the phone and dialed. He stepped away and started speaking.

Leo picked up the spec sheet again and continued reading.

"Charge, charge, charge... Here it is, every 12 hours. Okay, that's not too bad. We can make that work." She was trying to stay positive. "I hope..."

Dan hung up the phone. "Sam's on his way up to get the package. What's in the other box?"

"Same thing. He can use one while the other charges."

Dan nodded. "Of course."

There was a knock at the door. Dan walked over, cracked it open, peered out, then let Sam in. He was a young man, fresh out of college: not to mention young, thin and entirely out of place in his neat, grey, off-the-rack suit. Sam said nothing; he just stepped into the room and stood with his hands together in front of him.

Leo placed both earpieces back in their boxes and added a note to the package before standing up and walking over to Sam. "Okay, when you hand this to Davyn Daeger, you need to make sure you see him read the letter that's inside before you leave."

Sam nodded, took the package and left.

Dan went back to his desk. "Sam will text me after he delivers the package. In a little over an hour you should be speaking with Davyn." Dan looked up at Leo, but she was staring at the ground. "What's wrong? I thought you'd be relieved."

Leo looked up. "I'm worried the note is too cryptic. It might freak him out more than the voice did."

Dan shook his head. "You couldn't take the chance of revealing too much, too soon." Leo didn't look convinced, so Dan put his hands on his hips and sighed. "Do you want to role-play what you'll say to Davyn one more time?"

"I think we've covered it to death, but your safety posters are boring. Let's do it."

Davyn sat in a lounge chair under a floor lamp in a reading room on the second floor of the library. The hum of quiet activity drifted up from the main hall below. It had been a busy couple of days with far too many social interactions. He was glad to finally have the company of no one other than a book. He glanced up at the clock on the wall. It was 9:05 in the morning. He still had time before class, where he'd have to deal with students.

The door creaked open and a voice called, "Professor Daeger?"

Davyn looked up at a slender figure of a man standing in the doorway but said nothing.

The man stepped in, spilling light from the hallway into the small room. "Are the overhead lights out?" he asked.

"I like it that way. What is it you need?"

He walked over to Davyn. "I'm looking for you, professor."

The sky outside was dark grey, and rain slipped slowly down the window. The minimal natural light it allowed in illuminated the man's wiry frame. He was young, and looked out of his element in a suit. Davyn thought he might be a student there.

"I have an important package for you."

Davyn glanced at him, then at the package. He reached his hand out and took it, then set it on the end table next to him. The young man stood quietly. Davyn stared at him and tried to direct him to the door with his eyes.

Davyn strummed his fingers on the end table. "Am I supposed to sign or something?"

The young man fixed his gaze on Davyn. "They asked me to deliver this to you and ensure that you read the note inside. It's very important. Please read the note. It'll answer your questions."

"You sound like a fortune cookie." Davyn shifted his attention out the window. "It's fine, I'll look at it later." Davyn eyeballed the man. "Are you a student here?"

"No, I graduated two years ago, but I work with the engineering students on campus."

"Okay, well, thanks for the package. You can leave now." Davyn gestured toward the door and went back to reading.

The man stood for a moment. "Professor, I'm afraid I can't leave. Not until you've read the note."

Davyn looked at him, then at the package.

"It will provide some clarity on what happened yesterday," the man said, his voice rising at the end. He watched Davyn for a reaction. "The voice."

Davyn chewed gently on the inside of his lips and peered at the package. He opened it and pulled out the note and read it. He looked up at the man. "Who gave this to you?"

"I'm sorry, I can't say." The man turned and walked out the door, closing it behind him as he left.

Davyn set the package down on the large, heavy coffee table in front of him and rooted around for the contents. He pulled out two identical small boxes and opened one, then put his finger on the earpiece. He turned the box upside down and a small metal ring dropped out. He studied it briefly, then set it on the table. He leaned in and studied the earpiece, rotating it as he examined it. He set the earpiece on the table next to the ring, read the note again, and then opened the second small box. It contained the same earpiece as the first.

A knock on the door startled Davyn, and he jerked forward, dropping the second box. He picked up the earpiece from the table and put it in his pocket, then pushed the other box under the coffee table just as the door opened.

Davyn breathed a sigh of relief when Lily stepped in.

"Professor, are you okay? You look like you've seen a ghost." She clicked on a floor lamp. "Or maybe it's just the creepy lighting."

"Is there something you need, Lily? I'm very busy."

She looked him up and down. "Nope, it's not the lighting."

Davyn took a deep breath. "What is it you need?"

"Oh, sorry. I'll be quick. I left my notes here from earlier when I was grading papers. I'll just get them and be out of your way."

Lily picked up her notes and scooted out the door, leaving it open.

Davyn tried feeling around under the coffee table for the box, but the clearance between the bottom of the table and the floor was too narrow. He'd need Bukka to help him move it. Hearing a distant tinny sound, he stood up, looked around, then down. He patted his pocket before pulled the earpiece out and rotating it, trying to see which side the sound—no, it was a voice—was coming from. He held it to his ear, then with a swift motion stuck it in and scrunched his nose at the sensation. Then he heard the voice and his eyes opened wide.

"Davyn, when you're alone, say something. I have an important message for you."

He opened his mouth to speak, but Mrs. Dawit walked in.

"Davyn, you look like you've seen a ghost. Are you alright?"

The voice in his ear said, "He's got the earpiece in, but someone's with him."

"Davyn?" Mrs. Dawit said.

"I'm fine, the book I was reading was, um, intense."

She glanced down at the book: *Preparing Wild Game Using Stone Tools from The Pleistocene Era.*

"Hmm. Okay, if you say so."

The voice in his ear said, "It's okay, Davyn. When you can talk, let me know."

Mrs. Dawit waved a card for a free coffee and placed it on the table next to him. "Guess what Mr. Bakersfield gave me?"

Davyn's eyes bulged. He looked at the card, then back at Mrs. Dawit.

"I have to go," he said, starting for the door.

"Mr. Bakersfield really likes to see you over there, Davyn..."

Davyn stepped into the hallway and looked around to make sure he was alone. "Hello?" he whispered. "What the hell is going on?" He headed down the empty hallway, which overlooked the library's main hall below.

As he hit the elevator button, he noticed Mrs. Dawit staring at him. Davyn cracked a partial smile and raised his hand to wave, then looked back at the elevator button.

"Are you alone now?" The voice in his ear said.

The doors to the elevator opened and Davyn leaned into enter, then pulled back when students stepped off. The voice in his ear said, "Davyn. I have an important message for you."

His eyes darted around. "I have to get to my office," he whispered.

CHAPTER 7

Davyn stepped into his office, which was situated at the intersection of four main hallways. Windows ran the length of the entire perimeter of the office. It would have been a fishbowl, if not for the dark wood Venetian blinds installed on every window.

He drew a deep breath and said, "Okay, who is this and what's this about?"

"Davyn, I'm sorry for all of this, but I have important information. It's about your brother."

Davyn's heart sank. He looked down at a framed photo of his brother grinning on the beach, the sun setting behind him. It had sat on his desk for years, but everyone who saw it just figured it was a picture of Davyn. He'd never spoken of his brother to anyone other than Mrs. Dawit.

"What about him?"

The voice whispered, "Davyn, he's alive."

"What the hell kind of trick is this?" Davyn felt his face burning. He looked at the photo of his brother on his desk again. His heart pounded.

"Davyn, I know this is hard to hear. I'm sorry, but your brother is alive, and he needs your help." The voice was silent for a moment. "Desperately."

Davyn shook his head, his eyes welling up. "How the hell do I get this earpiece out?" He ripped the earbud out, but the core piece was deep in his ear canal.

The voice started pleading. "Please don't. I have more to tell you. I know how this must sound to you. But your brother didn't drown that day at the beach."

Davyn's eyes darted back and forth. He grabbed onto the armrest and fell down into his desk chair.

"You were both rescued," the voice continued.

It was in the newspapers. She could have read about it.

"Davyn, are you still there?"

He took a stuttering breath. "I'm here."

"Your brother didn't drown that day. Scouts from the agency were close by when you went into the water. They pulled you both out and administered CPR."

Davyn wanted to believe it, but it was just too extraordinary. He remembered waking up in the hospital by himself. *So they just took Magne?* He shook his head.

Leo pressed on. "Our agency works for the US government. What we do is tremendously vital."

Davyn leaned back in his chair, breathing heavily.

"Magne didn't want to cut off communication with you, or any others he loved. But he felt the duty, the obligation to serve, and he saw coming to work with us as his opportunity to do so. What we do here matters. We've taken out or provided intelligence to take out hundreds of terrorists and dozens of terrorist cells. And we've saved tens of thousands of lives."

Davyn scratched at his face and drew a deep breath. There was something in her voice. Her confident, compassionate demeanor sounded so convincing, and yet... "Look, how am I supposed to know that any of this is real? If he couldn't talk to me, why are you telling me this now? None of what you're saying makes sense."

"Davyn, please—"

"If Magne was alive, he'd have contacted me!" He reached into his ear again and tried to pry out the earpiece with his finger.

He heard a noise and looked up to see Mrs. Dawit standing in the doorway, her eyes wide and her mouth agape.

She looked at him sideways, and with a strained voice said, "What is going on with you? I'm worried."

Davyn took a deep breath. "Look, I'm tired of explaining myself. I know you mean well, but I need to get on a call now. Please shut the door on your way out."

Mrs. Dawit's face dropped. She turned toward the door, then turned back to Davyn. "You come see me as soon as you're done with that call, okay?"

Davyn nodded his head. "Yes, Mrs. Dawit. I promise."

She stepped out and closed the door while Davyn's eyes darted around the room.

"Davyn, your brother is alive, but he's been kidnapped. He needs your help."

In a monotone voice, Davyn said, "Kidnapped. Okay, that's new. What else do you have to tell me?"

"I understand how this must make you feel, but this is deadly serious. I hate to lay it out like this, but time is short. I can prove all of this to you, but you need, you need..." She stopped.

Davyn leaned forward. "What do I need?"

A sniffle came over the earpiece; she was crying. "I was hoping you'd be eager to help."

Davyn rolled his eyes. "Look, I don't respond well to crying. Just put it out there so we can move on."

She sniffed a couple of times and Davyn leaned back in his chair while he waited for her to compose herself, pushing against his desk with one leg. He actually tipped over backwards, but didn't get up. He just lay still, staring at the ceiling.

"I need you to get to Washington, D.C., and meet me there."

Davyn closed his eyes, trying to block out any further intrusions. "Okay, great, sounds like a plan. Is there a private jet or something? A helicopter? How about a jetpack? I'd really like one of those."

"There's no need to be sarcastic. And we have all of that, actually. Unfortunately, I can't use any agency resources at the moment. The agency can't know that Magne is missing."

"Look, this has been really fun, but you're out of your mind and you're making me crazy, too. I'm going to go now." Davyn reached in his ear with his finger and finally managed to pry the earpiece out. It fell to the floor. He stood up, grabbed his backpack and walked unsteadily toward the door.

Davyn walked through a small parking lot and on to the wooden plank walkway to the beach. The dry beach grass hissed softly in the salty breeze as the sound of the waves grew louder. The grey skies blocked the setting sun, making the ocean broody and dark, like wet charcoal ash. The waves rolled in gently. White foam writhed on the shore where the waves broke. He walked down the ramp toward the beach and stopped just before he reached the sand. He looked out over the water and hesitated at first, but then took a few steps to kneel and press the cool sand to his palms, between his fingers.

I haven't been to the beach since—

Davyn cut off his own thoughts and shifted his focus to the ocean. He knelt in the sand for a long while. A cool breeze scraped at his face like prickly fingers as he watched the waves crawl up the shore. The thought his brother was out there somewhere under the water had kept him from ever going back to the beach since that day he disappeared.

He stood up and took a few steps toward the ocean. He stood motionless, his eyes fixed on the water. The waves continued crashing, creeping further up the shore toward him. Their persistent sounds filled his ears, but his thoughts shifted to the pull of the current that had dragged Magne and him out and into the depths, four years ago to the day.

"Davyn, stop trying to swim to shore," Magne shouted. *"The current is too strong."*

"We're too far out." Davyn choked as a wave washed over him.

"Stop swimming, just tread. I'm coming for you."

Davyn tried to see over the waves to find Magne. The rain was already heavy, and only getting worse.

The sea was quiet when they entered the water just thirty minutes earlier, but a storm had moved in fast, churning the water into rolling cascades. Making matters worse, they found themselves being manipulated by the strong undertow. No one else was on the beach that day. It was too cold, but Magne and Davyn had gotten into an argument about who the faster swimmer was and ended up challenging each other to a race. Now, after three miles, exhaustion was setting in. Common sense would have motivated them out of the water sooner, but they were locked in competition, and neither would cede until it was too late.

The rain hammered down, reducing visibility to just a few dozen feet. Davyn struggled to stay above the water.

"I'm coming for you, baby brother. Hang on."

Davyn usually found Magne's pet name for him somewhat annoying. Magne would use it when he was being affectionate or when he was helping Davyn out, which was often. They were identical twins, but Magne was born two hours earlier than Davyn. Maybe that somehow put him over the top, because Magne always edged him out: ever so slightly, but enough that Magne was always the hero. He had all the charm, the social skills, the competence that made people feel he could do anything. You might think that would make Davyn resent Magne, but he had a warmth and charisma that made people, Davyn included, feel good just by being around him.

"I think I see a boat!" Davyn cried out.

With the heavy rain, the spray from the waves, the shadows and constant movement, he couldn't be sure what he saw. Davyn lurched up and down, sinking a little deeper with each roll of the waves. He tried to focus on where he thought he saw the boat, but he was too disorientated. Davyn felt something strike him on the back and he swung his body toward it. It was Magne—he'd found him. His heart lifted for a moment, but he could see Magne was exhausted, too. A swell lifted Magne up and away, back down, and then further away again. Magne tried to swim back toward Davyn, but the force of the waves made every move a struggle. Somehow, Magne managed to put his arm around Davyn and started pulling him along. The waves crashed around them and it was hard to hear, but Davyn made out some of what Magne was saying.

"We have to get—" Davyn heard Magne spit out water. "Out of the current."

Davyn was weak, and he could tell Magne was getting weaker, too. "Let me go, Magne." He sank below the water and struggled to resurface, but raised his head enough to say, "I'll follow you."

But Magne didn't let go. Davyn felt them sink deeper with each swell and it took longer to surface each time. He was running out of breath. On the next plunge, Davyn wasn't able to get enough of a breath before he went down, deeper than before. His lungs were almost empty, and he so desperately wanted to take a breath, but he couldn't reach the surface. He felt his chest try to expand, but there was no air. He reached his arm up, but felt nothing besides more water. Panicking, he thrashed and then a spasmodic breath he couldn't control drew water in. His throat burned, and the fire spread to his lungs. His limbs stopped moving, and he felt like a statue sinking. Please, Magne, please.

The pressure was gone, and Davyn was lying prone. Am I on the sea floor? No, it felt dry, warm.

He sucked in a deep breath and shot up to a sitting position to find himself in a hospital bed. How the hell did I get here? He reached out for the curtain and drew it back. The bed next to his was empty. Oh god, Magne?

"Nurse," he called to a nurse outside his door.

She turned to him and hurried into the room. "Calm down sir, you're okay. Lie down."

"Where's my brother? He was with me."

"I'm sure he's fine. You were the only one admitted." She placed her hands on his shoulders and tried to get him to lie back down.

"No, no, he was in the water with me. He was in the water with me, was in the water with me..."

A bright light blinded Davyn, and then it went dark again. He'd been so drawn into his thoughts that he'd lost touch of where he was until an old man shone a flashlight near his feet.

"Sir, are you alright?"

Davyn shook his head and looked at the man.

The man cleared his throat. "You were just standing here like a statue, looking at the water. And you're not wearing a coat. Do you need help?"

Davyn shook his head slowly and stared back at the water. "No, no—I'm okay."

The man continued down the beach.

They had never recovered Magne's body. Davyn wiped a tear from his cheek.

And I thought I saw a boat. He tried to drive his thoughts away, not wanting to consider it, but it couldn't be helped. Was it possible that Magne was alive?

CHAPTER 8

The next morning, Davyn was asleep in his office chair when a knock on the door awakened him. He opened his eyes, a bit surprised to find himself there. A banker's lamp did its best to light the space from the corner of his sprawling desk. The door creaked open and Mrs. Dawit peered inside.

"Davyn? Did you sleep here last night?"

He leaned back in his chair, stretching his back. "Ugh, I guess I did." He self-consciously ran his hand through his hair.

Leo jumped in over the earpiece. "Davyn, thank god, you're back."

Without thinking Davyn said, "Leo, I want to go to D.C. Tell me what to do."

Mrs. Dawit cocked her head. "Davyn, who are you talking to?"

Davyn stood up and ushered Mrs. Dawit out the door before closing it.

"Davyn, I'm so glad to hear your voice."

He walked back to his desk. "Tell me what to do."

"Grab the next flight to Dulles and I'll pick you up there."

"It'll be quicker if I take the train," he glanced at a clock on the wall. "There's one leaving in forty-five minutes. I'll swing by my apartment and grab some clothes and head out."

"No!" Leo exclaimed. "Um, there's no time. Just head to the train. I know where we can—" She paused. "Just get to D.C., we'll work out the rest when you're here."

Davyn grabbed his bag and headed out the door. "Okay, but I'll need clothes."

"Wait. The ring that came in the envelope: bring it with you. And make sure you have the charger for the earpieces. We're dead without that."

Davyn went back to his desk and grabbed the ring and headed out the door.

Bukka raised his hand as Davyn darted past. "Professor, the running book..."

But Davyn was already down the hall. He approached the elevator and noticed Mrs. Dawit waiting for it, too. The doors opened, and they both got in.

"Davyn, Mr. Puddington is looking for you. I think it's about the promotion."

Davyn glanced at her, then turned to face the elevator doors as he nodded. The elevator doors opened, and they stepped out. "I'll have to see him later. I have to be somewhere."

"It's about the promotion. He needs to see you..."

Davyn disappeared down the hall before he could hear the rest.

He jogged to the local train station: a small, traditional train station, no more than an outbuilding by the tracks. He planned to catch a ride to Central, then transfer to an express train to D.C. He bought a ticket and waited outside on the platform. The train pulled in and the train car looked empty. Perfect. When he stepped in, he noticed an old man sitting by the doorway. His skin was wrinkled and sallow. He wore a weather-beaten overcoat, his eyes were shut, and his head leaned against a pole. Davyn stepped around him and sat in the back.

"Okay, I'm on the train. I'll be at Central Station in about twenty minutes. They have runs to D.C. on the hour from there. I should arrive by eleven."

"Okay, we should get your earpiece charged. It's supposed to work for about twelve hours before it shuts off. Do you have somewhere to charge it?"

Davyn looked around the train. "I don't see anything."

"Okay, I'll power it down from here. We'll need it when you arrive."

"Wait, I have questions."

"We can't afford to let the earpiece run down. I will answer all of your questions when you get to D.C. I promise."

Two beeps sounded over the connection and his earpiece shut off.

Davyn reached in his bag and shuffled around for a book. He pulled out a bag of beet chips and set them on the seat next to him, then reached in again and pulled out a book and another earbud, which he placed in his ear. He wasn't listening to anything, but they sometimes helped keep interruptions at bay. As Davyn read, the train hummed along until it jerked suddenly and slowed.

It pulled into a station, the last stop before Central. The doors opened and three young men, who looked to be in their late teens, stepped into the train car. They strutted around the car like they owned it. Davyn glanced up. The tall one appeared to be the leader, wearing a sleeveless plaid black and white shirt over a grey t-shirt. He jutted his jaw out at Davyn and put his arms out as if inviting him to challenge him. Davyn put his nose in his book and ignored them. One of the other kids picked up the old man's walking cane and used it to poke him in the ribs.

Davyn kept his head down but watched them in his periphery. *Jesus, move on guys.*

One of them said, "What, you don't like us talking to this man?"

Davyn glanced up, then went back to his book.

"I'm just singing him a little song."

The kid put his cell phone near the homeless man's ear and cranked up the music, causing him to jump. Davyn kept reading.

"Want some more music, man?" He cranked up the radio again and the old man tried to move away, but the kid with the flannel shirt grabbed his arm and threw him back in his seat.

Davyn set his book down. "All right guys, you had your fun. Leave him alone."

Flannel-boy cranked the radio to full volume and jammed it in the old man's lap. "Don't touch it," he shouted over the music. "I want you to hold it for me while I dance."

Davyn pulled out his pocket watch and glanced at it. Still ten minutes from Central. The old man pushed the radio away and flannel-boy's eyes bulged before he punched the old man in the stomach. The man coughed, grabbing at his waist as he fell on his side.

"I said, hold it so I can dance. Are you deaf?"

That was enough. Davyn stood up and walked straight up to flannel-boy. He took him down with a rugby maneuver called a grapple tackle, then stood him up while holding him in a choke hold. The other two guys looked on, spreading their feet apart and raising their fists.

"Tell your buddies to move on," he whispered in the guy's ear as he pushed him forward, using him as both a shield and kind of as a hostage.

Flannel-boy tried to speak. "Mov, clk, clk."

Davyn loosened his grip, but used flannel-boy to push the other two toward a door to another train car. "Move, move," Davyn shuffled them to the car door and out to the next car. "Don't bother anyone else," he said and released him. The guys moved on through the next car as Davyn watched them go. He walked by the old man without looking at him, then sat in his seat and looked straight ahead.

Lily's words swam in his head. "*You need to get out more. You can feed the homeless.*"

Davyn looked down at his beet chips. His stomach growled. He looked over at the old man before picking up the bag of chips, walking over, and handing it to him.

"Here," he said, then walked back to his seat, sat down, and resumed reading.

The old man opened the bag and sniffed, his face pinching. He looked over at Davyn, who had his head in his book. The old man slid the bag into the garbage, keeping an eye on Davyn the whole time while Davyn pretended not to notice. When the old man was done, Davyn glanced up at him and he slid his hand away from the trash to give him a thumbs-up. "They're delicious," he said with a toothless grin.

The train car lurched as it slowed to approach the station. Davyn jerked forward and looked up from his book. *Oh, right, I'm on a train.*

He looked around the train car, then out the window. "Leo, are you there?"

There was no response. The train pulled into the station and came to a stop. Davyn grabbed his bag and stood up, heading for the exit. As he passed the old man, he slipped him another bag of beet chips. The old man nodded a thank you and wrinkled his nose. The doors swooshed open, and Davyn recoiled at the mishmash of greasy and sugar-sweet smells wafting from the food court, not to mention the indistinct sounds emanating from the parade of people on the station's platform. An onslaught of shoulders, torsos, and elbows pushed past him onto the train.

Davyn raised his arms in front of his face and pulled his shoulders in as he maneuvered his way off the train and onto the crowded platform. He hurried over to a clearing near a group of benches, where it was a little quieter, and tapped his ear. "Leo?"

"Davyn, good. We have a lot to do. Head up the escalator and turn left. Keep an eye out for the H Street exit. It's about 50 meters from where you get off the escalator. When you exit the station, you'll see a black Lincoln parked right outside, same side of the street as you. That's me. Get in that car."

Davyn peered around the station. The storefronts, kiosks, and hordes of people extended in every direction, further than he could see. There were at least two sets of escalators, going both up and down.

"Davyn? Did you hear me?"

"Yes, but I didn't follow. What street?"

"Head up the escalator—"

"Don't tell me how to get there, just tell me the street name and I'll find you."

"It's H Street. I'm in a black Lincoln. You have to go up the escalator—"

"H Street: got it." Davyn looked around for navigation signs but didn't see any. He headed for a kiosk that looked like it may have a map. Bingo. H Street. He memorized the directions and headed for a nearby escalator.

As soon he stepped outside, he spotted the Lincoln. As he approached, the passenger window opened. Davyn cocked his head and peered in as Leo said, "It's me, get in."

Nothing about this seemed right: strange city, getting in the car of someone he didn't know. But he'd come this far. Davyn started to speak, but his jaw went slack when he actually got a look at her. Leo was jarringly beautiful, and her emerald green eyes literally twinkled. Maybe it had something to do with them being opened so wide. She looked as surprised as he did as she studied his face. Her mouth hung open under high cheekbones, but the edges of her mouth quirked into hints of a smile above a rounded chin. He'd never seen anyone like her. And it was as if her expressions of shock and joy were duking it out.

Shock won. "My god, you're a disheveled Magne."

Davyn was still fixated on her green eyes, but his attention was stolen away by her curly brown hair. The stands of tight curls flowed out from her head like a fountain. Combined with the frosted red tips, it reminded him of something, but he couldn't decide what.

He squinted. "Hmm..."

Leo's mouth dropped open in apparent disbelief. "That's it?" She tilted her head. "Just 'hmm?'"

As he got in the car, his eyes danced over her face and hair. What was it she reminded him of? As soon as it hit him, he leaned back in his car seat, satisfied that he'd put his finger on it. "Your head looks like an erupting volcano."

Leo smiled. "Magne warned me your social skills might be a little rusty." She looked into her rearview mirror as they shot out into traffic, cutting across a blur of lanes then turning left on a cross street. Davyn pushed back in his seat and grabbed the door handle. The car raced ahead before settling into a relatively normal speed.

Davyn looked sideways at her. "What was that about?"

Leo turned the radio on and swayed gently to the rhythm of the soft music. "What, the rapid departure?"

Davyn loosened his grip on the door handle and cracked his neck. "Yes, that."

"I don't like lingering around target areas." She glanced in her side mirror for a bit longer than just a quick check. He figured she was watching to see if someone was following. She settled into her seat and gestured at the radio, then relaxed her arm on the center console. "This is Boccherini playing."

Davyn looked in his side mirror. The road was clear. "Wait, target area? What does that mean?"

"Sorry, work lingo. It just means the area where you pick up a specific person." She paused. "Or object."

Davyn looked over his shoulder out the rear window. "So, which am I?"

Leo laughed and shot a glance Davyn's way. "Relax, you're a person, silly."

Davyn's eyes narrowed. "Look, I'm gonna need more information. What is it I'm supposed to do, exactly?"

Leo clenched her jaw and let out a breath as she turned to Davyn. "I think someone within the company kidnapped your brother."

Davyn drew back. "Company? I thought you said you worked for a spy agency."

"Sorry, more work lingo. We can't go around saying spy agency. People take notice of that sort of thing."

He turned to look out the passenger window. "I almost didn't come."

Leo tightened her grip on the steering wheel but kept her eyes on the road. "I know this all sounds extraordinary, and I can't imagine what it must be like for you. But I'm afraid you're just going to have to trust me."

"No, that's not a good answer."

"I know, but you've come this far and for now it's all we have."

Davyn took a deep breath.

Leo nodded. "That's good. Deep breaths are a good way to relieve stress. But hold it in for a second or two before you blow out. Also, the out-breath should be longer than the in-breath. I can show you—"

"I wasn't doing breathing exercises, I was—well, I guess I was. Anyway, what am I supposed to do? What's the plan?"

"That's a little complicated. We're going to get you a haircut," she said as they approached a stop sign. She looked around before turning right. "I think it's this way."

She didn't strike Davyn as the secret agent type. The hairstyle, the billowy green blouse, and the big hoop earrings: none of it fit. But if none of it was real, what else could it be? A jolt of panic hit him hard in the chest. Was he on one of those hidden camera reality shows? Davyn spun in his seat and looked around the back of the car.

"Okay, where's the camera? Jig's up."

Leo laughed. "What are you going on about?"

"I know what this is. I'm on some stupid TV show."

Leo's jaw dropped, and she let out a laugh. "Uh, no. Look, you must be hungry. How about we get something to eat?"

Davyn thought about it for a moment. Maybe that was a little over the top. He didn't like any of this, but he was hungry. Show or not, he needed something to eat. He nodded, and they went through a drive through. Leo then pulled into a small, wooded park to stop in, got out, and stretched. She walked over to a picnic table and sat down. Davyn grabbed his bag of food and joined her. Leo kept her head down, but lifted her eyes to watch him, a half smile on her face.

"Uncanny, right?" he asked.

"I didn't want to be obvious, but it's like watching Magne in one of his disguises."

"What about you? You have a distinctive look. What's your ancestry?"

"That's an unusual question," she said as she squeezed ketchup out of a packet and onto her sandwich.

"Is it? I'm of Nordic descent. I don't see why people think it's unusual to talk about. I find the topic fascinating."

Davyn pulled the bun off of his sandwich. "Iceberg." He shook his head.

"What?" she replied and looked around the park. "Here?"

"The lettuce. It's iceberg. No nutrients."

"Sorry, there aren't a lot of choices out here." She took a sip of her soda. "You jumped from ancestry to iceberg lettuce pretty quick. You don't like staying on a single topic too long it seems."

"I asked. You didn't answer, so I figured you didn't want to talk about it."

"My mother's Irish and my father's Hawaiian."

"Ah, I see."

Leo shot him a curious glance, but Davyn didn't feel like explaining how it helped him understand her facial features, so he changed the topic.

"I don't have any clothes with me. We'll have to find a store.

Maybe there's a Kohl's."

Leo snorted, and her mouth expanded like a fishbowl before she turned her head to the side and spit out her drink so she could burst out laughing.

Davyn jerked back, out of the splash zone.

"I'm sorry, Davyn," she said, wiping her mouth with a napkin. "I needed a good laugh." She crumbled the napkin. "I've got something else in mind."

Leo turned off of the tree-lined rural street and pulled into an empty lot to park in front of a small two-story house. A neon "CLOSED" sign hung in a large window by the front door. Davyn's heart rate sped up as he anticipated going inside. Leo shut off the engine and turned to him. He stared at the sign for another moment, then shifted his attention to Leo. His throat was dry and tight as he swallowed. He didn't like the feeling of not having any control over what was happening. He considered calling the whole thing off, but if there was even a slight chance that Magne was alive—and it was sounding more and more like that was true—then he had no choice but to stick with the plan, whatever it was.

Davyn tried to ignore how Leo's eyes sparkled, and her crazy, erupting hair, but the new environment, the circumstances, and her wild appearance was a lot to process. Leo's eyes softened as she placed her hand on his, but he immediately pulled it away.

"Look Leo, I work better when I have all the information." His eyes tightened. "Don't try to give me the soft sell. I want to know the plan. Just say what you're going to say."

Leo drew a leg up under her and rested her hands on her lap. "Okay, I know this is going to sound crazy—"

"Everything you say sounds crazy." One side of Leo's mouth rose as she squinted at Davyn. He glanced away, then back. "Sorry, go ahead."

She squared her shoulders. "You want it straight, here it is. But this is Magne's plan. Keep that in mind." Leo took a deep breath.

"Just before he was kidnapped, he told me to contact you and have you—" She stopped and looked at the house.

"What?"

She glanced back at him. "Oh, for Pete's sake. He wants you to become him."

Davyn's jaw went slack and Leo's eyes darted across his face as he drew a deep breath.

"That's good. Deep—"

Davyn's hand shot up. "Don't."

"You said to just put it out there," she said, her voice rising.

"I know." He rubbed his temples. "But that's insane."

Leo opened the car door. "I love him, too, you know," she said softly. "I'll be waiting outside when you're ready."

Davyn lowered the seat back and put his arm over his eyes. He so desperately wanted to believe that Magne was alive and to find him, but what he didn't get was how he was supposed to help. *Become Magne? What, dress like him? Impersonate him? To what end?* He let out a deep breath, lowered his arm, and opened the door. Then he marched around the car toward Leo, who was standing on the porch.

"All right, I'm quite certain that what you've told me so far is true, but I also know you're holding back information."

She threw her hands up. "I'm not, I promise. I've told you everything I can."

"Then what's the plan? Why are we here?" He looked at the front door. "Why are we at this creepy little house in the woods?"

Leo frowned. "It's not creepy. It's...quaint."

Davyn smirked, but said nothing.

Leo sighed. "Okay, here's the rest of it. I didn't want to dump it on you all at once, but here it is."

Davyn leaned back and folded his arms, but Leo grabbed his arm and pulled him to the side, away from the door, and put her mouth near Davyn's ear. "We're here for a makeover," she whispered. "Inside this salon are some very dear and trusted friends of mine. They're going to give you a haircut and fit you with clothes. When they're done, you'll look like Magne."

Davyn let out a snarky laugh. "And what will that achieve, exactly?"

"I can't go into it all here, but let's just say that the people who took Magne have an interest in having the people on his team think he's gone."

Davyn leaned back and shot her a skeptical look. "How does me looking like Magne help rescue him?"

"You're going to help me figure out who did it and where he is, but in the meantime, no one can know he's missing."

"That doesn't even make sense."

"It will, in time. But for now," she glanced at the front door, "you're going to have to trust me."

Leo strolled through the door and into the beauty salon like a diva. "Hello boys."

Davyn waited on the porch, noticing a skinny young man peering out the door at him just before it closed. He walked over to a yellow Adirondack chair and sat down, but could still hear them speaking through the walls.

A husky male voice said, "O–M–G, girl. Is Magne 2.0 with you?"

Laughter and several other voices followed. *How many people are in there?* Davyn leaned forward and held his head in his hands.

After a few minutes of indistinct chatter, Leo opened the front door and stepped out. "They're ready for you now."

He kept his head down and stared at the ground. "There's no rush."

Leo walked over, smiled, and took his hand. "Come on."

Davyn pulled his hand away and stood up, taking several pained steps toward the door before pausing.

She gave him a gentle tug. "It's okay."

Davyn shook his head, causing his unruly hair to flop about. He inched up to the threshold and peered inside. A mix of hairspray and artificial fruit odors assaulted his nose. He leaned back, turned his head and drew in a breath of clean air before returning his attention to the room.

A group of three men stared back at him. Davyn ignored them and glanced around the salon. The dark wood paneling from the seventies made the room gloomy and drab. Piles of hairstyle magazines covered the coffee tables and chairs in the waiting area. He looked past the men at a single hair washing station in the back of the room.

Leo gave him a soft push, and he stepped inside, one hand still clinging to the doorframe. Leo ducked under his arm, then straightened her posture.

"Ladies and gentlemen, this is Davyn."

A heavyset man in too-tight jeans with a white pirate shirt clasped his hands together and smiled broadly. "O-M-G, it's uncanny." He looked Davyn up and down. "He's a messy Magne. I love it."

Leo pointed. "Davyn, that's Max."

Max raised a hand and wiggled his fingers. A wave, presumably. Davyn looked over at the other two men who were both beaming and appeared way too excited. He turned to Leo, his eyes wide.

"That's Sal over by the barber's chair. He'll be cutting your hair." She nodded at the other young man. "And this is Stefan."

The room went dead quiet.

Then, Max cleared his throat and approached Davyn. "It's very nice to meet you. We're going to start with a haircut, then I'll get you some spectacular clothes. It'll be fun." Max extended his hand toward the barber's chair.

Davyn didn't move; his eyes were vacant.

Sal reached a hand out toward Davyn. "Come, come, you magnificent beast. Oh, I love your look. Maybe Magne—" His eyes popped, and he glanced at Leo. "Oh dear, I mean when he gets back. Maybe Magne should be transformed into Davyn."

Davyn's heart raced as he stepped up like a wary traveler on to a decrepit suspension footbridge.

"Come, come, come." Sal took Davyn's arm and spun him around, like a ballroom dancer in slow motion. "Those clothes, those clothes. Ugh, we'll get to that. First, we have to cut off all of this fabulous hair. Darn." He pulled out drawer after drawer, apparently looking for something. "Why couldn't Magne wear his hair like you? Oh, never mind. Where are my clippers?" He looked around, arms flailing like one of those tubular balloon men outside a car dealership.

Davyn looked on, befuddled. It was like watching a pinball bouncing around.

Stefan stepped in and took Davyn's arm. "Sit here, honey. Sal will get you fixed up. Would you like coffee, tea, me?" He laughed a lot harder than the joke deserved.

Davyn grabbed an arm of the barber chair and eased himself into it.

Sal fluffed Davyn's hair. "Such a shame. You'll miss these beautiful locks. Hell, I'll miss 'em. Can I keep some?"

Leo sat near Davyn, offering only a sympathetic frown. The clippers buzzed, and Davyn closed his eyes and solemnly lowered his head, like a condemned man meeting his end.

Sal rolled the clipper over Davyn's head with a sigh. "Tsk, tsk, tsk."

Leo scrunched her shoulders and nose as she watched.

"This feels like a wake. I am going to get some espressos for everybody," Stefan said as he marched out the side door to a break room.

Sal buzzed away until Davyn emerged with a near crew cut.

Leo's mouth dropped and her eyes danced across Davyn's face. Max let out an audible gasp as Sal pulled a photo of Magne from a drawer and held it up by Davyn's face. His eyes shifted between Davyn and the photo. He spun Davyn's chair to face Leo and handed her the picture.

Stefan called from the break room, "You're finished? Damn the espresso, I want to see." He pranced in and stopped next to Leo to gawk. "He's the spitting image. Truly uncanny. Something about the expression is a little off though." Stefan leaned back. "Can you smile for us, Dav?"

Davyn's facial muscles twitched, like the Tin Man's when Dorothy first crossed his path. The muscles moved, not spontaneously but with begrudging force, and grew tight about his face.

Sal wrinkled his nose as he and Stefan drew back. "Is that the best you can do?"

Davyn rolled his eyes. "If you don't like this expression, you're going to hate my other one."

Sal set his clippers down. "Well, you're done. What do you think?"

Davyn stood up and pulled the haircut drape off, brushing the back of his neck with his hand.

Sal reached for Davyn with a brush. "Oh, let me do that."

"It's fine," Davyn said sharply, then he caught a glimpse of the photo Sal was holding. He reached his hand out it. "Let me see that."

Sal glanced at Leo, and the room fell silent again as Davyn pulled the photo from Sal's hand. His knees went slack when he saw it. He turned away from the mirror, bracing himself against the counter and then sliding down to sit on the floor. His eyes moved over the photo. Magne looked happy, healthy, but slightly older than he remembered him. Davyn blinked back tears as he drew a shallow, stuttering breath.

Leo moved beside him, resting on her knees. Davyn glanced at her, and her eyes were soft. She motioned to take his hand but stopped, her face hinting at a smile. She was learning to keep her distance, maybe. She didn't speak, just shared the space with him while Davyn looked back at the photo. He'd never say it, but he was glad Leo was with him. They had Magne in common, and he could tell she loved him, too.

Leo turned away for a moment. "Can you fellas give us a moment?" They shuffled into the other room.

Leo lifted off her knees and slid in next to Davyn. She didn't say anything, which was good. Words were the wrong tool for the moment, and she seemed to sense that. These feelings were unfamiliar: wanting someone to stay, and holding hope that he'd see Magne again.

He rubbed his hand over his head. The short hair was another familiar, but distant feeling.

Leo shifted her gaze toward Davyn. "What do you think?" she said softly.

"This is the first evidence I've seen that Magne's alive. We've got to get going. What's next?" He jumped to a standing position.

Leo called out, "Okay, fellas. It's dress-up time."

Davyn's eyes shot down to Leo's. He suddenly felt nauseous. He didn't want to be a doll. He needed some time by himself. Some people suck your social battery faster than others, but these guys were like industrial vacuums: way too exuberant.

Max stepped forward and clapped his hands. "The clothes make the man, and we are just getting started."

Davyn frowned as he ran his hand over his head and sighed.

Walking playfully up to him, Leo whispered in his ear. "Hang in there, baby. Try to have fun."

The next ninety minutes was a montage of what Davyn considered an overabundance of unnecessarily fancy clothes. Stuff right off the cover of GQ. He was completely out of his element and struggling to find his bearings. It all ended with him staring at himself in one of those triple mirrors so he could see every angle, but one was more than enough for his taste.

Leo stood just outside of the room talking with Max. Davyn could hear them, but didn't let on.

"It's amazing. He looks just like Magne. You guys did a wonderful job," she said.

"Honey, what, we did was simple compared to what you have to do." Max lowered his voice, but the walls were paper-thin. "This boy is as stiff as a board. He is no Magne. No charisma, no social grace. Where's Magne's winning smile? He can't even hold a convo."

It was all too familiar. They shared the same genes, but Magne was better than he was at everything. Especially social interactions.

"I think all the attention is overwhelming his social battery."

"His what?" Max replied.

"Oh, it's something he told me about being an introvert."

"Honey, I know some introverts. He ain't that. He's a subterranean-trovert."

"We'll get there. Thanks for everything. Remember, not a word of this to anyone."

"Don't you worry. We're gossips, but we all want you to get your man back."

"I need that picture of Magne back now, too."

"Oh, are you sure? Can't I at least take it to dinner, before I have to say goodbye?"

"Sorry, I need to get rid of any evidence of what happened here today."

"Okay, well, after Magne's back then. I'll take an 8x10 glossy and two wallet size."

"Thanks again."

"You'll find Magne. I know you will."

"Yes, we will."

"But send Davyn in there as a tank, not a diplomat. The boy's built for power, not grace."

Leo stepped around the corner and eyeballed Davyn. "Okay, fun's over. We've got a lot of work to do. Say your goodbyes."

Davyn mustered a wave as he walked for the exit.

Leo fell in behind him. "Thank you, friends. Wish us luck."

As they exited the salon, Davyn turned to Leo. She was beaming as Davyn reached behind her and pulled the door shut.

"How the hell are we going to make this work?"

Leo jerked back. "Whoa, what kind of attitude is that? We've only just gotten started."

"It's a hell of a start," he said, rubbing the top of his head. "I feel ridiculous in these clothes."

Leo stepped deliberately toward her car. "Well, you looked like a bag lady before. Now you look fab-u-lous."

Davyn followed her, rolling his eyes. "Fabulous? Great, my life's aspiration."

"Don't overthink it, *Magne*," she said with emphasis on the name. "From now on you're Magne."

He rolled his eyes. "I really don't see how this is going to work."

Leo opened the car door, but didn't get in. Instead, she rested her arms on the roof. "Social interaction is easy, and I'll be in your ear to help you."

Davyn opened the car door, too, and stared out at the woods. "I'm not feeling overly confident."

She climbed in and leaned over the passenger seat. "I already have a plan for that. Get in."

Davyn swallowed hard, his eyes bandying about. He didn't want to ask, but maybe it was better to know. "What did you have in mind?"

"We're going to do a little test run. There's a diner up the road, and you're going to go in there as Magne," she said. "Come on, get in."

Davyn sat down and she immediately backed out. The car took off down the road while Davyn stared out his window.

She rested her hand on his, but he pulled away again. "Look, I'll be with you. And I have some tips for you that should make it easier. Keep in mind that most of the time people aren't even listening. They're just waiting to talk."

Davyn turned to Leo. "People talk about stupid things. They can go on for hours. When I talk to someone, I want it to be something interesting. But when I bring up a topic, people immediately think I'm weird."

"Don't let people dictate what's weird. What's weird to them might not be weird to you, and vice versa. What makes them the best judge? You say something to someone, and they think you're weird? So what? Had you said it to someone else, they might have found it fascinating. Maybe you're just talking to the wrong people."

"I have a way of making things weird."

"Don't worry. If you slip up, most people will just assume that they misunderstood you or misheard you."

Davyn leaned his head against the headrest and let out a long breath.

"Sometimes you can learn from someone with a different perspective than you. You're an anthropologist. In the future, anthropologists will study the people living today. If it helps, think of people you meet as old bones and learn what they have to say."

"Okay, it's just up here on the right. Do you have your earbuds with you?"

Davyn reached into a pocket in his bag, "I think so. Yep, they're here."

"Good, put them in. If anyone sees you, they'll think you're talking on your phone." Leo cocked her head. "Wait a minute. If you don't have a phone, why do you have earbuds?"

Davyn sighed. "People bother you less when they're in."

"Ah, right. Boy, you really don't want people talking to you."

"Nope."

"All right, well, when you go inside, describe what you see. Just give me an idea of what we have to work with. Keep it quiet and brief."

"I don't know. This doesn't feel right."

Leo pulled her car into the diner's mostly empty parking lot and slipped into a space. "We have no choice. Magne is counting on us." She put the car in park and turned to him. "Counting on you."

It felt so weird to hear that. To consider the possibility, even that Magne was alive. It still hadn't fully sunk in yet. Learning someone so close was alive was similar in some ways to learning they'd died, especially given the circumstances.

Leo looked at Davyn. He raised his eyes to meet hers.

"I like what they did with your eyebrows," she said softly.

Davyn looked down. "They're too short. I look ridiculous."

She smiled. "You look fantastic."

Davyn sat motionless, his arms by his side, staring at the floor of the car.

"You'll get used to it. Now, head on in there."

Davyn entered the small diner. Seventies-style paneling covered the walls and the red vinyl booths looked original, too. The smell of fried food and old grease filled the air. He looked for a good place to sit; a booth would be better than a table, he decided.

A middle-aged man with a name tag that read STEVE stood at the register as an elderly couple settled up their bill. When they finished, they turned to head out and Davyn stepped aside to let them pass. Steve's attention then shifted to Davyn. He raised his eyebrows and looked out the door, then back at Davyn.

"Just one?"

Yeah, is that a crime? Davyn nodded.

"Give me just a minute and I'll get you seated." Steve walked toward the end of the diner and pulled out a dishrag to wipe down a table.

Davyn peered around the small diner.

"Davyn, tell me what you see?" Leo said in a hushed tone.

"It's a typical coffee shop."

"How many people are there?" she said, her voice sharpening. "Where are they sitting? How many in a group? Come on, we talked about this. I need some details, so I know what I'm working with."

Davyn let out a long breath. "Okay. I understand. Look at the outside. You see it?"

"Uh-huh."

"Okay, now picture the inside. It's exactly what you'd expect."

The background noise in his earpiece stopped. *She must have put herself on mute. I'm glad I'm not there to hear that rant.* He knew that he sometimes frustrated people, but this time it wasn't intentional. He just didn't have the patience to play spy and file an official report on what should be obvious.

His earpiece came back to life with what sounded like an agitated rhino snorting.

"Okay, I'm not enjoying this either," she said, sounding like the volcano erupting from the top of her head was actually getting ready to explode. "Just tell me if there are people there—" She took a measured breath and cleared her throat. "So that we can proceed."

Davyn smirked, but he knew when to stop; that's not to say that he always did, but in this case there was work to be done, and honestly, Leo was a pretty good sport about it. "It looks like three couples sitting in booths, and four people sitting on stools at the counter, in pairs."

A voice came from behind Davyn. "Are you government?"

Davyn jerked slightly and looked over his shoulder to see a man in a business suit that he didn't notice when he walked in. "Uh, sorry. Were you waiting for a seat?"

"No, I'm finished. Just waiting for a Lyft."

Davyn nodded and turned away to wait for his seat.

"So, you're Homeland or something?" the man continued.

"Tell him you're doing a location scout for a low budget indie movie," Leo prompted.

Davyn said nothing.

"I get it, you can't say. That's okay."

Steve finished wiping down the table and waved Davyn over.

As Davyn walked toward the table, the man added, "Keep up the good work."

Davyn didn't respond, but sat so that he faced the door. Steve set the menu and a glass of water down before he went back to his post.

"Why didn't you say what I told you?" Leo asked.

Davyn picked up the menu. "It's none of his business what, or who I am."

"Well, the 'sorry, were you waiting' line was a nice touch. You're not completely bereft of manners."

"Thanks, but I'm a little out of my element here. I feel like Frankenstein's monster."

"You're hardly that. You look amazing."

It wasn't a reference to how he looked. He wondered how Frankenstein's creature must have felt in those first hours, stripped of his clothes, his hair, his identity, and all alone in an unfamiliar land.

A waitress stepped beside his table. "Hi, I'm Sheila. What can I get for you?"

"Say, 'Hi, Sheila, I'd like a coffee.'" Leo paused, then added, "However you like it."

Davyn set the menu down. "Hi, I'd like a coffee. However you like it."

Sheila smiled at him. "However I like it? Well, I've never heard that one before. Are you new here? You don't look like you're from— ah, you're passing through, right?"

When Davyn realized what Leo meant his face flushed and he suddenly felt too warm. He grabbed the glass of water and drank it all in a single gulp before clearing his throat. "Sorry, black is fine. I'm on a call." He pointed to his earbuds.

"Oh, sorry. Hope it's not your girlfriend," she whispered, then walked away.

Davyn heard Leo suppress a laugh, then it fell quiet.

"You still there?"

Having apparently recovered from her laughing fit, Leo said, "Yes, sorry. Had to mute for a sec."

Davyn looked up and saw the man at the door was still there, and talking quietly to Steve. Steve nodded, then glanced over at Davyn before disappearing through a door into the kitchen.

Leo said, "I'm sorry, I meant—"

"I know what you meant. Just took me a second to process it. I was distracted. Anyway, we may have a bigger problem than conversational cues. I think we should go."

"What problem? The waitress incident?"

"The guy who asked if I was with Homeland Security. He just whispered something to the manager, and the manager looked at me and then went in the back."

"Okay, it's fine. Leave the agent stuff to me. He probably didn't like the salad or something. Let's talk to somebody at the counter while we wait for your coffee. We'll give the waitress a break."

"Funny. Alright, let's do this."

"Okay, good. I like the initiative."

"Don't patronize me. I just want to get this over with. I have to get back to work, assuming I still have a job when this is over."

"Sorry, Magne."

Davyn sighed. "Do you really have to do that?"

The waitress approached him from behind. "Still on the call?" she whispered, holding a hand to her ear like a phone.

Davyn stared at the menu and nodded.

"Do you know what you'd like to order?"

"Say, 'It all looks so good, I can't decide,'" Leo said.

Davyn shook his head. "Nope, I'm good for now."

The waitress nodded and gestured with her thumb toward the front of the diner. "I'll be over there if you need anything."

"Why didn't you say what I told you, Magne?"

"Because that was a ridiculous line. And stop calling me Magne."

"You'll have to get used to responding to it. And the line I gave you: that's how Magne speaks. If you're not convincing, this won't work. Just say it the way I say it."

Davyn clenched his jaw. "Okay, fine. But leave out the commentary. It's confusing."

"Sorry, Magne and I have been doing it for years and it just flows. You'll get used to it. I'll use the word 'say' in front of what I want you to say, then I'll say 'end' when I'm done with what you should say. What follows is informational. Sometimes it's important. Got it?"

Davyn rolled his eyes. "No, explain it again."

He understood her, but what got under his skin was that patronizing confirmation she'd tacked on at the end. He let her go over it again, anyway. She deserved it, and he had to admit he was a little curious about how someone would try to describe something so obvious again.

"Before I say something that I want you to repeat," she said, drawing out her words. "I will say the word 'say.' Repeat everything that I say until you hear me say 'end.' Anything that comes after I say 'end' is informational. Got it?"

Wow, that was fascinating. That couldn't happen twice, could it?
"Um, say the word 'say?' You say?"

"Davyn, it's so simple. What's not to get?"

"Well, 'and' is a conjunction, and you'll probably say 'and' a lot, and I think that might be an issue and it might be confusing and it's a bad 'end' word, because 'and' and 'end' occur frequently in spoken language."

"Wow, just...wow. Okay, what would you like me to use instead of 'end?'"

"Did you just say, '*and* move on?'"

Leo huffed. "How about we use, 'You're an ass?' Nope, I'll probably say that a lot, too."

Davyn paused for a moment then said, "Uh-oh."

"What? Uh-oh what?"

"That was good. Good comeback."

"Why's that an uh-oh?"

Davyn smiled. The "uh-oh" was because he was starting to like her. He wouldn't say that, though. "Let's use 'over.' It's short and clear and won't be confused with anything else."

"Okay, fine. *Over.*" Leo put an accent on the word 'over' but didn't call it out directly. She was apparently more nuanced in her jabs than Davyn. "Now in a minute, I want you to go over to one of the people sitting at the bar and stand next to them. Act like you're waiting to speak with the waitress. Then repeat what I tell you to the person at the bar."

"What do I say to the waitress when she comes?"

"I'll tell you when it's time. We'll start off simple. When you're ready, say, 'The coffee is good here. What kind did you get?'"

Davyn stood up and straightened his clothes, then walked over to stand at the counter. The person next to him stood up and nodded politely at Davyn, then walked over to the cash register. Davyn spun around quickly and went back to his seat. Steve looked over at him and furrowed his brow.

"Everything okay?" he asked.

Davyn nodded and waved him off.

"What are you waiting for?"

"The person I picked got up and left. I need to pick someone else. Give me a second."

"There aren't that many people left. Just pick one."

"Okay, okay. Here goes." Once again, he stood up, straightened his clothes, and walked over to the counter. This time, he ended up next to two men sitting next to each other. "The coffee is good here. What kind did you get?"

They eyed Davyn warily, then went back to talking to each other. Davyn stood there for a moment, then walked a few steps to another guy that was sitting alone.

"The coffee is good here. What kind did you get?"

"No thanks," the guy said and waved him off.

Davyn placed some money on the table and made for the door, not stopping until he reached the car and got in on the passenger side.

"What was that?"

"What do you mean? I said what you told me that time."

"You sounded like a robot. They probably thought you were selling something. Nobody wanted to speak to you."

He pulled a piece of paper from his pocket and placed it on the console. "The waitress gave me her number."

Leo's mouth dropped and she started laughing. "We've got some work to do, my friend. Looks will only get you so far."

As Leo prepared to pull out, a police car pulled in next to them.

"Time to go," Davyn whispered.

Leo put the car in reverse and started backing up, but the police car chirped its siren. An officer got out of the car and peered in through Davyn's window. The cop strode around to Leo's side of the car. Another police car pulled in behind them.

Leo watched the second car in her rearview mirror. "What the—"

She lowered her window when prompted, and the cop looked at Leo, then over to Davyn.

"Can I see each of your licenses? I'll need the vehicle registration and insurance as well."

Leo handed him her documents. "Is anything wrong, officer?"

"Sir, I'll need yours, too."

Davyn stared out the windshield. "But I'm not driving."

"Sir, I'll need to see your driver's license."

"I don't have one."

Leo turned and regarded Davyn with wide eyes. "Just give it to him," she whispered.

"I don't have one. I don't drive."

"State issued identification is fine," the officer said.

"I don't have that either. I'm sovereign."

The cop examined Leo's license. "Sovereign? What's that?"

"It means I don't carry papers."

A cop got out of the other police car and stood outside Davyn's door.

"Sir, please step out of the vehicle. Officer Rogers would like to have a few words."

"Be cool," Leo whispered.

Davyn opened the door and stood up accordingly.

"If you don't have ID, we'll need to take you downtown and figure out just who the hell you are."

"I didn't break any laws."

"We have reason to suspect you might pose a risk to the safety of the community. It's in your best interest to coperate."

"Do you mean, cooperate?"

"Sir, turn to the car and put your hands behind your back."

"I don't think you have the right to do that."

Leo leaned over the passenger seat and hissed, "Just cooperate. You can't help Magne from a jail cell."

Davyn shook his head and turned toward the car like he was told. The cop cuffed him and put him in the back of the patrol car.

CHAPTER 9

Leo pulled into a parking space at her agency's headquarters. The sun crept over the horizon, casting a warm glow over the expansive, mostly empty parking lot, as a few cars pulled in across the way. She turned to Davyn. "I was hoping to practice some more last night, but your stint in the slammer put the kibosh on that."

Davyn stared at the steel and mirrored building looming across the parking lot. He watched people getting out of their cars and head toward it. Alarmed by the sheer the number of them, he swallowed hard.

While he was busy observing, Leo put some things in her pocketbook and looked around to see if she'd missed anything. "We'll have to get you a badge. I'll work from my desk so I can tap into the security cameras and coach you through interactions with the staff. There are a couple of people I want you to meet. We'll start with the tech guys. That should be pretty easy. They're your quintessential IT guys, nerdy and socially awkward. You'll fit right in."

Davyn turned and looked at her but said nothing.

"I'll be with you the whole time, but I want to give you some pointers, so you can start flying on your own. I don't want you relying on me the whole time."

Davyn stared at the building again. "I don't know any of these people. I don't know their names, anything about them. You're going to have to live in my ear."

"I will, I will." She put some more items in her bag. "Baby steps. We need to get inside, get some practice, then we'll take a break before tonight."

"Tonight? What's tonight?"

"Davyn, look at me. There's no time for even a crash course. The good news is I have both eyes and ears on you, and I'll be in your ear coaching you on what to say. Our biggest challenge is you. You have issues with conflict, and you haven't been repeating what I say verbatim. That has to change now. I've only got two tips for you, but they're important."

Groaning, he slid down in his seat and put his hand on his forehead. "This is a nightmare."

Leo looked in the rearview mirror to put on lipstick. "No time for self-pity." She opened her car door. "Let's walk and talk on the way in."

Davyn got out of the car. His suit was tailored, and he looked sharp, but he stood, fidgeting like a toddler dressed up for Easter would. "I feel ridiculous in these clothes."

Leo came around to his side and handed Davyn a small box. "Use these and get rid of the wired earbuds you have." She took his hand and directed him toward the building before letting go. "Here are the two tips. Number one: if you don't agree with something the person is saying just say, 'I understand how you might feel that way,' and look them in the eye while you're doing it to show them you're listening. Got it?"

"Got it," he said as he walked behind her like a fledgling.

"Number two: ask open-ended questions and let the other person do the talking. The less you say, the better. And again, if you disagree with someone, tell them that you can understand how they could feel that way."

They approached a set of concrete stairs that spanned the front of the building, tapering in slightly at the edges to meet the courtyard in front of the twelve-story building. They climbed to the top and took a couple of steps before Leo stopped and faced Davyn, adjusting his tie. "Just follow my lead and you'll do fine. I'm switching the earpiece on now, so I can talk to you. Put in the earbuds, and I'll do the same so we look like we're on a phone and not just crazy people talking to ourselves. We'll go straight to the security desk to get your badge. I don't know who's working it today, but I'll let you know their name when we get closer. Once you're on your way to the desk, I'll step aside like I'm waiting for you and coach you through it. Okay?"

Davyn's heart pounded, but he took a deep, cleansing breath. "Okay."

Leo looked around the courtyard, then dragged him off to the side, away from the people entering the building. "Look, I know you're nervous, but this should be pretty easy."

Davyn looked at the ground and nodded, like a kid before his first day at school.

Leo put her hand under his chin and gently raised his face. "To be convincing, and to save Magne, you'll need to pull out all the stops. You need to be confident, charming and engaging. Pull yourself out of your funk and focus."

Davyn looked at the people streaming into the building. Some were talking and laughing, some were talking quietly, and some were walking alone. He glanced in and saw the security desk as he straightened his shoulders. "You're right, let's go."

After they stepped through the doors, Leo pulled Davyn to the side. There were eight lanes for staff to enter through metal detectors, and a security desk with a waiting area, complete with couches and lounge chairs. Beyond the metal detector lines, the building opened to a large windowed atrium with trees.

Leo leaned in and whispered, "Okay, it's Frank and Kevin working security. Head on over there and say hi, then let them know you lost your badge. Knowing these two, they'll probably give you a hard time, but it's all in fun. Go ahead."

"Yeah, fun," he said as he headed for the security station. Davyn approached the desk, which looked like a check-in at an upscale hotel, except the clerks wore badges and were armed with pistols and various takedown weapons and restraints. There was a heavy-set black guard sitting at the counter in a tall office chair, and a skinny white guard standing at the back of the station, about ten feet behind him, facing away and filing papers.

The seated guard smiled as Davyn approached. "Magne, my man. What are you doing here?"

Davyn cleared his throat. "Hi Kevin, I lost my badge. I need a new one."

Kevin looked up from the papers he was filing.

"No, that's not—"

Davyn saw Leo shaking her head out of the corner of his eye just as Kevin walked over to join Frank.

"Don't want Frank helping you? I understand. I'm everybody's favorite." He reached behind the counter, grabbed a new badge and flipped it over to scan it.

Frank's mouth dropped open in mock surprise. "No respect, man, no respect."

"I'll need to see some ID," Kevin said, and held out his hand.

Davyn glanced at Leo. Someone was talking to her, but he could see her face. Her eyes opened wide for a moment, but there was no way she could help him.

Kevin's face shifted from serious to delighted. "Oh my god, Magne—your face."

Frank barked out a laugh. "Serves you right for picking Kevin. Who picks Kevin when Frank's here?"

Leo let out a sigh. "Say, 'Speaking of the game, did you see last night's?' Over."

"Say, speaking of the game, did you see the one on last night?" Davyn said, sounding like a TV pitchman.

The guards guffawed. When they quieted down, Kevin wiped away a tear. "What is going on with you, Magne?"

Frank moved around like a robot, arms at his side and his forearms rising and falling mechanically.

Davyn stood motionless, speechless, until he heard Leo sigh in his earpiece.

"Say 'too much time in Salt Lake City.' Over. And liven it up a little, goddammit."

Davyn scratched behind his ear. "Well, I've been in Salt Lake City too long."

Frank was still laughing. "You're a hoot, Magne, and a good sport, for putting up with us."

Kevin handed Davyn the badge. "Better get your act together before tonight's big black tie affair. I heard you're giving a speech. Better drop your Salt Lake City shtick, too, or they'll be napping in the aisles."

"Or maybe rolling in them," Frank said.

Davyn stared at the two of them as they carried on. *Speech? Leo didn't say anything about a speech.* He gazed over to see her shaking her head, as if to dismiss it.

He imagined himself standing at the podium, all eyes on him, as he stood frozen, unable to speak. Kevin shook his new badge in front of his face, snapping him out of it. Davyn looked down at the photo of Magne with his name underneath. He stepped back, his eyes welling up before he could help it.

"Hey, you okay, Magne?" Kevin said as Frank looked on.

"Excuse me," Davyn said as he stepped away.

But he still heard Frank whisper to Kevin, "That was weird, but you never know what he's up to. He's probably setting us up for something."

Leo approached Davyn and put her hand on his elbow. "Are you alright?"

Davyn continued staring at the badge. "Seeing his name and picture—it's like when you go to a wake and it still hasn't sunk in until you see his name on the little marquee outside the viewing room." His head hung. "There wasn't even a body."

Leo glanced around the atrium then whispered, "But he's not dead. We're going to get him back. Come with me. We're going to my office. I have a plan."

Leo opened the door to her office and they stepped inside. Davyn looked around. He'd expected to see more high tech equipment at a spy headquarters, but it looked like any other middle management office. Standard mass-produced landscape paintings on the walls, devoid of style or feeling: check. The carpet was dark blue with speckles, probably to hide wear, dirt and spills. It was eerily quiet, though. The sounds from the hallway faded away completely once the door closed. Leo brushed passed him and sat at her desk, but Davyn hovered by the door. "Why was everyone staring at me?"

She sat up and eyeballed her monitors. "Well, for one thing, everyone here loves you. Secondly, you're extraordinarily good-looking. And three, you're never in this area of the building."

Davyn ignored the compliments. He wasn't all that interested in the reason to begin with, and they weren't really about him, anyway.

Leo started sorting her desk, then stopped abruptly. "Go ahead and sit down. Catch your breath. Things should go smoothly now that I'm at my command center."

Command center? It's a desk with a laptop and monitors. But Davyn kept his thoughts to himself. "So, what's the plan?"

"Well, you can go anywhere in the building and speak with anyone. There won't be any interruptions now, at least on my side. The building's blanketed with cameras, so I'll have eyes on you, too."

Davyn walked over and stood by her desk.

She glanced up at him. "Sit down, try to relax,"

He shook his head. "No, I'm more comfortable tense."

Leo chuckled and lifted a small tool from her desk drawer to pull her earpiece out and set it on a charging pad. "This will be so much better," she said, lifting a headset and putting it on.

Davyn pointed at the small tool she'd used. "What's that? I want one."

"You have one. It's inside your ring. Open the latch and pull out the wire. There's a tiny hook on the end for grabbing the earpiece."

"Thanks for telling me. I've been knocking my head off trying to get it out."

"Sorry, been a little busy." She closed her desk drawer and picked up a notepad covered in handwriting. "Here's what we know so far. Magne's been kidnapped."

Davyn's eyes rolled, and he shook his head dismissively as he scratched behind his ear. Leo glanced down at her earpiece, then up at Davyn holding the back of his head. "Don't do that."

"Do what? I'm just sitting here."

"Your hand—keep it away from your ear. The ring turns the earpiece off when you do that."

Davyn examined the ring. "Why didn't you tell me that?" He pulled the ring off and put it on his left hand.

Leo looked back at her notes while Davyn worked out how to turn the device off and on. He reached across his face with his left hand and put it near his right ear. He heard the beep when the earpiece turned back on. He nodded. Leo glanced at her earpiece, then up at Davyn, whose arm was still stretched across his face.

She watched him lower his arm and crack his neck, then shook her head and went back to her notes.

"We also know that it was almost certainly someone from inside the agency."

"Wait a minute. How do you know that, and how do you know he was kidnapped and not, not...something else?"

"I heard the people who took him—over his earpiece."

"Heard what? What did you hear?"

"I heard someone say, 'Hold your fire. We have him.'"

Davyn paused and considered what she just said. "How can you be sure that's what they said?"

She dropped her pen and cocked her head. "What rhymes with, 'Hold your fire. We have him?'"

"Hmm, nothing comes to mind."

"Right. I heard it correctly. That's what the guy said."

He gave a small nod, accepting her claim for the moment. "What makes you think it's someone who works here?"

Leo looked up from her notes. "Magne works overseas. There wouldn't be anyone stateside with an interest in him. And even if there were, they'd want him dead. They'd have no reason to kidnap him." She looked back at her notes. "Number three, the person with—"

"But why someone *here*?"

Leo blinked at Davyn twice.

Davyn nodded. "Okay, Sorry. Go ahead."

"Number three, Aluerd is up for chief, too, and he runs things a little differently than Magne. No, a lot differently. Maybe he wanted Magne out of the way."

"You mean dead."

"No. Aluerd's intense, but he wouldn't kill Magne."

"Wouldn't kill Magne? So he'd kill others?"

"He has a history of violence against targets. There've been investigations, but nothing conclusive. He flouts the rules and sometimes the law. In his mind, though, that's what it takes. He's not evil, just misguided."

"You said Aluerd is up for chief, too. Is Magne up for chief?"

"The decision about who makes chief is imminent. I think Aluerd may have kidnapped him to get him out of the way."

Davyn leaned back in his chair. "That's nuts. Why would he expect to get away with that?"

"He's got an interesting history. Well, tragic would be a better way to describe it." Leo's eyes bounced around as though she was pondering how to describe it. She shook her head. "Anyway, he has some serious health issues and I think he's getting desperate."

Davyn ran his hand back and forth over his head. "Okay, what else do you have?"

Leo looked at her list. "That's it. That's all I've got."

Davyn stood up. "Okay, we need to call the police. We're in over our heads. We can't do this by ourselves."

"No, Magne was very clear about that."

"It doesn't matter if he was or not. His life is in danger and he needs help. We're not prepared, or capable of doing that."

"Don't you think Magne knows that? But if you tell the police, or the chief, you'll destroy everything that Magne's built here. You'll take away the whole reason he gave up everything to join us. This is bigger than Magne. It's bigger than you."

Davyn shook his head, "So what do we do? Even if we figure it out, what do we do then?"

Leo sat quietly for a moment.

"Well?"

"I can't tell you. Not yet. You just have to trust me."

"Maybe you haven't picked up on this yet, but trusting people is not my thing. I don't trust anyone. That's why I don't leave campus, except to go back to my apartment. I don't like going out into the world, because when I do, shit like this happens. Well, not exactly like this. I mean, this is the pinnacle of shit, really. But bad things happen when I go places."

"Davyn, you don't really believe that, do you? Magne told me about what happened that night at the convenience store. And his disappearance must have really set you back, but people lose people close to them all the time. They don't become hermits because of it."

"Okay, therapy session's over." He put his hands on his hips and sighed. "Jesus, Leo. What are we going to do?"

"Well for starters, we're going to get in some practice."

Davyn turned a wary eye at Leo. "Practice? What do you mean?"

"You're going to talk to some ladies outside the office and I'm going to tell you what to say."

"No, that's dumb."

"Come on, step outside. It'll be fun and you'll get a big ego boost from all the attention."

"Yeah, right. They think I'm Magne."

"Well, do it anyway. I dare you."

Davyn squinted at her. "What are we, seven-year-olds on the playground?"

"Come on," Leo said, obviously trying to bait him. "You know you want to. You're a handsome, unattached, young bachelor. It'll be fun."

"No, it won't." Davyn scratched his head. "But we do need the practice."

Davyn began preparing for what he was about to do. He closed his eyes and took a few slow, deep breaths. He cracked his neck to the right, to the left, and then put his arms out in front of him for some power squats.

"What on earth are you doing?" Leo said.

"Just getting myself prepared."

"You're going to engage in small talk, not mortal combat."

Davyn returned to a standing position. "Small talk's worse." He reached up and around his head to turn on his earpiece.

"You're going to need to find a different way to do that. You look like Count Dracula."

Davyn heard the earpiece power up. "Okay," he said as he reached for the door handle. "Here goes."

"Wait!"

Davyn turned to her. "What?"

"What was the Frankenstein comment you made earlier?"

"Have you read the book?"

"No, but I saw the movie."

Davyn shook his head. "Then you wouldn't understand."

He pulled the door open and stepped out into the office cube farm as Leo's voice came over his earpiece. "The lady in the corner, wearing the pink blouse? That's Cindy. Go talk to her."

Davyn strolled over to Cindy's desk, stopping just short of it. He scratched behind his ear and opened his mouth to say something, but she beat him to the punch.

"Hey, Magne. What's up?"

Davyn listened for Leo's cue, but didn't hear anything. "Um, I don't know. What's up with you?"

Cindy raised her eyebrows. "Is there something I could help you with?"

With a rush of dread, it dawned on Davyn that he'd inadvertently turned off his earpiece. "Um, I was just in the neighborhood, so I thought I'd drop in." He went to casually turn his earpiece back on, leaning on her desk for effect, but slipped and fell on it instead.

"Oh my! Are you alright?"

The room was closing in on him, and his face was getting warm. Still sprawled across the desk, he reached his left arm across his face, trying to turn on the earpiece.

"Are you okay, Magne?" Cindy stood up and stepped back.

"Uh, yeah." He returned to a standing position. *Take a deep breath and say something normal.* "Oh, there's a new moon tomorrow."

Cindy bit her bottom lip and glanced over at her colleagues, then back at Davyn.

He forced a smile and forged ahead. "Tonight it's a waning crescent."

"What's a waning crescent?"

The air grew thick. Davyn scratched at his chin. "The moon. It's a moon phase. It's not very good for hunting nocturnal animals."

"I'm sure. Look, thanks for stopping by, but I have a lot of work to do."

"Sure, sure, okay. Bye." Davyn slunk back to Leo's office.

Leo looked up from her desk as the door shut behind him. "What the hell was that?"

"That's how conversations go with people I don't know." He pulled at his collar to loosen it. "She thought I was nuts."

"No doubt. Why did you turn off your earpiece? And what the

hell were you doing on her desk? It looked like the death scene from *Hamlet*."

"I was trying to turn the earpiece back on and I slipped."

"Well, what did you say to her?"

"I think I said a full moon is good for hunting."

"Why would you say that?"

"I don't know!" He threw his hands up. "I was supposed to be hunting in the woods this weekend, but instead I'm here, talking to you. And everyone else, apparently."

"Well, for the next encounter, keep your earpiece on. We can't afford any more weird conversations."

"You saw what happens when I say what I'm thinking." He folded his arms. "I just don't fit in."

Davyn lowered his head and stared at the ground.

Leo scratched her chin. "What was the Frankenstein reference you made earlier?"

"It has nothing to do with what you see in the movie. I was referring to the—never mind."

"No, I'm curious. Educate me."

Davyn sighed; there was way too much to cover if she hadn't read the book, so he'd have to keep it short. "It was in reference to me being stripped of my identity and thrown into a new world." *Ugh, too much. Back off.*

Leo, evidently making an earnest effort to understand him, studied his face. But it didn't last long. She looked back at her computer monitor but didn't say anything. The room was unnaturally quiet, completely dead.

Good opportunity to change the topic. "Is this room soundproof?" Davyn whispered, the thought having occurred to him in the relative silence.

Leo seemed relieved to move on to a new topic. "It's weird, right? The sound absorbing material sucks up the sound, so it immediately dissipates as soon as it leaves your lips. It's a little disorienting."

Davyn gazed at Leo. "Yeah, it is." He liked that she noticed it, too. *It's amazing how people go through life not noticing things, not thinking about them. They just think it's weird and move on.* He appreciated that Leo noticed even the little details.

"Oh my god, you almost smiled there for a second."

"Must have been a weak moment," he said, feeling a little embarrassed.

"You remind me of Magne sometimes. Not just your looks, but your mannerisms."

Davyn nodded, unsure how to reply.

"Why'd you grow your hair out?"

He didn't want to go into how, after Magne disappeared, he couldn't bear looking in the mirror and seeing someone who looked so much like his dead brother. It was like changing a routine to avoid running into someone you didn't want to see—except that someone was himself. So he shrugged and left it at that.

Leo broke the silence. "It must've been something when you guys hung out together."

Davyn thought back to a sunny day on a softball field, when they used to play on the same team.

"You're smiling. What are you thinking about?"

"Um, nothing."

"Come on," she said, trying to pull it out of him.

Davyn leaned in closer to Leo. "Okay, well, we were playing softball. Magne was pitching, I was covering first. We had to win this game, you know, because the guys we were playing were all pricks. I mean, every one of them. The game was intense, low score, and tight. Really aggressive pitching. Every inning, one or two guys were hit or nearly hit by a pitch. Fast pitch: it was fast pitch softball. The ump warned us twice. Any more and he'd call the game.

"Magne was on the pitcher's mound. It was the bottom of the last inning. We were up by one, but they had two guys on base: second and third. And there were no outs. Magne called me over to the mound to talk strategy, I thought. But he whispers, 'Look past first base. It's The Car.' I looked and, sure enough, there was this weird black car, with tinted windows. It kept showing up at different places we'd go, ever since we saw this schlocky seventies horror movie called *The Car*. I thought he had something important to say about winning the game, but leave it to Magne to horse around when things got intense.

"I asked him if that was all he'd wanted to say, but Magne got really serious all of a sudden and shook his head. It was a subtle shake, like pitchers do when they're communicating signals with the catcher. Then he looked me dead in the eyes, smiled—you know that winning smile, the kind of smile that made you glad to be his friend?"

Leo smiled.

"Yeah, you know what I'm talking about. It communicated confidence, warmth, but somehow that he'd be just as fine living on an island by himself. An 'everything is going to be fine' smile. You'd think I'd have that, too, us being identical twins and all, but nope. Anyway, Magne glanced over at the bleachers, and Sandy's sitting there. She was this girl I liked. So I asked him if there was anything else, and he nodded, then responds, 'Think they'll have any of those hot dogs left after the game?'

"The ump yells 'Alright, guys. Let's move it along or I'm calling the game.' He'd say that 'calling the game' line like two or three times during every game. We used to call him CTG because of it, and Magne always pushed him to the limit. I guess he wanted to find out if he'd ever actually call it. But that was Magne, always pushing to see how much he could get away with. Trouble was, he could get away with anything."

Leo smiled and cocked her head to the side. "And he'll be right back at it once we find him."

Davyn snapped out of his daze.

"Okay, we practiced with Cindy. What's next?"

Leo cleared her throat. "Well, I wouldn't call that practice." She set her notes aside. "But I'm curious about something. You're an introvert, yet you just opened up and told me a personal story. It's like sometimes you're an introvert and sometimes you're not."

"I think you're confusing being an introvert with being shy."

"What do you mean? I thought they were the same thing."

"That's not surprising. From the outside, I'm sure it looks the same. An introvert enjoys being alone and gets emotionally drained after spending time with people. A shy person doesn't necessarily want to be alone but is afraid to interact with people."

Leo squinted like she was trying to see the difference.

"It's really about motivation. I don't talk unless I have something to say, and I hate small talk. Introverts have a lot of thoughts going on. If you're going to interrupt, the conversation you bring up had better be more interesting than the one that they were already engaged in."

"Conversation?"

"Sometimes. If it's not a conversation, it's a thought or an idea they're working through internally. Either way, whatever you say would be perceived as an interruption. Think of it like this. If you're watching a movie and someone starts talking to you during an important scene, how does that make you feel?"

"Ugh, I hate that."

"There you go. Okay, so what's next?"

Leo appeared to be mulling over what Davyn said. Then, her look of concentration evaporated and she said, "We need to make some headway on the investigation, so you're going to go to Jordan's office. We can practice some more on the way."

Davyn wondered whether she understood, or had decided to just drop it without further thought—the latter being something he was incapable of doing. Once an idea set in, he had to process it.

"Davyn?"

Davyn tried to focus back on the matter at hand. "So, who's Jordan?"

She eyed him carefully. "Glad you're back. He's Aluerd's top guy. If Aluerd's behind Magne's kidnapping, Jordan's involved, too."

"And you want me to go see him? How do you know I won't kill him?"

"That wouldn't solve anything."

"I wasn't being literal. But if he's involved, I might not—our interaction might get a little heated."

"Well, he's scheduled to be off today, but that doesn't mean he will be. Agents' schedules can be fluid. If he's not there, I just want you to look around his office. See if you can find anything that might help us locate Magne."

"What if he is there?"

"If he is there, and, assuming he was involved in the kidnapping, he'll be shocked to see you. Either way, we're sure to get useful intelligence."

CHAPTER 10

As Davyn walked out of Leo's office, all eyes were fixed on him. But he didn't pay attention to them. He was focused on getting upstairs to Jordan's office. Finally, a chance to do something that might help find Magne! And it didn't hurt that he'd be getting away from Leo's area, where he'd made such a fool of himself in front of her and her colleagues.

As Davyn approached the elevator, he saw three people already waiting for it. He slowed down in the hope of avoiding any more social interaction than was necessary. Maybe the elevator would take them away before he arrived. He stopped and looked at his watch, stalling. Their backs were to him, so he'd just wait until they left and grab the next one. The elevator doors finally opened, and the people got on and turned around, facing out. He looked down at his watch again to avoid eye contact, but he could see in his periphery that the doors were still open. He fumbled with the watch buttons. How long could he do this without looking weird?

"Come on, Magne," someone in the elevator called.

Davyn looked up, his eyes wide. "Uh, go ahead. I—I forgot something."

The doors closed, and Davyn shuffled closer to the elevator. He pressed the button and looked around, hoping no one would join him before it came. Even a few minutes alone would help settle his nerves. A moment later, the doors opened. He peered in. Empty. *Thank god.* He stepped in, turned around and saw a man walking quickly toward him, clearly heading for the elevator. Davyn looked down at the buttons and pretended to try to hold the car, but pressed the 'close door' button and acted like he didn't know why it wasn't working. The doors closed, and Davyn took a deep breath. It felt good to finally be alone.

"How's the reception in the elevator? Can you hear me?" Leo asked.

Well, that didn't last long. "There are people here. I can't talk now," Davyn whispered hoping she'd buy it.

"No, there aren't. I've got eyes on you, remember? I can see you."

Davyn leaned back against the elevator car wall, closed his eyes, and let his head fall back.

"We're going to have to up the charm and grace a bit," Leo continued, "or someone will catch on. You're surrounded by people who love and respect you. They're happy to just be around you. Pretend you're an actor and you're playing a role, if that helps."

Nice advice. She's essentially saying don't be myself. Be someone better.

The elevator door opened and Davyn leaned forward to go out.

"Stay," Leo warned. "This isn't your floor. Remember, you're going to—oh that's Linda. Be friendly and say, 'Hey, Linda! How are the kids?' Over. She adores you."

A second later, Linda stepped into the elevator and smiled at Davyn.

"Hey, Linda. How are those kids...of yours?"

Linda chuckled. "Welcome back, Magne. You must have been in Salt Lake City, huh?"

"Say, 'Bill still coaching soccer? Season's wrapping up soon, isn't it?' Over."

Linda stood next to Davyn, facing the elevator door.

"How's Bill? Still coaching soccer? Season must be wrapping up soon, no?"

Linda smiled and pushed her hair behind her ear with her finger. She hesitated, blinking a couple of times. "Oh, he's fine. The kids made the playoffs. Billie's doing great as goalie. Low scores every game. Thanks for asking."

"Uh-oh, trouble with Bill. Say, 'Hang in there, Linda, and say hi to Billie and Tommy for me.' Over."

The doors opened, and they stepped out. Linda started to walk away when Davyn bumped her shoulder with his fist. Linda turned around and he said, "Hang in there, Linda. Tell Tommy and Billie I said hi."

Linda smiled somewhat tentatively. "Um, thanks, I will." Then she walked off.

"That was kind of okay. You need to work on your shoulder taps, though. More like petting a kitten and less like a rugby player."

"Uh-huh." Davyn gazed around the office space.

"That's Cynthia, at the reception desk. We're going to take it up a notch. Walk over there, lean confidently on the desk and say, 'I'm out of those writing thingies. You wouldn't have one I could borrow, would you?' Over."

Davyn shook his head and shuddered. *Oh boy.* But, he dutifully walked over to Cynthia's desk and leaned on it in a way that could be described as confident, though if you said it wasn't, nobody would call you out on it.

"Say, Cynthia, I'm out of those writing things. You wouldn't have a spare, by chance?"

Cynthia looked up at Davyn like she was surprised to see him. "Oh, Magne," she said, shaking her head. "I didn't recognize your voice. Do you have a cold?"

He forced a smile. "Just got back from Salt Lake City."

"Ah, probably the air there." She handed him a pen, which he took, wondering what he was supposed to do next.

"Okay," Leo said with a sigh. "Time to cut and run. Say, 'Thanks. See ya.' Over. Then head down the hall behind you. Jordan's office is all the way down at the end."

Davyn started down the hallway, his heart rate picking up. *This guy might be responsible for Magne's kidnapping.* His jaw clenched as he drew a deep breath. *Stay cool, or you'll blow it.*

"You forgot to say 'bye' to Cynthia, but that's okay. If Jordan's there, remember to check out his reaction when he sees you. Watch his eyes."

"Yep." Davyn saw Jordan's name on the door and stopped outside the office. He glanced in, then took a few steps back and whispered, "He's there."

"Act like nothing's wrong. You're just stopping in for a friendly visit. When you go in, say, "Hey Jordan, what's up?' Over."

Davyn stepped into Jordan's office, planting his feet just inside the doorway. The man he assumed was Jordan was at his desk, writing something on a notepad. His head was down, and he hadn't noticed Davyn yet.

"Hey Jordan, what's up?"

Jordan's head shot up. "Holy shit, you startled me."

"Ask him why. Just say, 'Why?' Over."

Davyn squinted. "Why?"

He looked down at his notepad. "You know why."

"Oh, wait. That's not Jordan. Say, 'Why are you in Jordan's office?' Over."

Not Jordan? Davyn's eyes darted around the room. "Why are you in Jordan's office?"

The guy, whoever he was, stood up and nudged the desk side drawer closed with his knee, then came around to leave, grabbing a sheet of paper from a notepad on the desk as he went. "I—I," he stammered. "I had to stop nearby to see someone, and I want to jot something down before I got back to my desk and forgot. Please don't tell anyone, Magne." He dashed past Davyn into the hallway.

"That's Madison. He works as an aid in intelligence. But what the hell was he doing in Jordan's office? You'd better follow him."

Davyn turned and did as he was told. Madison was already a hundred feet ahead and moving fast, so Davyn jogged a few steps until someone stepped out of an office in front of him. He stopped to avoid running into her.

"Hey, Magne. What's up?"

"Not now," he said and started jogging after Madison again, who had just turned the corner.

When Davyn reached the same corner, he turned and watched the elevator doors close.

"Never mind, we'll catch up to him later. Head back to Jordan's office."

Cynthia said, looked up from the reception desk. "Everything alright, Magne?"

Davyn turned to her. "Did you see Madison? How long was he up here?"

"Don't ask any more questions," Leo said. "I'm checking the video now."

Davyn walked over to Cynthia as she replied, "Um, I don't know, five minutes maybe. I'm sorry. Was I supposed to stop him? He had his pass with him."

"Say 'It's okay, thanks.' Over. Then go back to Jordan's—never mind. You look suspicious now. Take a seat on the couch on the other side of the elevator, away from reception while I think this through."

Davyn walked over and sat on the couch. When Cynthia wasn't looking, he whispered, "So, what do I do?"

"I'm sorry, Davyn, give me a minute. We need a way to learn more about why Magne was kidnapped and where they might be keeping him."

Davyn didn't feel like waiting and headed back down the hall toward Jordan's office.

"What are you doing?" Leo said.

Davyn didn't respond as he stopped outside Jordan's office and checked to see if it was clear. There were people at the other end of the hall, near reception, but no one with him in the hallway. He stepped into Jordan's office and closed the door behind him. He opened the desk drawer Madison had closed earlier and rifled through it.

"Okay, I guess since you're there, go ahead and tell me if you see anything interesting."

"Madison pushed a drawer closed and grabbed a sheet of paper as he was leaving. I'm looking in that drawer now, but I don't see anything I wouldn't expect." Davyn shuffled through a few more items in the drawer. "I'll take the legal pad with me. If he wrote anything down on the last page, we can probably pick up the leftover indentations. I assume you have someone here with the capability of analyzing it better than we could."

"No, we can't raise suspicion. We'll just do the pencil shading thing."

Davyn sat back in the chair, "Look, Leo, we don't have the luxury of time. The clock's ticking. We're going to have to take some chances. There's gotta be someone you trust, or maybe someone that Magne knows that he could—that I could ask."

Leo went quiet for a moment. "We can ask the tech guys."

"The tech guys?"

"That's what Magne calls them. There are two guys that he works with pretty regularly and he calls them the tech guys."

"All right, I'm going to keep looking around. I'll turn off the earpiece to save power. Be back soon."

Davyn turned his attention to the things on the desk, being careful not to move anything without putting it back where he found it. He looked at the pictures on the wall and on the shelves. Nothing that looked like family pictures, mostly just groups of men in suits—from work, presumably. He wished he knew how to identify the people in the photos, or that Leo could see them. Maybe they'd provide some insight. No pictures with Magne. That was something, anyway.

Davyn heard his earpiece blip back on and then Leo's voice. "Magne, the chief is heading your way. Not sure if he'll make it down there. He must know Jordan's off today. Maybe not, though. Don't leave the office, but be ready in case he comes in."

Davyn steeped over to the window and stared out.

"He's coming in," Leo warned.

The door opened and Davyn spun around. "Hi, chief." Davyn casually walked over to the chief as he let the door close behind him.

"Were you looking for Jordan? He's out today."

"I know, I was just getting a different view. Helps me think."

The chief smiled. "Well, maybe you'll have a better view very soon."

"Say, 'Sir?' Over," Leo said.

The Chief turned and looked at the closed door behind him as Davyn followed Leo's instruction. "Sir?"

The chief turned back to Davyn and pointed with his thumb behind him. "Was the door shut before I came in?" When Davyn just pushed his lips together and shrugged, the chief continued. "Anyway, I can't say anything officially until it's approved, but I think we both know where it's going." He extended his arm toward the chairs in front of the desk. "Sit down for a minute. Let's talk."

Davyn sat down and put his hands on his knees.

"Aluerd is a good man, but he's had some extraordinary tragedies, and I fear they've taken their toll. You two are a lot alike in some ways, but—" He paused and appeared to gather his thoughts.

"Your focus on achieving the agency's goals while staying within the limits of the law is part of what sets you apart. I have a lot more to say on that, after it's all official."

Davyn nodded.

"I expected you to be a little more excited, but I guess you saw the writing on the wall." The chief rubbed his chin. "Over the past week, especially."

"Whoa, did you hear that? Say, 'Do you think Aluerd knows?' Over."

"Do you think Aluerd—"

"Wait," Leo said, "Say 'suspects,' not 'knows.'"

Davyn sat quietly while Leo worked it out, but the unnatural pause was starting to feel awkward. "Do you think Aluerd suspects anything?" he blurted, then grimaced.

"Why the face? Oh, rugby injury acting up again?"

Davyn nodded.

"No matter, you'll be out of fieldwork and behind the desk growing fat soon enough." The chief patted his belly. "Like me." He stood up and adjusted the waistband on his pants. "Of course, I'm sure you'll make better use of the company gym than I did. Anyway, we'll talk more later."

The chief opened the door and stepped outside, waiting for Davyn to follow.

As he stepped out into the hallway, Davyn glanced at the plaque outside the office across the hall. "I have to stop and talk to Beth for a minute." He paused and waited for the chief to continue down the hall before he relaxed.

"Davyn," Leo said. "Quit standing around and bring that notepad to the lounge on the fifth floor. I'll meet you there, then we'll see the tech guys."

Davyn stood in a large atrium, facing the towering windows that stretched six stories tall and overlooked the park outside. The balconies in the building allowed all six floors access to the view.

Davyn looked past the park to the woods, wishing he was out there among the trees. When he said he didn't like being in the outside world, he really meant that he didn't like being in the outside world with people.

From the corner of his eye, he saw Leo step off the elevator. He held on to the quiet moment as long as he could until she walked past him, tapping him on the elbow as she went. He glanced her way, but his attention returned to the trees, past the park. His shoulders dropped as he finally turned to follow her. It was an unpleasant sensation. It reminded him of when he was a child and got dragged along to shop for clothes. Worse, now he had to go meet more new people.

He didn't enjoy meeting new people, except for maybe Leo. She was beginning to feel familiar, but he didn't like that she was essentially his puppet master.

"Okay, the lab is up here on the right." She was about fifty paces ahead of Davyn. "The tech guys are named Al and Phil. They do this sort of thing regularly, so it shouldn't raise any suspicion." Leo stopped at the entrance to the lab and waved her badge in front of a sensor. Its red light turned green and the door unlocked and they stepped inside.

She pointed past rows of lab tables to two men standing in white lab coats. "There they are," she whispered. "The skinny one is Phil."

Leo started toward them as Davyn followed, still feeling like he was being led around by his mother. He missed the feeling of autonomy he had on campus.

Phil, a balding man in his mid-thirties, held an object about the size of a softball, but with eight sides.

"Hi guys," Phil said cheerfully as he looked around for somewhere to put the object. Al, a large man in his mid-fifties, picked up a plastic case from a table behind them and held it out. Phil placed the object carefully into the foam-lined case, which looked crafted to fit it precisely.

"What's that?" Davyn asked, staring.

"It's top secret, but I guess I can tell you, it's an n-pulse gren—"

Al's hand shot in front of Phil's mouth and he closed the case. "We can't say yet, but once we can you'll be the first to know."

"You're from the Dominican Republic?"

"You are teasing me, Magne. You know this already." Al furrowed his brow, and Davyn nudged Leo as soon as he looked away.

Leo glanced at Davyn, then quickly addressed the tech guys, apparently to draw their gazes away from his tomato-red face. "We have a notepad we'd like you to take a look at."

"Just a moment," Phil said as he locked the case and walked it over to a cabinet. Al continued staring at Davyn until Phil cleared his throat. Apparently he needed him to open the cabinet door. Al jumped and hurried over to wave his badge in front of the lock before entering a code. Davyn made note of it, having a feeling it might be useful later. The door opened and Phil gently placed the object inside.

Davyn watched all of this closely. While he didn't usually like interacting with people, he sometimes found their interactions fascinating. The device that they locked away also held his attention. What could it be, and why were they so careful with it? Why couldn't they tell him what it was?

Phil put on latex gloves and took the notepad, examining it from several angles. "Hmm, same notepads we use here. That's not unusual. It's a common brand and available internationally. Even in third world countries. You've gotta wonder who their salesperson is."

Davyn chuckled. "Maybe it's the cranberry guy."

Phil looked up at him. "What do you mean?"

"The cranberry salesman. A couple years ago he got cranberries into everything. Cran-apple, cran-grape drinks, dried cranberries, cranberries and tropical nuts. Everything had cranberries in it."

Leo nudged him with her elbow.

Phil cocked his head. "So, what are we looking for?" Phil asked after an awkward beat.

"We think someone wrote something important on the page on top of this pad. We want to know what they wrote. If there're any pictures or doodles, we'll want to know about those, too."

Phil walked over to a square box, about the size of a microwave oven, sitting on a nearby table. He opened it and placed the notepad inside. "This will scan it. It should only take about fifteen minutes to go through the different wavelengths and interpret it. Where do you want me to send the image file?"

"You can send it to me," Leo said.

"Okay. As for the notepad, you can wait for it, I can send it by courier, or you can come back and pick it up later."

Leo looked at her watch. "Oh shoot, we have that black tie event tonight." She bit her bottom lip. "Just send it to my office."

Davyn leaned against a table, surveying the lab. "Can I just wait here?"

The tech guys seemed bewildered, but Phil also looked excited by the prospect of Magne hanging out with them.

Davyn walked over to Phil and pointed at the box. "How's this thing work?"

"Oh, this!" Phil exclaimed, apparently eager to talk about his gear. "It runs through different wavelengths of energy, including visible, ultraviolet, infrared, etc. Each wavelength's layer is saved as a separate image, then the images are interpolated into one. The report that I'll send to Leo will have the interpolated image, but she can drill down and look at the other images, too. Sometimes you see things there that you wouldn't see in the interpolated image, but not usually in this type of situation."

Davyn squinted and nodded as he examined the box. "Uh-huh. I guess it's spectral only, given its size. Can you do radiometric dating here?" He looked around the lab and then pointed across the room at a tall cabinet. "There. Is that one?"

"Yes. How did you know that?"

Leo shot a glare and gave a subtle shake of her head at Davyn. "Magne, can I talk to you for a moment? In private."

But Davyn and Phil were already on their way over to the radiometric dating machine. Leo tapped her ring to her ear, covered her mouth with her hand, and hissed, "Magne's not interested in any of this stuff. You're blowing your cover."

Davyn whispered back, "I'll be just a minute, Mother. I promise not to ask too many questions."

Phil stood in front of the machine like a kid on Christmas morning, ready to unwrap a present, and opened the door on the radiometric scanner.

"What kind of dating do you do? How far back can you go?"

"We don't get very many requests here, but sometimes other

agencies ask for a hand. Most of it's forensic: human remains, a weapon, or an old piece of equipment."

"Can you tell if a stone's been modified? Chipped, for instance? Can you tell when the modification took place?"

Leo approached from behind and clamped down on Davyn's arm. "We really need to get going. I'll keep an eye out for the report. Please send it as soon as you can, Phil. Thanks for your help."

Davyn nodded, stepping backward as Leo pulled him away. "Thanks, guys. It's been great."

"No problem, Magne. We love talking about our gear. Stop by anytime!"

Leo marched quickly for the lab exit, with Davyn in tow. He turned and waved. "I'll be back!"

"No, you won't," Leo whispered. They exited the lab, and the door closed behind them. Leo shot a glance up the empty hallway. "What the hell was that?"

"What? We were just standing around waiting."

"When Magne goes in there he's charming, he's nice, but he doesn't care how any of that stuff works. They were looking at you like you had grown a second head. From now on, you need to be seen and not heard. Got it?"

Davyn stood quietly and didn't respond. He wondered if he could send some of his artifacts to the lab and get them to examine them when all of this was over.

She tapped his forehead. "Hello, you in there?"

Davyn jerked back, then gave a soft nod.

Leo started walking toward the elevator. "Let's get to my office and take a look at that report. Maybe it'll tell us something. We need a lead."

Davyn's shoulders dropped. His social battery exhausted, he shuffled along toward the elevator.

"Come on, Magne," she said without turning around.

Davyn eventually caught up to her at the elevator.

"We have that black tie affair tonight," she said. "I'll take you to my place and you can shower there. We should be back here by 8:30 at the latest."

"I'll need to get a run in before that."

"I don't think we'll have time."

Davyn looked her in the eye. "You don't understand. I *need* to get a run in."

Leo must've noticed the expression on his face and nodded. "Okay but keep it short."

Davyn looked at his watch. "Fine, four miles then. Twenty-nine minutes. I've done it in twenty-seven minutes and eight seconds before, but I'm not familiar with the terrain here. It might take me thirty or thirty-one minutes. Maybe thirty-two. Then I'll need twenty-five minutes to cool off before showering."

Leo shook her head, "Why don't you just say half an hour to run, and half an hour too cool down?"

"Because it's not half an hour," he said, sounding simultaneously vulnerable and defiant.

The elevator doors opened, and they stepped inside and turned around.

"Shit," Davyn said. "One of the security guys said I'm giving a speech tonight. Why didn't you say anything?"

Leo rummaged through her bag and didn't bother to look up. "Don't worry, I'm going to talk to the event coordinator," she said, pulling out her car keys. "I'm sure you can skip it. It shouldn't be an issue."

CHAPTER 11

The event room at headquarters had been transformed into an extravagant ballroom for the evening. There were giant balloon archways, wait staff carrying fancy hors d'oeuvres on trays, at least four dance floors splashed by robo-lights, and a sea of people dressed to the nines. Just the sort of thing that made Davyn wish he was home instead, or to at least have Leo there with him. Technically she was, just in her office so she could keep an eye on things and feed him lines as needed.

"Keep in mind that you just need to be seen. Remember tip two. Ask open-ended questions and let them do the talking. The less you say, the better."

"Ten-four, captain."

"Well, you sound pretty relaxed. Maybe I should have gone on that run with you."

"I didn't know you run. Why didn't you?"

"Because I don't. I do Zumba, yoga, stuff like that."

"Maybe we'll dance later, once things loosen up and people get hammered. They won't notice."

"You mean, they won't notice you dancing alone? Because I'll be right here. In my office."

"Maybe you can slip out once I've met everyone."

"You sound like a different person, Davyn."

He did a little sashay across the dance floor. "I run hot and cold. Did you see that?"

"Yeah, pretty good, but keep your cool and don't embarrass yourself."

"I won't embarrass myself. I'll embarrass Magne."

"Have you been drinking?"

"Just a little one. First one in, um, five years, probably."

"Well, you're acting weird. Go back to your old weird. I think I like it better."

"It's just, I feel like some things may start to be getting a little better, maybe. Magne's alive." Davyn couldn't help but smile a little at that. "I made some new friends today."

"Davyn, I don't know what was in that drink, but it hit you hard. No more drinks, and—oh shit. Here comes the chief. He's with his wife, Deb. Pull your act together."

The chief and his wife worked their way through the crowd. Davyn smiled at him and the chief shot him a wink, mouthed some words Davyn couldn't make out, and pointed across the ballroom floor, then up to the ceiling.

"I didn't catch that on the video feed. What did the chief just say?"

"I can't read lips, so I have no idea what he said. I think he wants to dance with me to the ceiling."

"What? Ugh, Davyn. What did he do?"

"He pointed at the dance floor, then up to the ceiling."

"He probably wants to talk to someone across the room and he'll be back in a minute. Man, your social skills really are rusty."

"You're very perceptive, Leo. I like that. When I first saw you, I thought your hair reminded me of an erupting volcano. But it could also be the mane of a lion." He paused a moment. "Don't misunderstand—that's a compliment. You're a beautiful volcano and lion. Leo the lion. I'm sleepy."

"Dammit, Davyn, you've got to get out of there and get some coffee. You need some time to let that drink wear off. With your metabolism, it shouldn't take too long." Leo sighed. "Head out those exit doors to your left. I don't see anyone out on the balcony. If anyone tries to talk to you on the way there, tell them you'll be right back."

Davyn walked toward the doors and put his hand on the door release bar. "Hey, wait," he said, looking off toward the bar. "It's my new friends, Al and Phil."

"Davyn, no. You'll see them later. Go outside before they see you."
Phil saw Davyn and waved.

"Too late. They've spotted me."

"It was probably you're maniacal waving."

Davyn looked up and saw his arm stretched over his head and his hand swinging frantically. "Oh, I'm waving. That is rather maniacal, isn't it?" He pressed the bar on the door and stepped outside.

"You're getting worse. How do you feel?"

"I feel great. A little sleepy. Actually, a lotta sleepy. Maybe a bed would be good."

"You can't. Not yet. Let's see, it's 8:45. We'll get you out of there by 10:00. We'll say you're not feeling well or something. For now, we just need to get you some coffee, and some time alone."

"Boy, coffee and some time alone was my go-to thing back at the university. Tonight, though, I feel—"

Phil and Al stepped outside onto the balcony.

"Guys," Davyn shouted with more enthusiasm than he intended.

"Hi, Magne," Phil said as he walked toward him, smiling ear to ear like a puppy when his owner comes home.

"Get him started on that machine you two were talking about earlier. But let *him* do the talking. You need to stay quiet. Say, 'Tell me more about...' Ugh, whatever the name of the machine was. Over."

"Tell me more about ugh," Davyn said.

"Ugh?" Phil asked.

"Oh, that's what we call the one at the lab where I send samples. We call it ugh."

Phil looked shocked and hurt. "You use a different lab for your samples?"

"Davyn," Leo interrupted, "Say, 'Sometimes. Sorry, I probably shouldn't have mentioned it. It's classified.' Over."

He turned and leaned over the balcony, gazing out over the park. "I shouldn't have told you that. It's top secret stuff."

Phil nodded and walked over to Al, whispering something in his ear. Al nodded and headed back inside.

"It's a nice night for this time of year," Phil said.

"Say, 'Yes, it is. Tell me more about the radio metric—"

The line went dead, then a man's voice cut in. "West dock in fifteen—"

Leo's voice returned. "'It works.' Over."

"Whoa, that was weird," Davyn said.

Phil cocked his head. "What was weird?"

"The radio—uh, never mind. Oh, I know what I was going to ask you. Can you tell if a stone's been modified or chipped? And when the modification took place?"

"Don't talk about anthropology, they'll suspect something," Leo said.

"Oh, sure, we can date the time of the chip, if it's within the past fifty thousand years."

The balcony door flew open, and a man Davyn hadn't met stepped outside and shouted, "Magne, the chief's looking for you. He says it's time to give the speech."

Oh boy.

The chief saw Davyn step back inside and gave him a thumbs-up, then headed up to the stage.

Davyn turned to the man that had escorted him in. "The chief didn't want to dance with me after all. He was pointing at the stage."

The man slapped him on the back. "Magne, you're a nut. I hope you prepared something."

"No, actually. I didn't."

"That's okay, the mighty Magne can give speeches all day long with his hands tied behind his back, right?"

Davyn looked across the sea of people as the chief stepped up to the podium and asked for everyone's attention before beginning to speak, but it was all a blur to Davyn.

"How does tying someone's hands behind their back affect their speech?"

"Shh, the chief is speaking," the man whispered.

"Sorry."

"Davyn, stay calm. I'll talk you through this—" Leo said, but the line cut out again, and the same man's voice from before came on.

"The ship's been delayed."

Then he heard a blip, and Leo's voice returned. "Downloaded some generic stuff online. It won't be perfect, but good enough for tonight's speech."

"I feel pretty calm, actually. I'm starting to feel better. Not better, but more awake at least."

The man looked at Davyn and scrunched his eyebrows. "He's getting ready to call you up."

The chief said, "It's been a fine and rewarding experience to have worked with you all for so long. I'll be making my official announcement in a couple of days. For now, though, I'd like to introduce a man who needs no introduction. Everyone, please welcome Magne Daeger." He extended an arm out for Magne's entrance.

The audience broke into riotous applause, but it faded and turned to murmuring when Magne didn't materialize.

That's when the man pushed Davyn toward the stage. "Go, Magne, everyone's waiting."

The chief stepped back to the mic. "Ah, he's in the crowd talking everyone up, I'm sure. I shouldn't be surprised. Come on, Magne. Get on up here so you can talk to everyone at once."

Davyn worked his way through the crowd, then stumbled on his way up the stairs.

Leo said, "Stay calm, Davyn, we've got—"

The line went dead again, and the same unknown male voice came on. "Offloaded in—"

Another blip, and Leo's voice returned. "Should be good."

Davyn made his way across the stage and to the lectern. He peered out over the crowd, squinting as the bright lights shone in his eyes.

"Say, 'I'd like to thank you all for coming out to—" Again the blip, then dead air. Davyn stared out at the audience, trying to steady his legs by taking a deep breath.

The chief stepped up and covered the mic with his hand. "Are you okay?"

Davyn nodded, then pushed the chief's hand away. "I'd like to thank all you beautiful people for coming out this evening." The crowd laughed.

"Good. Say, 'As many of you know I've been with the company for four years and—" Blip.

Davyn cracked his neck. "As you all know, I've been here for four years." Davyn stopped and reached his left hand across his face, turning off the earpiece. "That's better."

The chief flashed a quick smile and looked sideways at the audience.

Davyn cleared his throat. "As I was saying, I've been with the company for four years now, and our beloved chief will be retiring soon. As many of you know, the company has been involved in an extensive search to try to find a suitable replacement. Given the excellent leadership displayed by our current chief, that job has not been an easy one."

The chief patted his forehead with a handkerchief.

Davyn put his hand on the mic, turned to the chief and smiled. "It's okay, I think I can do this," he said with a wink.

"Of course you can," the chief whispered, then stepped away to sit down.

Back in her office, Leo bit her lip, slumped in her chair, and watched the monitor as Davyn continued the speech. Her face contorted into a grimace as she listened to him sputter through.

"Replacing such a strong and consistent leader is not so simple," Davyn said, straightening his back and loosening his grip on the podium. "And, I understand, they are looking at some candidates internally." He turned to the chief. "I've got some ideas, if you need some."

The chief grimaced, then smiled out at the crowd as scattered laughter, mixed with some groans, wafted up from the audience.

"So, thank you again for coming out and helping us to celebrate the chief's pre-retirement party."

A smattering of applause rose from the audience. Davyn stepped away from the mic and headed for the stage stairs, where the chief caught up to him.

"That was a little risky, Magne. I guess that's your style, but I'll need you to not be quite so open about what we discussed from here on out. Understand?"

Davyn grabbed the chief's arm. "Of course, chief. I understand."

His brow furrowed as he looked at Davyn's hand, then back up at Davyn. "You seem different lately. Is everything alright?"

Davyn patted the chief's shoulder. "Yeah, fine. Just too much time in Salt Lake City, I guess."

The chief gave him a look reminiscent of the one Mr. Puddington gave him after Davyn's botched performance in class. He dropped his hand and forced a smile.

"Well, get some rest. I know you're on hiatus until next week, but I have a small mission for you, and I need you to be at the top of your game. We'll talk more tomorrow."

Davyn nodded as the chief walked off.

"Uh-oh," Leo said, as the earpiece flickered back to life. "What small mission?"

Jordan stepped into a quiet corner of the lobby and dialed one of the contacts in his cell phone. His heart raced as he continuously checked the area to make sure no one was around. When his contact picked up, he whispered, "I don't know how to tell you this, but I just watched Magne give a speech at headquarters."

He cupped his hand around the phone while he listened to the response. "Of course I'm sure it's him."

On the other end of the line, Aluerd stood under a lone light on the dock. He pulled his shoulders up and drew in the collar of his tailored blue uniform, as the wind blew spray from the waves that lashed at the docks. Several hundred yards out on the water, a midsize boat bobbed in the ocean as it headed toward him.

"That's impossible," Aluerd said. "Unless Boris got the wrong man. Wait there and don't move. I'll call you right back." He hit a button on his phone and waited for a response. "Do you still have him?" Aluerd listened. "Because I was just told he's at a party giving a speech. If you're trying to screw me over—" Aluerd pulled back from the phone, trying to rein in his irritation. "Send me a picture of him. Make sure it's clear, and that you're standing next to him. I want proof."

Aluerd dialed Jordan back.

"I'm waiting on proof that Magne's still in custody. If he isn't—" Aluerd stared out at the water without really seeing anything. "Did you set me up, Jordan?"

"What? No. Calm down, Aluerd. You're not thinking straight."

"*I'm* not thinking straight? You're the one seeing phantoms. Or you're trying to play me. I promise it won't go well for you if you are."

Aluerd hung up without waiting for a reply and looked at his phone as a photo came in via text. It was blurry at first, but then the image developed. He called the sender back. "I'm looking at it now, Boris. It looks like we got the right man. That means Jordan has double-crossed me. I want you to take him out next."

Aluerd listened for a moment, then said, "I don't care. It has to happen tonight. As soon as possible. If he tells anyone what—just take him out now." Despite the cold night air, sweat beaded on his forehead. "And I want Magne brought to the island... I know what I said. But I don't like how things are going. Get him here now. Call me when you're close and I'll meet you at the west dock."

CHAPTER 12

As Davyn walked away from the stage, the crowd clamored to get to him. He smiled as he passed through the dense crowd, a smattering of pats landing on his back among an assortment of compliments and well wishes. Someone even said, "You'll make a great chief."

Davyn heard a blip in his ear that told him Leo was back online, but he was talking with people and as far as he was concerned, he was getting along just fine—he might have even enjoyed the attention a little.

"Davyn, why do you keep turning off the earpiece?"

Davyn ignored her and focused on the people around him. A man next to him shook his hand and put his other hand on his shoulder. *Must be someone Magne knows. I wish these people had name tags.*

The man said, "These are exciting times, Magne. You must be thrilled."

"We'll see, we'll see. Don't want to assume too much," Davyn said with a wink.

"Oh, come on," the man insisted, slapping him on the shoulder. "I think we all know where this is going."

Davyn furrowed his brow for a moment. *That's exactly what the chief said.* He felt another rap on his back and turned around as yet another guy grabbed Davyn and gave him a big hug. "Bro!"

Davyn held his breath, eyes wide, searching for an appropriate response. "Uh, bro-ski."

"Bro-ski?" Leo snorted. "What's going on with you? You need to get somewhere alone."

Davyn reached across his face to turn off the earpiece.

Bro-ski shot him a pistol wink. "I don't know what this is," he said, mimicking Davyn's move, "but I can see it catching on." He followed it with an all too raucous laugh.

Davyn smiled and nodded, then turned back to his—or rather, Magne's—adoring crowd.

Compliments and more pats on the back followed. Everyone was sucking up, but some were probably genuinely happy for him. At the moment, it didn't matter. Davyn was having fun.

An hour later, while speaking with a woman, Davyn spotted Leo entering the ballroom. She seemed to be looking for some-one. Him, probably. As she got closer, he noticed she'd changed into a beautiful, long green dress that matched the color of her eyes. Her hair was more contained than it usually was, but still wild, matching her persona perfectly. She stopped to speak with someone, who pointed toward Davyn. Leo's gaze shifted and locked on him. The woman Davyn was talking to continued speaking while he pretended to pay attention—a skill he'd devel-oped out of necessity. When he was overwhelmed by outside stimulus, he'd escape into his head. In this case, he was focused on what Leo was up to.

She forced a smile as she approached. "Hi Beth," she said to the woman talking to Davyn.

"Leo!" She gave her a hug. "I wondered when you were going to get here."

After a brief, polite exchange, Leo fixed her gaze on Davyn. "I'm sorry to interrupt. Magne, can I speak with you for a moment?"

Davyn turned to Beth. "Can you excuse me, for a moment? I'm terribly sorry. We'll catch up later, okay?"

"Sure, okay," Beth said, eyeballing Leo before she turned to go.

As soon as Beth wasn't looking, Leo took Davyn's arm and pulled him along with her as she headed for the outdoor balcony. Davyn smiled, waved and winked at Magne's colleagues as he was dragged along. Then Leo hit the door release hard and flung him to the railing.

"What are you doing? Who are you? Why do you keep turning off your bloody earpiece?"

"Bloody earpiece?" Davyn feigned a shiver.

Leo shook her head and leaned in closer to Davyn's ear. "We're here to find out who kidnapped Magne. Remember?"

"Of course I remember, but that's kind of hard to do when *I'm* supposed to be Magne, and at a party."

"I saw Jordan earlier. I'll point him out to you, and you can go talk to him. We've lost the element of surprise, though. I'm sure he saw you giving your speech. I can only imagine how Aluerd reacted to the news, assuming he's our guy."

Leo leaned against the balcony railing and took a deep breath and Davyn stood quietly, observing her face for cues on how to proceed. He didn't want to argue and he saw no opportunity to make headway on the Magne investigation tonight. Just getting through the rest of the party would take all of his focus.

"The speech wasn't terrible. But it would have been better if you kept your earpiece on and let me help you."

"Thank you. I felt pretty okay giving it."

Leo looked at Davyn, really studying his face.

"What?"

"You're getting comfortable in your new skin. Too comfortable, maybe."

Davyn took a drink from his glass.

"That better not be—"

Davyn cracked a smile. "No, it's water."

"Oh. Good." Leo leaned over the balcony railing and looked out at the park.

"I'm glad you made it to the party."

"The earpiece. Why do you keep turning it off? What if I had something important to tell you?"

"The line kept breaking up. I would hear a word or two from you, then some longshoreman would pipe in."

"Longshoreman?"

"I don't know what he was. It sounded like he was directing boats or something."

"That doesn't make sense. The connection is encrypted and locked. There should be no outside interference. Certainly not some random voice."

The balcony door opened, and a small crowd poured out, laughing and carrying on.

Leo edged closer to Davyn and put her lips near his ear. "Let's go see if we can find Jordan," she whispered.

Davyn bit his bottom lip. Her breath was warm, and her hair tickled his face. He watched her walk toward the door and then followed her back inside. It was nice to feel close to somebody and share a common goal.

When they entered the ballroom, Davyn took a second to watch the people dancing. He looked at Leo's hand and thought about asking her to dance. As if she'd heard his thoughts, she flung her hand back and hit him in the chest.

"How did you—I didn't even—"

She took his hand. "There's Phil and Al. Let's go talk to them."

"Hey, guys," Phil said.

Leo stepped in front of Davyn, blocking out potential discussions on radiometric dating. "I've got a question for you guys."

"Sure, shoot."

"Magne and I have been using these new earpieces in the field, and he's been picking up another channel. Another voice that breaks up our communication."

"Oh, that's not possible," Phil said. Al stood behind him, nodding in agreement.

"No, I'm sure of it," Davyn said.

"It must be someone in the background."

Davyn shook his head. "No, we were both alone."

Leo backed him up. "Yep, I was in my office, and Magne was on the balcony."

"When was this? Tonight?" Phil asked.

"Yeah, like twenty minutes ago."

"They're upgrading and testing the communication systems tonight. Didn't you guys see the notice that went out?"

"Oh. No, I guess we didn't," Leo said. "How long is that going on?"

"The email said it would start tonight and will continue through the weekend."

Leo nodded. "Hmm, okay. Hey, have you guys seen Jordan, by any chance?"

Phil scratched his head. "I saw him earlier, in the lobby." He thought for a moment. "Yep, by the stairs. But that was like an hour ago and I saw him leave after that. He looked pretty shaken up. I hope everything's okay.'"

"Did he say where he was going?"

"No, he didn't."

"Thanks, guys," Leo said. She and Davyn excused themselves and worked their way into the crowd.

"Well, we can't do anything about it tonight," Davyn said. "Wanna dance?"

Leo shook her head, then glanced out at the dance floor, her eyes bandying about. "Oh, why the hell not."

Loud, frenetic music filled the ballroom, and Davyn had to squint against the pulsing colored lights. He held Leo's hand as they stepped onto the bustling dance floor. They were immediately drawn into the dance as the music coursed through him like electricity. She smiled, and he could tell she was surprised that his dancing wasn't half bad. They danced wildly and laughed freely. It was as if every care he'd ever had was gone, and he was finally living in the moment.

After a while, the music changed to something slow. They both stopped dancing and Davyn turned to walk off the floor. But Leo grabbed his hand and pulled him back. He turned to face her. She was asking him to slow dance, but he could tell she was unsure if it was a good idea. It was the first time he'd seen her look anything close to vulnerable. Her wild volcano hair had settled, and she glistened under the ever-changing lights. She was beautiful. After silently agreeing to her request, they began to dance.

"You're a really good dancer," she whispered in his ear.

"I used to dance all the time when I was young. Seemed like a stupid thing to do as I got older." He backtracked when Leo shot him a puzzled look. "This is fun, though," he said with a smile.

They didn't speak for a time. They were both feeling out the moment, enjoying it while they could. Leo rested her head on his shoulder and a sense of calm washed over him. He felt connected to someone for the first time in a very long while. After a few minutes, she lifted her head and he laughed under his breath.

"I have to say, I felt a little foolish bonding, if you can call it that, with a group of people I don't know."

"I guess, but they seemed to be enjoying their time with you. They may have thought you were Magne, but the experience was with you. I understand how you could feel that way."

That's what she coached me to say, when I didn't agree with someone, and—oh. A chill crept across Davyn's chest. He felt foolish for letting himself connect and wanted to back away from it without any fanfare. No reason to let on that he was feeling anything. Just having some fun.

He needed to get off the dance floor, away from Leo. Have some time by himself to finally be alone. Now.

She's using her lines on me, but I know the script. How much of this is a role to her? Is she even my friend? Ugh, she's a secret agent, you idiot. Am I just a tool? I'm a tool all right. Finally, Davyn backed away.

"I need some water," he said. "You want anything?" He hoped she didn't.

She furrowed her brow and shook her head. Davyn turned and beelined over to the bar.

Leo stepped off the dance floor and watched him walk away, scratching her head. She wondered what the hell had just happened. A woman slid up next to him. Davyn pointed at her and said something. She leaned back, laughed and put her hand on her chest like she'd received a compliment, then got nice and close again. Davyn held up two fingers to the bartender. *That had better be two waters you just ordered.* Her chest tightened. The last thing she needed was for Davyn to get sloppy and blow his cover.

Davyn was glad to be free of Leo and the question of whether or not she was being genuine with him. He took his drink and motioned for the woman to follow him. He looked back at her as they walked away from the dance floor and asked, "What's your name?"

She laughed. "Funny, Magne. You can't be that far gone this early."

Uh-oh, Magne must know her already. "Speaking of funny Magne, that reminds me of a story." He slowed to let her catch up then dropped onto a couch. She plopped down next to him.

She put her hand on his leg. "Okay, Funny Magne, I'll be Luscious Lilith. Now that we have our code names, tell me a story."

"When I was seventeen, my brother and I planned a huge party. Our parents—"

"Wait, you have a brother?"

"Um, yeah. Well, not my literal brother: my brother from another mother. You know."

Lilith laughed, and as Davyn told his story a crowd gathered around them. He was enjoying the attention. It was effortless. Everything he said made these people laugh, and everyone seemed to be having a good time.

Then he caught a glimpse of Leo working her way toward them. He pretended not to see her at first, but she was on him pretty fast, hissing in his ear. "What's in that glass?"

Davyn gulped what was left, looked at it, then looked at her. "Nothing."

She leaned in by his ear again. "Turn your earpiece on right now."

"Do you have any news?"

Leo pursed her lips. "No."

"Then it can wait 'til tomorrow."

"Yeah, Leo," Lilith said. "You can have him tomorrow, but tonight he's ours."

The crowd shouted out similar sentiments until Leo finally shook her head and stormed off. Davyn went on with his stories, getting more raucous with each passing hour.

Just after midnight, Davyn was starting to get tired. He stood up and said, "Anyway, once the police arrived, the place cleared out faster than if someone had dropped Phil's n-pulse."

Phil gasped, and everyone fell silent.

"What? What happened?" Davyn said as he looked at the faces surrounding him. He could see the disappointment in Phil's face, but it wasn't just him. Everyone seemed to know that he'd spilled something he shouldn't have. Davyn's skin prickled as he sunk back into his seat.

"Oh, that was supposed to be top secret." He scratched behind his ear. "Whoops."

One by one, everyone gradually walked away. A few shot him sympathetic smiles; one guy patted him on the back. A short time later, the ballroom was empty, except for Leo. She stood nearby with her arms folded.

Without making eye contact, she walked over to him and let out a long sigh. "You were something tonight. You almost got in a fist-fight with Roger—or Bro-ski, as you were calling him."

Davyn leaned over his knees, staring at the floor. "Ugh, I know."

"Do you even remember what it was about?"

He rubbed his temples. "Don't make me say it."

"You should. You deserve to have to say it."

He leaned back on the couch and stared at the ceiling. "He uses too many clichés."

"And that escalated into a fight?"

Davyn stood up and rubbed an eye with his palm. "Yup."

"I won't even get into the top secret information you revealed."

"I just mentioned it. No one actually knows what it is."

"That's not the point. People knew from Phil's reaction that it was a big deal. It was grossly negligent. In fact, it might even get Magne fired."

Davyn stood quietly and gave no response.

Leo adjusted her purse strap. "We should get going."

"Maybe I should just get a Lyft to a hotel."

"That would be my preference, too, but things are heating up and you shouldn't be alone. Feel free to sit in the back of the car, though. I could use a break." Leo glanced at the entryway. "I have to step outside for a moment. I'll be right back."

Davyn stood alone as the lights went out, then slowly shuffled out of the ballroom. He stopped and looked back at the dance floor, thinking about how good it felt to let loose and enjoy some time with friends. A smile crossed his face, but fell just as fast—like it was never even there.

The last couple of days were complete chaos, an erratic, emotional rollercoaster. From learning that his brother was alive, but had been kidnapped, to losing his identity to—what? Become Magne? No. Magne would have cracked the case by now. *Face it. I can't do anything without Magne's help.*

And there'd be repercussions after tonight. His actions would have consequences. He felt like both the perpetrator and the victim, not to mention foolish for trusting Leo with his thoughts and feelings. Was she just playing the role to get what she wanted? Highly likely. Or, maybe she liked Magne, and he was just the proxy for the moment. Both explanations felt gross, and he wished all of this had never happened. He wanted to be back at the university, safe in his reading room with his books and no one around to stir up trouble.

But he couldn't leave things like this. He couldn't live with himself if he had to carry that around. He'd have to find a way to get Magne back and undo the damage he'd done. Then he could return to his university, tucked away in the woods, and resume a quiet life.

The next morning, as Davyn slept in Leo's spare bedroom, he heard a blip in his earpiece.

Oh no, not Leo, not now. I need to sleep and then think about what I said and did last night. Ruminate on it for a decade or so. Just give me some more ti—

A man's voice interrupted his thoughts. "Put him in cell block five."

Davyn then heard another voice in the background. It was unmistakably Magne's. "Guys, if you don't mind, seven is my lucky number. And it looks a little more spacious, too. I think I'd like that—"

It was Magne's voice, all right. Davyn was sure of it. But it got cut off by what sounded like someone hitting him. Davyn shot up to a sitting position and put his hand over his ear to listen.

Magne's voice returned. Whatever hit him mustn't have been very hard, because he was definitely still up to being a wiseass. "Can we go to the beach tomorrow? I've heard that the new headquarters has the best beaches."

Another voice came in over the earpiece. "You idiots. He's somehow activated the broadcast. I can hear you, and so can anyone else with an earpiece."

"Oh shit!" said another voice. "Turn off the box."

Davyn heard a blip, and the voices fell silent.

Davyn jumped from his bed and ran to Leo's room, throwing the door open.

She rolled over to face him. "What the hell are you doing? What time is it?"

"It's 5:30. I have important news."

She sighed and turned on a lamp, blinking sleepily in the sudden light. "Can you tell me after I get dressed?" she asked, pulling her sheet up to her neck.

"It can't wait."

She growled under her breath like she'd already had enough. "What is it?"

"I heard Magne."

Leo shot up in her bed to face him. Her eyes darted around his face. "What? How?"

"Just now, in my earpiece. I thought it was you at first, but then I heard him. I heard Magne. He's alive. Holy shit, he really is alive." Davyn let out a laugh. Logically, he'd known this already, but hearing his voice was a completely different experience.

Leo leaned forward. "What all did you hear? What did he say?"

"He said something about a beach where they're building a new headquarters."

"The new headquarters are on an island off the coast. He was relaying his location."

"Do you know where it is?"

"Yes. Wait—they would have taken his earpiece. It doesn't make sense that you would hear him on yours."

"I don't know. It sounded like he was further away from the receiver. Like it was maybe picked up by someone else's earpiece? I don't know."

"Did you hear anything else?"

"No, it went dead after that. I heard another voice say something about a broadcast, then it went dead."

"He must have figured out a way to make an earpiece broadcast. I'll have to ask him how he pulled that off."

"Yeah, well, we have to get him back first. If he's on the island where they're building the new headquarters, it should be easy to find him, right? You tell the chief and he sends a squad of agents or whatever the hell you guys are."

Leo sat quietly, then motioned for him to leave. "I need to mull this over. Let me get dressed and we'll head to my office. It's Saturday, so the building won't be busy, but Jordan should be there. I want to see what else we can find out before we do anything drastic."

"Why not just send in the cavalry?"

"It's not that simple. Obviously there'd be an investigation, and you covering for—" Leo stopped. "Let's finish this discussion when we get to my office."

Leo stepped into her office, threw her bag on her desk, and sat down. She peered over at Davyn, who was still standing. "Sit down, Davyn."

"I'm fine where I am."

Leo let out a huff. "Why are you always so defiant? I just offered you a chair."

"Why do you micromanage everything?"

Leo rolled her eyes. "Anyway, as I was saying earlier, the investigation that would inevitably follow storming this island would reveal the timeline of events and blow your cover."

"So? Who cares? They'll go get Magne and I'll leave. Problem solved."

"Problem not solved. They'll figure out our little ruse and instead of becoming chief, Magne will get fired and probably be arrested. You and I will definitely be arrested."

Davyn put his hand on the arm of a chair and finally eased himself down.

"We have to learn more first. We've lost the element of surprise, but Jordan will still be uneasy seeing you. So, what I want you to do is to be sitting in his office, at his desk, when he arrives. Pay close attention to how he reacts when he sees you. Every move he makes could provide some information. I want you to grill him on why he's so surprised to see you, even if he doesn't *look* surprised. If he's involved, it'll throw him off his game and maybe he'll reveal something."

Davyn nodded. "Okay, we can try that, but if we learn nothing, what's next?"

"For now, that's it."

"Well, if we get nothing from this, then we need to talk to the chief. We can't wait any longer."

"I know it's hard, Davyn, but you have to be patient. Investigations take time and it's the best path forward."

"This isn't an investigation and we're not investigators. We're the Hardy Boys meet Nancy Drew, and frankly, they outclass us both by a wide margin."

"They may outclass you, but I've got a plan. You're just too stubborn and impatient to see it through." Leo shook her head and glanced at her watch. "Jordan will be in soon. We need to get you ready."

CHAPTER 13

Davyn sat waiting in Jordan's chair, his feet propped up on his desk while he stared at the door. *I can't wait for this SOB to show up.*

"Any sign of him, Leo?"

"No, and I've got eyes on the parking lot. It's still mostly empty. I suspect a lot of people are sleeping in after last night's party. He's not in the building yet."

Davyn stood up and stretched as he examined the framed photos on the wall. "Give me a heads-up when you see him."

"Of course."

He turned to the window, surveying the parking lot. *I hate waiting.* He walked over to the desk and shuffled through some of the same items he looked at the day before.

"It's 9:20. This guy's an ass." He paused, then emphatically added, as if to imply that his next statement would be the more serious offense, "*And* he's not punctual."

Leo laughed. "He's an ass, *and* he leaves parties before they get going."

"Yeah," Davyn said with mock incredulity. "That's normally my thing." Davyn scratched behind his ear. "Let's see. He's an ass, *and* he doesn't cover his mouth when he sneezes."

"Ugh, I hate that," she said with disgust. "What else? Ah, he's an ass, *and* he sniffs where a pause should go."

"Wait, what?"

"You know the type. They use sniffs in place of pauses when they speak." Leo sniffed, "And then they'll say something." She sniffed. "Then they'll go on until—" She sniffed again. "It becomes very, very irritating."

"Huh, I never noticed that before. But I'm sure I will now. Thanks."

Leo sniffed, and said, "They'll do it before they start talking." She sniffed. "And sometimes at the end." She sniffed again.

"Okay, that's enough of that one. He's an ass, *and* he reads out loud to himself."

"Hey, that's my thing, and there's nothing wrong with it."

Davyn smiled and looked back out at the parking lot. "Are you sure he's coming in today?"

"He's on the docket."

"Hey, Leo?"

"Yeah."

"He's an ass, *and* he has no books in his office. I'm going to go to the restroom. Holler if you see him."

Davyn reached his left hand across his face and turned off his earpiece, then stepped out of the room.

A few minutes later, Davyn walked back in the office and looked out at the parking lot. He turned his earpiece back on only to hear Leo say, "Dogs have a way... Dogs have a way of telling their owner it's time to go outside. Even if, even if they don't really need to."

Davyn furrowed his eyebrows, then smiled.

"I can't say for sure, but I think the poop look differs from the—"

The laugh that Davyn was suppressing burst out.

"Hey, you were eavesdropping on me!"

"I'm so sorry," Davyn said through his laughter. "I didn't mean to. I just turned my earpiece back on."

"Huh, I didn't hear the blip."

"What on earth are you reading?"

"I'm not reading anything. I'm watching the monitors, looking for Jordan. I was composing sentences for a book I'm writing on dogs."

"Oh, I see."

"He's an ass, *and* he eavesdrops."

"Hey, I told you, I just turned it on. It wasn't deliberate."

"Uh-huh, and how long did you wait before you—wait, I think that's his car. Yep, that's Jordan. Get ready."

Davyn's heart thumped in his chest. "How long 'til he gets here?"

"I don't know, maybe five minutes. Just be ready. I'll give you updates on his movements as I see them."

Davyn went to the window to wait.

Leo said, "Hey, Davyn?"

"What?"

"He's an ass, *and* his pants are too short."

Leo's comment reminded him of how Magne always cracked jokes and stayed cool when things were getting serious. It was something he'd missed, and he admired Leo for doing it then.

"Okay, the elevator doors just opened, and he's getting off. Sixty seconds. Remember. Say, 'Why do you look so surprised to see me, Jordan?' Over."

Davyn took Jordan's desk chair again and put his feet back up on the desk.

Jordan entered and froze. He stepped backward and looked up the hallway, then back at Davyn and forced a smile. "Magne? I thought you were on leave."

"Why do you look so surprised to see me, Jordan?"

"Like I said, I thought you were out on leave. No big deal."

Davyn stood up and walked toward him. Jordan looked down the hallway again. "What's down the hall? Why do you keep checking?" He took another step toward him.

Jordan stammered. "I'm—I'm not—What are you doing in my office—" He sniffed. "Anyway?" Another sniff.

"You have a cold?"

"No." Sniff, "Why?"

"Say, 'I know what you did.' Over."

Davyn tightened his gaze. "I know what you did, Jordan."

"Nice," Leo said.

"What I did? What do you mean?"

"Say, 'The Chief knows, too.' Over."

Davyn inched closer, crowding Jordan's space. "The chief knows, too. He's on his way here."

"I don't know what you're talking about."

"Say, 'Yes you do.' Over."

Davyn put his hand on the wall behind Jordan's head, pinning him in place. "Yes. You do."

Jordan stepped to the side and back into the hall. "You're nuts, Magne. I heard about last night. You're losing it." He dashed past Davyn into his office.

Leo said, "Step outside the office and make like you're signaling to someone."

Keeping one eye on Jordan to make sure he was watching, Davyn stepped into the hallway and gave a signal.

A second later, Jordan pushed him out of his way and ran out the door and into the stairwell.

Davyn started after him until he heard Leo in his ear.

"Wait, don't—that's good for now. Head back to my office."

Davyn stepped out of Jordan's office and immediately spotted the chief heading his way. No way to dodge him: the chief had already seen him hovering outside Jordan's office. Still, Davyn tried to appear as though he was visiting the office next door. *Play it cool and see what he says. Maybe just walk past him with a smile and a nod.*

As the chief got closer, though, it became clear he had something on his mind. He stopped a few feet short of Davyn. "Magne, may I have a word with you?"

"Sure, chief."

The chief looked behind him and then gestured toward Jordan's door. "Is Jordan in there?"

"No. In fact, I was just looking for him."

"Let's step inside for a moment. We need to speak confidentially." The chief stepped into the office, followed by Davyn, then leaned on Jordan's desk, his face was pulled tight. Strained. "Close the door, please," he said as he motioned with his hand.

Leo spoke over the earpiece. "Davyn, stay cool. I'm here if you need me."

Davyn closed the door, then turned back to the chief and forced a smile. "You look like you have something on your mind."

"Yes." The chief cleared his throat. "I wasn't too happy with what you said in your speech last night. How you alluded to being the top choice for the next chief." He watched Davyn, apparently looking for a reaction, but Davyn wore his poker face—which was to say, his usual expression. The chief continued, "And I heard you stated the name of a weapon we have in development, to a group of people who aren't authorized to know about it. That's not like you. If this is part of some kind of spiral, I'll have to reconsider my decision."

Davyn looked down at the ground, then back up at the chief.

"Chief, I can assure you that my behavior last night was a one time mistake. I took the lesson hard. I assure you that it will never happen again."

The chief sighed. "I'm confident of that, Magne, but because of the sensitivity of the subject matter you disclosed, it's already gone to the board for review. Your record, at least until last night, was unassailable. Now there will be questions. I know you were deep undercover recently, with an assumed identity. I know how that can play with someone's head, but being chief has its own pressures. You have to be able to manage them."

There had to be something Davyn could say, but he was drawing a blank. Nodding was all he could come up with.

The chief looked away, then back at him. "I'll make sure that the board takes your recent mission in to consideration, before they make a decision."

Cutting the conversation short seemed to be the best course of action. "Thanks, chief. Anything else?"

"Yes, there is one more thing."

"Yes, of course. What is it?"

"I know you're on mandatory leave now, but there's a fundraising event on the island tonight. If you were there doing a little glad-handing, I think it would go a long way toward securing funding for the new headquarters. And, if all goes well, that'll also help you regain your footing with the board."

"Say, 'After last night, I think I need more downtime before I engage in any more social affairs.' Over."

Davyn ignored her. "Sure, chief. You can count on me."

"What? No. Are you nuts? You can't go to the island. Say, 'Hey, wait chief. I think I need some more downtime.' Over."

The chief smiled and nodded. "Keep it quiet, though. No one at the organization knows about the event. Fundraising for spy agencies is, like so much of what we do, a covert affair. Only a couple of people here know about it."

"I won't let you down, chief."

"I know. I'll send you the details within the hour, including the guest list."

The chief turned to leave.

"Hey, chief!"

The chief turned to Davyn.

"Does Aluerd know about tonight's affair?"

The chief shook his head. "No, he doesn't."

"Can I ask where he is?"

The chief furrowed his brow. "You know better than to ask that," he said as he walked out the door.

"Davyn, what on earth do you think you're doing?"

"I'm going to the island. I'm going to get Magne."

When Davyn reentered Leo's office, she marched up to him and punched his arm. It was a hard punch, too. He took a step back, rubbing it.

"What the hell do you think you're doing?" she said.

"You're the one committing assault. You tell me."

"You know what I mean."

"Going to the island?"

"Yeah."

"I'm tired of pussyfooting around here. We're not getting anywhere. So what if we get a confession from Jordan? What then?"

"At least we know."

"What good is that?" Davyn shook his head. "I should have told the chief when I saw him."

"Oh, that would have been interesting." Leo rubbed her shoulder, mimicking Davyn. "Hey, chief, guess what? I've been kidnapped and I think I'm being held on an island, but we don't have any proof."

"Damn the proof. You saw how Jordan reacted. I'm going."

"To do what? You going to research him out of there?" Leo jeered. "You're not an agent, Davyn."

"Oh, so *now* I'm not an agent? I'm posing as an agent. I'm undercover. Secret identity and all." He rubbed his injured arm. "Why'd you really bring me here, huh?"

Leo bit her lip and closed her eyes. Davyn could see the frustration welling up in her. She blinked a few times, then started sorting items on her desk and looking anywhere other than at Davyn.

"Well?" Davyn shouted.

"It wasn't for your investigatory skills or your ability to step in as a secret agent. You're here to parade around as Magne, so no one knows he's missing. You're here to buy time for Magne to escape. That's it."

Davyn's face dropped. He wasn't here to rescue Magne. He was there as a distraction. He couldn't believe what he was hearing, and he could tell by the expression on Leo's face that she'd just realized what she said.

"Oh my god, Davyn. I'm so sorry. That sounds terrible when I say it out loud."

Davyn sank into a chair. "The two of you concocted this plan to—*that's* why I'm here?"

Leo approached with a hand extended but stopped when he immediately pulled away. She sat down across from him, keeping a few feet between them. Her eyes scanned the room, clearly searching for something to say. She'd already shown her hand. What could she possibly have to say after that?

After a few seconds, Davyn stood up and stretched the arm she'd punched. "I'm wasting my time here." He headed for the door, barely sparing her a glance. "I'm going to go get ready."

"Davyn, wait," she said, her voice quivering.

He stopped to listen, but didn't turn around.

"A few years ago, Aluerd would have been a shoo-in for chief. Magne would say the same. He was a model agent, smart, dedicated. He has a brilliant mind for strategy, and he was once an inspiring leader. He had the respect and admiration of everyone at the agency."

Davyn turned and looked at Leo. "Why are you telling me this?"

"Because you need to know the whole story. Aluerd, Magne, this agency—we've
saved thousands of lives. What we do here matters."

Davyn stood still, listening. So far it sounded like a propaganda piece, but the claim of having saved so many human lives held his attention. Here he was, the misanthrope that loved humanity—just not the people in it—contemplating his role in helping to protect them.

Leo continued. "Over the past year, Aluerd has been rotting the agency from the inside. He no longer has any regard for rules or laws. If he takes over, the agency will become lawless, until it's operating like a group of mercenaries. Everything Magne joined for, everything he gave up, would be for nothing."

Davyn wasn't buying it. It was becoming clear that Leo had uprooted his life, and by the sound of it, it was at Magne's behest. And for what? To address personnel issues at the agency that let his family believe he was dead?

"You two are really something," he said as fire spread from his chest and filled his eyes with hot, bitter tears. "Magne's disappearance ruined my life." He stepped toward Leo and leaned down until he could meet her eye. "I thought I was responsible for his death. I thought his death was *my fault*." He jabbed repeatedly at his chest and straightened back up. "Then you tell me he's not dead, that he's been playing dead all this time. And I believed it. But now you stand here and tell me he—that both of you put me through all of that. And all of this—what could be worth it?" Davyn took a deep breath as he turned to leave. "What you have is an HR problem. You had no right to drag me into this."

"It's not like that, Davyn." Leo rose from her chair and moved toward him, her tone hardening with every word. "People will die. If Aluerd takes over running the agency, innocent people *will* suffer. He doesn't care about collateral damage. He inflicts it willfully, deliberately. In his mind, what they did to his wife and to his daughter has to be avenged. He's obsessed, and he'll stop at nothing to exact—well, he would call it justice, but it's nothing more than revenge. Without the chief to keep him in line, there's no telling what he'd do. This is bigger than us, Davyn. It's bigger than everyone here. What happens next will—"

"Enough! Enough flag waving already."

"You know it's more than that."

They stood quietly for a time. Finally, Davyn looked up at Leo. "What happened to Aluerd's wife and daughter?"

"They were killed in separate terrorist attacks. His wife, ten years ago in Egypt. Then, his daughter, two years ago in France. One man was responsible for both attacks and a dozen others. His name's Abdullah Sheikh Abdullah, and Aluerd is singularly focused on taking him out before he dies of cancer."

"Jesus, what are the odds of one, never mind two?" Davyn drew a long breath. "Did you say Aluerd has cancer?"

Leo nodded. "He was diagnosed last week. I think he's known for longer. And I think his imminent demise is what's driving his erratic behavior."

"Well, maybe Aluerd's right. Maybe tough tactics are what's needed. Who are you to judge?"

Leo glared at Davyn, then her expression softened. "You're upset, but you know better."

What a trite way to frame what I've been through. My brother's dead. No, my brother's alive, but he let me believe he's dead. They duped me into coming here. Never mind that it's turned me inside out. It was as if all the pain and angst that had been simmering beneath had at once erupted.

"I'm *upset*?" Davyn huffed. "Yeah, I'm upset. I don't usually get upset. I'm normally the calmest, serenest son of a bitch in the room. Now I'm goddamn Frankenstein's monster." He grabbed Leo's bag and rifled around inside.

"What are you doing?"

He pulled her car keys out and threw the bag on the floor.

"It's time for Frankenstein's monster to wreak havoc on the village," he spat as he stormed through the doorway.

"Davyn, wait!" Leo called, but he was already gone.

Davyn ran through the mostly empty parking lot to Leo's car. The wind was blowing harder now and the cold rain struck his face like grains of sand. He stopped at her car, popped the trunk, pulled his bag out, and changed into his running gear.

Don't think, just run. Davyn raced through the woods, maneuvering around the trees effortlessly. Years of hunting and chasing prey had honed his skills. He came out of the woods on a service road and continued running, heading east. He didn't know exactly where to head, but he knew he needed to get out of there, and the beach was dead ahead.

He tried to piece it all together as he ran, but his thoughts were too fragmented. None of it made sense. He thought about Aluerd and what happened to him. Maybe he should be chief. Maybe he deserved justice. *Or maybe nobody's right and we're all just battling primates. We should have stayed in the trees.*

Davyn kept running as the rain fell harder. The darkening sky and sheets of rain reduced his visibility to just a dozen feet. It was cold, and there wasn't any sign of civilization anywhere.

Do I even know the way back? How long have I been running? A mile, maybe. This is good. Just what I need. Focus on breathing. In, out, in, out. Magne's alive. Magne's alive. Magne's alive.

Davyn ran down the dirt road, dodging the puddles until it wasn't possible. His feet splashed with every step on the saturated dirt road. All the while, he imagined Leo talking to Magne, concocting their plan to draw him in when it suited them.

We'll just get Davyn to cover for you while you escape, Magne. He just needs to talk to people. Sure, that's a tall order for him, but I can train him. The little monkey. I'll even tell him what to say. All he has to do is repeat it. Maybe I'll pretend to be his friend. Good little monkey.

Davyn stopped dead in his tracks and shook his head wildly, sending water in every direction. He put his hands on his hips, struggling to catch his breath. He'd been racing hard for the past mile.

He took the ring off of his left hand, pulling the wire out and removing the earpiece entirely. He looked at it for a moment, then pitched it into the woods along with the ring. He started running again, squinting through the cold rain to make out what appeared to be a bridge in the distance.

Magne's alive, Magne's alive. He needs your help. Davyn stopped again and caught his breath. *Focus on your breaths. In, out, in, out.* He began to run again. *It's a bridge for sure, running north and south. It's probably the highway. The beach can't be too far past it.*

When Davyn reached the sands of the beach, he spotted a lone bench. Walking through the rain and the mist, he sat down to look around for somewhere to grab some water, but there was nothing. Not as far as he could see, anyway.

Water: water everywhere, and not a drop to drink. He put his head in his hands and braced his elbows on his knees. His clothes were soaked and he had nothing on him. No wallet, no cash, nothing. It was fine, at least for now. He needed to be alone, and frankly, the weather suited him. He caught his breath and still felt warm, hot even. But soon he'd begin to cool off. What then?

I'll head north. I better get going. But I'm so tired. I'll just lay down here for a minute. He lowered himself down onto the bench. *It feels so good, so warm, so comfortable.*

Almost two hours later, headlights swept across his face, waking him with a jolt. *What am I doing here? It's freezing. Oh, I ran off.* His arms and legs were tight. It was hard to move; the cold had really set in. *Idiot. Never fall asleep when you're cold. I need help.*

As soon as he had that thought, he saw the silhouette of a figure in the headlights and fog, and Leo called out, "Davyn! Is that you?"

Davyn tried to turn his body to get up, but struggled to move at all. Leo came around to the front of the bench and peered down at him.

"Oh my god, Davyn. What have you done to yourself?"

CHAPTER 14

Davyn stood in the empty hallway outside of the lab, appreciating the feel of warm, dry clothes after getting a shower and warming up at the hotel. He planned to use this visit to figure out how to steal the n-pulse. Well, borrow. He'd bring it back, of course. But he'd need it on the island if he was going to get Magne out of there. The n-pulse was nonlethal, but would incapacitate anyone in the area when triggered: the perfect weapon for his mission. He'd pried its details out of Phil when Al was supervising the installation of a surveillance camera near the lab's door.

Davyn knocked on the door to the lab. The top half of Phil's face popped up on a monitor mounted at his head's height next to the door.

Phil's eyes were wide. He looked left, then right. "Who is it?"

Davyn took a step back, looking for the camera. "Um, it's me, Magne."

Phil looked straight ahead. "Ah, so it is." A buzzer sounded, and the door latch clicked. "Do come in, sir." He extended an arm out toward the lab as the door swung open.

When Davyn stepped inside, he noticed Al standing near the back, shaking his head.

Phil pointed to the monitor. "They just installed the video doorbell. Isn't it cool?"

"Yeah, that's—that's pretty cool."

"The camera's a little high, though. They installed it while Al was here. Works fine for him, but I'll need to get a step stool."

How much longer are we going to discuss the damn camera? Okay, be nice. You're here to apologize. "Well, I guess it'll prevent any surprises." Davyn forced a smile.

"It's always a surprise to see you down here. A treat, really."

"You're too kind, Phil, especially after—hey, I'd like to talk to you and Al if you have a couple of minutes."

"Sure. Hey, Al, come over here. Magne wants to speak with us." Phil called with the same level of excitement one would expect to hear from a child meeting Spider-Man.

Davyn peered at Al, who was standing next to the cabinet housing the n-pulse. His eyes shifted to the keypad lock on the cabinet's front door. He remembered the code, but he'd also need one of their security badges to get it open.

"Never mind, Al. We're coming to you," Davyn strode toward Al, scanning the room for any other cameras as he went. Stopping just in front of Al, he extended a hand to shake. Al hesitated before reaching out and accepting it. "Yeah, I get that. I want to apologize for what I did at the chief's party. I feel—I feel terrible. You trusted me with some information, I told you I'd keep it quiet, then I let it slip out to a crowd, no less. I had no right to do that, and I betrayed your trust. I may even lose my job."

Al watched with no expression, but Phil's mouth dropped open and he had to cover it.

"It's by no means certain, but if it happens, it's my own fault. I take full responsibility." Davyn held his breath and waited for a reaction, but it was quiet for a few long moments.

Finally, Al said, "We may lose our jobs too, Magne. We shouldn't have told you about the—the device."

"I'll make sure that doesn't happen. I will take care of that when I—" Davyn paused. *Ugh, I can't tell them I'll fix it after I rescue myself.* "I still have a lot of sway around here. I've taken full responsibility for what happened, and I'll tell the board I tricked you into revealing the information or something."

Phil glanced at Al. "You don't have to do that."

"You can do that." Al cracked a hint of a smile. Then his face hardened. "You can do that, Magne. You should do that. It is your responsibility. We did nothing wrong."

"Well, we told him the name of the—"

Davyn cut Phil off. "No, Al's right. I'll talk to the chief today."

"You do that, and if we keep our jobs, then I will forgive you," Al said. "You will have earned it then."

"I forgive you, Magne."

Al glared at Phil. "Okay, Magne. I think you should go now. It's not good for you to be in the lab. Especially now."

"Sure, sure." Davyn stared at the cabinet that held the n-pulse. "You know, I just have one question about the, uh, the device."

Phil seemed enthused by the opportunity to share more information. "Oh, sure!"

Davyn glanced at Al's clenched jaw. "Um, actually, maybe another time."

Davyn walked down the hallway toward Leo's office and picked up the earpiece from where'd he'd hid it after leaving her earlier. He knocked on the door, then stepped inside and shut it behind him.

"There you are," she said. "I couldn't reach you. Where did you go? What happened?"

Davyn sat in the chair in front of her. "I had to apologize to Phil and Al."

Leo pursed her lips. "The damn cameras have been up and down all morning. I couldn't find or hear you. You should have been looking for Jordan."

"Jordan can't help us. We already know who took Magne and where he is."

"We need evidence, Davyn. We can't do anything without evidence."

"Maybe *you* can't do anything without evidence, but I'm going to the island. I have a plan."

"What?" she scoffed. "You have a plan?"

"You won't like it, but you're not involved. You can keep your nose clean, and I'll fix it on my own."

Leo let out a sigh. "You're infuriating, and extraordinarily naïve."

"Yeah, you're not the first person to tell me that. Well, the naïve thing is new."

"Davyn, if you rush in there and get Magne killed—"

"That won't happen."

"How can you be so certain?"

"Certain? What kind of world do you live in?"

"Look, the event on the island isn't until tonight, so for now, let's focus on finding Jordan. There's no way of knowing how any of this will go down. If we get found out, we'll need evidence to build a defense."

Davyn mulled her response. "Alright, captain. What's the plan?"

"Do you always have to be so flippant?"

"That was rhetorical, I presume."

Leo scanned her monitors, then pulled out a small disk shaped device about the size of a marble from her desk drawer. "I want you to stick this somewhere on your person." She eyed him up and down, searching for the right spot. "Maybe your jacket pocket."

She stuck her hand out for him to take it but turned her eyes back to the monitors.

Davyn sat back in his chair. "I don't know where that's been."

"Oh, for Pete's sake, it's brand new. Put it in your pocket."

"What is it?"

"A recording device. It works with the earpiece, but they need to be within ten feet of each other."

"There isn't one built into the earpiece?"

She shook her hand. "No, not yet. They're still developing stuff. The new headquarters will be state-of-the art, and all the equipment that's here is being replaced or upgraded. Now take the damn thing."

Davyn reached out and took the device and put it in his inside jacket pocket.

"That's why communication has been screwy. They're upgrading and testing new equipment."

"So I can use this on the island?"

"You can use it anywhere, but the island isn't up and running yet. Only one building is even complete, and none of the electronics are installed yet. If you end up going there, take a charging brick. Other than the main building, there's no reliable source of power."

"So, you're on board with me going?"

She peered at her monitors. "I don't have any way to stop you. But if we can get some evidence between now and when you leave, we'll at least have some cover."

Davyn nodded. "So where the hell is Jordan? Have you seen him since earlier?"

"No. I don't even know if he's on site. His car's still there, though."

"I'll need some way to hold off or distract the guys that are holding him on the island."

Leo's face drew tight as she squinted at him. "And what did you have in mind?"

"Do you remember that device we saw Phil put away?"

"Yeah," she said with a distinct tone of someone who didn't like where the conversation was going.

"I asked Phil about it and I got some more info. It can take out a whole room of people. Just knock them out. They'd be out while Magne and I escape."

"You're a college professor, Davyn. You don't have the skills required for something like this."

"I have skills. I can live off the land. I can hunt. I know how to move stealthily without detection."

"Taking out trained agents isn't quite the same thing as taking out Bambi."

Davyn recoiled at her dismissive tone. He didn't have to share that with her, and she'd dismissed it like it was nothing. *I don't know why I bother explaining things to her. There's a lot more to hunting with primitive tools and weapons than she'll ever know.*

"Even if you had training," she went on, "there're no cameras on the island yet. I wouldn't be able to help you." Leo scanned her monitors and sighed. "This is nuts."

"You're just catching on to that now?"

Several minutes of silence passed before Davyn spoke up again. "Leo?"

"What?"

"What can you tell me about the day Magne disappeared?"

Leo looked at Davyn and then moved some things on her desk to get a better view of his expression. "Well, I wasn't here when he came on board, but he shared some things with me."

"Did he say anything about me?"

Leo's tone softened. "Not initially. You know how he is—everything's a joke. He's never too serious."

Davyn sat back and nodded. "Yeah, I do."

Leo gave him a sympathetic smile. "Sometimes he opens up, but it took a awhile. At first it was just stories about the two of you. Funny stories. But I could tell you were special to him. Just the way he spoke about you. I could tell."

Davyn looked down at the ground.

"He always wants to project confidence, like nothing bothers him, but after we got to know each other—we've been through some real shit together mission-wise. It has a way of making you close, like family. He eventually opened up some more."

Davyn's eyes darted back and forth, but he didn't look back up at her.

"How much do you want to hear?" Leo asked.

He took a deep breath. "Go ahead."

"He told me about the night you two went to the convenience store. Um, Jim's store. He said you changed after that."

Davyn looked away. "Anything else?"

"Sure, lots of stuff. Maybe this isn't the best time to go into it, though." Her eyes went back to scanning the screens.

"Yeah, you're right. But I'm just going to say this, then we'll be done with it. I'm sorry for how I've behaved. I made mistakes. I'm trying to own them, but other people might take the fall for what I've done. I don't like that. I don't want to carry that around."

"I know. Thank you for that."

"I will do whatever it takes to make this right, then I'm going home."

"Home? You mean back to the university."

Davyn cocked his head to the side. "Maybe home's not the right word."

Leo shifted her gaze back to Davyn. "I should apologize, too. What we asked of you was—it wasn't fair. We had no business intruding in your life in such a way."

Davyn rocked back in his seat opposite Leo's desk.

Without looking away from her monitors, Leo said, "Don't do that."

"Do what?"

"You know what. You're going to fall."

"But I'm so bored. Where's Jordan?"

"Hey, look at this. I think that's him, heading for his car. Wait. Why'd he stop?"

Davyn got up and leaned closer to the screen so he could focus on an image of a man standing in the middle of the parking lot.

"Can you get a closer look? I can't tell who that is."

Leo made some adjustments. Just as the image adjusted to a tighter shot of Jordan, he turned and ran back toward the main building.

"Where's he going? Can you follow him?"

"Yeah, hang on." Leo flipped through some screens.

"There." She hit a switch. "Center monitor. See him?"

"I'm heading out there. I've got my ears on. Call out when you know something." Davyn ran out the door, past the elevators to the stairs and up to the lobby, then outside. "Leo, anything?"

"No, not yet."

He scanned the parking lot. Nothing. His heart was racing. He took a couple of deep breaths, undid his top shirt button, then took off his tie and jacket and threw them on the ground.

"Wait, I see him. Run toward Building D. It's the building with the glass dome on top. See it?"

"Yeah, on it."

Davyn ran to the top of a grassy hill and peered across a field. "I see Jordan. He's running toward the entrance of the parking garage."

"That's weird. His car's in the lot."

"Wait, I see someone else running, too. Is he chasing him?"

"What the—better stay out of sight. I'll follow with the cameras."

"Yeah, he's chasing him. Jordan's heading up the exterior stairs."

"I see them now. Where's he going?"

"I can't tell. Maybe there's something in the garage they're after?"

Jordan took the stairs, two at a time, with his pursuer on his heels. The concrete stairs ran up the outside of the building, all six stories, and by all appearances they were heading for the top. Jordan cleared the fourth floor platform and kept going. Turning the corner to the next riser, he slipped, slamming his leg into the step. He grabbed at his shin and tried to keep running, but stumbled and fell. His pursuer closed in fast and pulled his gun, aiming right at Jordan's head.

Davyn braced himself. "Leo, you seeing this? What do we do?"

"Just hang tight, I'm afraid. There's nothing we can do."

Jesus, I can't just sit here and watch this. Davyn stood up, waving his arms and shouting. "Hey, Jordan! Jordan, what's up?" he screamed, jumping up and down.

The gunman turned his head in Davyn's direction as Jordan called for help. The man struck Jordan in the head with the butt of his pistol. Jordan crumpled in a heap, and the gunman holstered his pistol, looked over the railing's edge to the ground four stories below.

"Hey!" Davyn shouted. "Get away from him!"

Then Davyn sprinted for the garage. The man picked Jordan up from under his arms, hoisting him to the railing.

"Davyn, stop. He's armed."

Davyn felt like he was moving in slow motion as he crossed the open field and watched helplessly as the man flopped Jordan's torso over the railing and lifted his legs. "No!"

Davyn started up the stairs. As he passed the second floor platform, the sound of a crash reverberated against the railing. Jordan's flailing body plunged toward the ground, bouncing off railings as it dropped, then landed with a sickening thud.

"Davyn, stay where you are. That man's got a gun."

"Keep an eye on him." Davyn flew back down the stairs. Jordan was on the grass, blood running from his head. Davyn looked up and saw the gunman climb over the railing and jump onto the garage roof. "Jordan, can you hear me? Leo, call 911. He's breathing."

"Already done."

"Jordan, we've called 911. They're on their way."

Jordan coughed, spewing blood and spit from his mouth. "Magne, tell everyone I'm sorry. Aluerd's come unglued. I never thought—I don't know how it got so out of control."

"Aluerd did this?"

Jordan's eyes closed, and he didn't respond.

"Who was chasing you?"

Jordan opened his eyes but they wandered around listlessly. "I'm glad you escaped, Magne. I didn't mean for—" Jordan's eyes shut again.

"Jordan, who was chasing you?"

Jordan's breath slowed. "Aluerd put out a hit—"

His breathing grew slower.

"A hit on you?"

Jordan's breathing stopped.

"He's gone, Leo. Did you hear what he said? Aluerd doesn't kill his own, huh?"

"Yeah, I heard him. We're running out of time. I've got to speak with the chief."

"No, wait. I have an idea."

Davyn headed for the lab. His plan for saving Magne depended on him having a way to incapacitate the people that were holding him while they made their escape, but at least three obstacles stood in his way. Once on the island, he'd have to find Magne without being spotted. This one he felt pretty good about. He'd spent many hours moving stealthily through the forest, hunting game with primitive weapons. But the other two challenges—those he didn't feel so good about.

He'd be on an island surrounded by ocean. He's been terrified of water since the drowning incident that took—at least, so he'd believed until recently—the life of his beloved brother. Lastly, how was Davyn going to get his hand on a top secret n-pulse that was locked in a cabinet, which was locked in the lab? They weren't going to just give it to him, which meant that he'd have to steal it. Well, borrow.

As he approached the lab, the door swung open and out walked Phil, followed by Al. "Oh, hey Magne, were you coming to see us?"

"Um, no, I was down here to see someone else, actually."

Phil looked past him, down the hallway. "Oh, okay. Well, we were just heading to get something to eat. Want to join us?"

"I actually did want to talk to the two of you about something, but it can wait. When will you be back?"

Phil shrugged. "An hour, probably."

That would give him time to get the grenade, but he'd need a way to get in the lab first. He glanced down at Phil's badge, then put his hands on his shoulders and rotated him so he could place himself between Phil and Al.

"I want you to know that I've spoken to the chief and your jobs are secure." Davyn turned his head to Al and forced a smile. "And I want you to know how much I appreciate your trust in me."

His heart dropped at that last statement, but he had to get the grenade. Besides, once Magne was back, he'd be able to set things straight.

Davyn hit Phil with some playful punches while Phil giggled like a toddler and wrenched his body away. "Ah, I'm ticklish!"

Davyn laughed and turned to Al. "How about you, Al?" Davyn put his hands out like he was going to tickle him. "You ticklish?"

Al turned away, apparently not amused. "Come on, Magne, we are not all children." He shot a critical glare Phil's way. "What did the chief say?"

"He said he understood what happened and that there wouldn't be any action taken against the two of you."

Al studied Davyn's face warily. "Really?"

"Yeah, really."

Not really, but Magne would fix it when he returned.

Phil, having gathered himself, broke in. "Uh, Magne, why don't you come to lunch with us?"

Davyn hesitated like he was considering it, then pointed over his shoulder. "Ah, I can't. I have to speak to—" He cleared his throat. "Someone down here."

Al squinted at Davyn and looked like he wanted to ask more, but Phil took Al's arm and started leading him away. "Okay. Come on, Al."

Davyn watched them walk away, then turned and headed down the hallway. He passed the lab and kept going. *Now to burn some time while they clear out.* He glanced at the tags over each of the doors as he passed, then stopped and looked through the glass window of one door before peeking out of the corner of his eye to see if the tech guys were gone. Al was standing in the middle of the hallway watching him. Phil was further up the hall, apparently waiting for him.

Holding his breath, Davyn walked up to the next door and knocked. There was no response. *That's a relief.* Still, he waited some more and then checked on Al again. No change. With no other options, he started back toward Al and Phil. "Not in, I guess."

The three of them headed for the elevator together. When they got to the lobby, Phil and Al made for the exit, while Davyn went the opposite way to circle back to the lab.

"You really shouldn't give Magne a hard time," Phil said. "He saved our jobs."

"You are naïve, my friend. He's up to something."

"He's a secret agent. He's always up to something."

Al sneered. "Hmm, but maybe this is something he's not supposed to be doing."

"If he was up to something, he'd have been found out by now."

"You don't think it was strange that Magne was meeting someone in a maintenance room?"

"Is that what that was? Are you sure?"

"I've been here longer than Magne. Yes, I am sure."

"Well, you know how secret agents are. It's all cloak and dagger. I'm sure it's fine. Come on, I'm hungry."

As they passed security, heading for the exit, a guard standing outside the lobby nodded at them. Phil smiled and nodded back, but the guard stepped in front of them. "Hey, Phil. Where's your badge, man? You're supposed to have it on at all times."

Phil patted his waist. "It must have fallen off. I'll go back and look for it."

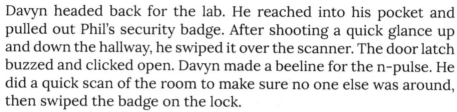

Davyn headed back for the lab. He reached into his pocket and pulled out Phil's security badge. After shooting a quick glance up and down the hallway, he swiped it over the scanner. The door latch buzzed and clicked open. Davyn made a beeline for the n-pulse. He did a quick scan of the room to make sure no one else was around, then swiped the badge on the lock.

He stared at the numbered keypad. *I think it was 7,5,9,3.* He mimicked the movements without pressing the keys and nodded. *Yep, that's it.* He punched the keys, and the cabinet popped open with a clank. He heard a clatter outside in the hallway. Someone was coming. He ducked behind one of the lab tables and pushed the cabinet door until it was almost closed and held it in place.

The lab door latch buzzed, then Phil said, "I must have dropped it somewhere in here then. Give me a sec to look."

Damn, they're back. The squeak of footsteps on the tile grew louder. How was he going to explain this? He couldn't let the door go, or it would spring open. Davyn held the cabinet door with one hand and flung the pass to the next row with the other, hoping Phil would see it, grab it, and leave. It fell short of the aisle and lay against a lab table.

Crap. He'd have to move. He pressed the door shut and flinched as the lock audibly engaged.

Al's hurried steps clomped down the aisle toward Davyn. "What was that?"

Davyn slid his prone body across the tile and pushed the badge out to the next row. He tucked his legs in and lay in a fetal position, mostly shielded from view by the lab tables. He couldn't see anything, but he could tell by the sound of Al's heavy steps that he was approaching the cabinet.

"It's locked. But why did it make that sound?"

Davyn covered his head like a kid hiding under a blanket.

"Oh, there it is."

Perfect, Phil. Now please go back the way you came. Please, please. Davyn lay motionless. He heard Phil's footsteps stop and the scrape of the pass on the floor as he picked it up.

"It's probably just the testing they're doing. They said it'd be going on all weekend."

"I don't know. It's very suspicious."

A shadow crept over Davyn. He held his breath as he peered up with one eye and saw Al hovering over him and rubbing his hand over the side of the cabinet.

As he turned toward Davyn's makeshift hiding spot, Phil said, "Oh my god."

Al stopped and looked at Phil. "What is it?"

"I'm starving. Let's go."

Al laughed and walked off. Davyn let out a breath as their steps moved away. When he heard the door close, he jumped up and punched the code into the cabinet's keypad. Nothing. He'd need the security badge to try it again, but time had run out.

It was time to get ready to go, and all he knew was that he was headed to a remote island where enemy agents held his brother captive. He had no idea how many agents there were, what the topography of the island was like, or what types of weapons they had. And worse, Aluerd was growing more unpredictable and dangerous. Suddenly being able to incapacitate a rabbit with a sling seemed less reassuring than it did before. He needed a new plan. But what?

CHAPTER 15

Davyn stood by the railing at the stern of the yacht, waiting to embark on the voyage to the island. The sun had slipped behind the trees and the breeze was colder now. He watched as security personnel moved around, exploring all one hundred twenty feet of the vessel. His heart rate quickened, and his stomach turned sour when he peered out over the water, so he tried to focus on the dock and savor this moment of solitude, knowing it wouldn't last.

Sure enough, Davyn heard the blip in his earpiece. *So much for solitude.* But honestly, any distraction from the water was welcome. He moved away from the railing and stepped toward the dining area, a large room in the middle of the deck. He didn't dare step inside for fear the smells would further unsettle his already churning gut.

"Ahoy, Magne," Leo said with undue enthusiasm.

"We're back to calling me Magne now?"

"To get you back in the role. You've got to be Magne tonight."

"Right. How long will it take to get there?"

"Not sure, depends on their speed. Probably three hours. The second ship with the investors will be close behind, but will wait for confirmation that the security staff is in position before they dock."

"If they think the island's empty, why so much security?"

"It's SOP."

"SOP?"

"Standard operating procedure. Remote island, lots of bigwigs, therefore lots of muscle," she explained. "You'll probably have about an hour to look for where they're holding Magne. After that, you'll have to glad-hand the investors for a couple of hours. Then you can pick up looking where you left off."

"Security seems eager to get there. They've all moved to the front of the ship."

"Did you hear what I said?"

"Yes, one hour to look. Plus the other things you said."

"Ugh, why can't you just repeat it back like a good agent."

"Uh, because I'm not an agent, as you like to remind me. I heard you."

"We'll continue to go over it until I hear you confirm it."

"One hour to look, glad-hand for two hours. Look for Magne some more. Got it."

"It would be so much easier if you'd just cooperate. Anyway, the guards are at the bow because you're near the stern. That's also SOP. In a scenario like this, they keep their distance from the agents."

"Wow, you mean everyone on the ship will leave me alone? Maybe I *should* become a secret agent."

"Until you get to the island and have to talk up the investors, yes, they'll leave you alone."

"Right. Never mind. I'll stick to research. Assuming I still have a job when I get back."

"Oh, yeah. How'd you leave that?"

"I called in sick. Hopefully, people know enough by now not to stop by and bring soup."

"If my experience with you is any indication, they won't."

"Thank you." Davyn looked down at the small crowd that had gathered on the dock. "Hey, there's a group of about ten people congregating on the dock. They don't look like security or crew."

Davyn took a few steps toward the bow to get a better look and noticed a guard standing in that area tap the one next to him, then jerk his head toward Davyn. The other guard looked his way, then they both moved toward the port side of the ship.

"I see them," Leo said. "They're part of the maintenance crew. Nothing to worry about."

But Davyn was distracted by how the security personnel moved away from him when he moved closer to them, and didn't bother responding to Leo.

That's interesting. I wonder if the security crew has to stay out of my line of sight, too. This needs some investigation. If I move toward them, will they move away again?

Davyn ambled toward the bow of the ship, pretending not to notice the guards. One by one, they'd see him and move away. He continued this until he was standing at the bow and all of the guards had moved to the ship's stern.

Oh, I like this. It's like an introvert superpower. I'll miss this.

Leo broke in, "Davyn, what are you doing?"

"I'm just standing at the bow of the ship. Alone."

"Did you do that on purpose?"

"What?"

"Chase those men off."

"I didn't chase them. I just—" He scratched his chin. "Took a walk."

"You're taking advantage."

"I got curious. Humans, especially when you add social and workplace rules, can be very interesting. They're heading downstairs now, anyway."

"Ugh, you can take the man out of the anthropology lab..."

The ship jerked as it backed away from the dock. Davyn grabbed the railing to stabilize himself, then placed a hand on his stomach. The ship lurched as it turned and pointed its bow toward the open water.

"Hey, where can I go inside the ship? I don't like seeing the water."

"Oh, right." Leo's voice sounded alarmed, with a pinch of compassion. "You can go just about anywhere on the ship. There are plenty of meeting rooms downstairs. Just find one that's not being used."

Davyn pushed his back to the wall. His heart pounded, and the sounds of the water slamming against the side of the ship were amplified in his head.

"Davyn, did you hear me?"

He jerked his head to his left, looking for a way downstairs. Then to the right. He saw the stairs when he boarded. But where were they now? *Did I imagine them? Stop, think. You're having a panic attack. Of course the stairs are still there.*

"Davyn?"

He didn't remember where they were, but he couldn't stay where he was. He slid to the floor and began crawling, leaning against the mess hall wall as he inched toward the stern.

"Davyn, why aren't you responding?"

His heart raced as he inched along the wall. His ears filled with the sound of the waves as they crashed against the ship and brought back mental images of similar waves slamming into him, of Magne riding up and down, appearing then vanishing beneath the water.

Focus, breathe. Deep breaths. Davyn heard footsteps climbing the stairs. *Thank god, the stairs. I'm almost there.*

"Sir," a voice said.

With his head down, Davyn could only see the lower half of the neatly pressed, dark blue uniform slacks and shined black shoes as someone stepped in front of him.

The man knelt down beside him. "Are you okay? What happened?"

Davyn wiped the sweat from his face with his shirtsleeve. "Nothing, I'm fine." He didn't sound at all fine. His stomach churned as he struggled to keep his dinner down.

The man took his arm. "Here, let me help you."

"No." Davyn pulled his arm away. "Just—just give me a minute."

Davyn peered up at the man's badge for a name: Lieutenant Robert Shuller.

"Sure, sure. Take your time." Shuller remained beside him.

Davyn loosened his collar to get some air. "You don't need to stay."

"I don't mind."

"I mean you should leave. I'm fine."

"Are you sure?"

Davyn lowered his head and drew another deep breath. "Uh, maybe you could help me to the stairs. Slowly."

Shuller took his arm and helped him up, but Davyn stopped midway, hunching over and clinging to the handrail with both hands. He kept his face to the wall, feeling his way, reaching hand over hand until he came to the end of the wall. He followed it around the corner, his legs shaking, struggling to support him. His stomach lurched as his head swam. Halfway down the stairs, Davyn stopped to sit on a step.

"I need a minute."

"Sure, Mr. Daeger, take all—"

Davyn's dinner would stay down no more, and without warning it spewed all over Shuller's pants and shoes. He wiped his mouth. "Sorry."

Shuller cleared his throat. "Um, that's okay. It's not your fault."

"You're too understanding. Why don't you find me a conference room—without windows, preferably, and definitely near a bathroom. Then go get yourself cleaned up. I'll wait here."

A young man wearing fatigues sat at one of the fifty workstations spaced more or less evenly across the sprawling communications center at the new headquarters. The name stitched on his shirt was Brian Hilgo.

Hilgo tapped his ear. "I'm picking up a communication device forty-six miles due west of here and it's heading toward the island. It's one of ours."

About a dozen of the fifty or so men turned away from their screens and watched Hilgo to see what he'd say next.

Aluerd walked over to Hilgo, and shot a harsh look at the onlookers. They simultaneously went back to their screens as Aluerd looked down his nose at Hilgo and said, "You'll address me as 'sir.'"

Hilgo just pointed to his monitor, which showed a map with a flashing beacon. "I'll put it on the wall so you can see it better."

The image appeared on one of the eight giant monitors mounted on the front wall. Aluerd glared at him for a moment, then shifted his gaze to the map.

"Are you sure it's one of ours?"

"Yes," he said, then cleared his throat. "It's one of the new models, like the ones we use here. It's curious because they haven't started issuing them back at headquarters yet. Must be one of the prototypes."

"Keep tracking them. See if you can patch them through to me, so I can hear what they're saying."

"Yes, sir."

Aluerd grabbed a pair of binoculars and headed out the door.

Davyn sat at a table in a small, empty conference room three flights below deck.

Leo said, "Let's go over the plan again."

"Ugh, really?"

"Hey, at least you're feeling better. And it'll keep your mind busy."

"My mind's busy enough, thank you."

"Well, let's hope it's been busy on the plan. Repeat it back to me."

"When we dock, I do a quick inventory of the buildings and their locations. Look for a building that looks fortified. Be back at the main building by 9:30 at the latest."

"Which one is the main building?"

"You're going to make me say it?"

"Come on, it's important. Secret agents have to do this on every mission."

Davyn said nothing.

"I know you're still there. I can hear you breathing. How do you know which is the main building?"

"Fine." Davyn let out a heavy sigh. "The main building will be the one with the lights on."

"See, that wasn't so hard."

Davyn turned his earpiece off, but heard a telltale blip a second later.

"Hey, don't do that. I need to have ears on you the whole time."

"Don't make me say pointless things and I'll keep it on."

"You go back and forth between being an intellect and a four-year-old, faster than a jackrabbit."

"Faster than a jackrabbit what?"

"What?"

"You said faster than a jackrabbit."

"Right."

"Never mind."

Leo laughed. "I can do it, too, you know."

"Ah, touché."

Aluerd stood with his hands behind his back in the communication center, rocking on his heels.

Agent Hilgo put his hand to his ear and listened. "Sir, I'm picking up an intermittent signal now. Would you like me to patch you in?"

"Yes, patch it through."

A voice on the earpiece said, "He's an ass, *and* he laughs too hard at his own jokes."

Aluerd grimaced. "What the—"

"He's an ass, *and*—oh, the ship's approaching the island. Remember, after the ship docks, let the security personnel get off before you. Then you can start looking around for where they may be keeping Magne."

Aluerd's eyes grew big. "Leo?" he said softly. "She knows." He glanced around to make sure no one heard him. His chest tightened as he worked through the possible implications. *Does she know it was me?*

"Copy that."

Aluerd's brows furrowed. He didn't recognize that other voice. *Is the ship coming for me?* He called to Agent Hilgo, "Give the order to shut everything down, and go directly to the ship at the east dock. We need to be out of here by 8:40. Leave no evidence. No one can know we were here."

"Uh, sir, what about Magne?"

"What did I tell everyone? You're to refer to him as the prisoner. Leave him in the cell with a guard—no, better make it two. And tell them to keep him quiet."

"We're not guards, we're agents. Also, it would be helpful if you told me which agents you'd like to stay."

"Watch your tone, boy. One more word from you and you're off my team. We have big plans and you'll be left out in the cold if you're not careful."

"Yes, sir. Sorry, sir."

Agent Hilgo hated sucking up like that, but he was stuck now. He never should have helped Aluerd with such an off-the-wall plan, and it never should have gone this far. His buddy Bill Chambers at the workstation opposite him stood up, peered over at him, and rolled his eyes. Hilgo nodded, then glanced over at Aluerd as he picked up a pair of binoculars and walked out the door.

Agent Chambers, who was neatly manicured and wore his hat with the brim high, stood in sharp contrast to Hilgo. "You look like shit."

Hilgo rubbed his eye with the palm of his hand. "Thanks, man."

Chambers put his hands on his hips and leaned in closer. "Don't let that prick drag you down."

He ignored the comment for the time being. "I don't know how he thinks he's going to get away with it."

"You mean operating out of the new headquarters without permission, or holding Magne against his will?"

"He thinks once he's chief he can make it all go away, but I don't think he's making chief, and we're all tangled up in it now."

"I used to sympathize with the dude, but he's lost his marbles. We're going to find him in here one day just sitting in a corner, diddling his lips."

Hilgo laughed. "Yeah, he'll end up in some posh psych retreat while we're serving time at Leavenworth."

"Don't you know it." Chambers leaned down and whispered in Hilgo's ear, "Did you hear anything about Jordan?"

Hilgo shook his head. "What'd you hear?"

Chambers pursed his lips. "Something crazy. It's probably nothing."

"We're in it. Deep. I don't know what's next. I just hope he doesn't snap and take us all out."

Davyn stood on the ship's deck between the bow and the exit. He glanced down at the crew on the dock as they prepared the ropes. The ship was almost docked. He returned his gaze to what he could see of the island in the dark, through the tangle of trees.

The dock was well lit, as was the roadway leading toward the main building, where the fundraiser gala was to be held, but everything else was nearly drowned by a sea of black on this dreary, overcast night. The land rose gently from the water's edge, and the terrain appeared to be similar for the rest of the island—at least from what he could see—but there was no telling what it was really like.

The main building wasn't the only one with power, though. At least two other buildings had lights on.

"Leo, I see at least three buildings with lights on."

"Are you sure they're not part of the main one?"

"Seriously?" As if he couldn't tell one building from three.

"Look, the exchange of information will be more efficient if you stop being so defensive."

Davyn could tell her patience was wearing thin, and it would probably be a good idea to just play nice. He watched the crewmen securing the ship to the dock while he pondered her response. *I like that she's direct and doesn't sew nuance into every sentence. And maybe she has a point.* "The buildings aren't connected to each other. Maybe they're the same building, but different buildings."

"Davyn, that doesn't make any sense."

"I know, right?" he said with uncharacteristic enthusiasm. Davyn enjoyed hearing the sound of her exasperated grunt, even if he was being a bit of a jerk. "Hey Leo?"

"What?"

"They're separate buildings."

"You're an ass, *and* you should be disembarking any minute now."

She modulated her voice to sound like a flight attendant and slipped the word "ass" in there quite nicely. Points for that. Davyn didn't want to admit it, but he was starting to like her—as a friend. Well, not really a friend, more of an acquaintance. He didn't have room in his life for friends, and then there was the distance—

Davyn felt the ship jerk and peered over the side to see the boarding ramp unfold toward the dock. "They just lowered the ramp, Leo."

"Okay, the security team will signal you once they're ready. Get ready, and remember you'll only have an hour to search the campus before you need to be at the gala."

After Davyn made his way down the ramp, he looked up the roadway to the main building. The road forked about halfway up the hill. Davyn couldn't see where either road led, so he picked the one that looked like it would wind furthest away from the main building. As he reached the top of the first hill, he saw a small out-building. He walked around it, but saw nothing unusual.

"Leo, there's a small outbuilding with no windows. He could be in there, but I have no way of telling. Should I knock on the door?"

"Funny. Keep looking. If you see nothing else, we'll circle back. Stay low, too. I don't like that Aluerd's been there. He may even still be on the island."

Davyn continued along the roadway, looking for any sign of where they might be holding Magne. "I see a building at the bottom of the hill, north of my current position. There's a guy sitting outside with a rifle. I don't think he saw me."

"Okay, you're almost out of time. I made note of where it is, so head back to the main building. We'll circle back later."

"Um, okay. Sure. Magne out." Davyn shut his earpiece off. He was sure that's where Magne was being held and he wasn't about to pack it in to go to a party, of all things. He looked up the hill at a dense cluster of trees to the east; that could be used as his cover to get closer to the building. He crept up the hill and heard the Leo blip, as he'd come to call it, in his ear.

"Are you heading back to the main building?"

"Shh. I'll be running on silent for a while." He tapped his ear and shut off the earpiece again before inching through the brush, not making a sound.

Inside the guardhouse, Agent Larry Page leaned back in a hardwood chair, adjusting his position to try and get comfortable, which he was finding to be nearly impossible.

Agent Tim Mathers entered carrying a brown paper grocery bag. "When are they coming back?"

"Shh, you'll wake him."

"What do you care?" Mathers set the bag down on an end table in the tiny makeshift jail.

"He's a pain in the ass when he's awake. I want to eat my dinner in peace," Page whispered as he glared at Magne sleeping on the cot. "I don't know when they'll be back. They'll tell us, but keep it low."

Mathers quietly opened the exterior door and slipped out. In the next instant, he yelled, "Hey, it's Magne! He's escaped. He's on the hill!"

Page shot a quick glance at Magne's alleged blanket covered body. "Damn—are you sure?"

"I'm looking right at him. I don't know how he did it, but he's out here."

Page grabbed his rifle and ran out the door.

The commotion woke Magne, and he pushed his cover off. "What's all the racket?" He noticed the open cell and exterior doors and jumped up, leaning a hand on the doorframe as he peeked outside.

"What the—" He scurried out and positioned himself between the guards and a thick oak tree. He took a quick look around, but the guards had already fled. *Not sure what the hell's going on, but I think I'll take this lovely opportunity to escape.*

Magne peered out from between the trees. A crowd of people in tuxes and long dresses streamed into a large white convention building. He looked down at his grey jumpsuit, then moved closer and saw a member of the security team that he recognized. Magne snuck up and grabbed him, yanking him behind a shipping container.

"Hey, David. Sorry if I scared you."

David regarded Magne with wild eyes and adjusted his belt. "Ha, no problem Magne. I wasn't scared."

"Good, good. Look, I need you to keep this quiet."

"Keep what quiet?"

"What I'm about to say."

"Okay."

"I need to get back to the to the mainland, uh, cloak and dagger style, you know. No one should see me. Unless you see me later and I'm dressed in a tux." Magne cleared his throat. "Then it's fine."

"Um, I'm not sure I understand what you're saying."

"Did you see me on the boat on the way over here?"

"Yeah, sure."

"How was I dressed?"

"You were wearing a tux. What happened to your clothes, anyway?"

"David, you know better than to ask that."

"Sorry, it's just—"

Magne stared him down.

"Sorry, never mind. Whatever you need, Magne."

"Great."

"Uh, what was it you needed me to do?"

"I'm going to board the ship now and stay out of sight."

"Okay."

"I need you to distract the guys so I can slip on."

"I can do that."

"And if you see me later, in a tux. That's all part of the plan."

"Um, okay." The guard looked a tad confused, but moved toward an outbuilding near the dock. "Hey, guys! Come over here a minute."

The guards followed David, while Magne slipped on to the boat.

CHAPTER 16

Davyn emerged from the woods about two hundred yards away from the outbuilding. Still no sign of the agents pursuing him. He crouched down and turned his earpiece back on. "My shoes and the bottoms of my pants are caked in mud. I can't go in."

"I told you to head back to the party. You're lucky you weren't killed." Leo sounded more annoyed than concerned.

"Security needs to check out that building."

"Yeah, I was thinking about that. If they're holding Magne there, it could get very dicey."

"Why can't they just bust in with overwhelming force?"

"That would require all of them. We don't know if Aluerd is still on the island or how many guys he has with him. Or how they're armed. After Aluerd put the hit on Jordan, there's no telling what he'll do next."

"Damn, I wish I had that n-pulse."

"What?"

"Nothing." Davyn turned off his earpiece and ran back to the outbuilding. Positioning himself behind a dirt mound, he maneuvered closer to the building and scanned the area. No one was around. He stayed low and worked his way closer. No sign of anyone and the building's door stood wide open.

He gave one last survey of the area, then slipped inside. It was clear that someone was being kept in that cell recently, but it was empty. He turned to leave when he heard footsteps.

"Magne, turn around slowly," Page said.

Davyn did so and saw his rifle pointed at his chest.

"Thank you so much for coming back." Page prodded him with the end of his rifle. "In the cell, my friend." Page pushed the cell door open as he took a step back and stepped into the cell. Page closed the cell door. "You've got to tell me what brought you back here."

Mathers ran in and stopped, trying to catch his breath. "How did you get him back here so fast?"

"He came back on his own. He's about to tell the story." He turned to Davyn. "Aren't you Magne?"

Davyn sat down on the cot and put his hand near his ear. "Well, I'm no Tolstoy, but..."

As he drove his Land Rover into an empty parking lot at the beach, Magne dialed Dan McQue. He'd already been to his apartment to see what he could learn about his kidnapping nearly a week earlier. The clumsy but effective job was not carried out by trained agents—more likely hired goons. Questions raced through his head. Who ordered it? Why?

But right now, his priority was to find out where Davyn was so he could return him to his normal life. Then he'd focus on the investigation. To do that, he'd need to speak with Leo. It's not like he could just stroll through headquarters and risk running into himself.

Dan answered in his traditional laid-back manner. "It's Dan."

"Dan, it's Magne. Sorry to call so late."

"Oh, thank god! I'm so glad you're okay. How's Leo?"

"That's a very good question. I don't know. I haven't spoken with her since Monday. It sounds like she spoke to you, though."

"Yes, she was here. Haven't you called her?"

"Of course, but she didn't answer."

"How did you—never mind. You'll buy me a brandy when this is over and tell me all about it. What can I do to help?"

Magne stopped his car and gazed out over the dark water. A storm was moving in from the east, blotting out the rising sun. "Did she get in touch with Davyn?"

Dan chuckled. "Yes, we tried using a hypersonic sound transmitter at first, before the new earpieces showed up. That didn't go too well, I'm sorry to say."

"Earpieces?"

"Yes. She didn't want to use the standard-issued ones for fear they'd be detected. She said they'd developed new ones and managed to get some prototypes. Outside of regular channels, I think. Anyway, she had them couriered over."

"I see, very smart. Did she send them to Davyn or—"

"Yes, she sent two. One to use, one to charge."

Magne looked out over the breaking waves. An uneasy feeling crept in. Not the full memory, but the sensation that rises before a memory takes shape, like it's stalking you and closing in. He tried to put it out of his mind.

"Magne, you still there?"

"Yeah, sorry, Dan. I need to get in touch with her, but I can't reach her and obviously I can't go to headquarters."

"Right. I can see the chief now. 'Hi Magne. Hi Magne. Wait, what?'"

"Right, it would be a disaster. I'll have to find another way."

"Do you think they're in any danger?"

"No," Magne said merrily. "He's just attending social events and glad-handing investors. I'm sure he's frazzled, but he's not in any real danger. Same for Leo. I'm sure she's loving the banquets. Anyway, thanks for all your help, Dan."

"Sure, I wish I could do more."

"I know you do. I won't forget that brandy either. So long, Dan."

"Wait, Magne, you just reminded me of something."

"What's that?"

"Davyn forgot one of the earpieces when he left for D.C. Leo was pissed."

Magne scratched his chin as he thought about that. "So it'd still be at the university. Or maybe his apartment. Did she say where he left it?"

"No, sorry. If I had more information, I could probably locate it, except—"

"Except what?"

"It's probably dead now. Leo said it only stays powered for twelve hours."

They both fell silent.

"Magne, you still there?"

"Yeah, I have an idea, but—did Leo say anything about what Davyn looks like these days?"

"No, but the messenger I sent said something about him dressing like a young H.G. Wells."

"Oh boy."

"What is it?"

"I'll keep you posted, Dan. Bye."

Davyn was sitting on a small cot in the jail cell when he heard the Leo blip. He glanced at Page, who was leaning back in a chair against the bare concrete wall, with his head down and a hat over his face. Davyn scratched behind his ear as he glanced over at the other agent, Mathers, who stood near the exterior door.

"Don't respond if you think they may hear you," Leo said. "Just clear your throat if you can hear me loud and clear."

Davyn covered his mouth and cleared his throat. Agent Page tilted his hat up and peered at him, followed by Mathers. Two sets of eyes on him felt like an intrusion.

"Just clearing my throat, Larry." Davyn looked at Mathers standing by the door. "Go back to what you were doing, Tim-o-thy."

There was a knock on the door, causing Mathers to jump. Page swung an arm out and hit Mathers in the leg. "You're supposed to be standing guard outside."

"It's cold out there, man." He lifted the cover from the peephole and looked out. He leaned left and right, then turned to Davyn. "I go by Tim." He opened the door.

Agent Hilgo stepped in and eyeballed the three of them, then focused his attention on Page. "Aluerd wants to know if there were any issues while we were gone."

Mathers glanced over at Page and then Davyn. "Nope, it was pretty quiet."

Davyn raised his eyebrows at Page and tilted his head to the side.

Hilgo took notice and looked Page up and down. "Nobody from that ship came around?"

"Nope," Mathers shot back.

Hilgo cast a skeptical eye at Davyn, then stepped over to the cell to get a better look at him. "Where'd he get these clothes?"

Page shot a stare at Mathers and cleared his throat. "Uh, he spilled soup on his jumpsuit and, so, you know."

Hilgo spun around and surveyed their faces. They both looked like preschoolers caught by their teacher with their hands in a cookie jar.

Davyn found it amusing. "Yeah, thanks for that, guys. The fit is remarkably spot-on."

Hilgo shook his head. "All right, you guys are dismissed. We've got this watch."

He continued to eyeball the two agents as they fumbled their way out the door.

Leo said, "I heard all of that. Just lie low. If they think you're Magne, then he must have escaped, and he'll be contacting me. If I don't hear from him soon, I'll contact the chief and pull the plug on this whole crazy thing."

We've come too far to give up now. But how to communicate it to Leo?

"He's an ass," Davyn whispered, "*and* he gives up too easy."

Hilgo shot a quizzical look at Davyn. "What?"

"The guards you just relieved. He's crap at twenty questions and he—" Davyn switched to a deeper, more deliberate tone, "He gives up too easy."

"I know," Leo said softly. "It's just gotten too risky. Aluerd's unhinged and now your life's in danger."

"Don't give up," Davyn said.

Hilgo shook his head. "We're not playing twenty questions, Magne."

"You can give up if you want to, but I'm in this 'til the end."

Hilgo slid down into his chair and pulled his hat over his face. "Fine, just play by yourself."

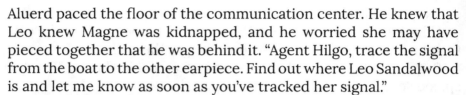

Aluerd paced the floor of the communication center. He knew that Leo knew Magne was kidnapped, and he worried she may have pieced together that he was behind it. "Agent Hilgo, trace the signal from the boat to the other earpiece. Find out where Leo Sandalwood is and let me know as soon as you've tracked her signal."

"Sir, Hilgo was sent to guard Magne."

"I sent Page and Mathers. And you're to refer to him as the prisoner." Aluerd said in disgust. "Get Hilgo back here. Now."

"Who do you want to send?"

Aluerd threw his hat down. "I don't care."

The agents looked at each other with blank stares.

"Now," Aluerd yelled.

Magne pulled into the tree-lined visitor overflow parking area at the edge of the university campus. He could have parked closer, in the faculty lot, but didn't have a sticker and wanted to slip in as casually as possible so as not to draw attention to himself. If he was going to assume Davyn's identity without being discovered, he'd need to collect some basic information before classes resumed tomorrow morning—assuming Davyn held Monday morning classes.

He stepped out of his Range Rover and put his hands in the pockets of his brown trench coat. The rain had cleared out, but the sun was setting and the temperature was dropping. He headed down the sidewalk toward the center of campus. He figured Davyn's office was probably the best place to start looking for the spare earpiece.

As he passed a field where some students looked to be playing a pick-up game of football, he noticed a muscular young man running toward him. He stopped and eyed the figure, sizing him up quickly. *Looks like a student, doesn't appear hostile. Likely a student wanting to talk to Davyn. Ah, he's waving.*

Squinting, Magne pulled a hand from his pocket and waved back in a way that he hoped matched the student's expectation. Magne hadn't seen Davyn in over four years, but he knew that he had started withdrawing socially just before he disappeared. *Better act aloof when he gets here.*

The young man stopped in front of him. "Hey, professor."

"Uh, hey." Magne put his hand back in his pocket and kept his gaze fixed on the ground.

"I'm glad you're feeling better. Lily and I came by to check on you, but you must have been at the doctor or something. You didn't answer the door."

"Yeah, probably. Look, I'm in a bit of a hurry." Magne looked up and motioned with his head toward the main building.

"Sure. Um, hey, did I see you pull into the parking lot just now?"

Magne cleared his throat and glanced toward the lot. "Yeah, I—I felt like a bit of a walk."

"Oh, okay, it's just that I thought you didn't—ah never mind. Nice ride, though."

Magne nodded and said, "Okay, see you." He started to walk past him.

"You got a haircut." The student leaned down and around to look up at Magne's face.

Magne returned a cool stare, then, remembering his role, softened his expression and returned his focus to the ground. "Uh-huh."

"Looks good. Well, see you later."

This guy didn't strike Magne as being very sharp, but he might have useful information about Davyn and he could probably get away with asking questions that might, with someone else, trigger suspicion.

"Wait—when did you see me last?"

"Uh, I guess it was Wednesday night, when we were running. No—Thursday morning, outside your office. You were rushing off and—" The student scratched the top of his head, then jutted his pointer finger out as if struck by an epiphany. "You were going to recommend a book on running."

"Right. Did I say where I was heading?"

"No, but you seemed busy."

Magne nodded. *Sounds like he left on Thursday then.* "Did you see me after that?"

"No, professor. Lily said you called in sick. I like the new threads, too. It's like you got a makeover." He stared at Magne's face. "Oh, and nice manscaping on the brows."

I should have picked up a skullcap, too, but then I'd look like a punk instead of a hippie. Not sure which look I like less. I wonder if Davyn wears a skullcap. Magne gave another nod as he turned away and headed toward the main building, pulling his collar up around his ears. It was weird, going on assignment with next to no intelligence on the subject, and even stranger to think that subject was his own twin brother.

Magne stopped in front of a sign with a map of the campus. *Let's see, Anthropology. Would that be humanities or social sciences?* He opted to start with the humanities building. He climbed the brick stairs, and tugged on the door and stepped inside and up to a directory on the wall and scanned it.

A woman's voice caught him off guard. "Hi, professor."

He spun around.

She laughed. "Sorry, I didn't mean to startle—wait a minute." She looked him up and down and then grinned. "You got a haircut. I like it." She circled him slowly, taking in his appearance. "And new clothes." Her mouth dropped open. "Did you get a makeover?"

Young woman, familiar with Davyn, identified him as professor: probably a student. Dressed entirely in blue, except for purple running shoes. Hmm.

Magne pulled his hands out of his pocket and rubbed them together. "It's getting cold outside. Where's your coat?"

"Aw, that's nice of you to ask. I left it in your office."

"My office? Are you going there now?"

She raised an eyebrow. "Um, yeah. What were you looking for?"

"Hmm?"

"You were looking at the directory."

"Oh, nothing."

"Well, okay, after you."

Magne smiled and extended his hand. "No, after you, please." He followed up with a little bow.

"My, my, professor, you're in a good mood today." She started down the hallway as Magne fell into step beside her. The student turned her head to him as they walked. "This is funny. I'm usually the one chasing you."

Magne smiled. "Well, it's Sunday. I thought I'd take it easy."

When they stopped in front of what he presumed was the office's door, Magne looked down at the nameplate: Professor Davyn Daeger, Associate Professor.

"Something wrong, professor?"

"No, no." The edge of his mouth curled up with amusement as he walked inside.

She shot him a puzzled look, shrugged, then followed him in. Magne went straight to the desk and started looking for the earpiece. He opened each drawer, rifling through them one by one before moving to the next.

"Can I help you find something, professor?"

Magne looked up from the drawer he was searching. "You haven't seen a small earpiece, have you?"

"An earpiece? You mean like earbuds?"

Magne looked back in the drawer and pushed some items around. "No, this would be smaller. Tiny." He held his thumb and pointer finger close together to approximate the size. "Like a hearing aid."

She scrunched her nose. "You wear a hearing aid?"

"Um, it's not for me."

"Whose is it?"

He stood up and peered across the room. "They'd prefer I didn't say, I think."

"Oh, is it Mrs. Dawit's?" The student backtracked when Magne shot a wry expression her way, trying to wordlessly point out that she'd completely missed the point in what he'd said. "Right, sorry. Um, no, I haven't seen anything like that. Is it in a box or anything?"

He scratched his head. "I don't know."

"You don't know if it was in a box?"

"There were two. One was not in a box. I don't recall if, um, I took the other one out or not."

She pinched her lips together and shrugged. "I'll keep an eye out for it. If I see it, I'll definitely let you know." She grabbed her coat and headed for the office door.

"Great, put the word out, too, would you?"

"Sure, professor. I'll tell everyone, except Mrs. Dawit." She put her finger to her lips. "Mum's the word on that." Magne shot her a pistol wink and she laughed. "I like when you're in this mood."

Being on campus gave Magne a strange feeling of guilt. Leaving Davyn alone, without so much as a word to indicate that he was alive. He'd always told himself it was for the greater good. His work at the agency made it all worth it. But maybe while he was here, he could help him out a little. Like he'd always done for him in the past.

"Say, uh—" Magne paused. This was an easy trick that he'd picked up. Act as though he'd forgotten her name, let her say it, then act like he'd paused for a different reason. He'd follow it by saying that of course he knew her name.

"Yes, professor?"

Shoot. Try again. "Say, uh—"

She put her hands on her hips, her coat slipping through the crook of her elbow.

"What is it, professor?"

He grinned. "Um, I just wanted to wish you a wonderful day. That's all."

She bit her bottom lip. "Is everything alright, professor?" she said with a hint of concern.

"Sure. I just appreciate you more than I think I've let on. If I haven't said it before, I'm saying it now," he added with an affirming nod.

She put her hand to her heart. "I've suspected that you feel that way about Mrs. Dawit, Bukka and me, but never let it show." Her eyes misted, and she smiled. "This is a very positive step, professor. I'm proud of you." She marched up to him and gave him a big hug.

Magne gasped when she squeezed, then returned the hug with a couple of gentle pats on her back.

She stepped back and smiled, still holding his arms, her eyes beaming. "You have a wonderful day too, professor."

She turned and walked out the door. Magne wasted no time in closing and locking it, then went back to searching through the desk. Without the earpiece he had no way to reach Leo or Davyn, and if he didn't find it here, he'd have to venture out on campus. He figured he'd better find out what Davyn's schedule was for tomorrow, just in case. Hopefully, he wouldn't be teaching any classes.

CHAPTER 17

L ily knocked on Professor Daeger's office door and then pushed to try and open it, but it didn't budge. She stepped back, then leaned in, managing to gain some ground that way, but was surprised at how heavy it was. She peered around behind the door and saw the reason. She'd been pushing a stack of books. Glancing around the office, she finally spotted Professor Daeger standing near one of the dark wood bookshelves.

"Professor, why are you here?" She looked at her watch. "Class starts in five minutes."

Lily surveyed the empty shelves and stacks of books scattered across the floor. The professor set down a picture frame that he'd been holding. All the desk drawers and cabinet doors were open, most of them having been emptied like the bookshelves. The place was a mess.

"Yes, I know. Actually, I'm still not feeling well. I may have to cancel, I'm afraid."

"Oh, that's too bad," she said, still scanning the messy room.

"Unless someone can cover for me?"

"Um, normally that would be the teaching assistant, but I don't think I'm ready to do that."

"Oh, right, because you're my teaching assistant. Well, all you need is the syllabus and the notes for today's lesson."

"Notes? Today's lesson?" *What was he talking about? His notes are all in his head.*

"How long is the class?"

"Um, the usual," Lily said, sounding a bit perplexed.

"The usual...?"

"One hour."

The professor scratched his stubbled cheek. "Do you have a syllabus?"

I've never seen him with five o'clock shadow. He's acting weird. She walked over, grabbed a syllabus from her notebook, and handed it to him.

He flipped through it. "Hmm, should be fun." He placed his hand on her shoulder and gently guided her to the door. "You're going, right?"

"Yes, of course."

"Great, lead the way." He gave her a gentle push to cast her ahead of him.

When they arrived, the professor looked around at the students, some of whom were still filtering in at the door. Others stood around talking. The professor glanced at his watch and clapped his hands. "Let's go, chaps, ladies. Take your seats and we'll get this class started. It's already after ten."

The students all looked up, apparently shocked by their professor's demeanor, then they all sat down.

"Is everything alright, Professor Daeger?" one student asked.

He chuckled, shook his head and repeated, "Professor Daeger," under his breath. Lily shot a bewildered look his way. "Yeah, yeah, everything's great. Somebody bring me up to speed on where we left off. I was out—" He motioned with his extended thumb behind him. "Out for a bit."

One student raised their hand. "You were telling us about how you use primitive tools and hunted like the Clovis people."

"Ah, right. The Clovis people. How could I forget them? Great bunch of hunters, them."

Lily looked up from her seat and pushed aside the papers she was supposed to be grading. *The papers can wait. This is too good to miss.*

"Well, let's see. Hunting like Clovis people is—well, it's a lot like hunting terrorists."

Lily pursed her lips and took in the students' bewildered expressions.

"Let's say you're a secret agent, and your job is to hunt terrorists." The professor strode around the room with uncharacteristic confidence, gesturing as he went. "Sometimes, the terrorists can be located using high tech gadgets like satellites, but a lot of it is gathering intelligence on the ground."

At once, several hands shot up.

The professor stopped pacing and put his hands on his hips. "You're a curious bunch." He looked around at their faces. "You can just call out your questions. No need to raise your hands. One at a time, though. We want to be polite."

Then he flashed a smile that Lily hadn't seen before. A confident and charming smile. It was as if the professor had spent his days away from campus at a world-class finishing school.

A student stood up. "How do you know about being a secret agent?"

"You guys never saw a documentary or a movie? Ah, of course you have." He waved the thought away. "I'm using a simile. You must've learned about that in your—what? English classes, I'd guess. Yeah?"

The student nodded slowly and sat back down.

"Right, who else?"

The students sat quietly.

"Where are all those hands that were just up? No matter. I guess you all had the same question then." He resumed striding around the room.

Lily's mouth hung open as she stared at the professor and felt around in her bag for her phone. She found it, pulled it out, and quietly started texting.

"My teaching assistant, for example. She's fit and lean. She'd be able to move stealthily and quietly through the brush." He turned to her. "Isn't that right, Miss, uh, Miss—"

Lily heard him, but was too busy texting Bukka to immediately respond: **Get to Professor Daeger's class NOW. You have to see this!**

A student near the professor whispered, "It's Lily."

"Yes, of course it is. It's just that she's distracted." He boomed, "Lily, isn't that right?"

Lily jumped nearly out of her seat, sending her phone into the air. She sat up straight in her chair. "Sorry, important text." She gathered herself. "What was the question?"

The professor walked over to where her phone had landed and picked it up. He waved it around. "These'll get you killed out in the field. We call them 'mind leeches' because they'll suck the attention right out of you." He walked over, set the phone on her desk, and winked at her. "You're safe where you are, though. Carry on." He turned back to the class.

Lily leaned back in her chair. The professor's behavior was quite unusual, even for him. She put her hand on her chest. "We?"

He turned back to her. "Sorry?"

"You said 'we' call them mind leeches. Like you were once an agent?"

The professor smiled. "I used to pretend when I was a kid, but no, everything I've told you comes from books or documentaries."

The door in the back of the lecture hall opened and Bukka peered in. Lily gestured for him to use the side door near the front.

"Ah, come in young man. You're the fellow from yesterday. Have a seat."

Lily scratched her head. *Fellow from yesterday?*

Bukka stepped inside, looking like he was trying very hard to appear inconspicuous as he made his way to an open chair.

"Come on, son," the professor boomed. "We're just getting started."

Davyn sat on the cot in his cell. A single light fixture in the middle of the ceiling lit the small, windowless room. It would be easy to take it out and plunge the room into darkness, but then what? There wasn't a lot to work with here. But if he couldn't escape, he could at least try to get them to talk while he recorded them. See what evidence he could collect.

Hilgo stood by the exterior door with his rifle leaning nearby, eyeballing Davyn. "I'll be right back. Don't try anything."

Davyn looked around the cell. "Like what?"

Hilgo squinted at him, then stepped outside. Davyn heard the two guards talking, but couldn't make out what they were saying. Then they fell silent.

Davyn whispered to Leo, "Hey, the guard stepped out. I've got the recorder. I'm going to try to get them to talk. Can you upload the recording in case something happens?"

"Yes, but it may take some time. Keep it close."

Hilgo opened the door, poking his head in and looking around. "Who were you talking to?"

"You jealous?" Davyn said, raising his eyebrows. "I bet you say that to all the prisoners."

"You are one crazy son of a bitch, Magne. I don't know how you haven't ended up with a bullet in your head. You talk shit to people who can fire you, kill you, have you put away for life. You even say 'sir' like a wiseass."

Davyn shot Hilgo a wink. "Don't take offense, Brian. We're on the same team. We're just having a little fun."

Brian shook his head and chuckled. He set his rifle down and sat in a chair facing Davyn. His facial expression shifted from annoyed to...curious?

"Something on your mind, Brian?"

Brian glanced at the door, then leaned closer to Davyn and looked him up and down. "I don't like this situation."

Davyn leaned in, too, and nodded, but said nothing.

"Aluerd," Brian whispered, "is a competitive SOB. But this—this is a whole new level."

"Yes, it is, and now he's got you involved. I'm sure you're not happy about that," Davyn said.

Brian's gaze shifted back and forth rapidly between Davyn's eyes, looking as if he was about to say something, then he let out a breath and slumped back in his chair.

"What is it?"

Brian pressed his lips tight as if trying to hold back what he was going to say. "I hope the weather changes soon. I hate rainy weekends." He pulled his hat over his eyes.

"Don't feel like talking, Brian?"

"I know your tricks, Magne. I don't know how you pull them off, but you do."

Davyn grit his teeth. "What's your favorite one so far?"

Brian grunted. "Well, broadcasting your location was pretty good. Unfortunately for you, it only reached the new spectrum, so nobody off the island would have heard it."

Yeah, except for maybe me. Brian seems comfortable. Maybe I should shake him up a little.

"How can you be so sure?"

"What do you mean?"

"How can you be sure no one off the island heard it? There could be an extraction team on their way right now."

"Nice try. I analyzed the signal myself. The spectrum used on the island only works with the new earpieces, and nobody else has any."

"You sure?"

"Actually, we picked one up on a ship headed this way, but they've already come and gone. No extraction team. I mean, you're still locked up here, aren't you?"

Probably should let him believe that and let the discussion about earpieces drop. Time to change the subject.

"Pretty smart. I could use a guy like you on my team."

Brian didn't react for a moment, but then lifted his hat and peered at him with one eye. Davyn stood up and stretched, deliberately avoiding eye contact and letting what he said sink in.

"Are you serious?"

"Yes, absolutely. You're obviously very smart. I mean, aside from letting Aluerd rope you into this." Davyn paused and waited for a response. Nothing. "I'm good in the field, but I can't analyze signals and do all the high tech stuff that you do."

Brian took off his hat and put it aside. He stood up and cocked his head while Davyn pretended not to notice his interest.

"Are you just screwing with me?"

"No, I'm lost when it comes to technology."

"Not about that. I mean about wanting me on your team. If all this somehow works out, of course." He paused. "Is that still a possibility?"

Davyn stretched his right arm over his shoulder. "You know, this cot isn't very comfortable."

"Come on, stop messing with me. If I help you, would you consider helping me?"

Davyn turned to him. "I don't know what you mean, exactly."

"Jesus, Magne. If I help you to escape, will you testify on my behalf?"

The door opened, and Bill poked his head in. "Everything okay in here?"

Davyn smiled. "Brian wants a soda. Did you bring anything, Bill?"

Bill looked at Brian and Brian waved him off. He stepped back out and closed the door.

Davyn sat down on the cot and looked at Brian. "Look, if you get me off this island safely, I'll do everything I can to ensure you don't do time and I'll see about getting you on my team."

Brian scratched his chin, apparently contemplating the possibility. "Let me see what I can figure out."

"It would help if you told me how you got caught up in this mess."

Brian squinted at that. "Why?"

"I'll need to know when I testify on your behalf."

Brian nodded but fixed his skeptical gaze on Davyn.

Suddenly, Davyn heard Leo over his earpiece. "What's with the gun?"

A man's voice in the background replied, "Leo, you'll have to come with us."

"Leo?" Davyn called without thinking.

Brian looked him up and down. "What?"

"They've taken Leo. Get me out of here. I need to help her."

Brian bit his bottom lip and rubbed his chin, then stood up and stepped outside. When he came back, he approached the cell door. "Magne, come here. Listen up."

"I'm listening."

"Bill is with me on this. Neither of us likes what's going on and we want to let you out. Aluerd ordered us here to get everything up and running, but he's getting nuttier by the day." He stopped and stared at Davyn for a moment. "If I let you out, you need to tell the judge, the chief, everybody that we had nothing to do with you being taken—or Leo. And you tell them Bill and I helped you. Got it?"

Davyn put his hand on the cell door. "Yes, of course. Open the door."

"Promise me you'll get off the island and tell the chief what's going on, and that we helped you. I don't know what he's going to be able to do, but let him know we've got thirty guys here and everybody's armed."

"Armed with what?"

"Rifles, pistols, semiautomatics. That's it, but Aluerd is crazy, and I don't want to be here if a gun battle goes down against friendlies."

"I get it."

"I'll try to get as many of the guys to go with me as possible, but you gotta let the chief know that Aluerd is the bad guy here, not us. You gotta testify to that."

"Yes, of course."

"There's a small craft inflatable Zodiac at the east dock. Here's a radio." Hilgo looked around the small room and pulled a first aid kit from the wall. "Take this, and..." He pulled off his hat. "Wear this. It'll help you blend in if someone sees you. I'll let you know when the coast is clear."

Davyn stood, hat askew and arms full of assorted supplies like a cart-less shopper at Walmart. "Wait, wait, wait. There's gotta be some other way to get to land. What about a bigger boat? There's gotta be a bigger boat, right?"

"You sound like Sheriff Brody. You afraid of sharks or something?"

Davyn stared off with a dazed look in his eyes. "It's a long trip and the weather's bad. Come on, there has to be a bigger boat."

Hilgo glanced at him, shook his head, then picked up his backpack and set it on the chair. He took the items from Davyn, one by one, and stuffed them into the pack.

"The inside of the backpack's bulletproof. It'll provide some protection. Hopefully you won't need it. There's some paracord, a compass, and some nuts in here, too."

Davyn swallowed hard. "What about a bigger boat?" he muttered.

"Aluerd has the keys to the ship. The Zodiac's keys are in its center console by the steering wheel. I'm sorry, but it's the only option."

CHAPTER 18

"All I'm saying, professor, is that the way you engaged with the class today was really great," Lily said as they walked down the crowded hallway to Davyn's office.

"Good, good," Magne replied. "Hey, you think you could help me look for that earpiece I mentioned? I'm not having any luck and it's very important that I find it."

"I suppose, professor. I have some time before my next class, but these papers are due back by Wednesday, and you said that I need to finish them by then."

Magne glanced at the stack of papers in her arms. "Well, this is more important, and I need your help."

They walked into Davyn's office and Lily set the stack of papers on his desk as she peered around the room. "Well, let's see what we can find." She knelt and looked under a coffee table. "Have you looked under the desk and tables?"

"Yes, I've looked everywhere. It's almost like he hid it."

"Why would *he* hide it and who is he?"

Magne stared into a corner and scratched his head. "I don't know."

Lily's eyebrows raised, and she puffed out her cheeks before letting out a long breath. She picked up a wooden yardstick and used it to reach into a small gap behind a bookcase.

Magne scratched his chin. "Maybe it's not in the office. Where else do I like to hang out?" He was trying to sound like he was thinking out loud, but hoped for a response from Lily, who had her arm fully extended behind the bookcase and her face pressed up to its side.

"I don't think there's anywhere that you *like* hanging out."

Magne looked at her, then at the photo of himself on the desk. He picked it up as Lily continued on about something, but he wasn't listening. He thought back to that fateful day they took the photo. How Davyn was eager to get in the water and resisted Magne's insistence on stopping to take a picture.

"Wouldn't you agree, professor?"

Magne jumped out of his thoughts and looked at her. "Yes, I suppose," he said.

"Maybe we should look there, then."

"I'm sorry, where did you say?"

Lily sighed. "The conference room you're always hiding in."

Magne set the picture down and rubbed his eyes. "Which conference room?"

"Are you alright, professor?"

"Yes. Fine. What's the name of the conference room?"

"Grimm, the one you're always in."

"Ah, yes, of course. Well, let's go."

"Um, I just said I can't join you right now. I have to go see Professor Anne remember?"

Magne looked at the photo again, then back at Lily as he turned it around to show her. "Did I ever tell you about the day we took this photo, Lily?"

Lily briefly surveyed it, then shook her head. "No, I've seen it dozens of times on your desk, but you never talk about anything like that. At least not to me."

Magne rubbed his razor stubbled face. "But I've told you about my family, right?"

Lily laughed as she looked him up and down. When he didn't seem to get the joke, she furrowed her brows. "Are you feeling okay, professor?"

Magne sighed. "Maybe I'm just feeling a little nostalgic."

"It must be the medicine they gave you for—what was it you said you had?"

"Um, it was a cold, I think."

"It must have been one nasty cold to have you out for three days. Maybe it was the flu."

"Probably."

"Well, I really have to get going. I don't want to keep Professor Throp waiting." She picked up her bag and headed for the door.

Magne smiled and waved. "I hope her first name isn't Anne."

Lily snorted a laugh, then looked back at him. "You really have a strange sense of humor." She stopped and adjusted her bag on her shoulder. "You know she really likes you, and you two would make a great couple. You really should give it another try with her. Anyone can have a bad first impression. My grandfather—oh, I'll tell you later. I have to get going, and you never want to hear my stories anyway."

Magne thought he might be able to help Davyn with both Professor Anne and Lily's less than stellar impression of him. Perhaps after he got back to the university and knew that his brother was okay, he could get a fresh start.

"Say, Lily, do you mind if I walk with you? I'd like to hear that story."

Lily tilted her head and appeared to mull over his request. "Are you sure? I thought you'd be getting ready for Dean Puddington."

"What do you mean?"

"He's sitting in on your class today. To observe, remember?"

Magne stopped cold. *How am I going to pull this off? A group of college kids is one thing, but the dean?*

"Professor?"

Magne shook his head. "That's today?"

"Yes, today at four."

Magne glanced at his watch. "Well then, why don't I walk with you and on the way, you can tell me the story about your grandfather. Then I'll prepare for today's class on—" He snapped his fingers. "What were those hunter people called?"

Lily hugged her books and winced. "Uh, Clovis people."

"Yes, Clovis, that's it. Funny name, Clovis," he said with a deep voice, stretching the word out as he uttered it.

Lily bit her bottom lip and stared at him until Magne cracked a reassuring smile and tapped her elbow. She released the stranglehold on her books.

"Well, let's get going. I'm eager to hear about your grandfather."

She smiled as she started for the door. Magne reached out and opened it for her.

"Thank you, professor."

"You're welcome, Lily."

They walked down the hallway, side by side. "Are you sure you want to hear this?"

"Yes, absolutely. It's why I came with you."

Lily shrugged. "Okay, well, I was saying that first impressions aren't everything. My grandfather and grandmother kept journals when they were young. My grandfather told me a story about how, after they got married, they looked at their journal entries for the day they met. He wrote, 'Today I met the woman I will marry,' but she wrote, 'I met the most annoying boy today.'"

Magne burst out laughing. "Oh my god, that is the most charming story. What a delight."

Lily beamed. "Really? You liked it?"

He stopped and turned to her, shaking his head. "Yes, of course. It's a wonderful story."

"I don't mean to imply that she thinks you're annoying, just that first impressions aren't as important as people say. That's all."

Magne touched her elbow. "You're a treasure, and I've been a fool. I hope you and Professor Throp will give me another chance."

Lily smiled, then pressed her lips together like a curious kid. "Well, this is a side of you I haven't seen. I have to say I like it very much."

"I've turned over a new leaf, Lily. Put in a good word for me with Professor Throp, won't you?"

She reached for the door to Professor Throp's office. "I certainly will, professor."

After the door closed, Magne peered at its placard: Professor Anne Throp. Magne's eyes grew big. *Oh boy, I hope Davyn knew that before he talked to her.*

Magne tilted his head to peek through the door's window. Anne was sitting at her desk and smiling at Lily. *She's lovely.* She noticed him, smiled, and held up a hand to wave. She kept her eyes on him for a moment, then Lily said something and it drew Anne's attention back to her. Magne wanted to stop and say hello, but he had work to do if he was going to make a favorable impression on the dean. But maybe taking an extra minute or two wouldn't hurt.

He popped open the door and stuck his head in. "I don't mean to interrupt, ladies. I just wanted to say a quick hello to Professor Throp and wish her a lovely afternoon." He smiled. "You too, Miss Lily."

Anne pushed her bottom lip out and cocked her head, seemingly impressed or amused. He wasn't sure which. "Well thank you, Professor Daeger. It's nice to see you, too."

"I'd love to stay and chat, but I have to be somewhere. Perhaps I could stop by after my class?"

Lily smiled and turned to her as Anne shook her head slowly. "Um, we could give that another go, I suppose."

Magne winked and closed the door. He glanced in briefly and saw Lily turn to Anne, mouth open wide in delight, like a child at Christmas. Anne smiled back and pushed her shoulder, playfully.

Now to find a book on the Clovis people. The library seemed like a good place to start.

Magne walked through the library's double doors and gazed around to get his bearings. An older woman, who looked like she might work there, spotted him and waved. *She might be helpful.* He waved back and made his way toward her.

"Good morning, Davyn. It's good to see you back here. You're feeling better, I trust?"

"Good morning," he replied, glancing at her name tag. "Yes, I'm feeling a lot better. Thank you, Mrs. Dawit."

Mrs. Dawit furrowed her brow. "I see you got your hair cut. It's quite a change."

"Yes, yes, I did," he said, then quickly changed the subject. "Say, I wonder if you could help me find a couple of books."

Mrs. Dawit rubbed her chin. "Um, you want me to help *you* find a book?"

Magne read between the lines. "Yes, I know, it's just that I'm in a terrible rush. The dean is coming to observe me today."

Mrs. Dawit's posture stiffened. "And what type of books are you looking for?"

"Some books on the, uh, Clovis people. Something for beginners. Maybe one that's more advanced, too. I don't have a lot of time."

"We have two books on Clovis people," she said, examining his face.

"Oh, is that all?"

"Two that you authored," she continued, giving him a sideways glance. "And we have some others that mention them as well." She pulled a piece of paper and wrote something down. "Might I inquire why you need them, and why you've forgotten where they are?" She handed him the slip of paper.

"You're a tough cookie," he said, with a smile, then headed off to look for the books.

"Davyn," she called out. He stopped and turned back just as she pointed. "You might want to use the stairs."

He waved and changed direction, heading for the stairs. When he reached the top, he stopped a passing student. Quickly checking to make sure Mrs. Dawit wasn't watching, Magne slipped her the piece of paper. "Hello, young lady. I wonder if you could point me in the right direction to find these."

She gave a gentle laugh and handed it back to him, then headed down the stairs. Magne walked between the bookcases, rubbing his chin as he searched for some signage.

"Davyn?" a voice called out. He turned to see Anne Throp. "What are you up to?"

"I uh—" Magne glanced down at the slip of paper and considered asking for help, but then thought better of it. He wanted to make a good impression, and based on his encounters with Mrs. Dawit and the student, he figured it was safer just to slip the paper in his pocket.

"Oh, you know, sometimes it's just nice to meander." Magne elaborated when Anne cocked her head. "You never know what you'll find. You, for instance. That was a very pleasant and unexpected surprise. Had I been off studying somewhere, I'd have missed the opportunity."

She smiled. "Opportunity?"

"Well, to say hello and ask if you have time to go for a walk later."

"A walk and a chat? Hmm, maybe. What time were you thinking?"

Magne scratched the back of his neck. "How about after my class? It starts at four. How does five or five-thirty sound?"

Anne rubbed her chin as if considering the proposal. "That sounds fine. I'll be in my classroom. I'll see you then."

"Great." He started to leave, then turned back. "Uh, so five or five-thirty?"

"Surprise me," she said with a smile, then turned and walked away.

Magne looked at his watch and growled. He grabbed the paper from his pocket and started looking again. Who knew being a professor could be so difficult?

Mrs. Dawit stood at her station and checked in books, a task normally done by other members of the library's staff. But she couldn't shake the feeling that something was off with Davyn, and checking in books served as a distraction. His behavior over the past week had grown more peculiar by the day. At first it was just unusual, but now it was almost dissociative. Like he was someone else entirely. Mrs. Dawit reflected on how Davyn had said he heard a voice tell him that his twin brother was alive, but at the time, she'd immediately dismissed the idea as being too outrageous.

She was sure the cause for his behavior was something more down-to-earth. Perhaps he was suffering from dissociative amnesia. She knew that stress or trauma could trigger it. Whatever the cause, she was worried about him, and now seemed like a good time to pay him a visit and see how he was doing.

Pausing behind a column, she found him sitting in a lounge chair in an open area of the library. That by itself was unusual. He normally tried to hide away in a reading room. She recognized the cover of the book he had his nose buried in. It was one of his. *That's curious.* He pulled a pen from behind his ear and drew on the page. *What on earth?*

When she stepped out from behind the column, he stopped reading and looked up. He put his pen behind his ear. "Don't worry. I've been meaning to replace this one. It's getting a little worn."

She flashed a quick smile. "I just came to check on you. Have you been reading your book this whole time?"

"Sure, sure, just catching up on my work. It's actually very interesting. Well-written."

Mrs. Dawit furrowed her brow. "Yes, they are. Same as always. They haven't changed."

He smiled. "Anyway, thanks for checking in, but I've got to get back to it. I have class—" He glanced at his watch. "In just about an hour." He rubbed his eye with his palm and blinked a few times, then stood and raised a finger skyward. "Oh, while you're here, I mentioned that I have the dean coming to observe me today. I wonder if you had some tips that you could share."

She thought for a moment. "Well, you know the subject better than anyone. That's never been an issue. I would focus on interacting with the students in a positive way. Really try to engage them."

His eyes darted around like he was contemplating the idea.

"I know that can be difficult for you, Davyn. But engaging with the students—that's what the dean will want to see. He already knows you know the material."

His face brightened. "Yes, that's it. You're brilliant, Mrs. Dawit. That's what I'll focus on. Student engagement. Really get the kids involved. It'll be fun." He leaned over and collected his book. A smile crossed his face, like a cloud had been lifted from the sun.

His enthusiasm for engaging students struck her as very out of character. He looked different, dressed different, and now he was definitely acting differently, too. This idea that his brother was actually alive—outrageous as it seemed—kept creeping back in. It was just too crazy to consider, but still, something strange was happening. She just didn't know what, or how to approach the topic with him.

Mrs. Dawit gazed at the floor, her face taught. "Um, Davyn," she started.

He patted his pocket and pulled out car keys. "Yes?"

Seeing him there, holding car keys, was just too much. This was a man that never drove in his life, or so he'd said. It was so very uncanny, and she felt uncomfortable asking, but she couldn't help herself. "What was it you said about your brother the other day?"

He squinted at her for a moment, then said, "Uh, I don't recall specifically."

How could he not recall saying that some voice told him his brother was alive? Mrs. Dawit mustered her courage to ask a question that until then would have been preposterous. "You wouldn't be Magne, would you?"

His eyes grew wide, and he tripped over a chair leg as he stumbled backwards. "Mrs. Dawit, why would you say such a thing? I know that I've been out of sorts lately, but really." He straightened the front of his coat.

She felt a rush of heat warming her cheeks with that disquieting feeling of a blush coming on. She'd overstepped. "Oh, I'm sorry, Davyn. I don't know what I was thinking." She reached a hand out to comfort him, or maybe herself.

He cleared his throat. "That's okay, Mrs. Dawit. It's been a strange week for all of us, but I have a feeling things will get better soon. I really have to go now. I have to get ready for my class."

As he hurried away, Mrs. Dawit put her hand on her chest and tried to steady her breath. She watched him descend the stairs from the balcony and retraced their brief conversation, parsing it for something that might be useful. But the library's book alarm interrupted her thoughts, and she looked over the balcony at the doorway. Davyn had triggered it as he raced by, his book still clutched in his hand.

Lily stepped into the lecture hall via an exterior door. Her shoulders relaxed when the warm air hit her face. The temperature outside was dropping, and it felt good to be indoors where the heat was circulating. She walked over to her desk, set her things down, and shook off the cold.

The professor stood at the front of the hall arranging his artifacts on a table. *That's odd.* She'd never known him to bring them out in public before. She walked over to investigate.

He looked up with a warm smile. "Hello, Lilly," he said as he set an artifact down.

It was an interesting array of goodies, but she had some big news for the professor. She held up a small box. "I found something that you were looking for."

His mouth dropped open. "Oh, you wonderful person, you. Thank you so much." He took the box and tore into it, pulling out an earpiece and charger.

Why'd he open it? Maybe it's for him and he doesn't want people to know? Or maybe he's charging it for somebody who is too frail to do it themselves. That's sweet, but kind of unusual for him.

Lily's attention shifted to the back of the lecture hall as Mr. Puddington stepped in and stood just inside the doorway. A dreary aura seemed to surround him, like Pig Pen in the comics. She winced and cleared her throat to get the professor's attention. He was kneeling by a power outlet, having just set the earpiece to charge. He peered at Lily, who motioned with her head toward Puddington. The professor glanced his way, then at his watch. It was two minutes before four o'clock. He smiled and winked at Lily.

"It's show time," he whispered.

The professor stepped to the center of the lecture hall and watched the students file in and find seats. He appeared uncharacteristically confident, engaged. He smiled when students made eye contact with him. He gave a nod to the dean.

"All right, let's get settled in, we'll be starting in a just minute."

Lily sat down at her desk and slid a pile of papers in front of her. For the sake of the dean's good opinion, she wanted to give the appearance of being busy, but the professor's new persona fascinated her. She wanted to see what he would do next and was on the lookout for any opportunities to assist.

"Welcome, everyone," the professor started. "I noticed during my last class that there was a lot of interest in my hunting expeditions. So today I thought I'd show you some tools I use and let you have a closer look." He gestured toward the artifact-covered tables. On display were various stone and wood tools, slings, ropes and blades. The students leaned forward, and even the dean seemed intrigued.

The professor smiled. "You'll all get a chance. I promise." He paused for a moment. "You, too, Mr. Puddington."

Everyone laughed, including the dean, who gave a nod of approval. Lily sat up and smiled. It felt good to see the professor so animated, not to mention he was making a wonderful impression on Mr. Puddington.

"Before we do that, though, I want to tell you a little about the people who used these tools. You'll remember from your reading of Chapter 8," he looked around the room for reactions, "that no one is quite certain who the first people to inhabit the Americas were, or when they arrived. The Clovis people were thought to be, but a recent discovery in—" He paused and looked at his handwritten notes. He lifted the top page and scanned several pages after it before continuing. Puddington scrunched his brow. "Chile—a discovery in Chile show that there were people here before them."

The professor walked over to the table and picked up a nine-inch arrowhead and held it up. "The Clovis point was a new and innovative tool then. Think of it as the Swiss Army knife of its day. They'd place it on a spear to stab at prey, or used it as a knife to cut up meat or clean the hide. It could also be used to cut vines or wood." He picked up another arrowhead that was much smaller. "They could be anywhere from small to large in size." He looked out at the crowd of students. "Who'd like to come down here and help me?" Dozens of hands shot up. He pointed to a young woman sitting in the front row. "Madam, please come down." She hurried to the stage as he asked, "What's your name?"

"Amy."

The professor handed her the large arrowhead. She held it in one hand, then the other, and lifted it up and down.

He nodded. "Heavy, right?"

"Very heavy," she replied with a laugh.

"Now if you were hunting a rabbit, would you use this?"

She shook her head. "Definitely not."

He walked over to the other table and gestured to her to follow.

Amy waddled over, carrying the arrowhead in front of her like a bowling ball. "Unless the rabbit was sleeping," she said. "Then I might drop it on it."

The professor laughed. "That might be a very effective method, actually."

The class and the dean laughed, too. Lily smiled at their enthusiastic reactions.

"Now, if the rabbit were awake and hopping about, what one do you think you'd use?"

She set the larger arrowhead down and scanned the table before picking up a smaller one and holding it up. "This one."

"You seem very confident in your choice."

She pointed it at the professor as if lining him up in her sight, then scanned down to his feet. "I am."

He backed up, raising his hands in the air. "Okay, don't shoot," he said with a smile.

Lily beamed. She loved seeing the professor engage with the students.

"What are these little curved features on the edges?" Amy asked. "And there's a channel at the base. Is that so they could make a spear?"

"Wow, great questions." He picked up the large arrowhead to show the class. "You can see how that groove makes the arrowhead thin here." He ran his finger along the channel at the arrowhead's base. "Archeologists have debated the purpose of this for years. Some argue that the channel acts as an attachment point for a spear, as you suggested, Amy. But tests in physics labs have shown that this channel also acts as a shock absorber, increasing the strength of the point and its ability to withstand stress."

Another student raised their hand as the professor turned to Amy and extended his arm toward her seat. "Thank you for your help, Amy." He turned back to the student with his hand up. "Young man, you had a question?"

"Yes. Why do you make your own tools instead of just studying the artifacts?"

"Another great question. I do something called 'experimental archaeology,' which means I make my own tools and use them how ancient people did for a more hands-on study. I can also experiment on the tools in ways that I couldn't if they were genuine artifacts. I might, for example, apply pressure to an arrowhead until it breaks to determine how strong it is. That sheds some light on how they used them. By making them and using them, I learn more than I would by just viewing them or reading about them."

The professor pointed to another student.

"What's that board with the hook on the end?"

The professor walked over to the table and held up a narrow, two-foot-long board, about two inches wide with a small wooden dowel at one end, and a loop carved out at the other.

"We call this an atlatl." He pointed at the end with a loop. "You grip it on this end," he said, demonstrating, then picked up a six-foot spear and slipped it onto the atlatl. He rested the spear on his shoulder with the spear tip pointing out toward the students. "Think of the atlatl as an extension of the arm. It allows you to increase the force and deadly precision of the throw." He took a big step and prepared to throw it. Gasps erupted across the room. "Of course, Mom told me to never use an atlatl indoors." He smiled and returned the spear to the table as the group let out a collective breath.

He invited another student down. "What's your name, son?"

"Rolland, sir."

"Rolland, why don't you pick out a tool or weapon?"

"What's this thing made of string?" he asked.

"That looks harmless, but it's actually a very precise and deadly weapon. It's made from—" He paused and riffled through his notes. "Maguey fibers. Now, hold on to the two ends and let the pouch in the middle hang," the professor said, showing the proper movements.

Rolland slipped the fibers through his hands and let the pouch hang down, holding one string in each hand. He furrowed his brow and looked at the professor.

"That's right, now put both ends into your throwing hand." When the student hesitated, the professor winked and added, "The hand that you throw with."

The student smiled and nodded, then put both ends in his right hand and held it.

"Okay, good. Now swing it around in a circle." The pouch moved slowly around in a circle as the professor continued. "If we were outside, and you put a small stone in that pouch, it would swing much, much faster. And when you released it, the stone would travel at up to 150 miles an hour toward its target."

Rolland looked at the sling, then did a double take at the professor.

"I know, surprising, right?"

"What's it called?"

The professor turned to the class. "You're familiar with the story of David and Goliath? When we hear the story, we think of poor little David and his sling, which most people think of as slingshot or something. Well, a slingshot can wing ya pretty good and might take out a window on occasion, but a sling is different. As I said, it's a precise and deadly in the right hands."

Rolland picked up a small stone. "Is this the kind of stone they'd use?"

The professor looked at the stone and squinted. "Yeah, probably about that size. What's great about these tools and weapons is that they can be made quickly with the materials found in the woods around here. Once you know how to make them, you can build an arsenal pretty quickly. That's why I rarely take them with me on my hunting trips. I just make them out in the field like our ancient ancestors did."

"Can we go outside, and you can demonstrate?" Rolland asked.

"Yes, certainly. But not today. We'll plan that for a future class."

When the class wrapped up, the professor thanked the students for their participation and dismissed them. But instead of leaving, most of the students filed down to the tables where the tools and weapons lay. Dean Puddington came down as well and pulled the professor aside, while Lily shuffled closer to listen.

"Well done," the dean said. "The students loved it. Hell, I loved it. If you keep teaching like this, you'll definitely improve your chances for that promotion."

"Thank you. I've been working hard."

"I can see that. Keep it up." He swatted him on the arm and smiled.

The professor glanced over at the earpiece, then back at the dean. "Anything else?"

"Um, no."

"Great. Well, thanks for stopping by," he said, side-eying the earpiece again.

The dean shook a finger. "Well, there is one thing. Your use of notes was unusual. You looked at them for things that I know you already know."

Lily's eyes darted back and forth quickly, before she went back to staring down at her papers.

"Uh-oh," the professor whispered. "You figured out my secret."

Lily slumped down in her chair, eyes wide, wishing she could disappear.

The professor pulled Puddington away from the students, and glanced over the dean's shoulder, like he was about to tell a secret and didn't want any eavesdroppers.

"I'm often on the students about the importance of taking notes. I always have mine handy," the professor continued when the dean nodded. "And I'll reference them during class to drive the point home."

The dean nodded approvingly, while Lily breathed a sigh of relief.

The professor turned back to the students. "Okay, everyone, we'll do this again soon, but please exit now. I have some important matters to attend to." He waved them toward the door with big, broad strokes.

They started filing out as Professor Anne edged her way in. Professor Daeger dashed over to the earpiece and picked it up.

"Lily, would you entertain Professor Throp for me for a moment, and please let her know I'll be right back," he said, as he made his way to the exterior door.

"Yes, of course," she said, looking him up and down. "But you're not going out there without your coat, are you?"

"I'll be quick." He stepped through the door and slipped the earpiece in just as the door closed behind him. Lily watched him through the window.

So, it is his hearing aid, but he looks to be using it like a phone. I don't get it.

As the last student filed out, Professor Anne made her way to Lily. "Hi, Lily."

Lily smiled, then looked over Professor Anne's shoulder and through the window. Professor Daeger paced back and forth with one hand covering his ear. He was saying something, but she couldn't tell what.

"Professor Daeger will be right back," she said, as she watched and wondered what on earth the professor was up to now.

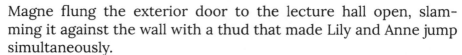

Magne flung the exterior door to the lecture hall open, slamming it against the wall with a thud that made Lily and Anne jump simultaneously.

"My apologies, ladies," he said as he cast his gaze to the ground and shook his head. "The door got away from me."

Anne flashed a wry grin. "I can see that."

Lily's bulging eyes and drawn lips gave way to a relieved smile.

Magne laughed as he walked over to join them. "My apologies, again. I was trying to reach someone and had no luck."

Lily perked up. "Was it Mrs. Dawit?"

"Uh, no, actually."

"I didn't know you knew anyone besides us three," Lily teased.

Anne laughed and peered at him like she was watching for a reaction, but the comment took a few moments to register.

"I'm sorry," Lily said. "It's just that I've been trying to get you to get out more and now, suddenly, you've gone through this transformation and we don't quite know what to think."

Magne scratched his chin and glanced over at Anne, letting Lily's comment go unacknowledged. "And what brings you here, Anne?"

Anne put her hands on her hips. "I'm not sure you responded to Lily. I think we're both a little curious about your transformation, Davyn. Have you been going to charm school?" she asked in feigned shock.

Magne laughed. "You caught me."

The room fell silent as Anne and Lily both raised an eyebrow.

"Uh, the dean suggested it would be a good way to work on my—oh, what do they call it these days? Shyness, maybe? Something like that. Anyway, it's good to see you, Anne."

Anne furrowed her brows and looked as though she was about to say something. She gave the distinct impression she didn't agree with his assessment, but perhaps she was saving the topic for another time.

Magne was still trying to sort out how to behave as Davyn. He wasn't quite sure what a reclusive introvert was or how one would act. When he went undercover as an agent, his team would provide all of this information. But for this, he'd just have to figure it out as he went along.

Anne glanced at Lily, then back to Magne. "You mentioned that you wanted to talk earlier, so I thought I'd stop by on my way out."

"Oh, yes," Magne said. "How does a walk sound?"

"That's a chilly choice, as cold as it is. Why don't we grab a coffee at Bakersfield's instead?"

Lily held a smile as she looked on, her wide eyes shifting back and forth between Anne and Magne.

"Sounds great," he said as they headed for the door.

Anne stopped and looked down at his suit. "Don't you need your coat?"

"I guess I probably do." He turned and walked toward the far side of the lecture hall to grab his coat.

Magne lingered there, pondering his next move. He didn't want to blow his cover, and he'd continue trying to reach Leo, but while he was there, he could use the time to help Davyn with that promotion and also give his social life a bit of a much-needed boost.

When he returned, Anne and Lily were talking about something that she needed Lily to work on, so he cleared his throat. "Say, I parked out in the south forty today. Why don't I bring the car to the front while you two talk?"

Lily's head jerked back. "The car? You're driving now, too?"

Magne paused a moment before answering. "Yep. Figured it was about time."

Anne slung her coat over her arm. "Hmm. Well, I don't think we need the car for such a short walk,"

Magne flashed a quick smile and hurried to compensate for not really knowing the area. "No, of course not. But I was hoping maybe we could grab dinner afterwards."

Anne glanced at Lily, who nodded her head subtly, eyes wide.

"What the heck. You bring the car around and we can go straight to dinner. We'll save Bakersfield's for another time."

"Great. I'll wait for you out front. By that statue."

"Perfect, statue location it is."

Lily shook her head. "But professor, there isn't any other—"

Anne waved her off. "See you soon, Professor Daeger."

Magne pursed his lips. "Right then. I'll see you there."

Davyn's going to have to step up his game to keep up with Anne. That is, when he's done playing around at headquarters. I'll bet he's having fun.

CHAPTER 19

D avyn crouched in the woods just outside the communication building. Jumping into a small inflatable motorboat and navigating through tumultuous seas to the mainland was out of the question. If he could get the drop on Aluerd, he'd need just enough time to play the recorded evidence against him. Then he'd have no option but to surrender.

As Davyn peered through the trees, Aluerd stood on the exterior balcony of the watchtower, staring out at the ocean. He wore the same indignant expression he had in the photo that Leo showed him, like his surroundings were beneath his pedigree. But this was Davyn's chance. He slipped quietly through underbrush. The damp night air coated everything, including the plants, and helped muffle his movements. He'd hunted in worse conditions, and he scarcely noticed it as he moved like a panther, singularly focused on his prey. He closed in on the stone stairwell that wound around the exterior to the balcony where Aluerd stood. Creeping out of the brush, he ascended without a sound. Footsteps on the wet concrete stopped him dead, and then a creak followed by a door slamming put him back in motion. As he reached the balcony, he stopped and leaned his head past the edge of the stone tower wall. There was no one around, and aside from water dripping from the railing, the air was quiet and still.

Davyn slunk on to the balcony and cracked the door open to peak inside. Aluerd stood just a few feet away with his back to him. The glow from his phone cast him in an eerie light. The small room was so quiet that any sound would alert him of Davyn's presence. Davyn would have to be on Aluerd in a single, swift movement or— no time to consider the alternative. He shoved the door and threw an arm around Aluerd, pressing his arrowhead to his throat.

"Don't move. I've gutted pigs this way before. You won't be the first."

"I'm not moving," he said so calmly that it sent a shiver up Davyn's spine. Aluerd put his hands in the air. "What do you want?" he asked with the dispassionate ease of someone responding to a knock on the door.

Davyn got straight to the point. "I want you to surrender. Your team is turning against you and I have evidence of what you've done. Your plan has fallen to pieces. It's time to call it off."

"You have no idea what you're doing. I'm not the enemy."

Davyn laughed. "Okay, someone else kidnapped me."

"Your heart is racing. You should try to relax."

Davyn pulled Aluerd's gun from the holster on his hip and pushed him into a chair.

"You're not Magne. You can stop the charade."

"Whether I am or not, it's time to end this."

"End it? Why? No one even knows we're here."

"Give me your cell phone."

"It doesn't work out here."

Davyn peered around the room. "I'll decide that. Let me have it."

"It's not here. It doesn't work. Why would I carry it?"

"You have some means of communicating. Stop playing games and get the chief on the line."

"You're out of your depth, Davyn." Aluerd watched him as if waiting for a reaction.

Davyn glanced away. He didn't like how this was going, and he hadn't thought past calling the chief. Still, Davyn kept the gun trained on Aluerd to remind him who was in charge.

"I'm not the enemy, Davyn."

He knows my name? What else does he know?

Aluerd leaned back in his chair. "Our country has lots of enemies, but I'm here to protect you. You and all the other citizens."

Davyn's mind raced. Strange as it sounded even in his head, Aluerd seemed to be the only one making sense. What now?

"The terrorists. They're the enemies." Aluerd said matter-of-factly. His polite, almost gracious tone was unsettling.

"Spare me your rationalizations," Davyn said, trying to sound dismissive. Trouble was, Davyn wasn't sure Aluerd was wrong. But he pressed on anyway. "They won't work on an objective observer."

"Philosophy professor? I thought you were in anthropology. Maybe you bounce back and forth in that ivory tower of yours."

Davyn swallowed hard and thought about what his next move should be. Listening to Aluerd pontificate was going to wear him down fast. Self-righteous indulgence was a major social battery drain.

"It must be nice to be tucked away on your little college campus, while others protect you." Even with the gun on him, Aluerd's voice remained even, steady. "We put our lives on the line every day. Risk everything while you share your ideas about the world and how it works with the children."

Davyn shook his head. "Okay, and kidnapping colleagues?"

Aluerd's eyes remained fixed on Davyn's. "It can get competitive out here in the world I inhabit. Sometimes it gets ugly. But I didn't hurt your brother. He just needed to be out of the way so I could take care of some things that needed to be done. I know that's not how you would do it. You have the luxury of just filing a complaint when your feelings get hurt. But out here, it's not so easy."

"Well, you've got it all figured out, don't you? A little kidnapping here, a little collateral damage there. Must make rational lies pretty essential."

Aluerd's expression changed for the first time. He smiled. "Rational lies, rationalize. That's brilliant. It must be nice to have time to sit around thinking up these things. Let me go so I can go back to protecting you and your freedom to spend your days with your nose in a book. I promise you, my team and I will continue to put our lives on the line to guarantee it."

"Sure, and the next time someone gets in your way—what then? Maybe kill them, if that's what you think needs to happen. What about Jordan?"

"Jordan? What do you mean?" Aluerd's voice was tight, strained. He actually sounded surprised.

Damn, he's good. "Jesus, Aluerd. You killed him. Or had him killed. Whatever you want to call it, he's dead."

Aluerd's eyes grew big. "What? Jordan's dead? I've heard nothing."

"Nice try, Aluerd. I'm not an idiot."

"No. You aren't. You wouldn't have gotten this far if you were. You and your brother are obviously very talented. Very smart. You escaped capture and got the drop on me. I must say, it's all very impressive."

The door flung open, and an agent stepped in. He looked at Aluerd, then at Davyn, then slipped a hand behind his back.

Davyn cocked his gun and pointed it at him. "Don't."

The agent put his hands up and Davyn glanced at the gun, trying to catch a glimpse of a safety switch. He had no idea if the gun would even fire, but knew he'd better act like he did.

Aluerd turned his attention to the agent. "What was it you wanted, Agent Williams?"

Williams shot a puzzled look at Davyn. "Uh, we've located Magne."

Aluerd smiled. "Ah, good. We have his brother Davyn to thank for that." He tipped a nod to Davyn. "I don't know why he'd be at your university, but we picked up his location by tracking his earbud."

Davyn knew why, and he knew it wouldn't have happened if he hadn't come to the island. He had to warn him. But first, he had to get out of there.

"Close the door," Davyn said.

The agent turned around, grasped the handle, then ran out the door before Davyn had time to react.

Davyn turned back to Aluerd, who shrugged. "That was unfortunate. My offer still stands. I suggest you take it. They'll be back in force in a moment, and then you'll be out of options."

"I still have evidence on you, Aluerd." Davyn glanced back, looking for an escape route.

"I know. Leo has it, but we have Leo, so..." He said, raising an eyebrow.

Davyn backed up slowly. "Come over here, Aluerd."

"No. You're out of options and I rescind my offer. You should have taken it while you had the chance."

Once his back hit the other door, Davyn eased it open and peered out. There was no one in sight. "Get down on the ground, Aluerd."

Aluerd didn't move. He just stared at Davyn as shouts and

footsteps of men approached. Then he shouted, "Find him and bring him back: dead or alive!"

Davyn winced. He hated clichés.

The tower stairway led to an empty hallway as Davyn raced back down. A quick scan of the perimeter didn't reveal a way out. He glanced over the balcony's edge, peering down five floors to the atrium below. That didn't look like a good option. The area was empty, but men shouting and boots pounding on the steel catwalks above meant he'd better keep moving or it wouldn't be that way for long.

Before he could move, a bullet sliced his ear like a razor. Time froze as all sights and sounds vanished. His heart pounding in his chest drew his attention back to the present, followed by an urgent moment of clarity as he realized what had happened. Fight, flee or freeze. No time to look back. He had to move. Now.

Had it been a tiger or any other apex predator, freezing might have been a good strategy. Freeze and you may not be seen. But it didn't work with armed men. Davyn forced himself into action and ran. Glancing across the balcony to the other side, he made a quick calculation and then dove over the balcony as another gunshot filled the air.

The bullet missed, but he had a new problem. He just dove off a balcony, five stories off the ground, and used the banister to swing around and down to the floor below. But he'd misjudged, and instead of landing on the next floor down, he'd slammed hard into a solid wall. He held tight and kicked with his feet, feeling around for an opening. He looked up to see a gunman reaching over the balcony and steadying his aim. He was a sitting duck. Davyn closed his eyes tight.

A shot rang out. It missed. *Thank god for awkward angles.* Davyn put his legs on the wall, and in a single motion, pushed out and up, pulling with his arms and landing back on to the floor he'd just jumped from.

The gunman stood ten feet away, arms at his side, and smiled. Gun holstered. "I never liked you, Magne. Thanks for the opportunity to kill you." He glanced at the balcony's edge. "Why'd you do that?"

This guy was cold, and clearly toying with him. Davyn needed to buy some time. The two men stared, sizing each other up. The gunman reached down and unsnapped the holster. He held all the cards, and he knew it. He pulled out the gun, raised it, and aligned

Davyn in its sight. He closed one eye as the other hovered just over the barrel. "I could shoot you now."

Davyn tried to channel Magne. He squared his shoulders and forced a smile. At least he thought he did. He could never really tell what his face was doing unless he was looking in a mirror. "That's not very sporting."

"Screw sporting. I might mount your head on a wall."

This guy's a real ass. Davyn considered his options. *Action always beats reaction. What if I charge him? No, he's too far away.*

"I have an idea."

The gunman continued to stare down the barrel, then cocked the hammer back.

Davyn had to act fast. "Hang on," he said, feeling his way through. "I've beat you before."

Davyn didn't know this for sure, but based on this guy's attitude, it was probably true. Baiting him might buy some time to come up with a plan, or maybe a bargain.

The gunman squinted. "Not this time."

Ugh, what an obvious response. This guy's an ass, and he's not very creative.

"You don't want to end it like this. You want to take me out like a man." Davyn cleared his throat. "Like you're a man, I mean."

The gunman sneered. "What do you have in mind?"

Davyn thought for a moment. He needed five strides, maybe more, to reach a spot where he could jump. "Give me ten paces, then you can shoot."

"Ten? I know what you're thinking and I'm not stupid."

Yes you are, but that's beside the point. "Okay, five then."

"How about you run, and I shoot when I'm ready? You're not in a position to bargain, Magne."

Davyn squinted. "Hardly seems fair."

The gunman shrugged.

Davyn saw more agents rounding the corner at the opposite end of the hall. He doubted the gunman would wait before he opened fire, but there was no other option than to jump early and hope it'd be hard to shoot a moving target. He turned, took two steps, then jumped over the railing.

As he dove, a gun blast shattered the silence. He clung to the rail and shimmied toward the opening that had damn well better be where he'd guessed it was. If not, would he die before the fall killed him? His heart pounded, the swish of blood pulsing filled his ears. *No time to think. Just move, man.*

Another blast. This one cut through Davyn's leg. He recoiled as the pain shot up his body. Another shot grazed his arm. His foot slipped on the lip of an opening, but he wasn't close enough. *Almost there.* Another shot grazed his leg. His grip loosened. He was being ripped to pieces. *Last chance.* He kicked out with his good leg and swung, slamming to the floor.

Davyn staggered to his feet. More men at the other end of the hall were heading his way. He leaned on his injured leg, testing it in the hope he could still run. Pain shot up his leg and through his torso. Two shots fired in rapid succession. Davyn ran, but his leg gave out, and he slammed to the floor. Another shot—

He could give up there and just let it end. It felt like that was what was going to happen either way. Another shot cut through his arm. *Hell no, I'm not just going to get shot to pieces.* Gritting his teeth Davyn pulled himself up and ran, zigzagging left and right, making his way for the stairs. His erratic pattern stemmed partly from his injuries, partly from the adrenaline cocktail in his blood, and partly from the desire to make himself a harder target to hit.

Agents swarmed out from the stairs. Out of options again, he flung himself over the balcony edge, plummeting into the floor below. *Can't keep doing that, but there's nowhere else to go.*

Davyn crouched in the woods and peered over a rocky cliff's edge to the east dock below. The cold, damp breeze felt good for the moment, but now that he was outside, he knew he'd cool off quickly. He was still catching his breath from the chase. It wasn't until he slipped out of the building and reached the tree line that he managed to outpace the agents that were pursuing him.

The air was still and quiet, and there was no sign of anyone.

Finally, a break. The glow from the dock lights illuminated steam rising from his sweaty clothes. If the agents didn't take him out, he'd have to worry about hypothermia. The tapping of raindrops descended through the tree canopy, gently washing away the silence. A moment later, he felt the cold sting of them on his face.

Maybe there was something to cover up with on the Zodiac. That was if he could get to it, force himself to get on it, and head out into the open ocean. Short of swimming, that tiny boat was the only way off the island. *One step at a time, buddy.*

Davyn stood up. He winced as stabbing pain shot through his leg and up to his chest. It hurt like hell, but it wasn't bleeding and the improvised antiseptic and bandages on his leg were holding up, at least for the moment.

As he stepped out from the relative protection of the tree line, the sound of what he thought were voices reached his ears. It was hard to tell over the sound of falling rain. He held his position, waiting and listening. After a few minutes, he was sure it was just the sound of rain, but either way he couldn't stay there. He had to get to the university to warn Magne and get him out of there before agents arrived, putting everyone else there in peril, too.

He stepped out from the tree line, took a deep breath, and prepared to run. *Wait.* A sputtering engine made its way toward the dock. Something small. It was the strained, muted whining of an off-road quad. He slipped back into the brush and watched as two armed men drove, weapons drawn, toward the dock.

They stopped their vehicle by a small outbuilding at the dock's entrance and got out to scan the area. Then, they assumed a post—right where Davyn needed to go. They appeared to be talking. Were they discussing him? A movie they saw recently? They gave the distinct impression that it was business as usual. Just another day of hunting a human.

Davyn pushed the thought away as he slipped the rope from the crude sling he'd fashioned from the paracord around his hand and felt through his bag for stones. No time to shape them, he just collected what he could find. He pulled them out and slipped them in his pocket. He'd have felt a lot better if he had the sling and round stones he fashioned at the university, but these would have to do.

Maybe he could take one guy out before the other guy knew what happened. To do that he'd have to get close and be ready to fire again at a moment's notice.

The parallels between his actions and theirs poked at his brain, but they weren't remotely the same. He was just trying to survive. They were hunting him.

He slipped out of the woods and took a deep breath before lowering a leg over the cliff's edge. He reached for a jutting tree root, grabbed hold, and slid the other leg over. His foot hit the cliff's soft slope, sending some sand tumbling below. He instinctively clutched the tree root for stability, but the ground gave way beneath him. He grabbed at anything he could get his hands on: grass, roots, sand. A cascade of sand and rocks plummeted beneath him. Davyn froze as he watched the agents for their reactions. At once, they looked both his way, but did they see him? They stared for too long in his direction. Maybe right at him. He couldn't tell. He remained motionless, trying to slow his breathing. Finally, they looked away and started talking again.

Davyn continued his descent while keeping a close eye on the agents. Eventually he'd be close enough that they'd see him, even in the dark, so he moved as far away as he could on the way. He was almost halfway down the cliff when streams of water gushed from above, covering him and filling his already soaked shoes.

As he neared the bottom of the hill, the agents appeared no wiser to his presence, but the rock fall earlier likely left them on edge. His feet sloshed in his shoes as he touched down on solid ground, and he was prepared to run if spotted. Did the agents really not see him, or were they toying with him?

Davyn crouched down below the brush line and thickets and placed a rock in his sling. He knew that as soon as he started to swing it, the agents would see him or hear it and he'd be an immediate target. He'd have to be ready to move. The rain and the darkness would provide some cover, but a single shot could take him out in an instant. He crouched down on the ground for traction and prepared to fire off a shot.

Two quick swings and Davyn let it fly, then sprinted for the tree line. He didn't have time to look behind to see if he'd hit his target.

His heart raced as he ran as fast as he could, but it was as if he was moving in slow motion, and the tree line didn't look like it was getting any closer.

He swerved left, then right, mimicking the maneuvers of a fleeing prey animal. Unpredictable movements were his only option. He didn't have time to stop and prepare his sling to fire again. He could only run.

Davyn glanced over his shoulder. No one appeared to be following. No one was firing at him. What was going on? He stopped and turned to get a better look. His leg was on fire. He knelt down to get his weight off of it and brushed the rain and sweat from his eyes so he could make out one of the agents standing over a slumped figure. He could only see their silhouettes flanked by the faint glow of the dark grey sky behind them.

Why wasn't the agent firing on him or shouting for backup? The agent knelt down. Was he tending to him? Davyn couldn't tell, but he was, to the best of his knowledge, out of immediate danger. Gratitude bubbled up in his chest, but he quelled it. *Too soon.*

He headed toward the brush near the ocean. He'd seek shelter there while figuring out his next move, and maybe build another sling as a backup. As soon as he reached the brush line, he checked his bandages. The wraps were coming undone, and blood ran down his leg, filling his already soaked shoe. He worked to stem the bleeding, then pulled some salve from his pouch in his bag. It was liquid fire as it spread, but with some luck it would prevent an infection. He reaffixed the wrap as the rain fell around him. He quivered from the cold, or maybe shock—he didn't know which. But he knew he had better keep moving.

He moved along the edge of the scrub brush, keeping it between him and the remaining agent until he was in position to fire another shot. He prepared his sling, ready to take out the remaining agent. He swung, but it snagged on the brushwood. The agent must have heard the sound because he turned to him and raised his gun to fire. The shot whizzed by Davyn as he yanked the sling free and let fly, hitting the agent in the shoulder. Davyn watched as he dropped to his knees. He prepped another stone and fired again, striking him in the face this time. The sickening thud made Davyn gag. The agent slumped over on the dock. Davyn looked up the hill and saw other agents reach the edge and start down the side, moving a lot faster than he could.

Davyn ran down the dock for the Zodiac. The waves crashed against its sides. He stopped and looked out over the churning ocean. The ocean closed in from the east and the agents from the west. He dropped to his knees as his head filled with images of the waves that took him and his brother. Magne's bobbing body as he struggled to stay above the waves that in a short span of time swallowed them both. He closed his eyes as the sound of his pounding heart filled his ears.

But he couldn't let the ocean stop him from warning his brother and the others. He took two deep breaths, letting them out slowly. He'd have to press on before the agents arrived. Their shouts were getting closer. He pulled a leg out from under him and steadied himself. Focusing his attention on the Zodiac boat, he stood up and hobbled the few feet to the vessel, taking a moment to examine it. Who made an inflatable boat? Fine for a pool, but the ocean?

Stay focused. What's next? Start the engine, release the ropes. Focus on the steps. Forget the water.

Davyn stepped into the boat, pulled the keys from the console, and started it. He looked up at the hill. He figured he had just enough time to sabotage the ship next to him. He jumped off the Zodiac and ran up the plank to the ship. As he reached for the door, he heard a splash. The agent that was slumped over on the dock was gone. Davyn looked in the water and saw the agent bobbing up and down in the swells.

Shit. Do I just leave him there? He was trying to kill me.

The agents on the hill had reached the bottom of it. The fallen agent was too far away to reach, even from the dock. He'd need something to pull him in. He looked around and pulled a grab tool from inside the ship. He returned to the agent and used it to snag his collar and haul him on to the dock. The other agents were almost on him. He turned the one he'd rescued on to his stomach. Hopefully, the other agents knew CPR.

There was no time to sabotage the ship now. Davyn ran back for the Zodiac as the agents closed in. He pulled the ropes free, revved the engine, and threw it into drive. The boat jerked forward, then raced into the crashing waves. Gunshots rang out around him and he ducked for cover, peering over the console as the boat rode further out to sea.

The waves pushed hard, and he felt the boat slam down as he pushed through each onslaught. One of its running lights exploded as shots ricocheted off the Zodiac. He stayed low and maneuvered the boat until the gunfire finally ceased.

As the waves grew smaller further from shore, Davyn looked back and saw the lights from the ship come on. He killed his boat's remaining running lights and pushed the throttle to full. He'd have to once again count on the cloak of darkness to provide some cover as he headed into the gathering storm.

The rain stopped, but the night sky was still overcast. Davyn had no way to confirm that he was heading in the right direction. If he could see the stars, or at least the right ones, he could orient himself and head west, toward land. If he went east, he'd find nothing but open ocean, and would eventually run out of gas. He ducked behind the boat's windshield to seek some shelter from the cold, cutting wind. On the bright side, there was no sign of the other boat.

He pulled the blanket he'd found tightly around him: a moment of warmth and calm. He took a few deep, slow breaths and pushed his darker thoughts aside. There'd be time later to ruminate on those. For a few short minutes, he'd focus on quieting his mind and replenishing his soul.

A crash, then a relentless buzzing jerked him out of his short reprieve. *What the hell was that?* The sound was coming from the back of the boat. Davyn reached over and pulled the throttle back, idling the engine. The Zodiac slowed abruptly and stopped. He worked his way to the back.

The buzzing sound had stopped, too, but now he smelled gas. He checked the tank cap. It was closed tight. Davyn looked out at the water and his heart raced. Everywhere he looked was inky black, rolling sea. He shifted his gaze to the night sky, hoping for a break in the clouds, and that he could orient himself, but it was just a muddle of grays.

At least the sky was brighter in the direction he was headed. It was too late in the evening to be the remnants of the setting sun, so he hoped it was light from the mainland's coast. Still, it would be nice to see some stars to confirm it.

He shifted his focus back to the buzzing sound. What would cause that? He saw nothing obvious, so he worked his way to the throttle and pushed it forward. The buzzing got louder as he sped up. He pulled the throttle back and slowed. As the boat crept across the water, he worked his way to the back. The water level in the boat was higher than it was just a few moments earlier. Was it coming in over the sides? He grabbed the side of the inflatable boat and squeezed. It crumpled in his hand. Not good. He tried it on the opposite side. Hard as rock. *Oh boy.*

It must have taken a bullet—and the gas smell? He lurched forward at the helm and peered at the gas gauge. It was less than half full. It shouldn't have been so low. There must have been a leak in the gas tank. *Think. Is there anything that could cause a spark?* He looked around. *Just a—crap—combustion engine.* He idled the boat and shut off the engine.

Still no sign of the ship at least. He considered his options. Stop and try to repair the leak, or keep moving? The boat would sink, but maybe he could make land before it did. Or, maybe he'd run out of fuel. *Or maybe I'm heading in the wrong direction and nothing I do at this point matters.* Davyn's soul seemed to drain right out of his feet, mixing into the slimy water in the boat. *You're probably better off there than where you were. It's hopeless.* He sat at the back of the boat and watched the water swell around him. It was calm, quiet.

The boat rocked harder, sending Davyn forward to land on his face and covering him in a mix of seawater, dirt and gasoline. *What now?* Davyn got up on his knees and looked around. Either the boat hit something in the water, or something hit the boat, and he wasn't sure he wanted to know which it was. He got to his feet, reached over, and hit the ignition to start the engine. It rumbled, but faltered. Something bumped the underside of the boat.

Predators could sense when prey was injured and weak. He looked down at his bloodstained leg and adjusted the bandage. The wound would need attention, but he had more immediate concerns. The only weapon he had—the sling—wouldn't help him now.

Davyn lowered his head and looked at the water. He grimaced. Thoughts of drowning filled his head. Of Magne struggling to stay above water. He forced himself back to the present. He looked out at the grey mist on the horizon and considered trying to start the engine again, but didn't want to draw the attention of whatever was beneath the boat. Maybe it would find some other sea creature in distress or get bored and move on. He could only sit quietly and wait.

Davyn jerked awake as water from the boat splashed in his mouth. He gagged and spit as he sprung up to a sitting position. The water was up to his waist now; the boat was sinking. His heart raced as panic sunk in. As he got to his feet, the boat gave way beneath him, dipping beneath each step.

He tried to focus, but knew only one thing for sure. Panicking was the pathway to doom. He stopped and assessed his surroundings.

The fog wasn't as thick as before, but there was still no sign of land. He glanced at his watch. It was almost eleven o'clock. He'd been unconscious for more than an hour. The ship hadn't made an appearance. He wanted to think that was good news, but it would have followed him west, toward land. Maybe he'd drifted off course. He looked up at the sky. Still overcast, with no visible stars. He waded over to the engine. Maybe he could find the gas leak and stem it. But the boat was losing air and that would need attention first. He'd need to feel around for the leak, but that meant putting his hand in the water and that might draw the attention of whatever was hitting the boat earlier? He didn't want to admit it, but it was likely a shark. Or sharks. What else could it be?

Maybe if I get the engine running, I can make land before it deflates. Davyn lifted the cover off the engine and scanned it for signs of damage. Nothing. He considered the angle that the gun-shots would have come from and followed the hoses down to the waterline.

He had to reach in, but hesitated. The image of his hand going in the water and straight into a shark's mouth popped to mind. He never should have watched the movie *Jaws*.

He leaned back, resting his arms on his bent knees. *Damnit. I can't just sit here. I'll end up in the water anyway.* He put his hand on the hose and followed it down, splashing water as he went. *Just ignore it, sharks. It's not a fishy.* The fuel line was smooth except— there. A rough spot, but he couldn't tell if it was the fuel line or the engine casing. He grabbed a roll of duct tape from the console and set it aside. Putting tape on under water wouldn't work. He'd have to focus on patching the hole in the boat.

As he leaned on the side of the boat, it collapsed beneath him and plunged him headlong into the freezing water. The icy water enveloped him like a million stabbing needles. He forced his way to the surface and grabbed the boat's side, but as he pulled, it sank and sent more water rushing in. The back of the boat was now under water, bobbing like a dead fish. He'd have to stay in the water and make his way to the front.

As he kicked his legs, it immediately brought to mind that scene in the movie. *Don't think about* Jaws. *Not now.* He worked his way past the engine. *Stay focused. You can do this. Stay calm, keep moving. What the—*

Something bumped his leg. He latched onto the boat's side, but as he squeezed it into a choke hold, the boat gave way, dunking him back in the water. The sides wouldn't hold him; he needed to get to the bow.

He swung his arms one over the other as fast as he could and kicked his way to the bow, then pulled himself up. The boat held, but he couldn't make it in over the side. He tried again. This time he hung in space for a moment before plummeting back into the water. *Come on, man.* He paused for a moment to gain his strength then tried again. His arms burned, but he managed to get his good leg up and flung it over the boat's side. The boat shuddered as he slid back to the water, but he forced himself forward and dragged his other leg up until he collapsed into the bow.

As the front of the boat settled under his weight, he lay motion-less and caught his breath. The grimy water in the boat was even higher than before and the boat would sink soon. What then? But what more could he do? He couldn't stem the water's advance and the engine wouldn't start.

What would Magne do? Davyn lay in the water as it rose around him. *Let's be honest. He'd drown with me. It's hopeless.* He thought back to how he'd escaped the gunmen, how he'd even rescued one. *But now Magne and everyone at the university are at risk and it's my fault. I never should have gone to the island. How could I come so far and fail?*

Davyn gazed up at the grey sky. The clouds were parting. The cold was gone, and he felt warm. Peaceful. He'd done all he could. There was nothing left to do but sink slowly. He stopped worry-ing about the sharks, the water. He was at peace. He looked up at the sky and watched the light pole sway slowly back and forth in a rhythmic motion. It glimmered as the light from the stars bounced off it. The stars were out now, but it was too late.

A bright light reflected in the globe at the pole's tip. *The moon must be out now, too.* He closed his eyes and waited for the inev-itable. *Wait—it's a new moon. What's that light?* Davyn shot up to a sitting position and looked out at the horizon. Lights from the mainland. *Holy shit!* He squinted. It couldn't be more than three miles off. He looked up and down the shoreline. *I've come this far. I bested those agents. I got on to this ridiculous tiny boat and crossed an ocean. I can do this.*

How quickly his thoughts veered from drowning to survival as he grabbed a tactical knife from the console and used the duct tape to fix it to his upper arm. If a shark attacked now, it would have to earn its meal, because he wasn't going down without a fight. Not now.

He looked out at the water. A boat's running lights cut through the thinning fog. He squinted. Two lights, a space and another light. It was Aluerd's ship, headed right toward him.

Davyn grabbed his sling and used it to tie his flashlight to the mast. *You want this boat? You can have it.* He turned the flashlight on, took a deep breath, and slipped into the water and swam for shore. The boat's engine grew louder. *No time to stop and look. Just keep swimming.*

He'd be there soon if he wasn't spotted. Out of the corner of his eye, a light cut across the water. They'd spotted the boat. *Tell ya what, fellas. You head for my crappy sinking boat while I make my way for shore.* A search light crossed the water again, closer to him, so he dove and stayed under as long as he could, then broke the surface.

He gazed back at Aluerd's boat. The men stood on deck, talking as they looked out at the water. Davyn stayed low, his eyes just above the surface. His foot kicked something. He pulled the knife from his arm, unfolded it, and went under again. His leg hit something solid. It was land.

He continued toward shore, swimming underwater and surfacing briefly to get air, then heading back down out of sight. He clenched the knife in his hand until his chest bumped against the sand. He raised his head above the water's surface, facing the ship and watched as it bobbed up and down in the distance. They hadn't spotted him. Not yet.

Still warm from the long swim, Davyn knew he would cool off fast in the cold night air and should get out and dry himself, but he couldn't do it just then. The water provided cover, and they'd see his movement against the sand on the beach if he made a break for it. Instead, he stayed low and watched. The ship's engine roared as it made for the shore.

The sand squeezed between Davyn's toes as he walked up the beach. It was good to be on land. The air was cold, but he was still hot from the exertion of swimming almost three miles. He'd have to find some shelter and dry off soon, though. As he got out of the water, he noticed headlights cutting through the dunes from the parking lot. He veered for the cover of the woods. There was no way of knowing where the agents were or if they had radioed others his whereabouts.

As he approached the woods, the car door swung open and a woman's voice called out. "Davyn!"

He dove into the woods and peered out at the figure on the beach, walking straight for him.

"Davyn," the voice called again. The light from the parking lot was enough to highlight her silhouette. "Davyn, it's Leo."

He stayed quiet and watched, just to be safe. She appeared to be alone, but there was no way to be sure. The figure kept looking at her phone. She tapped the screen and Davyn heard a blip in his earpiece.

"Davyn, did you hear that? It's me, Leo."

It sounded like her, but—

"Take off your hood," he whispered.

The figure lowered her hood, still peering into the woods. It was Leo, all right. No mistaking the outline of that hair. Davyn stepped out and she immediately rushed him.

"Davyn, thank god you're safe." She threw her arms around him and gave him a big hug. "Ugh, you're wet."

He looked down at her and smiled. "Yeah, the ocean's wet."

"And you smell like gasoline. Yuck." She took a step back and looked him up and down, her lip curled with disgust.

He smirked. "I'm glad you're safe, too. I thought they'd kidnapped you."

She pinned her hair back; even then it was wild, but Davyn liked it. "They tried. Now let's get you into some dry clothes." She started back toward the car.

He hobbled after her. "Magne's at the university. Have you spoken with him?"

Leo stopped and turned to him. "What university?"

"My university."

"What the hell is he doing there?"

"How should I know?" He paused. "Aluerd and his men followed me here. I saw their ship just offshore. They'll be heading there next."

"Are you sure it was him?"

"Yeah, I saw the ship." He paused. "I saw the agents and recognized one of the men, but I didn't see Aluerd, now that I think of it."

"I'll drive, you try to call the university and get a hold of Magne."

Davyn struggled to keep up, but his leg was on fire and wasn't cooperating.

Leo turned back to him. "Come on, we're in a hurry."

"It's my leg."

"Let me see." Leo waited while he reached down and pulled up his torn pant leg.

"Oh my god, what happened?"

"It's a long story."

"I have a first aid kit in the car that's provisioned better than most walk-in clinics. And there are some of your clothes in the trunk. You can change, and I'll have a look at it. Your ear needs some attention, too. It's just up here. Take it slow."

Davyn limped up to the car, and Leo opened the trunk so he could get to his bag and pull out some clothes. He peeled off his shirt. "I hope you have aspirin." Leo turned away as Davyn proceeded to change. "Oh my god, this feels good." He opened the passenger side door and got in.

Leo came around to his side. "I know you just put them on, but pull down your pants. I have to clean up that leg."

"But we have to get to the university."

"It can wait ten minutes. You could develop an infection. Maybe gangrene."

Davyn shook his head and unzipped his pants, then pulled them down around his ankles.

Leo laughed. "Ooh, nice boxers."

"I know," he said with uncharacteristic enthusiasm. "Max picked these out for me. Nice, right?"

Leo leaned back and made a face. "Did you just sort of make a joke?"

"Huh, I guess I did. Anyway..."

"Hmm?"

"Dress the leg. We have to go." Davyn grabbed the bandage and unwound it until it was off. Blood oozed out from the wounds.

Leo's eyes grew big. "Did you get shot?"

"Good eye."

"Yeah, I see the entry and exit wounds. It looks clean, though.

No sign of infection. What did you put on it?"

"An herb in the pyrola family. It grows on the island, and—"

"Mhmm." She pulled his leg to the side and out of the car. "Watch the leather."

A hot sting shot up his leg and he grimaced. "Sorry."

She placed a bandage on his leg and put his hand over it. "Hold this tight. I'm going to have to sew it up."

Davyn pressed down on the bandage and took a deep breath. His palm warmed as blood soaked through the material.

"On the count of three, you lift it off the top but keep pressure on the bottom. Ready?" Without waiting for Leo's count, Davyn lifted the bandage. "Okay, we'll just do this then." She wiped the wound and pushed the skin together. Davyn's head shot backward and his eyes clenched shut as he shook a fist with his free hand. "Hang in there. It looks pretty good, considering."

Davyn let out a breath. "You can hold the commentary 'til later," he said, his voice straining.

Leo pierced his skin with a needle and pulled a long black thread through. "Seriously, though. This could have been a lot worse."

Davyn leaned back, bit his lip, and let a "mm-hmm" escape.

"There, there. Almost done." Leo pulled the needle through a few more times and wiped the wound. She smiled at him. "All done."

He let out a long breath.

"Now the bottom. Ready?"

Davyn shook his head. "Give me a second."

She leaned back and drew a breath. "Okay. There's water in the console. You should drink some."

He grabbed the bottle, then leaned forward to examine the stitches. "Where'd you learn to do this?"

"I trained as a field agent before I moved to support."

"There's story there, I'm sure. You'll have to tell me sometime." He adjusted his position and leaned back. "Okay, let's get this over with."

A few minutes later, Leo put the finishing touches on his leg and wrapped it up. "Okay, it's done."

Davyn leaned forward and looked at it. "I wish I knew Lily's phone number. I've never had to call her before." He gazed out at the ocean. "She always just shows up when I need her."

Leo nodded. "Let's get you there. We can figure out how to reach her on the way." She lifted his leg and eased it into the car and patted his shoulder.

"I can call the library." He looked at his watch. "It's closed now, but tomorrow's Tuesday... Mrs. Dawit comes in at eight. Lily and Bukka will arrive at around nine."

Leo smiled knowingly at him. He glanced away for a moment, then mustered the courage to look back. Leo blinked twice and shut the door, then came around to the driver's side and got in.

He cleared his throat. "I mean, probably nine. Nine-ish, maybe."

"It's okay, Davyn. Caring's not a crime." She threw the car in to drive and sped off for the university.

CHAPTER 20

Leo turned into the university parking lot and hit the brakes, jerking to a stop in the first spot she saw. Davyn's body lurched forward, waking him with a jolt as he snapped back to a sitting position. Still groggy, he gazed out at the campus. The warm sunlight slipped over the horizon through the morning mist, giving it an otherworldly feel—like a setting in a storybook. It all looked very quaint, the rustic campus nestled snugly in the autumn woods.

"Sorry, I didn't mean to stop that hard."

Davyn patted his chest, looking for his pocket watch. "What time is it?"

Leo adjusted the rearview mirror and primped her hair. "Check your wrist."

Davyn's eyes shot to his watch. "Just after seven. If Magne's on campus, he could be anywhere. We should start at the library."

He unlatched his seat belt and gingerly got out of the car.

Leo leaned over the center console and looked up at him. "We should split up and look separately. We'll cover more ground that way."

"Yeah, good idea. The library's that big brick building," he said, pointing. "You start there. I'll look in my office." He gestured with his head. "It's in that that stone building over there."

Leo stepped out of the car and stretched. "I see it. I'll call you on the earpiece if I find anything."

She headed for the library and Davyn started off toward his office. As he passed one of his students, he looked at him like he'd just seen a ghost.

That's weird. Davyn stopped him. "Hey, everything okay?"

"Uh, hi, professor. Sorry, I uh—nothing." He shook his head.

"What is it?"

"It's just—I thought I just saw you upstairs."

"Where?" Davyn snapped back.

"Uh, no, I mean, I thought it was you, but it couldn't have been, right?"

Davyn let out a small laugh. "No, no, obviously it wasn't." He peered at the building, then back at the student. "Uh, second floor?" The student nodded and Davyn slapped the student's arm. "Thanks," he said, then ran off, hopefully to where he'd find Magne.

He flung the door wide and jogged up the two flights of stairs before stepping out into the hallway. Lily was walking his way with her head down, unaware of his presence. It was good to see a familiar face. She stopped and stepped into his office.

Davyn walked over to his office door and stopped to peer through the window. Lily gathered some papers from her desk. Davyn's eyes moved around the room. No sign of Magne. Maybe Lily had seen him. It was all so familiar, yet strange at the same time. Like going to your childhood home as an adult and getting that feeling that everything seemed smaller than it once was. He turned the handle and pushed the door open.

Lily looked up from her desk. "Professor?"

"Hi, Lily." Davyn stood in the doorway, arms dangling at his sides, unsure what to expect. He'd been gone for almost a week. Who knew what had transpired in his absence? The idea of stepping back into his life seemed comforting, terrifying and foreign all at once. Like putting on a baseball glove that fit perfectly in junior high, an extension of his hand. But now it felt stiff and small.

"Professor, are you alright? You look a thousand miles away. Not that that would be unusual for—"

"Yes, I'm fine."

Lily nodded. "So, did you forget something?"

The chest where he kept his tools was open. *That's strange.*

"Professor?"

He shifted his focus back to Lily. "I was just going to grab some things before class begins." He glanced back at the open chest.

"Did you change your shirt?"

Davyn put his hand on his chest and looked down at what he was wearing. "Um, yes. I, uh, spilled coffee." Davyn grimaced. *Whoops, that's a Magne thing.*

"Oh, you're drinking coffee now?" She looked him up and down. "I don't blame you. I couldn't live without it myself. Speaking of coffee, thanks for the gift cards. Bukka and I used one last night."

Magne must have given them to her. That's fine. I don't use them anyway. That's Magne for you. Always helping somebody out.

She squinted and scanned his face. "You got your eyebrows done again? I guess I didn't notice earlier."

"Earlier? Today?"

Lily cocked her head. "Yes. Just before."

"Lily, just before, when? When did you see me last?"

Lily's eyebrows rose. "When you were here. You remember. I know you're always deep in thought, but honestly, professor, you worry me sometimes."

"Lily, where was I heading?"

Lily snorted a laugh, amused until she realized Davyn was still looking intently at her. "Oh, you're serious." She scratched her head. "I don't know, you didn't say. Um, well, where *did* you go?"

Davyn turned to the open chest against the wall. "Lily, where are my hunting tools?"

Lily's brows furrowed. "Professor, you left them in the lecture hall. Last night..."

Why would Magne bring my hunting tools to the lecture hall?

"Look, Lily, I know this will sound strange, but did I teach a class last night?"

"Of course you did. It went very well, too," she said with a broad smile that evaporated when she saw him just standing there, staring at his things. She crinkled her nose. "Um, anything else?"

Davyn needed to get to the lecture room and grab his hunting weapons, so he was at least armed with something. Magne might be there, too. He stepped over to Lily and put his hand on her arm, looking her in the eyes. "Lily, I want you to find Bukka and I want you both to get off campus right away."

Her eyes opened wide. "Why? Is something bad going to happen?"

"I can't get into why right now. Just promise me you'll do it."

Lily looked in his eyes and shook her head slowly.

"Lily, promise me."

"What about my friends? If something's going to happen—what about Professor Anne, and the others? Should we evacuate the campus?" The pitch of her voice rose with each question.

It dawned on Davyn that this wasn't going to work. *Mrs. Dawit would never listen to Lily telling her to leave work without an explanation. Same for Anne.* His best bet was to find Magne and for both of them to get the hell out of there.

Davyn tried his best to recover, even forced what might have passed for a real smile. "Whoa, hey, that's not what I meant. I meant you should go out on a date. Get off campus. It'll, uh, do you both good."

Lily let out a breath. "Professor, you scared me. That was a really bad way to phrase that."

Davyn's eyes darted back and forth. She was right. It was a clumsy recovery, but with Lily it would probably work just fine. *She thinks I'm weird, anyway.*

As soon as she was on her way, he turned and ran out the door, headed for the lecture hall. When he arrived, Anne Throp was just stepping out. *Oh boy.*

"Hi, Anne," he said, flashing a sheepish smile as he recalled their last awkward encounter. He held the door for her, but his attention was on where he was headed.

Then she stopped in front of him. He glanced up the hall then back to her.

"So, have you decided where we're going on our next date?" she asked.

Davyn looked at her like a deer in headlights. His eyes darted around as he tried to summon a response, but drew a blank. His awkward porcupine suit was feeling less useful as he cast an awkward smile. "Um, yes, but it's a surprise."

Anne didn't seem bothered by his clumsy response. Her focus had shifted, and she squinted as she examined his face. "Hey, did you get your eyebrows done again?"

Davyn ran a finger along his brow and scrunched his nose, responding like a little boy who had just gotten a haircut.

Anne put her hand on his face and smiled. His first instinct was to pull back, but her hand was warm, and her eyes smiled at him. Her mouth, too. *She's really lovely.*

"They look very nice." She cocked her head. "Frankly, I'm a little partial to your old look, but you look very handsome this way, too."

Davyn gazed in her eyes. "You liked the way I looked before?"

She nodded.

"Me, too." He grinned and tried to think of something else to say. "They'll grow back. Um, I have to run."

"Too bad. See you later."

"Yep, see you later," he said with uncharacteristic enthusiasm as he dashed off into the lecture hall.

Davyn didn't know what had happened, but he was glad to be back in Anne's good graces. Then it dawned on him. *Magne's back to being a fixer.* Davyn used to welcome it, but now—he rounded a corner and stopped. Dean Puddington was speaking with a colleague. Davyn tried to slip past them unnoticed, but Mr. Puddington excused himself and stopped him.

"Davyn, good to see you." Puddington appeared uncharacteristically upbeat. *What's this about?*

"Good to see you too, sir."

He pulled Davyn aside and whispered. "If you keep teaching your class like you did yesterday—well, let's just say it'll go a long way in getting you that promotion."

Davyn nodded as the dean beamed at him. "Great, that's the way I plan to, uh, to do that, going forward..." The dean furrowed his brow and Davyn gestured up the hall with his head. "I'm sorry, I'm in a bit of a rush."

The dean squinted. "Did you get your eyebrows done?"

Davyn put a finger on his brow and looked away. "Um, yes," he said, thinking of what Anne said earlier. "They'll grow back, though."

No time to chat. Time was running out, and he had to find Magne before the agents did. Davyn quickly waved, then turned and ran for the lecture hall.

When he turned a corner, Davyn saw Leo heading into the lecture room. He jogged to the doorway but stopped before entering. *What if Magne's there? How will he react? How will I react?* He stood just outside the doorway and listened.

Leo said, "Magne, thank god."

"Leo? What on earth are you doing here? Where's Davyn?"

"Davyn's here on campus. We've been looking for you, to warn you. Aluerd's agents are on their way."

It was quiet for a moment.

"Then you and I need to leave."

"Magne, no. They'll think Davyn is you."

"Oh, right. Duh. Hmm. Well then, you and Davyn get out of here and I'll wait for the agents."

That was enough to spur Davyn through the doorway.

"No, Magne. We all need to leave together."

There was no time to think, to process before Magne ran across the room and grabbed him into a bear hug. Davyn was stiff and didn't reciprocate. Magne let go and took a step back.

"Baby brother," he said, looking him up and down. "You look great," he added, much like a salesman pitching some new product. "My god, you look like me!" Magne laughed and slapped Davyn's arm.

A thousand thoughts raced through Davyn's head, but all he said was, "Where are my weapons?"

Magne cocked his head. "What?"

"My weapons. Lily said you brought them here."

Magne scratched the back of his head. "Uh, well. They're on the table." He pointed across the room. "Honestly, I thought you'd be a little happier to see me."

Davyn glanced over at the sheet-covered table. "I've got mixed feelings." He walked over and drew the sheet back.

Leo bit her bottom lip and glanced at Magne. Both appeared a little taken aback by Davyn's reaction.

"You can't just leave them," Davyn shouted. He looked down at the table, realizing how that must have sounded. But he had every right to be mad. He picked up the atlatl, cradling it in his arms like a lifeline.

Magne looked to Leo as if seeking guidance, but she seemed as lost as he did.

Davyn set the atlatl down and made his way around the table, inspecting each of the tools.

Magne took a step toward him. "Look, little brother, obviously we have a lot to discuss."

Davyn glared at Magne, then shifted his gaze to Leo and took a deep breath, letting it out slowly as he looked away. "I put a lot of effort and care into making these. You should be more careful."

Magne gave a slow nod and cleared his throat. "You're right, Davyn. I'm sorry."

Davyn continued his slow walk around the table. Magne always knew exactly what to say, but now, for once, he seemed to be at a loss for words.

"I did cover them... And I locked the room. They were safe," he said, gesturing at the door with his head.

Leo flashed a quick sympathetic smile at Magne, then walked over to Davyn and put her hand on his arm. Davyn glanced at her hand and, for once, didn't pull away. "You and Magne have a lot to talk about," she said, her tone soft. "But right now we need to focus on Aluerd and his men."

She was right. The conversation could wait. They needed to get out of there. Davyn lifted his eyes to hers and nodded.

Magne shifted his attention to the field outside. "Leo, do we have any idea what weapons they have?"

"No, but so far they've used nonlethal force."

"Nonlethal?" Davyn said, tapping the atlatl against his hand. "Someone should have told that to the agents who shot me."

Magne glanced wide-eyed at Davyn, then at Leo. "What?"

Leo stared at the floor. "Let's just say that your plan didn't go as expected—not by a long shot."

Magne watched Davyn for a reaction, but none came. "Well, you must tell me about that sometime," he said as he headed for the exterior door.

Davyn picked up a small arrowhead and put the sling in his pocket along with some rocks. "Where are you going?"

"We need to get out of here, out of this room. They'll end up coming this way and it'll be filled with students soon." Magne glanced at the weapons on the table. "We don't have any good options. We need to get out of here before agents arrive, and we have to assume that they may already be here."

Leo put a hand up. "Hang on, who still has their earpiece?"

Magne raised his hand. Davyn covered his ear with his hand. "Mine's good."

Leo extended her hand. "Let's have 'em."

An airburst followed by a clang drew Davyn's attention to the door as an agent stepped in, his arm extended with a gun pointed at Magne. Magne dropped behind the podium as the agent fired again. Davyn pulled a rock from his pocket and threw it, hitting the agent directly in the back of the head. The blow sent him to the floor, spilling his gun right in front of Magne, who wasted no time reaching out and grabbing it.

Wow, that couldn't have played out better if I'd planned it. Davyn was shocked but played it cool, walking over to the fallen agent. "You can use the gun," he said. Magne looked at Leo, as if expecting an explanation, but she just shrugged. Davyn pulled out a packet of darts from one of the agent's pockets, opened it, removed four, and, without looking at him, extended the pack to Magne. Magne's mouth dropped open, but Davyn just continued rifling through the agent's other pockets and shook the pack of darts at Magne.

Leo ran to the door and assumed a defensive position as she peered down the hallway. "It's clear."

"Okay, now I have a gun, but what about you?" Magne laughed as Davyn shook his atlatl. "You can't use that."

"I'm a lot more practiced with this than I am with a gun," Davyn pointed out. "And I just took out an agent with a rock. Don't presume to know so much."

Leo shrugged when Magne looked to her. "Hard to argue with that." She fixed her gaze back on the hallway. "Put your earpieces on the table."

Davyn reached up to remove his. "Why do you want them?"

"Cover me," she said to Magne, then picked up the earpieces, sat down and splayed them on the desk in front of her.

Davyn watched her, and Magne answered his question as he stared up the hallway. "She's re-syncing them."

They say it's a twin thing. Magne had a habit of answering questions sometimes even before Davyn asked them. Funny thing was, it only worked one way with them. It was not a skill Davyn possessed, at least not since he was very young. It was a function related to empathy. Something Magne was simply better at.

"It'll only take her a minute." Magne turned to him. "Hey, Davyn?"

Ugh, can we talk about this later? Sadly, Magne's mind reading trick never seemed to work when Davyn needed some personal space. Davyn kept his attention on Leo, hoping his twin would get the message.

"I swear, I thought you'd be glad-handing investors at black tie fundraisers. I had no idea you'd be in any danger." Magne cleared his throat. "And I want you to know that the decision to leave, to serve—it wasn't easy."

Davyn put his hand up to silence him. Now wasn't the time. "I'm sure."

Magne sighed. "How's it going, Leo?"

"I'm done." She collected the earpieces and handed them out.

Davyn slipped his in. "Test, test."

Magne shook his head.

"I don't hear you, Davyn." Leo looked at Magne. "Can you hear me?"

Magne shook his head. "What's wrong with them?"

"I don't know. I'm starting to think the equipment Aluerd's been provisioning is funky."

"Funky?"

"We don't have time to troubleshoot them. We have to go." She picked up her bag and stood, ready to leave.

Magne looked out the window. "We need to get off campus. How did you guys get here?"

"I drove. My car's in the lot by the entrance. Now we just have to get there without being seen."

Davyn side-eyed her. "Or shot."

Magne tucked the pistol in his pants. "Davyn, what's the best way to get to the car without being seen?"

Davyn pointed out the window. "We'll head to the woods, just over there. It's only about 175 meters. Once we're out there, we'll have some cover and we can head south toward the park. It should be empty now, so we can take the path from there to the parking lot."

Leo threw her bag over her shoulder. "If we get split up, we'll meet at my car in the south lot. Magne knows what it looks like."

Magne cracked the door. "Okay, everyone stay low and keep sharp."

Davyn leaned over to Leo and whispered, "Does he talk to the other agents this way?"

Leo shushed him.

Magne stepped out and assumed a defensive position. "I'll make a beeline for the woods. Once I get there, I'll take a position to cover you and the two of you follow."

Davyn watched as Magne sprinted for the woods. He thought back to his own mad dash on the beach, how it felt during those moments, when he was just waiting to be shot. His stomach sank, and he wished he was nicer to Magne when he first saw him, especially after being apart for so long. *He's fast. I wonder if he still runs. I should have asked.*

He reached the woods and crouched by a tree, peering out over the field, gun ready. Davyn doubted the dart gun had enough range to cover them the entire way. He looked around for any sign of enemy agents.

"Okay, he's in position. Are you ready?"

Davyn nodded, and they dashed through the field. It was a newly familiar and unsettling feeling, this sense of being prey. It always seemed more sportsmanlike when he was the hunter, but running and just being picked off by a sniper—surely it was different because he used primitive weapons. Right?

A few minutes later they reached the parking lot and headed for Leo's car.

Leo caught her breath. "That wasn't too bad, and I don't think anyone saw us."

Davyn kept an eye out for signs of trouble as they approached the car and glanced at his watch. "We're getting out at a good time. The campus will be crawling with people soon."

Magne reached for the car door handle. "Once we get a good distance from the campus, we can stop, get a burner phone, and call the chief."

Leo came around to the driver's side and looked down at her front tire. "Uh, Magne, we have a problem."

He walked around the car. "Don't tell me you have a flat."

They all stared at the rhino-booted tire.

Davyn scratched his jaw. "No sticker. We should have parked in the visitor lot." He looked around for a guard. "Well, I guess we'll have to make a stop at the security office."

"Where's that?"

"In the library's basement."

It was clear from Magne's expression he didn't think that was a good idea.

"We don't have to go into the library. There are exterior stairs in the back that lead down to the security office. We'll make our way back the way we came." He paused for a moment. "The woods head east when we get close to the library. We'll have to cut across a field and then walk on campus for a bit."

"Well, baby brother, we'll have to split up when we get to that point. We can't be seen together."

"I hardly think that matters now."

Magne smiled. "Ah, but it does. While you were off on your adventures, I was back here getting your life straightened out."

Davyn had an idea of what he meant, but wanted to hear him say it. "What do you mean?"

"Well, I gave a very impressive classroom performance for your dean or whatever he is. Uh, Puddington. So your promotion's looking good. And I also made a very favorable impression on Anne Throp for you," he said with a laugh. "You've already got your first date out of the way."

Just like in high school: Mr. Perfect, always helping others. Well, that explains Puddington's exuberance earlier. And Anne's question about a second date. Davyn didn't respond, but Magne seemed pretty pleased with himself.

"You know," Magne said, still chuckling. "When you add 'Miss' in front of her full name, it sounds like—"

"Yes. I know," Davyn said, shaking his head. "We better get going." He turned and headed back for the woods.

Magne followed. "What, no thank you?"

CHAPTER 21

As they arrived at the edge of the woods, Davyn peered down the small, grassy hill at the library. The campus was getting busy with students and faculty. Some were strolling, others rushing. Some sat on benches or stood in groups and talked among the trees and neatly mowed lawns. He'd never seen the campus from this perspective. Not just the broad bird's-eye view he had now, but from any perspective other than the narrow view of the sidewalk in front of him as he moved from isolated room to isolated room. Everyone appeared to be enjoying themselves.

Davyn might have tried to take a moment to reflect on it, but if they didn't get out of there before the agents arrived, the setting might not stay so nice.

"There's no reason for you two to come with me," Leo said. "Lie low here. I'll go down and get the car sorted. Watch for me to come out, and I'll head back to the car and meet you there."

Magne handed the tranquilizer gun to Leo. "Take this, just in case."

Leo stepped out of the woods and descended the hill. Davyn kept his eyes peeled for any sign of trouble as she made her way along the sidewalk toward the library.

"Does anything look amiss? Do you see anyone that you don't recognize?" Magne asked.

Davyn shook his head. "I wouldn't know. I've never really paid attention."

Magne's eyes narrowed. "Do you think things will be different for you now that—well, now that you know I'm okay?"

"It's hard to say," was all he could think of as a response. He was still processing it all, and to say there was a lot to process would be putting it mildly. *My brother's dead. He's alive. He betrayed me and put my life at risk. He didn't know he was putting my life at risk.* It felt like being sprayed with a fire hose.

Magne offered a sympathetic nod. Not what Davyn was looking for. Time and space to process would have been the ticket, but Magne looked as though he was getting ready to frame everything that had happened in a way that made sense and would make everything okay. Somehow he always did, but Davyn wasn't up for it.

"Davyn, when the agency approached me, I felt an obligation, a duty, to serve my country—to do my part. To do something, anything, to stop these people who were attacking us, Mom and Dad, our family."

He had to mention Mom and Dad. Bugger. Fine, we'll go there.

"I get it, Magne. But you could have said something. Maybe let me know you weren't dead. A note. Something."

"No. I couldn't. I had to cut off ties with everyone I knew. Any communication between my old life and this one would put the mission, and the people I cared about most, at risk."

"You could have let me know you were alright, then cut off communication. I thought you drowned trying to rescue me." Davyn's voice rose. He glanced down at the bustling campus and lowered his tone. "My last memory before I blacked out was you trying to keep me afloat. Of you sinking below the water. When I woke up on the beach, I thought you saved me and that you drowned. I thought it was my fault."

Magne took a deep breath. "I'm sorry, Davyn, I didn't know. The agents that were scouting me, they saved us both."

They fell silent and watched the scene below.

Magne stood up to stretch. "We should see Leo with someone from security soon, right?" He narrowed his eyes. "Do they carry guns here?"

"What?"

"Campus security. Do they carry guns?"

"I don't know. Maybe."

"How do you not know? Haven't you seen them walking around?"

"I never paid attention."

Magne scanned Davyn's face as if trying to puzzle out what he had become over the past four years. He shook his head. "Tell me what happened at headquarters. You were supposed to attend a black tie affair, and that was supposed to be the extent of it. What the hell happened?"

"Oh, I attended. I even gave a speech."

Magne laughed. "How'd that go?"

"Not too bad, actually. The speech, anyway. I got a little carried away afterwards."

Magne's eyes widened.

"You should probably buy something nice for Phil and Al."

Magne squinted. "Hmm. We'll come back to that. How'd you end up—you said someone shot at you?"

"Oh, that," Davyn said matter-of-factly. "Well, they were doing a fundraiser with the investors on the island. The chief asked me— uh you—to go. Leo tried to stop me, but I'd picked up some cross chatter, or whatever you call it, and heard you say that you were on the island."

"Holy shit, you heard that?"

"Yeah, I heard it."

"Wow, I never dreamed that would work. I was just giving the guys shit." Magne's mouth dropped open. "And you were the one to hear it. Wow. Reminds me of that time you wanted to ask out Sandy but couldn't get up the nerve, so I—"

Davyn glanced at Magne. "Yeah, yeah. I remember."

They both laughed. Davyn found himself enjoying his time with Magne, despite his best efforts to remain aloof.

"Hey, Magne."

"Yeah?"

"Phil and Al. They're good guys. I—" Davyn stopped and stared at the ground looking for the best way to say this. "When I learned I was coming to the island, they showed me something they shouldn't have. At least Phil did. But it was only because I manipulated him into doing it."

Magne stared at Davyn, eyes wide. "What did you do?"

"I got Phil to tell me about something called a n-pulse."

Magne shrugged. "He should know better than to tell you, but no big deal."

"That's not the end of it. I was planning on, um, borrowing it, and

I—" He scratched the back of his neck. "I blurted out the name of it at the party to a bunch of people."

Magne shook his head. "Why, exactly?"

"It doesn't matter. The point is Phil and Al's jobs are at risk and it's my fault. You need to make sure they aren't fired over this. It was my fault."

"They both told you?"

"No, just Phil, but Al stood by him and is willing to take the fall along with him."

"Anything else?"

"Yeah, maybe."

Magne's lips tightened as he stared at Davyn.

"The chief knows about what you—um, I—did. Revealing the name of the top secret device, and it went to the board for review."

"Jesus, Davyn."

Davyn thought about reminding him he only did it to rescue him and he was only at headquarters as Magne because Magne pulled him from his normal, quiet life into this mess. But Davyn had dragged Phil and Al into a mess, too, and they didn't deserve to lose their jobs for it.

"Just make sure Phil and Al keep their jobs. And when you see them—when you see them, ask them how they're doing. They really like you. Phil especially."

Magne reluctantly smiled and gave a nod.

"Seriously. If you have any appreciation for getting rescued, show it to them. Make it right."

"Okay Davyn. You're right. I will." Magne scanned the campus below, then turned to his brother. "So, you came to the island with the investors. Then what?"

"I came with the security team, ahead of the investors. When I got to the island, I started looking for where they might be holding you. I found a small outbuilding with a guard holding a rifle posted outside. I figured that was the place, so I made my way toward it. They spotted me and I disappeared into the woods."

Magne's head jerked back. "That must be when I woke up and found the cell door open and no one around. Holy crap. They must have thought you were me and that I escaped, so they went after you—uh, me." Magne hit Davyn on the arm. "You rescued me."

Davyn shifted to a sitting position. His wounds from the escape were catching up with him and he couldn't get comfortable. "Anyway, I circled back to the building a short while later and went in."

Magne's eyes bugged out. "You didn't."

"I did. And they locked me up, thinking I was you."

Magne shook his head. "I can't believe this."

Davyn smirked, then went on with his tale. "An agent named, uh, Brian, and another one named Bill. They let me go. They want you to testify to that effect when this is all over."

Magne rubbed the back of his neck, apparently still trying to wrap his head around it. "I knew Aluerd's men weren't sold on the kidnapping. They must have been tricked or coerced. Some of them, anyway." Magne sat up and pulled in his knees, looking more like a kid listening to a campfire story than an agent. "How did you get off the island? Did you ride back on the security transport?"

Davyn laughed. "I wish."

"Then how?"

"There was a small Zodiac that ended up getting pretty shot up. It sank about three miles offshore. Not that the engine was running at that point, anyway."

Magne raked his hand through his short hair. "You're lucky to be alive. My god, I'm so sorry I dragged you into this, baby brother."

"Hang on now. One, it wasn't luck. Two, if you didn't then you might not be here. And three, stop calling me baby brother."

Magne nodded as if to concede the point. "Yeah, okay." He looked down at the library and squinted. "I'm still the oldest, though," he said under his breath.

Davyn smiled, but it still didn't sit well with him. Yeah, it was tongue-in-cheek, but still kind of arrogant. *Just because he was born two hours before me, doesn't give him the right to hold it over me forever.*

Davyn set his attention on the library. "What's taking so long?"

"Give it a few minutes. I'm sure she's fine."

"That's what you thought about me on the island."

Magne's face dropped before he stood up from his crouched position. "You're right. I don't like this. It's been too long. I'm going down there to find Leo. Wait here."

"Wait, what, so they can pick us off one by one? Forget it. I'm going, too."

"But we can't be seen together."

"Screw that." Davyn stood up and faced him. "I can fix my own life, thank you very much. Whatever you did here, it wasn't necessary."

"Not based on what I saw."

"You arrogant bastard."

Magne's head jerked back. "Look, if I'm a bastard then technically, so are you. Also, I was only trying to help."

"Well, I don't need your help. I can fix things on my own now, big brother."

Magne smiled and slapped Davyn on the arm. By all appearances, he was proud of him, and Davyn's hold on his grudge was starting to slip. His eyes darted around Magne's face as he examined his expression. Then, without a word, he nodded and turned back toward the campus.

They stepped out of the woods, walked down the hill and on to campus, heading for the library. Students and staff looked on in disbelief as they passed. It must have appeared to them like they were seeing double. Davyn was a recluse, to be sure, but everyone on campus knew who he was. Before long, everyone was looking and pointing.

"I think our cover's blown," Magne said out of the side of his mouth.

"Nah, they probably just think they need glasses."

Magne let out a laugh, then put a hand on Davyn's shoulder and squeezed. "Keep your eyes peeled for anything unusual."

"Sure. I'll watch for anything that doesn't look like a book."

Magne let out an audible sigh and they picked up their pace. As they approached the library, a man in a dark grey suit emerged from behind one of the columns near the front doors.

Magne stopped and grabbed Davyn's arm. "You see that guy?"

Davyn nodded.

"You recognize him?"

"Nope, but that's not saying much."

Magne gave Davyn a push, directing him toward the side of the library. "He's communicating to someone."

"Well, that's obvious. They don't teach you guys ventriloquism in spy school? What's the point of a covert earpiece if they yap, yap, yap like that?" Davyn mocked the man's mouth movements.

"I'll pass your recommendation on to the chief. Come on, we have to find another way in." Magne pulled Davyn along as he started running for the back of the library.

The man ran after them, then two more joined the chase. Davyn and Magne sprinted to the back of the library. As they rounded the corner, Davyn stopped and turned around.

"What the hell are you doing?"

Davyn took a few steps back and pulled out his atlatl and loaded a dart.

"No way. Come on, let's go."

But Davyn watched and waited. An agent rounded the corner and Davyn let a dart fly, striking the agent in the center of his chest. His legs turned to jelly and he face-planted on the ground right in front of Davyn. He grabbed the agent's gun and tossed it behind him to Magne, then stepped to the side. "Your turn."

The two other agents rounded the corner and stopped when they saw Magne walking at them, gun drawn.

"Hold on, fellas. Set your guns down," Magne said. "You know the routine."

The men set their guns down and raised their hands over their heads.

"Good. Now back up." He reached under his belt with his free hand and pulled out two plastic straps, extending them to Davyn.

Davyn grabbed them as he moved toward the agents. "Where'd you get the restraints?"

"I always carry them. You never know when you might need 'em. I'm a bit of a shot magnet sometimes."

"You, too, huh?" Davyn said as he pulled a strap tight around an agent's wrists.

A moment later the two men had their hands strapped behind them. Magne glanced down at the dart gun.

"You're using *poison* darts now, Steve? Really?"

Steve shook his head as he gazed past Magne, but gave no reply.

"Grab their guns, Davyn."

Magne walked the agents toward the security office. When they reached the top of the stairs, he stopped. "Wait," he told the men. "Davyn, head down and see if you can tell what's going on inside. Make sure no one sees you. We don't know who might be down there."

Steve glanced at the other agent, sending a chill down Davyn's spine. It was like they knew exactly what he'd see when he got down there. He moved down the stairs, then pressed himself against the wall and peered in through the window. The small security office appeared empty. The hallway to the stairs leading up to the library was empty, too.

"I don't see anyone," Davyn called out.

"Okay, head back up here."

Magne pushed the agents off the sidewalk and onto the grass. "On the ground, face down. And no peeking."

Magne waited for them to lie down, then took the two guns from Davyn. He glanced at the dart loaded in the chamber, then tilted it toward Davyn. "You see this label? That means it's loaded with poison. If the label is yellow, it's a tranquilizer. They're not using nonlethal force anymore."

Davyn took one of the guns and tucked it in his pants. "You don't have to tell me. They were definitely using real guns on the island."

Magne trained his gaze on Davyn for a few moments before turning to the agents on the ground. "Watch these guys and wait for me to give the all clear." He headed down the stairs.

Davyn didn't recognize either of the men from the island. Magne seemed to know Steve pretty well. Enough to be disappointed in him, anyway. They weren't out to kidnap Magne this time, but to kill him. He'd already lost his brother once, and thinking about it made his blood boil.

"Hey, Steve. Want something to drink?"

Steve looked at the other agent but didn't respond.

"What's your buddy's name, Steve?"

Neither responded. Davyn lifted the other agent's arm with his foot, then set it down. "What's your name, friend?"

Davyn wanted to know where Leo was, but these guys weren't responding to anything.

Magne came back up the stairs and walked over to the agents, nudging Steve with his foot. "Get up." He pulled Davyn over toward the stairs, all while keeping an eye on the agents. "I'll go in first, followed by these two. You follow us in. Copy?"

The proper response was probably "copy," and Magne likely didn't realize he was using lingo, but Davyn didn't feel like playing along.

"Yeah, sure. Anything else?"

Magne shook his head.

"Okay, fellas. Follow me. My doppelgänger will be right behind you, so no tricks."

The agents filed into position behind Magne.

"You guys don't talk much," Davyn said. "We should hang out sometime."

Magne flashed his eyes and shook his head at Davyn, who responded with a shrug. Magne started down the stairs.

When they got inside, they did a quick search, but the place was deserted.

Davyn stepped up to the counter. "Should I ring the bell?"

Magne looked at the counter, too. "What bell?"

Davyn pushed the agents, directing them into a couple of seats.

Magne asked again, "What bell?"

"I guess they don't have one. I'm taking a star off their Yelp review."

Magne shook his head and looked behind the counter before ducking around to the other side. "Is it always this empty?"

"I have no idea."

"There should be someone here. Watch the guys while I have a look around."

He disappeared into a back room. Davyn held his gun on the agents as he stepped over to the hallway to have a look.

"There's someone here!" Magne called out.

Davy went back to the counter and cocked his head to listen in.

"What happened?" Magne said.

"Five men came in, tied me up, and left. I don't know where they went. Are you guys cops?"

"Sort of. We have two of their guys in restraints. Let's get you untied, and you can tell me if they were part of that group that you saw."

A few moments later, a security guard emerged, followed by Magne. He looked at the agents on the bench and shook his head. "Nope, I don't think they were with them."

Magne shot a glance at Davyn. "That would be at least seven here now. We need to find Leo and get off campus." He glanced over at the two agents on the bench. "No telling how many more may be coming."

Davyn walked back to the hallway to keep an eye out.

Magne turned to the guard. "Do you have somewhere we can hold these guys?"

The guard picked up a set of keys. "There's a room over there," he said, nodding at a door in the corner.

Magne collected the two agents and shuffled them into the holding room, shutting the door behind them. "Okay, they're secure. Go ahead and call the police. Tell them what happened here."

The guard picked up the phone, listened, then tapped the receiver. "There's no dial tone."

"Try your cell phone."

"There's no signal. It stopped working a few hours ago."

"I need to have a look around," Magne said and headed down the hallway. He opened the first door and turned on the light as Davyn looked on. Magne opened the next door, and immediately slammed it shut.

"Davyn, run!" he yelled as he threw his weight against the door. Davyn ran toward him. "The other way! There's too many. Get out of here."

But Davyn planted his feet and drew his gun as the door flew open, slamming Magne against the opposite wall. As the agents streamed out, Davyn pointed his gun at each, but there were too many and they all pulled their guns on Davyn. As Magne emerged from behind them, Davyn kept his eyes on the agents and watched Magne in his periphery so as not to give him away.

Magne gestured at the exit door behind Davyn, then shouted, "Nobody move! You're under arrest."

The agents all turned around at once, and Davyn took the

opportunity to fly out the door and up the stairs. *Oh Jesus, not again.* He stopped running and eyed another set of stairs leading to an emergency exit. *No good. It's alarmed. How do I get him out of there?*

Holding his gun low beside his leg to shield it from view, he moved past the stairs and around to the front of the library. He entered through the main doors. Mrs. Dawit stood at her kiosk, shuffling through papers. Students sat at tables in the main hall. Mrs. Dawit looked up at him and smiled and raised a hand as a wave. Everything appeared to be normal.

Davyn made his way through the main hall toward the stairs leading down to the security office. Maybe he could surprise them or distract them and free Magne, but it would be nice to have some help. Davyn wondered if the group that stormed Magne was also holding Leo. The hallway was quiet; he hoped it stayed that way as he pulled out his tranquilizer gun and pointed it ahead.

Bukka turned the corner, heading straight for him. *Oh boy.*

Bukka eyed the gun curiously as he closed in. "Hey, professor."

"Hey, Bukka," Davyn replied, looking past him down the hallway.

Bukka adjusted his backpack as he stared at the gun. "What's with the toy gun?"

Davyn grabbed Bukka by the arm and pulled him into a side room, closing the door behind them. "It's not a toy. We have a situation. There are some bad men on campus. Do you have your cell phone?"

"What? Wow, really?" He squinted at Davyn. "Wait, are you just kidding with me again?"

"No, Bukka, I wouldn't kid about something like this. Do you have your cell phone?"

"Yeah, but it's not getting a signal. Same for everybody else," he said, gesturing with his head toward where he'd just come from.

"They must be jamming the signal."

"Who?"

"The bad men." Davyn put his hand on Bukka's shoulder. "I have an important mission for you, Bukka." When Bukka just stood there like a toddler fidgeting with the placement of his backpack, Davyn took that as his cue to continue. "You need to get off campus." He still looked as if he was trying to work out whether Davyn was messing with him. "I'm serious. This is important, and it's not something I would joke about. Once you're off campus, call 911. Tell them there's a—Jesus, tell them there's a bunch of enemy agents—no, just say people—people on the campus and they're carrying guns."

"Are you sure about this, professor? It sounds a little crazy."

Davyn reached for the door handle. "Oh, it's crazy. But it's also true." He pressed his back to the wall and took a deep breath. "Okay, I'm going to check to see if it's clear. If it is, I'll head out, then you head straight out the front of the library."

Davyn cracked the door and peered out, then glanced at Bukka, gave a nod, and crept out. When he got to the stairs, he peaked around the corner. An agent spotted him and started up after him. Davyn ran back the way he came and Bukka opened the door as he ran by and yelled, "Go back in! Lock the door."

But Bukka stuck out an arm and clotheslined the agent, sending him in a heap to the floor.

Davyn ran back to Bukka. "Whoa, nice work. He's out cold."

Bukka smiled. "You're not allowed to do that in football. You can see why," he said, looking down at the fallen agent. "He'll be okay, though. Right, professor?"

Davyn knelt next to the agent and pulled a pack of darts from his pocket. Yellow label: tranquilizers. "I'm sure he'll be fine. He's just knocked out, but I'm going to give him a tranquilizer to hold him until this is over."

Bukka watched Davyn as he opened the pack and pull out a dart. "What's going on, professor?"

Davyn pulled the protective tip off the dart, reached down, and injected it in the agent's arm. "Bad men, Bukka, bad men. I'll explain later. For now, I need you to get off campus and call the police. Tell them what you saw here. Tell them there are more of them. We don't know how many."

Bukka looked at the agent, then at the professor, and nodded as he stood up.

"Bukka."

"What?"

"If you come across any more of these guys, don't engage them. Just get off campus and call the police. We'll let them handle this."

"Okay."

"Oh, and Bukka—"

"What?"

"I haven't been the nicest. I know you think I was making fun of you, and I never took the time to explain that I wasn't, but you still helped me out." Davyn hesitated for a moment, then looked Bukka in the eye. "I guess I'm wondering why."

Bukka bit his lips and looked up at the ceiling. "Um." He appeared to be debating whether to say what was on his mind.

"It's okay, Bukka. You can say it."

Bukka looked down at the ground and gripped his backpack strap. "This stuff is really too complicated for me, professor, but Lily says deep down you're a nice person, and past hurts have made you seem mean." Davyn flashed a tentative smile. "But she says some of the things you do are nice, even if they don't always seem like it at the time." Bukka continued adjusting his grip on his backpack straps as he recounted what Lily told him. "She says you're just pushing people to do better." He stole a glance at Davyn, then his eyes shot back to the ground. "Um, she says you don't have the courage to be kind, but one day you will and maybe her, um, she and I can help you."

Davyn's mouth hung open for a moment before he shook off his surprise. "Wow, that's a lot to process," he said, scratching his chin. "Well, thanks for that. You—you better get going."

Bukka rose on his toes and back down, then nodded at the professor before he turned to leave.

"Bukka."

Bukka stopped but didn't turn around. "What?"

"I'm sorry about not taking the time to explain what happened."

"Okay, professor. I better go call the police now."

Davyn nodded as Bukka continued down the hallway, but called him back once more.

Bukka stopped and turned his head toward Davyn. "What?"

Davyn let out a small laugh. "Thank you."

Bukka nodded and ran off as Davyn stood and headed down the hallway toward the stairway that would take him back to the security office. Once there, Davyn peered down the stairway. Apparently, no one had noticed the agent's absence. That might provide an opportunity to slip down unnoticed and get the jump on the others. He eased his foot on to the wooden step, and as his weight bore down, a loud creak filled the space. He stopped and pointed his gun down the stairway and waited. No one heard, or at least no one responded.

He leaned his head back and looked up the hallway, catching the tail end of someone crossing the intersection. Leo? He could have sworn it was her and wanted to call out, but worried the agents might hear. If they were holding Magne, he'd be outgunned if he tried to go in alone. He'd need her help. He took off down the hall after her.

Soon, he was in a part of the library he hadn't seen before. The wall to his right curved outward, broadening the hall as he went. Wait, he had been here before, when he just started working on campus. He remembered the hall led to a large, open reading area overlooking an atrium with a nice view of the woods. He remembered liking the space, except that it was always crowded.

Sure enough, the hallway spilled into an open area with lounge chairs. The wall to his right was covered with bookshelves, and the glass to his left provided a view to the atrium below.

Davyn gazed down and saw several armed agents stood guarding about a dozen students and faculty. A side door opened, and an agent pushed two more students into the atrium before closing the door. Davyn looked across the reading area to see Leo on the far end, still walking away. He looked back to the atrium. *Lily? What the hell is she doing here? She should be in class.*

A door across the way swung open, drawing Davyn's attention. Bukka stepped in and glanced down the stairs. Davyn waved his hands, motioning to Bukka to get out of sight. He had to get the message across before Bukka saw Lily.

Bukka spotted him, smiled, and waved back. Davyn rolled his eyes, then motioned again, but something caught Bukka's attention and he looked back down to the atrium. His eyes grew big, then shot back to Davyn. Too late—he'd seen Lily and there'd be no stopping him now. Still, Davyn shook his head to signal him not to go down, but Bukka took off stairs like a steamroller.

"Leave her alone!" he shouted as he plowed into an agent, tackling him to the floor. Two nearby agents immediately aimed their guns at him. Bukka looked up and let go of the agent. His rescue attempt ended as quickly as it began.

Aluerd stuck his head out from an adjoining room, then stepped out into the atrium. "What's all the commotion?" he asked with a chilling, calm voice.

Davyn leaned back to avoid being seen as Aluerd began pacing around Bukka like a panther.

"Tsk, tsk. Now I have to make an example of you. I didn't want to do this. I just wanted to get Magne and go, but now I have a hero trying to spoil my plan."

This wasn't fair. Aluerd was a master at manipulating people's emotions and playing on their fears, and Bukka was just an affable kid. Davyn wanted to jump into the fray, but that would only result in his being captured, too.

Bukka cringed as Aluerd circled back in front of him. Davyn's eyes moved from Bukka to Lily as she looked on in horror. Then she looked up at Davyn, as though trying to figure out why her mild-mannered professor was holding a gun on—well, she had no idea who these people were or why Davyn would be involved.

He pulled back, not just because he couldn't bear to have Lily look at him like that, but because if Lily saw him, the agents might, too. It was Davyn's fault the agents were there, and he felt the full weight of it then.

"What do you want?" Bukka said.

"What I wanted was to protect all of you good people, but as happens, things don't always go as planned. So now we have to take extreme measures, once again, to set things right."

Davyn peeked over the balcony's edge as Aluerd pulled a gun from behind his back and aimed it at Bukka's head.

That was too much. Davyn stood up and aimed his own gun at Aluerd. "Let him go, Aluerd!" he shouted. "Magne's left campus. You may as well collect your men and go, too."

Aluerd looked up at Davyn and smiled as he pushed Bukka into a chair. "Are you sure Magne's left, Davyn?"

Davyn nodded slowly. He had no idea where Magne was, but Aluerd didn't necessarily know that. "I know you're trying to get me to say something that will reveal where he went, but I'm not saying anything more."

Aluerd shook his head. "I'm only asking because I don't think you're one of a set of triplets, and we have this guy right here."

He motioned, and two agents walked out with Magne in front of them.

Magne looked up at Davyn. "I'm sorry, Davyn. Things were getting out of hand. I turned myself in to end this."

Aluerd turned the gun on Magne. "Well, end it you have."

"You won't get away with it," Davyn said. "The chief will know what you've done."

Aluerd looked up at Davyn, ignoring the gun fixed on him. "Unfortunately, the chief is about to meet an untimely natural death."

Davyn shook his head. *He's completely lost his mind.* "What's your plan for Magne?"

"Magne? Well, he's wanted out of the agency for some time now. You see, he wanted a break from all the violence. A fresh start. He told me so himself. Turns out your life would do nicely. He planned to kill you, which he will, then take over your life. Now I know you think he would never do a thing like that, but being an agent can make you ruthless over time. I can attest to that."

Davyn needed to try another tack. "You're not a bad person, Aluerd. You're one of the good guys. You don't want to kill anyone. Certainly not your own people, or these students."

"Yes, well, unfortunately this is bigger than me, and it's bigger than what I want. With a terrorist like Abdullah out there, many more lives will be lost if I don't do this. It's my duty, difficult as it may seem."

"There are too many witnesses."

"That's easily taken care of."

Davyn wasn't going to be able to talk Aluerd down by himself. There was no choice but to try to surprise them. He counted the agents—six, plus Aluerd. He looked at Magne. There was a hand signal they used in rugby. Magne would remember it.

He made eye contact with Magne and put his thumb and pointer finger together, then slowly drew them apart. Magne nodded. Now to wait for the right moment.

Aluerd stopped in front of Bukka. "I'm out there every day, protecting you, your families, the community. But do I get any appreciation?" He stared at Bukka, waiting for a response.

Bukka tried to stand, but the agent behind him forced him back into the chair. "Well, I don't really know you, but from what I've seen, you're not protecting anybody. You're the one making threats."

"Typical," Aluerd said, glancing up at the agent. "You haven't been listening. I'm what keeps this country safe. But no one wants me to do my job anymore. It's always, 'You can't do this. That's not legal.'" Aluerd resumed pacing. "My time is short, and I have important work to do. I was hoping to do it as chief and really clean things up. But once again, it falls to me to get the job done on my own."

Sounds like Aluerd is wrapping up his speech. Time to act. How to do this? Aluerd holstered his gun. There were two agents behind Magne, one behind Bukka, and three in the crowd. Davyn locked eyes with Magne, and when he knew he had his attention, shifted his gaze to his gun, then to the agent over Magne's left shoulder. Magne nodded, and Davyn adjusted his aim from Aluerd to the agent. The agent must have noticed because he stepped back and drew his gun. Davyn fired as Magne threw his arms around the other agent behind him and slammed his head into his knee.

Davyn yelled, "Bukka, fight!"

Bukka jumped up and took out the agent directly behind him as Davyn jammed another dart in the gun and got ready to fire. An agent aimed at Bukka, but Davyn fired, knocking him out. He went to reload as Aluerd drew his gun on Magne and fired. Davyn's eyes darted to Magne. The shot missed, but Aluerd had already taken aim, ready to fire again. Magne was a sitting duck. A shot rang out from the balcony and Aluerd recoiled as the bullet struck his shoulder. He turned and sprinted out the door.

Leo shouted to the remaining agents, "Drop your weapons!"

Davyn looked over to see Leo pointing her gun at the men as they scattered and ran out the doors.

Magne called out, "They'll be back for me. We need to get off campus, even if it's on foot. What's the best way out of here?"

Davyn ran down the stairs and pointed to a door. "Down that

hallway, then straight out. Once we're outside, it's a short run to the woods."

Magne nodded. "Which direction to the main road?"

"I'll show you."

"No, stay here and watch out for your friends. It's better I go alone."

"There are more agents out there. You need my help."

He looked Davyn up and down. "It's too dangerous. And you're not an agent."

"I was this week. Anyway, you can't stop me. I'll follow you."

Magne hesitated only a second, then slapped Davyn's arm and nodded. "Okay, let's go."

Bukka stepped forward. "I can go too, professor."

"No, you stay here with Leo and look after everyone until the police arrive. Barricade the doors, including the one we're using."

Davyn crouched low as he opened the door and peered down the hallway to see if it was clear. No one was around, but Davyn heard the catch on the door beside him. He leaned back and aimed his gun as two agents stepped out. He fired at one and drove the butt of his palm into the jaw of the other, knocking him senseless and sending him to the ground.

"Okay, it's clear. Let's go."

Magne stepped out, gun drawn, and stared at the agents on the floor as he moved by. "How the hell are you so good at this?" he whispered.

Davyn didn't answer; he just kept his eyes on each door they passed.

"I've got our flanks, Davyn, you keep your eyes ahead."

Four more doors and they would be out of the building. The handle jiggled on a door just ahead. They froze and aimed their guns, but the door didn't open. Weird. They glanced at each other, then continued on. The stairwell door swung open, slamming into the wall with a bang. At least two agents turned and ran back up.

Magne pushed Davyn forward. "Let them go. We need to get out of here."

The end of the hall lay just ahead. Almost there, then it was into the woods.

"Run!" Magne shouted. "Agents behind us."

Just then, the doorway to the outside opened and filled with even more of them.

Davyn turned around. "Agents in front. Quick— head up the stairs." They raced toward stairs, as agents closed in from both sides. Davyn reached out and pulled the door open and pushed Magne through, then stepped inside and turned a deadbolt on the door, locking it behind them. "That'll slow them, but what now?"

"We'll have to find another way." Magne looked round. "Looks like up is our only option."

They climbed to the second floor and paused on the platform. Magne glanced at the lock. "Better not lock this one in case somebody tries to get out of the building. Let's go up another flight. I suspect those agents went out this door."

"They teach you *that* in spy school?"

"Actually, yes, they did."

When they reached the next platform, Magne stuck his head out and peered around. "It's quiet. Maybe too quiet. I'll go out first. You watch our backs. And stay close."

They moved through a reading area, stepping around the chairs and tables without a sound.

Magne whispered, "These desks up here in front have short walls around them."

Davyn eyed them. "They're listening stations."

"They're also a good place to hide. Let's find another way."

"We'll have to cross the library and go down the stairs on the other side. It'll be harder to reach the woods, but at least we'll be out of the building."

"Agreed."

They approached a long row of bookcases with an aisle running down the middle and both sides.

Magne grabbed his arm and nodded toward the books. "We'll have to take these one at a time. You cover the right side, and I'll take the middle and left. Remember, one row at a time and stay close. Don't get ahead of me."

Davyn nodded, and they started moving. Magne glanced past the first bookcase "Clear."

Davyn peered around a wall of books. "Looks clear here, too."

"Good. We'll take each one the same way."

They moved to the next row and repeated the process. Clear, clear, next. One after the other, until Davyn heard a whistle. "Stop. I hear something."

A rustling sound came from ahead. Magne nodded at it and crouched low before moving to the far side of the bookcases. Davyn continued on his side, but remained standing. The crouching struck him as a little theatrical. The bookcases were taller than both of them, so he didn't see the point. He could also cover more ground this way.

The sound stopped, and the room fell dead quiet. Davyn looked over at Magne and watched him crouch-walk; he was very methodical. They were almost across the library when Davyn spotted a book and paused to pull it out. As soon as he had it, a dart hit the back with a dull *thwack*. He tossed the book, knocking the agent's gun to the floor, and ran.

"Magne, agent behind me."

Magne started after them, catching up quickly. He grabbed the agent's shoulder, taking him down with a grapple tackle. Davyn turned around, looking for a way to help. An agent jumped Davyn from behind, sending them both to the ground and knocking his gun away from him. He clawed his way toward it as the agent went for it, too. The struggle nudged it under one of the bookcases. Davyn jerked back as the agent threw a right hook, but recovered and threw a punch straight out, grazing his chin. Another agent appeared and fired at Davyn, but nothing came out of the gun.

"God, these things suck!" the agent screamed. "Can we go back to using real guns now?"

Davyn looked at him and laughed. *What a drama queen.*

Apparently, the agent didn't like that and charged him. "What, you want some of this?"

Magne jumped him and tackled him to the floor, putting him in a stranglehold.

Davyn asked Magne, "Where's your gun?"

"Indisposed," he grunted.

Davyn pulled a dart from his pocket and stuck it in the agent's arm. He went limp and dropped to the ground. Four more agents stepped out.

Magne backed up slowly. "Come on, fellas. What are you doing this for, anyway? Aluerd is clearly off his rocker. What do you say we call it quits?"

"He'll make it worth our while," one of the agents said.

"Not if you're in prison."

"That's why we're going to take you out and get out of here."

Davyn and Magne continued backing up. Apparently, no one had a working gun anymore.

They all rushed Davyn and Magne, and they fell to the ground, punches flying. Davyn wriggled out of the fray and stood up to land a punch to the side of one agent's head, knocking him to the ground. He struggled to get up, stunned by the blow. But he shook it off and rushed Davyn. They fell backward and hit the floor. Davyn rolled into a student who was sitting at one of the listening stations, apparently unaware of the events that had been unfolding around him. The student lifted his headphones and shushed Davyn.

"I know, right? I'm so sorry." Davyn glanced at the title of the audio book he was listening to. "Oh, that's a good one, you'll love it," he said as he backed away, between rows of bookcases. The student shook his head and put his headphones back on.

Davyn grabbed one of the guns from the floor and pulled a dart. An agent jumped on his back, slamming him against a bookrack. Davyn slipped the cover off the dart and jabbed it in the agent's leg, knocking him out. The fight continued until Davyn and Magne stood battered and bruised inside a circle of crumpled men.

Magne staggered over to the window and looked out. "Calvary's here, Dav. Police, fire and ambulances streaming into the parking lot."

Davyn made his way over to the window and watched with him. "Where do you think Aluerd is?"

"I don't know, but if he hasn't fled yet, he will now. We've got most, if not all, of his agents." Magne leaned against the windowsill. "He's given up on us. He'll probably head to Europe and use what time he has left trying to find Abdullah."

"So it's finally over?"

"For you, yes. Come on, let's go back downstairs. I'm sure the police will want to speak with both of us." Davyn started for the stairwell, but Magne's voice pulled him up short. "Hey Davyn?" Davyn stopped and turned to Magne. "Say nothing about the agency."

Davyn looked him in the eye. "Uh, it's kind of an agency thing. Bad guys, agents and all."

"Just tell the police you don't know who these people are or why they were here. I'll get things sorted once I'm back to the agency's headquarters."

With the university cleared of agents and police investigating the scene, a small crowd gathered around Davyn and Magne in the library's main hall. Bukka and Lily joined them, and Davyn reached out and patted Bukka on the back before he gave Lily a quick hug.

Lily's brows furrowed as she glanced between Davyn and Magne. "Professor?"

Davyn ran a finger over an eyebrow. "Yes, it's me."

"Am I seeing double?"

Anne joined the group, "Are you guys okay? Is everyone okay?" She looked at Davyn, then Magne, and back again. She looked at Lily and jabbed her thumb toward Magne, apparently looking for an explanation, but Lily just shrugged.

Davyn pointed at Magne. "This is my brother, Magne."

Magne raised a hand and smiled. "Hello."

"I knew it." Mrs. Dawit had made her way to them, and stood looking back and forth between the two. "I knew it."

"I was just telling everyone, this is my brother Magne."

They all began talking at once.

"How long's he been here?"

"I can tell you," Mrs. Dawit chimed in.

"I knew something was weird!"

"Was that Magne teaching class yesterday?"

"Who did I go out on a date with last night?"

Magne stepped forward. "I arrived this morning. I've been

overseas and just got back stateside this week. I came by to see my brother. Sadly, duty calls and I can't stay." He looked around at the puzzled faces. "Although, this was quite the welcome and I'm glad I got to at least meet some of Davyn's friends before I go."

Davyn turned to Magne and grabbed his shoulders. "I know what you're trying to do, but I can take care of things for myself."

There was some movement, and Davyn squinted, trying to make out who was moving through the crowd behind Magne and heading right for him. It was Aluerd. As he closed in, he raised a knife and brought it down on Magne. Acting on pure instinct, Davyn pushed Magne to the side and swung both hands up, intercepting Aluerd's thrust and diverting the knife so that it just grazed his head as they tumbled to the ground. Davyn pulled his legs in and jammed his feet under Aluerd, then pushed with everything he had, sending Aluerd straight up in the air. Davyn rolled out as Aluerd slammed to the ground and put his knee on Aluerd's back as he pulled his arms back and cinched them with a tie.

"God, what I wouldn't give for some quiet reading time." Davyn shook his head. "It's over, Aluerd."

Several officers noticed the commotion and ran over, cuffing Aluerd properly and taking him away.

"You know I have pretty good patience," Davyn said. "Very good actually, but there comes a time when—" Davyn looked around at the bewildered faces. He took a deep breath and let his cheeks puff out. "How do I explain this?"

Magne stepped in. "Just a crazy man randomly attacking people. Good work broth—"

"Magne, I appreciate what you're trying to do. You did it through my entire childhood, but I'm an adult now." He looked out at the group. "As I was saying, Magne's been here for a few days. It wasn't me teaching class yesterday." He glanced at Anne. "And it wasn't me who took you out last night."

The group fell silent. Magne whispered into Davyn's ear. "I'm proud of you, brother."

Anne walked up and used a handkerchief to gently wipe the blood from Davyn's forehead. "Someone find an EMT, please. This might need stitches."

"I don't think so. A bandage should do the trick," Leo said with a smile as she materialized from the gathered crowd.

Davyn flashed a quick smile her way but pretended not to recognize her. He'd have to let the past few days disappear from his history and keep Magne's role with the agency, including his own brief stint within its ranks, a mystery.

Magne winked at Davyn and pointed to the scratch on his own forehead. "We match again." Davyn winked back as Magne cleared his throat. "Well, I apologize, but I have to say goodbye to you and my little brother—I mean, my brother. Maybe next visit we can just do lunch instead," he said with a laugh. The joke fell flat; Magne was used to a life of action and joking about it, but no one else there was. "Ah, yes, well, I should get going." He slapped Davyn on the shoulder and walked off.

Davyn took Anne's hand to stop her from tending to his cut, but not before he slipped the handkerchief into his own grasp. He gave her hand a squeeze, then ran after Magne. When he caught up to him, he grabbed his shoulder to stop him.

"So are you going back into hiding? Will I see you again?"

"I don't know, Davyn. I have to try and clean up the mess back at the agency. If I make chief, I might be able to make some changes, but—" He flashed a sympathetic smile. "I'm sorry. That's just how it has to be."

Davyn looked at him for a moment, then nodded slowly. "I hope you can send me a note from time to time. I missed you, brother."

Magne hugged Davyn. "I miss you, too."

They separated and looked at each other for a moment, then Magne walked off. Davyn took a deep breath as he watched him go. Leo joined Magne and threw a quick behind the back wave. Moments later, they were both gone.

Leo, his social coach and mentor had helped him navigate his relationships, even taught him a bit, would disappear like none of it ever happened. But it did happen, and Davyn knew he was better for it. He realized he cared for Lily and even Bukka more than he knew. Of course, in a couple of years they'd graduate and be gone as well. Mrs. Dawit was probably only two or three years from retirement. He carried these thoughts with him as he walked back to the crowd. They swirled around him like autumn leaves on a blustery day. Anne, though... If he played his cards right, she might stick around. That idea excited and intrigued him.

Change and loss were inevitable. People would come and go. He knew he couldn't control that. But what he could control was how he reacted.

Davyn rejoined the group. "I'm glad everyone's alright."

Lily returned with an EMT, who wiped Davyn's forehead and slapped on a bandage before dashing off. Davyn put his fingers on the bandage and shrugged before he turned to Lily. "What brought you back to the library? You were supposed to be in class."

"Yeah, well, so were you, professor," she said with a snort. Davyn grinned. She was right, after all. Then she looked at Bukka. "I heard something was happening here, so I came to check on Bukka."

Davyn glanced at Anne. Their eyes met, and Davyn smiled as he directed his attention to Bukka. "What about you, Bukka? What brought you back to campus?"

Bukka sat up straight and stretched his neck. "As I was leaving, I saw Lily going into the library. I couldn't just let her go in there, not with everything going on."

Davyn smiled and returned his gaze to Anne for a moment, then back to the young couple. "Reminds me of *The Gift of the Magi*."

Bukka's brow crinkled. "What's that?"

Davyn looked at Lily. "Have you read it, Lily?" Lily shook her head. "I'll get the book for you for Christmas, but I want you to read it together, okay?"

Lily grinned as she hugged Bukka. "That sounds so nice, professor."

Anne took Davyn's hand. "I have some more questions for you. Can we talk?"

Davyn looked at Anne, then his gathered group of friends and sighed. It was nice to be back, but he needed to escape into solitude for a while. "I'm sure you all have questions, and I owe you an explanation and an apology. But right now, I need to get some rest. I promise I'll talk to each of you tomorrow."

Anne nodded and let go of his hand as she walked away.

Davyn sighed as he watched her go. As the crowd broke up

and wandered off, he turned to see Puddington heading right for him.

Wait, what am I doing? He went after Anne as fast as his aching leg would allow and reached out for her hand.

She turned to him, her eyes warm and inquisitive.

Davyn gazed back at her. "Um, would you like to go for a walk with me?"

A playful smile blossomed across her face as she gave a hint of a nod. "Let's go out the back. Puddington's right behind us and trying to explain this to him can definitely wait 'til tomorrow."

They laughed like kids as they snuck out the back of the library, up the stairs, and into the sun-soaked park.

Davyn held her hand and gazed ahead. "I've liked you for a long time. I'm sorry I never said anything."

"Well, I wouldn't have guessed. You're good at keeping secrets." She stopped and turned to him.

He pursed his lips. "It's a very long story. I'll tell you sometime."

She pulled him closer. "Will you take me on a second, first date sometime?"

"How's tomorrow sound?"

She looked away. "Maybe."

A grin spread across Davyn's face. He had it coming, and he knew it. He'd have to earn his way back into her good graces. And that was okay.

CHAPTER 22

As the library was closing up, the second floor reading room where Davyn spent most of his time was dark and quiet. He was in the main hall chatting with Anne, Lily, Bukka and Mrs. Dawit. As they laughed and talked, their voices wafted up and drifted through the empty reading room.

Davyn said, "We can do that the following weekend."

"But isn't that the weekend you wanted to go hunting?" Anne replied.

"Uh, yeah, but I'm not so sure I—well, let's just say I'd rather go apple picking with you. Oh, and while I'm thinking about it, Mrs. Dawit, is the conference room available tomorrow night?"

"Yes, why? I thought you were over your introversion."

Davyn laughed. "I never want to be *over* my introversion. Book it for me, won't you? I'll need some alone time after tomorrow afternoon's outing."

"Well, you'll have to ask Linda. I'm leaving for a date."

"With Mr. Bakersfield?"

"Yes. Don't you remember? You set us up." She paused and Davyn waited for it to dawn on her. "Oh, wait, I guess it was Magne. He's so helpful. Thank him for us, would you?"

ABOUT THE AUTHOR

John Catan writes stories about his fellow introverts who are thrown into the perilous and unfamiliar world of extroverts. He likes to push himself out of his comfort zone by speaking at Toastmasters, and sometimes shakes things up even more by throwing in twists like juggling and using accents in his speeches—neither of which he's particularly good at. But that's the point; it's through our struggles that we learn and grow. At his first Toastmasters meeting, he laid low, hoping not to be called on to speak, but now mentors new members, serves as the club's president, and coaches other Toastmasters clubs.

What does an author stand to gain by asking for reader feedback? A lot. In fact, what we can gain is so important in the publishing world, that they've coined a catchy name for it.

It's called "social proof." And in this age of social media sharing, without social proof, an author may as well be invisible.

So if you've enjoyed *The Substitute*, please consider giving it some visibility by reviewing it on Amazon or Goodreads. A review doesn't have to be a long critical essay. Just a few words expressing your thoughts, which could help potential readers decide whether they would enjoy it, too.

CPSIA information can be obtained
at www.ICGtesting.com
Printed in the USA
FSHW020731221220
76857FS